◆

DISCOVER WHY CRITICS—AND READERS— LOVE **KAREN ROBARDS** AND HER IRRESISTIBLE ROMANCES

◆ ◆ ◆

"Ms. Robards [has] the marvelous talent to zero in on the heart of erotic fantasy. She seems to know instinctively our most secret thoughts and then dreams up the perfect scenario to give them free rein. . . . The result is pure magic."
—*Romantic Times*

◆

"Karen Robards writes an absolutely splendid tale, and is among the best for giving the reader incomparable sexual tension. . . . She is certainly one of the few authors who successfully moves from historical to contemporary fiction and back again with gifted ease . . . [she writes] romantic adventure that will leave you breathless."
—*Affaire de Coeur*

◆

[Ms. Robards writes] "spellbinding romance."
—*Publishers Weekly*

Also by Karen Robards

◇

Amanda Rose
Dark Torment
Loving Julia
To Love a Man
Wild Orchids

Published by
WARNER BOOKS

KAREN ROBARDS

NIGHT MAGIC

WARNER BOOKS

A Time Warner Company

WARNER BOOKS EDITION

Copyright © 1987 by Karen Robards
All rights reserved.

Cover design by Diane Luger
Cover illustration by Don Brautigam

Warner Books, Inc.
1271 Avenue of the Americas
New York, N.Y. 10020

Visit our Web site at
www.warnerbooks.com

W A Time Warner Company

Printed in the United States of America

First Printing: October, 1987

Reissued: June, 1993

20 19 18 17

With love to the real "Puff"—my sister Lee Ann,
who inspired this book.
And, as always, to Doug and Peter

Friday, October 2, 8 P.M.

He had maybe a minute to live.

Jack McClain felt a rush of terror override the drug that was dulling his body's responses. The accompanying adrenaline somewhat cleared his head, enough so that he could at least weigh his chances of avoiding being shot in the head at point-blank range. Conclusion: not good.

The bozos dragging him from the trawler's lantern lit cabin to the pitching, spray-wet darkness of the deck were the size of gorillas. Even at full strength, unarmed as he was he would have stood about as much chance of overpowering them as Texas Christian University's Horned Frogs had of defeating Alabama's Crimson Tide the year he had been the Frogs' star quarterback. In other word's, a snowball's chance in hell.

Which left his brains. He'd always prided himself on his brains. If only the squishy mass of gray matter were functioning normally. . . .

The bow plunged into a trough left by a rolling wave and

1

reared out again. His head swam. Nausea caused as much by the drug as the motion of the sea made his stomach churn. He staggered, nearly falling to his knees as his city shoes lost purchase on the slippery wood. The resulting yanks on his arms twisted behind him made him cry out.

The gorillas reached the railing. Thrown hard against the iron bar, McClain stared groggily down at the dark, choppy waters of the Atlantic. How many miles out to sea were they? It had been maybe an hour before that they had passed beneath the Chesapeake Bay Bridge. Doing about seven knots, as they were, that meant they'd come . . . Hell, his brain wouldn't perform even that simple calculation. Forcing himself to concentrate, he tried again.

The trawler plunged again and his stomach plunged with it. God, he couldn't think. At least the rush of the wind drowned out Yuropov's blubbering. They'd crushed the knuckles of the Russian's right hand, one by one, with a pair of pliers. The man had screamed until one of their captors had slammed a rifle butt into his face. After that they had heard only a sobbing punctuated by the bubbling of blood as Yuropov tried to breathe through the pulp of what had once been his nose and mouth. Which was probably a good thing, McClain had thought at the time. At least it kept the Soviet from spilling his guts about the microfilm concealed in a secret compartment in McClain's belt. If Rostov had had any inkling of the existence of a microfilm, he would have tortured its whereabouts out of one of them, if a simple strip search hadn't revealed it, which it probably would have. Rostov was a pro, after all. He was no stranger to secret hiding places, and the belt was a garden-variety money belt that didn't work half the time with the muggers it was designed to circumvent.

Yuropov's life wasn't worth a penny now that the Soviets

had him back. Yuropov knew that as well as McClain did. Defectors weren't exactly popular with the Central Committee, and defectors who happened to be former KGB officers with the information that Yuropov had told him could be assured of a very long, painful death while the KGB used its innumerable wiles to find out exactly what beans he had spilled.

Behind him, out of the corner of his eye, McClain saw a white-soled deck shoe beneath the perfectly creased leg of a white canvas trouser. Colonel Andrei Rostov, KGB. A graduate of the Moscow State Institute for International Relations, and formally a diplomatic attaché at the Russian Embassy in Washington. Informally he was deputy to the Washington Rezident, or KGB chief. McClain had known Rostov, or at least known of him, for years. They were close to the same age, and for a while had been rising at about the same speed through the intelligence ranks on their respective sides. But Rostov had far outstripped him in the last few years.

A sharp dresser, was Rostov, which was unusual for a Soviet, and a damned good agent. Intelligent, ruthless, efficient. McClain had been like that once, before the monumental screw up of Budapest. Now he was nothing more than a boozed up, burned-out shell.

He couldn't believe he'd been careless enough to let them be taken. That he'd been entrusted to debrief Yuropov, the agency's prize catch, at all had come about through a combination of Yuropov's own request (McClain had met Yuropov briefly when both had been posted to West Germany at the same time years before) and a personal vote of confidence on the part of Hammersmith. Tim Hammersmith had his own ass to cover as the newly appointed acting head of the foreign intelligence gathering arm of the Central Intelligence Agency, but he had stuck his neck out for

McClain, who had worked for him before when both had had far more elite, deep-cover overseas assignments. Now Hammersmith was paunchy and balding, the flame that had driven him burned down into ordinariness just as McClain's had. But he still retained his irreverent sense of humor, dubbing his group the Redbusters and playing a tape of the theme to the movie *Ghostbusters* with "Redbusters" inserted at appropriate spots at the conclusion of every staff meeting. The secretaries were going ape, vowing to strike if they were subjected to the song one more time, but McClain thought it was funny. Gave the whole intelligence gathering bit, which tended to be deadly dull routine, and dry as dust, a little comic relief.

"You can get more information out of him than anyone else I know, Jack. First, he seems to trust you. And people open up to you, for some reason I can't begin to fathom. Must be that ugly mug of yours." Hammersmith had grinned as he had told McClain of the plum assignment that, if carried out successfully, would restore some of McClain's lost lustre in the intelligence service. McClain knew that Hammersmith had had to lobby hard to get the assignment for him, despite Yuropov's request. It was symptomatic of Hammersmith's basic softheartedness that he would do what he could to get his old friend and long-time subordinate back on the fast track. Burned-out agents were usually put out to pasture in some nice desk job; McClain himself had been stuck monitoring intercepts for the past three years. Rarely were they offered the chance of a come-back. But McClain knew he'd been an unusually effective operative. The agency was loathe to lose him to mediocrity unless there was no alternative. So it had come: his chance to work his way back to where he had been.

Hammersmith had been right. Yuropov had opened up.

He'd spilled lots of little secrets over the six weeks that McClain had been handling him. Tonight, over linguine with clam sauce at a pricey D.C. restaurant, he'd parted almost casually with the granddaddy of them all, a secret so big that McClain had called Hammersmith from the restaurant to tell him they had to see him immediately. Without revealing what it was that Yuropov had given up (even public telephones were not proof against interception, as McClain well knew), he had then bundled Yuropov into his beat up Chevy Nova and lit out for Hammersmith's Gaithersburg home. Hammersmith wouldn't believe this one unless he got it straight from the horse's mouth.

Only they hadn't made it. A car running without lights had come hurtling out of nowhere on the dark twisty road. McClain had been driving the familiar route with only half his mind on the road. The other half he had given over to weighing the bombshell that Yuropov had dropped. The previous intelligence Yuropov had passed along had proven to be right on target, but even so it was nearly inconceivable that a deep cover Soviet mole had managed to worm his way into a high-level position deep within the CIA itself.

The mole's codename was Bigfoot. If what Yuropov had said was true the mole's existence was a catastrophe of monstrous proportions. His identity was unknown to Yuropov, although the information Bigfoot had passed along was mind boggling in its scope, accuracy, and ability to compromise the entire U.S. intelligence apparatus. It had had to come from someone at the very top. Someone who had access to a broad range of secrets. Someone who was above the "need to know" basis for the dissemination of highly classified information. But even more urgent than the possibility of Bigfoot's existence was the operation Yuropov swore the mole was even then in the process of carrying out:

nothing less than the imminent assassination of the secretary of state.

According to Yuropov, Bigfoot had passed the word to Moscow about a top secret summit to be held at an undisclosed location in the U.S. in two weeks time. The meeting was between Chinese and American leaders; its purpose was to execute a mutual defense treaty between the two super-powers. The Soviets perceived such a treaty as an extreme danger to themselves. The secretary of state, Franklin Conrad, was an archconservative known to be strongly in favor of it. Without his urging, it was felt, the waffling president would not agree to such a treaty. The solution, therefore, was obvious: eliminate the secretary of state. But Yuropov didn't know the exact details of the plot. Only that while the assassination had been approved at the highest levels in Moscow, the plan itself was being activated by Bigfoot.

McClain had been preoccupied with silently sifting through the possibilities when the car had overtaken them and crashed into the side of the Nova, slamming it into a ditch. McClain had put up a fight of course, but one of the thugs had stabbed a needle into his thigh, and that had been that. Now he and Yuropov were going to die, and there didn't seem to be a thing he could do about it. He had blown it . . . God, had he blown it. And he was about to pay with his life for the monumental sin of a few moments of carelessness. The worst of it was that he hadn't given Hammersmith a clue as to the nature of Yuropov's bomb-shell. So what Yuropov had told him would die with him. And no one in Washington would ever know about the danger to national security. Bigfoot would live long and prosper, the secretary of state would die, and the American-Sino mutual defense pact would be no more than a Soviet nightmare once again.

"Do svidaniya, Mr. Magic Dragon.'' The mocking use of his old codename along with the Russian's good-bye was barely audible over the sharp slap of a wave against the hull as the trawler heeled again. Rostov was directly behind him. McClain could see moonlight gleaming on the barrel of the pistol as Rostov raised it. It was now or never.

Terror and rage combined to give him a burst of superhuman strength; another sharp yawning of the trawler didn't hurt any, either. The gorillas' attention had shifted to Rostov. They expected no further resistance from McClain. With a sudden, desperate jerk, he managed to break free and launch himself in a low, fast dive over the rail.

"Nyet!" Rostov howled as McClain jack-knifed toward the frothy black water. A bright streak of light flashed across his peripheral vision. There was a muffled *thwack*! and the sensation of a baseball bat slamming into his skull behind his left ear. Momentarily he blacked out. The shock of icy water closing over his head brought him to his senses as he disappeared with a splash beneath the waves.

He was not dead. That fact was born in on him as he sank deeper and deeper into the bone chilling turbulence of the sea. His eyes opened wide, trying vainly to see through the salty blackness that was as dense as oil. His head hurt like hell, ached and burned just behind his ear. He could neither see nor hear nor breathe, but he was not dead. Yet. To live, he had to fight his way out of the undertow that sent him tumbling head over heels through the ocean's pitch dark middle. He must first have air; then he would take the business of surviving from there. He forced himself to touch the place behind his ear where the throbbing was centered. His exploring fingers found a shallow gash about three inches long that slanted sharply upward, slightly above and behind his ear. Rostov must have fired as he hurtled downward; the bullet had just creased his flesh. He'd done as much to himself shaving. Lucky. He'd been lucky.

Lungs burning, he tried to swim. It was impossible. The ocean had him in its grasp, tossing and tumbling him as a child would toss a ball. Blind panic caused him to thrash wildly. He felt himself sinking further. With a tremendous effort of will he forced himself to calm down and try again to swim. A shoe went; the small loss lightened him. He kicked off the other one and felt immediately more buoyant. His arms and legs made weak paddling motions that affected his plight not at all. But at least they seemed to keep him from plummeting further toward the bottom of the sea. He paddled, holding his breath until he could hold it no longer and then holding it some more, praying all the while that the sea would spit him up before he drowned.

A sudden upsurge caught him and he surfaced. Retching and gasping, he looked around. Not more than a hundred feet to his left the trawler chugged through the water; on its deck stood Rostov, scanning the waves with a flashlight. At each end of the boat his henchmen were doing likewise. They were looking for him, McClain realized. Taking a deep breath he dove down again, deep into the sea.

When he was forced to surface, the trawler was much farther in the distance. It was barely moving through the water. As McClain watched, blinking against the sting of the saltwater in his eyes, he saw that it was moving around so that it would be between him and the shore. Of course, Rostov must hope that the shot had killed him, or wounded him so much that he would drown, but he could hardly take that chance. He would have to find him if he was anywhere to be found. . . .

A beam of light swung in his direction. McClain knew that it was too far away to find him, tiny speck that he was in a vast black ocean of pitching waves, but then he heard the faintest sound of a shout and seconds later the trawler seemed to be turning in his direction. It was only then that McClain realized his white face must stand out like a beacon against the inky water. Gulping a lungful of air, he prepared to dive. But before he could do so, a huge wave washed over him and sent him crashing down head over heels into the ocean's depths to flail about as helplessly as a rag doll.

Through the blackness all around him, he realized that he could see cylindrical shapes of an even denser blackness. Squinting against the searing sting of the saltwater, he tried to believe that his eyes were playing tricks on him. Even as his body tumbled, his eyes searched. Then the black shapes drew closer. McClain felt panic surge again. Sharks! Of course, the blood that must still be flowing from his head had attracted them. To be torn to pieces by these primitive feeding machines had been one of his secret nightmares since he had seen *Jaws*. He wanted to flail blindly, but he knew that if he did the motion would likely lure them to attack at once. He must not panic. Somewhere he had read that their noses were their vulnerable points. He would try to punch their noses with his fist, hoping to scare them off. As a defense, it was pitiable in its weakness, but it was all he could think of. Eyes straining to make out the shapes through the darkness, he clenched one hand into a fist, paddling with the other. Fear tasted sour on his tongue. . . .

The undertow chose that moment to tumble him upwards. His head popped through the surface. For a moment McClain thought of nothing but filling his starving lungs as he sucked in great gulps of air. The lights that marked the trawler bobbed some three hundred feet away. Instead of cruising a straight line between where they had lost him and shore, or heading on out to sea where Yuropov would be handed over to a ship that would carry him back to Russia, the trawler seemed to be traveling in concentric circles. He was just to the north of its epicenter.

Rostov must have seen the flash of his face against the water when he had surfaced before. They were zeroing in on him with characteristically systematic efficiency. Rostov would not rest until he was sure that his target was dead.

Overhead the moon peeped from behind a moving mass of dark clouds. McClain instinctively lowered his face to the water, knowing that his skin would reflect the light and be visible to anyone who happened to look in his direction. Though being shot to death was preferable to some other deaths he could think of.

Suddenly a wave rolled over his head and he simultaneously felt the weight of a smooth, sleek body as it hurtled past his thigh.

"Oh, God," he prayed, unable to form a more coherent plea as he was sucked down into the ocean's belly again. The sharks would be near, he knew. The scent of blood would keep them from losing him despite the undertow's machinations. The pass of that body had doubtless meant that they were circling him, closing in for the kill. . . .

He felt one brush his leg, and would have screamed if he had been anywhere else. Frantically he twisted about, trying to keep the aggressor in his view. Five or six of the black hulking shapes were circling him. He tried to swim away, knowing that it was useless, that he was as helpless against these predators of the deep as he had been against Rostov and his thugs earlier. At any moment one would attack. Those razor sharp teeth would tear off an arm or leg.

They were drawing closer together, sandwiching him between them, but made no move to hurt him as they carried him along with them. McClain's head burst through to the surface even as the truth dawned on him: He was not being menaced by sharks. They were dolphins, and, miracle of miracles, the creatures seemed to be intent on helping him.

Although he had never really believed them, he had heard tales of dolphins bearing drowning swimmers to shore. Still disbelieving, he grasped a shiny dorsal fin as a sleek powerful body surged past him, and was carried with it. Great rolling waves of salty seawater threatened to drown him anew as they engulfed his mouth and nose. Would the creature head for the depths again? But no, it was skimming along the surface, speeding away from where the trawler still bobbed in that pattern of ever widening circles, with its mates jumping and diving beside it and McClain being towed in its wake. Locking both hands in a death grip around the slippery fin, he concentrated on staying conscious and keeping his mouth and nose above water.

The saltwater burned like kerosene in his eyes. He closed them and entrusted himself to God. And the dolphin.

Hours could have passed. Or days. Or centuries. What brought McClain out of the trancelike state he had entered was the feel of the fin slipping through his hands as the dolphin unexpectedly dived. One moment he was being pulled through the water at what felt like light speed. The next he was floundering, sinking, swallowing what seemed to be half the ocean as he fought to keep his head above the waves.

Dog paddling, he saw a flash of light as the moon hit an arching, leaping curve already several hundred feet away. Then there was only a phosphorescent trail on the ocean's surface that shimmered like green wildfire in the moonlight.

They were leaving him, he thought, panicking, leaving him to drown as they headed back out to sea. . . .

"Hang on, buddy, we'll have you safe in a minute."

Something hit his back as he thrashed, then landed with a splash beside him. Turning his head, he saw the white doughnut shape of a life preserver bobbing in the water a few feet away. For a moment he thought that Rostov had found him after all. Then he realized that this was not the trawler. It was much smaller, perhaps a three-man fishing vessel. In any case, Rostov would certainly not be throwing him a life preserver. Narrowing his eyes into the beam of the flashlight, he saw that the two men leaning over the side were strangers. One was fair-haired, young, dressed like all the young in jeans and a flannel shirt. The other was older, grizzled. But they were almost certainly not Soviet, or any other kind of, agents.

Breathing a wordless prayer of thanks, McClain managed the short swim to the life preserver. They hauled him to the side of the boat, dragging him over the side. Then he fainted.

When he woke again he was in an ambulance, bouncing up and down as it rushed toward a hospital. Bending over him were the intent faces of paramedics. As his eyes opened, one of them fastened a clear plastic bag half full of liquid to a hook over the bed. McClain saw that the tubing led down to a needle that disappeared into his arm. His head felt like it was about to explode. Attempting to lift a hand toward it, McClain was surprised to find that he was restrained by a strap that crossed over his arms and chest and held him to the bed.

"What," he began.

"Just lie still, man." The paramedic was black, with dark brown eyes that gleamed at him over a white surgical mask.

McClain could barely hear him over the screaming of the siren. "You're going to be okay. You got lucky. The bullet wound's just a graze. What you're suffering from is basically exposure, but it won't kill you. Can you tell us your name, give us the name of somebody to call? You know, next of kin?"

An answer was on the tip of his tongue. Then a lifetime of caution and training asserted themselves. No one in the agency, not even Hammersmith, knew of the existence of his mother and sisters. They were safer so, and he would not compromise them now. Rostov clearly had a strong suspicion that he was not dead; an all-out search and destroy effort would be mounted. Of course, Rostov might think he was at the bottom of the ocean, but Rostov was a careful man. He would do his utmost to make sure. And the fishing boat that had picked him up had very likely summoned an ambulance with a ship-to-shore radio. Being the man he was, Rostov had probably been monitoring the air waves.

"Where . . ." Funny, he couldn't seem to talk. His tongue felt like it was swollen to about three times its normal size, and he couldn't manipulate it well enough to form words. The paramedic frowned. McClain could see the deepening of the creases between his brows.

"Lie still, man," he said again, impatiently. Since he could do nothing else, McClain lay still as the man taped a gauze pad to the wound behind his ear. His mind worked, he was glad to discover. Slowly, painfully, but it worked. And what it was telling him was that there was every chance that Rostov was even now hot on his trail.

McClain knew he had to survive, had to get the word back. It was a matter of national security—and personal pride—as well as a way to make up for the blunders he had made. And a matter of his life, which he was kind of surprised to find he valued so greatly. But McClain also knew that Rostov would give his own life to stop him. Rostov was more machine than man; he let nothing stand in the way of getting the job done.

The ambulance screeched to a halt. Immediately the doors were jerked open from the outside and McClain, in his mobile bed, was bundled out. He could just make out the words Bethesda Naval Hospital Emergency Room on the brick wall as they wheeled him toward it. Just before he disappeared into the bowels of the emergency room, a nondescript brown Volvo screeched to a stop behind the ambulance. McClain craned his neck in time to see two men get out. Men in ill-fitting suits and bulky overcoats who stared after him as he passed through the hospital's brightly lit portals.

There were only a few people in the emergency room. A mother with her child in fuzzy, footed pajamas cuddled on her lap, an old couple, a man clutching his arm. McClain was wheeled straight on through another set of swinging doors. Doctors in white coats and nurses in white uniforms bustled around him as he was pushed into the treatment area.

"Shit!" McClain was glad to find that his tongue was functioning again. As he was wheeled into a curtained cubicle, his escort dropped off until he was attended by one intern and one nurse. Which made what he had to do that much easier, he thought. He'd been in the game long enough to recognize KGB men when he saw them, and his still sluggish brain had finally picked up on what had bothered him about the two men in the Volvo: they were vintage KGB. Just as he had hypothesized, Rostov must have been monitoring the ship-to-shore air waves in case another boat picked him up. Unless he got out of the hospital fast he would be dead.

The nurse unfastened the straps that held him to the stretcher.

"Thank you," McClain said politely, sitting up and pulling the IV needle from his arm.

"You mustn't!" The nurse tried to push him back, but he shoved her aside. "Doctor!"

There was no time to be polite. As the young intern came to the nurse's aid, McClain socked him in the jaw. Under normal circumstances the man would have dropped like a stone. As weak as McClain felt, he was relieved to see the fellow go staggering back, then lose his footing and fall.

"Help!"

The frightened nurse called for reinforcements, lunging for the call button beside the bed. McClain lurched to his feet and staggered toward the rear of the treatment ward, shouldering past hospital personnel who were running to the aid of the nurse. The nurse emerged from the cubicle, shrieking and pointing after him, just as he burst through the door that led from the emergency room into the hospital proper. Immediately to his left was an open elevator. It was empty, McClain was relieved to see. He stepped inside, sagging against the wall and pushing the button for the top floor. The doors closed just as two white-coated interns, the nurse he had run out on and the KGB men erupted into the hall.

The elevator began to ascend with a speed that made his stomach lurch. Halfway up, he pushed the emergency stop button. With any luck the goons from the KGB would imagine him, hurt and panicking, thinking he could hold them at bay while marooning himself in an elevator. While they waited for the elevator to be restarted and brought up, he would have time to escape. Goons at the level his present pursuers appeared to occupy were not selected for their intelligence, in his experience. With luck, it should not occur to them that he might be able to escape from an elevator trapped between floors.

If only he weren't so damned weak, McClain thought as he jumped up, once, twice, three times before managing to grab the edge of the trapdoor in the ceiling of the elevator. Wincing, panting, he nevertheless succeeded in pulling himself up and through it, dislodging the door at the same time. He caught the metal door just before it could go skittering over the edge of the roof. If it had fallen, it would have landed with a crash on the concrete floor four stories below, and that crash might clue an alert listener in on what he was trying to do.

Thank God it was a double shaft. Now all he had to do was pray he had the strength to catch himself and hang on. Trying not to think of the four-story drop below him, he peeled off his thick, soaking wet athletic socks and wound them around the palms of his hands. Then, taking a deep breath, he jumped from the roof of the car toward the concrete block wall. He fell like a stone, but managed to catch hold of the steel cable of the adjoining elevator as he did so. The pain in his hands was excruciating even with the meager padding of the socks, but he hung on, wrapping his body around the cable and using his blue-jeaned legs to stop his precipitate slide before his hands were sliced to the bone. The strategy worked, and his downward rush stopped abruptly.

Panting with the pain in his hands and his head, praying that loss of blood would not cause him to lose consciousness and fall, McClain clung to the cable with one hand and the entire rest of his body while he loosened his belt with the other. Fastening the sturdy leather so that it encircled the cable as well as his waist, he grasped the cable again and stretched his legs out until his bare feet were braced against the rough cement block wall. He would catwalk down. Willing himself to ignore the terrible burning behind his ear, he gripped the steel cable with desperate strength, lowering himself down the shaft with an efficiency sprung from years of training and some weekend rappeling. If only he wouldn't pass out—or the elevator belonging to this particular cable wouldn't hurtle down from the heights before he could get out of the shaft. . . .

He made it. Opening the emergency access door, he staggered out into the deserted basement. His wet jeans left a trail of drips on the terrazzo floor. He could only hope that the trail would dry before anyone who could connect it to him found it. It was a short walk to an unlocked side door which led to a set of outside stairs. He climbed them and found himself on a sidewalk facing the hospital parking lot.

Unbinding his hands and tossing the soggy, lacerated socks behind a convenient bush, he examined his hands for an instant under the bright glare of the streetlights around the parking lot. He had suffered the equivalent of rope burns across both palms. Blood beaded slowly along a razor-blade thin slice in the exact center of the burns. Minor damage, was his assessment. He would live. He would definitely live. Wrapping his arms around his bare chest (the paramedic must have discarded his shirt in the ambulance, because he couldn't account for its loss otherwise), McClain stood shivering in the cold night air as he weighed the possibilities.

He felt surprisingly good. An adrenaline rush, he supposed, that came from meeting danger and surviving. McClain discovered that he was whistling through his teeth, and

grinned as he recognized the tune "Ghostbusters." Hammersmith and his ridiculous tapes.

Moving swiftly toward the parking lot, he surveyed its
contents with detached assessment. Like many hospital
parking lots, this one was almost half full of unattended
cars. Like taking candy from a baby, he thought, and for the
hell of it selected a candy red Corvette to hot wire. He
deserved some pleasure out of this godawful day.

II

Saturday, October 3, 12:45 A.M.

Clara Winston yawned. It was late, past her usual bedtime of eleven P.M., and she was dead tired. She had stayed up to finish some last minute editing on her newest book. *A Summer Kiss* was one of her better efforts, she thought. Light, frothy, romantic, with believable characters. She didn't want to be immodest, but she thought that it was really very good. As she ran her eyes over the last page of her ninth romance, she felt that indefinable tingle that always accompanied the completion of another book. Now she had a few months of leisure coming. . . .

Setting the proofs aside, she turned off the light and headed down the stairs. Puff, the gigantic ball of gray fur that ruled her with a rod of iron, greeted her at the foot of the stairs and weaved meowing about her ankles as she walked down the hall toward the bathroom of the small, two-story former carriage house that she had converted into her personal residence some four years before. Even with a mother as loving as Clara's was, one needed one's privacy, and there was no way to dislodge her mother from the big house that had been in the Jolly family for generations. Not that she would want to, anyway. Emily Jolly Winston Crawleigh Hays Seidel *was* Jollymead. A dyed-in-the-wool Southern belle who at age fifty-two had gone through four husbands and was working on landing number five, her mother was the last of a vanishing breed. Clara loved her dearly, but she could not live in the same house with her. Not unless she wanted to go insane. Besides, as she'd told her mother four years before, she needed privacy to work. Emily had been unconvinced—in her view Clara didn't need to work, she should instead direct her energies toward finding a suitable husband—but Clara had been adamant, and in the end she had won out. The carriage house was hers. Compared to the fading magnificence of the porticoed big house it was small and insignificant and even a little shabby, but Clara loved it anyway. She had converted the entire upstairs into an office. Keeping the two sides of her life separate had seemed a good idea. Downstairs she lived, slept, and ate. Upstairs she worked.

"You just ate an entire can of seafood dinner!" Clara protested at the bathroom door, determined to ignore Puff's protestations of starvation. The greedy monster yowled, pressing against her insistently. Clara sighed. "Look at Amy and Iris! You don't see them begging for seconds!"

The two cream and gray Siamese cats she referred to, a gift from her aunt on Clara's twenty-ninth birthday, were sitting side by side on the braided kitchen rug, daintily washing themselves after their evening meal. Puff spared their slender shapes not so much as a glance. Instead he sank his needle sharp teeth into Clara's pink terry mule, as if to chide her for comparing his majestic Persian girth with their Oriental slenderness.

"Youch! Stop it, Puff!" Clara glared down at him, shoved him aside with her leg, marched into the bathroom and locked the door. Living alone as she did, locking the bathroom door would seem an unnecessary precaution. But not if she hoped for a moment's peace. That dratted cat could open any door that was not securely locked. To keep him out, every cabinet had to have a childproof catch on it. She'd even had to slide a ruler through the twin handles of the side by side refrigerator after he'd learned to open that. Come to think of it, maybe she should have left the refrigerator alone. For a while there, he hadn't been yowling at her every time he felt the need of sustenance in addition to his daily (gigantic) meal. He'd been opening the refrigerator and helping himself, once even knocking a carton of milk over so he and Iris and Amy could have a drink.

The cat was a menace, no doubt about it, Clara told herself as she tied a scarf around her head to keep her shoulder-length, baby fine blonde hair out of her face. Rubbing a thick white cleansing cream into her skin, she grimaced at her reflection. Puff had been with her for ten years now, and for all his many faults she loved him dearly. But since the vet had told her to put him on a diet . . . Clara rinsed the cream off with warm water and followed it with a splash of cold to close her pores. She just wished the vet could try putting Puff on a diet. Be firm, she silently mimicked the instructions she'd been given. The man obviously had no conception of the lengths to which Puff would go to get what he considered a decent meal.

"Yowl!"

Clara sighed. Now he would howl until she came out. She'd ignored the rattling of the door as he'd tried to jimmy it open with his paw, but his yowling was something else. The deep throated cry was as grating as fingernails across a blackboard. But she would ignore that, too. Fixing her eyes firmly on her reflection, she smoothed moisturizing cream into the soft white skin of her face and neck. Her complexion was her one real claim to beauty, and she took care of it. Good skin made up for a lot of beauty failings, she thought, looking resignedly at her overlong nose, mismatched lips and pointy chin. The proper use of cosmetics camouflaged the rest. Her ordinary blue eyes took on a lovely sparkle when carefully framed by tangerine eyeshadow, charcoal-brown liner and deep brown mascara. And her straggly eyebrows acquired elan when cunningly filled in with a taupe pencil. In fact, when she had the time and motivation to effect the transformation, she could be quite an attractive woman. But when she was just schlepping around. . . .

"Yowl!"

Clara grimaced and turned away from her reflection, knowing that she could ignore the howling no longer without going mad.

"All right, Puff!" Gritting her teeth with exasperation, she retied the belt of the pink terry robe so that it was cinched even more firmly about her middle, opened the door and marched toward the kitchen. Puff, the maddening creature, purred like a motor as he followed sedately behind. He was getting his way again, and Clara had to shake her head at herself. It was a good thing she didn't have any children, she thought as she extracted the milk from the refrigerator and poured a modest amount into Puff's bowl. She couldn't even control a too-fat cat!

With his motor running at high speed, Puff settled himself in front of his dish and attacked the milk with greedy laps. Amy and Iris, Clara was glad to see as she returned the milk to the refrigerator and shut the door, were already curled up on the rug together, fast asleep. If only Puff were as well mannered as they.

A sharp knock sounded at the kitchen door. Clara started, and turned to stare. Who on earth would be knocking on her door at this time of night, so far out in the country? Her mother had left on a Carribbean cruise with her latest conquest two days before. Mrs. Mullins, the woman who kept house for her mother, was away too. The antebellum tobacco farm that was Jollymead was located along a narrow road that wound through the horse country of Virginia without ever going anywhere in particular. There was nearly half a mile between Jollymead and its nearest neighbor. So who could be—

The knock sounded again, louder this time, impatient. Amy and Iris sat up, staring at the door. Puff even looked up briefly before returning his attention to his milk.

Clara crossed to the door, hesitated, then pulled the blue gingham curtain aside so that she could look out. A man's face stared back at her. A strange man, with short blond hair, looking at her expressionlessly through the glass. A man in a beige raincoat, who was holding something in his hand.

"Miss Winston? Claire Winston?"

The words were muffled, coming from the other side of the door, but Clara had no trouble recognizing her nom de plume. As Claire Winston, she was a fairly well-known author of romances, and since she had started putting her address in the backs of her books so that fans would know where to write her she had received a few impromptu visits as well as letters. But this man didn't look like a romance fan—not by any stretch of the imagination. A spurt of fright caused her to drop the curtain and back hurriedly toward the kitchen phone. As much as she hated to bother Mitch so late at night, she wanted the sheriff out there in a hurry.

Glass shattered; shards flew across the kitchen to land with a clatter on the lovingly restored brick floor. A black-gloved hand shot through the top half of the door, groping for the knob below. Gasping at the horror of it—she didn't have enough breath to scream—Clara dropped the phone and ran for the bedroom, which had a sturdy, lockable door, another phone, and a can of mace. The cats scattered as she did. There was a tremendous crash as the door was flung back on its hinges. Her heart was pounding so fiercely that she could feel each panicked beat. She was going to make it, she was going to make it, she was go—

She stumbled over something and fell to her knees just a foot short of her bedroom. Even as she crawled frantically forward, nails digging into the plush mauve carpet, a protesting yowl told her what the something had been. Curse you, Puff! she swore silently just as a hand closed painfully over the back of her neck and hauled her to her feet.

She screamed—ear splittingly. Only to have the sound cut off by a slap so vicious that it sent her head snapping back and weakened her knees. Silenced, stunned, terrified, barely aware of the taste of blood on her tongue from a cut lip, she was forced into her bedroom by a grimly silent monster in the shape of a man who was twisting her arm behind her back as though he meant to break it. The pain shot through her body like hot swords, but even worse than the physical agony was the mental. Who was he? What did he want with her? Oh, God, was he a rapist? A killer? What could she do?

She thought about trying to kick backwards at him, then thought again. She was not even sure she could kick that far in her present bent position, and even if her foot made contact with his leg she doubted that it would hurt him. Her slippers were soft terrycloth. In retaliation for the attempt, he might very well break her arm. He pushed her through the bedroom door, his grip on her arm tightening brutally as he forced her to her knees beside the bed. Tears formed in her eyes and clogged her throat. She was in so much pain. . . .

"Search the house. Everywhere," he said over his shoulder in a cold hard voice with the faintest hint of an accent that she couldn't, in her agony, quite place. It was then that she realized he was not alone. Crashes of overturning furniture told her that his confederates were tearing her home apart.

"You will tell me where he is and I will let you go." Her captor was leaning over her, holding her arm in a vice grip. Bright shafts of agony shot along her nerve endings. Then he slackened his grip a degree, leaving her almost gasping in relief.

"Who—who?" The word was a squeak, but Clara was surprised she could talk at all. Her arm was twisted so viciously that she cried out.

"The Magic Dragon. Where is he?"

"The magic dragon?" Was the man insane? Oh, God, this couldn't be happening. It was the stuff of her worst nightmares. Half sobbing, she rested her head against the soft plush covering the floor. He was going to kill her, she knew it. There was a cold viciousness about the way he deliberately caused her pain. She would die—and she wouldn't even know why, or the identity of her killer. Clara was afraid to look at the man's face, afraid of what he would do to her if she tried to get a glimpse of his features.

"Yes, the Magic Dragon!" He wrenched her arm again,

then slackened his grip as she cried out. "Do not play games with me! Where is he?"

"The magic dragon?" Clara thought frantically, but she had not the least idea of what he was talking about. "Uh, what magic dragon?"

Clara screamed as he twisted her arm with methodical ferocity. He would break it for sure if she didn't tell him—what? The pain was so excruciating that she couldn't even think clearly.

"The Magic Dragon! The Magic Dragon! *This* Magic Dragon!" He extracted something from his pocket and thrust it in front of her eyes. Clara saw that it was a copy of her latest book, *The Magic Dragon*. Her hero had been a secret agent who had used the song title as a code name. But what did her book have to do with anything?

"I'm sorry, but I don't understand what you want." She tried to speak clearly and reasonably, hoping that some of her reason would rub off on the maniac who was breaking her arm.

"I want to know where the Magic Dragon is!" he said in a voice more terrifying than a roar. "This Magic Dragon!" He opened the book to the title page, holding it in front of her eyes so that she could read the dedication. "With love to the real Magic Dragon, who inspired this book—and me" she'd written.

"This Magic Dragon!" he hissed. "Where is he? You will tell me *now*!"

"Uh, under the bed," Clara whispered, closing her eyes. If he was going to kill her, she didn't want to watch him do it.

"Under the . . ." His voice trailed off. His grip tightened on her arm and she braced herself as he twisted it with slow relish. Searing pain shot from her shoulder blade through her midsection and back up again. Clara whimpered, utterly defeated. "I want the truth, and I want it now! Where is the Magic Dragon?"

"He's under the bed. I swear it," Clara whispered, the pain nauseating her. His grip tightened for a moment, and then he was releasing her, pushing her away so that she fell onto the carpet before pulling herself up on her hands and knees. Her arm ached so that it would not hold her weight, and Clara cradled it against her body as she clambered warily around to face him. He was on his knees too, she saw, and she also saw that he was holding an ugly black pistol. Her heartbeat speeded up and she could scarcely hear anything over its drumbeat.

"Make a move and I kill you," he said between his teeth. Looking into icy blue eyes that glared at her from a face that would have been palely handsome if it had not been on the other end of a gun, Clara knew that he meant what he said. She also realized that, whatever this lunatic wanted, he was going to kill her sooner or later, whether he got it or not. Her fate was there in his eyes.

Somehow she managed to shake her head. But already his attention was shifting from her. She had to do something, now, she thought as he lifted the dotted swiss bed ruffle and scanned the space beneath the bed. Clara watched him, afraid to move. She had to do something, but what could she possibly do against a tall, vicious maniac with a gun?

"There is no one here!" The voice with its slight foreign accent was taut with anger and accusation. Clara swallowed. There was a can of mace in her top drawer. . . .

"He—he was there. He hid there. I saw him. I—he must be under there."

The man pulled up the dust ruffle again. A fat gray paw

darted out, batting at the shifting material. Puff loved to take a swing at moving objects.

"You see, he is there!" Relief rang in her voice.

"There is nothing here but a cat!"

"That's Puff."

"I am not interested in the beast's name! Enough of this foolishness! You will tell me where the Magic Dragon is, now. Or I will force you to talk in ways that you will not enjoy, I promise you." He rose to his feet, his eyes narrowing until they were icy blue slits.

Clara had no difficulty believing him. She cowered, cradling her arm protectively against her as she watched him approach with growing terror.

"But—but Puff *is* the magic dragon. You know the song. 'Puff, the magic dragon, lives by the sea,'" she babbled, singing a few bars for emphasis. "I named him for the dragon in the song, and I named the character in my book for Puff. Because his name gave me the idea..." Her voice trailed off and she shrank against the nightstand. In a second he would reach her. He would hurt her, she knew. Should she make a grab for the mace now? Even if she could get to the chemical, would she dare use it on this man? She remembered hearing somewhere that mace didn't always work on lunatics—and this man seemed to be totally around the bend.

"I want the Magic Dragon!" The words were a hiss. Clara cringed as he took another step toward her. As he closed in on her she pressed herself backward until her spine felt as if it would meld with the flowery paper covering the wall. Her hand shot down toward her nightstand and closed around a framed picture of her mother—framed in padded fabric, naturally. It was the only object she could reach...But before she could throw it or hit him with it or whatever she intended to do, he stumbled, falling heavily, cursing in a foreign language as the side of his head hit the nightstand with a resounding crack. An indignant yowl and a flash of gray fur gave her the identity of her rescuer, but Clara didn't wait around to see how long her attacker would be down. This was her chance, her only chance, and she took it with a speed born of desperation. Leaping to her feet, picking up the skirts of her robe, she cleared the man's back with the agility of a running back and darted down the hall toward the kitchen door, leaving her pink mules behind her as she went. He had left it standing wide open.

"Stop her!" he roared, and his two confederates burst out of rooms on either side of the hall. Terror gave her a speed and agility she had never imagined she possessed as she dodged them both and the glass on the floor as well to fly through the door with them hot on her heels, shouting curses in a foreign language that was not French or Spanish or Arabic but Russian. (The "nyet, nyet" she heard one of them shout to another was unmistakable.) The cold wash of an autumn rain fell about her head, but she didn't even feel it, or hear the companionable rumble of thunder. She ran for her life, darting across the yard into the tobacco field across the road, leaping and dodging amongst the stalks of tobacco that had thankfully not been harvested because there was no money in it this year and were therefore higher than her head. They would have a hard time finding her in the field at night. Behind her she could hear them crashing about, and she was glad of the noise. At least she could keep track of their whereabouts, and the noise they made would drown out her own less cumbersome passing. . . .

A tall, shadowy figure holding a gun materialized directly in front of her. No, it couldn't be, it was impossible. They could not have gotten in front of her. Clara opened her mouth to scream with mindless, soul shattering terror. She would be killed now, she knew. He was on her in an instant, whirling her around so that her back was to him, his hand slamming over her mouth, stifling the scream before it was born. He yanked her back against his chest, then threw her to the ground. Her breath was knocked from her as he fell with her, landing heavily on top of her, pressing her face into the pebbly mud between the rows. Tears fell from Clara's eyes to mingle with the rain on her face as she felt the hard muzzle of a gun pressed to her temple.

III

McClain felt the soft body of the woman beneath him and cursed under his breath. He hated hurting women. It was a weakness of his that must have been instilled in him by his female relatives. But this one was one of the bad guys, had to be if she was involved with Rostov. And she *was* involved with Rostov. McClain had tailed him to this farm in the middle of nowhere, having discovered the Russian and his henchmen systematically searching his apartment when he had driven the Corvette up outside, only a half hour or so after he had made it safely away from the hospital. He had stopped only to buy a Saturday night special from a guy on the streets. At the last minute he'd thought to offer the man an extra twenty if he'd throw in his sweatshirt and sneakers and the man had obliged. He might smell a little bit—the sweatshirt was definitely well-worn—but at least he was armed and decently covered.

The disadvantage of being as much machine as man was that your moves were predictable, McClain thought. He had expected Rostov to show up at his place, although he had thought it would take a little longer than it had. He

31

had already decided that his best course was to go on the
offensive and take out Rostov before the Russian could take
him out.

Thanking God that he and Gloria had had a fight that
morning and she had stormed home to her mother for the
umpteenth time that month, McClain had settled in to watch
what happened. His first thought upon driving away from
the hospital parking lot, with a relatively whole skin, had
been to contact Hammersmith, but an innate sense of
caution had caused him to hesitate. After all, his last
conversation with Hammersmith had had very unpleasant
consequences. Somehow, that telephone call had been
intercepted by the KGB. The odds on Hammersmith being
involved with the Soviets were minimal, but not nonexistent. Good agents had turned before. With his life on the
line, McClain preferred to err on the side of caution. Until
he had had a chance to sort this whole thing out in his own
mind, he felt safer going it alone. The thought had occurred
to him that he might just be able to use Rostov to get to
Bigfoot. If he was lucky, when the search was finished and
a guard posted on the off chance that McClain was stupid
enough to waltz back into his apartment, Rostov would
report to his superior. And if he was really lucky, Rostov's
superior might turn out to be in contact with Bigfoot. Of
course, it had been a long time since he'd been that lucky,
but then luck had a way of changing. Sometimes.

"Shut up!" he hissed in response to the woman's gasping
efforts to breathe, and stealed himself for what he was
probably going to have to do to her to make her talk.

Clara shut up. This man's accent was definitely American, and he seemed both shorter and more muscular than the
one who had attacked her in the house. He was also not

wearing gloves. She felt the hard warmth of his palm over her mouth. The salt of his skin burned against her cut lip.

She lay unmoving beneath his crushing weight for what seemed like an eternity, trying not to think of the gun that was still pressed to her temple. Would she know when he pulled the trigger, or would it all happen so fast that she could be dead before the action could register?

Finally he shifted, lifting his head as if he were listening. Oh, God, were the others still looking for her? For them? For he had seemed as anxious as she to hide. . . .

"Make a single sound and I blow your head off. Got it?"

Clara nodded. She was no longer even aware of feeling frightened. She had gone beyond that to numbness. Nothing mattered any longer. If he was going to kill her, let him kill her and be done with it.

To her surprise, he rolled off her to crouch by her side. The gun was no longer pressed to her temple, but balanced loosely in his hand. He jerked her up so that she was kneeling in front of him, facing away from him. The gun settled behind her ear. Clara cringed.

"What have you got to do with Rostov?"

"Who?" Her voice sounded rusty because her throat and tongue and lips were so dry. The cold rain had slackened, but her face, like the rest of her, was soaking wet. She ran her tongue around her lips to catch some of that precious moisture, swallowed, then tried again. "Who?"

He was impatient. "The man in your house just now. You do remember him?"

"Oh." Clara licked her parched lips. The pressure of the gun's muzzle behind her ear increased. "He—he broke into my house. But—"

"Now why would he do that? Break into a strange woman's house? Pretty unusual, that, wouldn't you say?"

He paused for a moment, then his hand twisted in the wet knot of hair at the nape of her neck. "Tell the truth. What are you to Rostov? His contact?"

"I am telling the truth!" Clara was almost in despair. Why would no one believe her? Crouching amidst towering stalks of tobacco in a freezing rain in the middle of the night with a madman who had a gun pressed to her head was making her feel lightheaded. What else could happen to her? Then she thought, he could kill me, and she started to shake.

"You are telling me that Rostov drove thirty miles into the country and then broke into your house for no reason? Sweetheart, I should warn you that I'm perfectly aware of Rostov's game. He's KGB, and he wouldn't have driven out to the middle of nowhere at this time of night without a reason. But he did drive directly to your house and went inside. So tell me, what did he want?"

"He kept asking me about a Magic Dragon!" Clara wailed. This man was as crazy as the other. She had escaped from one only to fall victim to his doppelganger. She had to figure out a way to escape from him too.

"A Magic Dragon?" There was a curious note in his voice. He went very still, almost seeming to forget to breathe. "He was asking you about a Magic Dragon? What precisely did he say?"

"He—he wanted to know where the Magic Dragon was. He kept asking me over and over. So I told him."

"You *told* him?"

"Puff was under the bed. I told him so."

"Who the hell is Puff?"

"My cat. I named him Puff, as in 'Puff the Magic Dragon.' That lunatic in there—Rostov?—was waving my book around and demanding that I tell him where the Magic Dragon was. So I told him.''

There was a moment's silence. Then, "Tell me precisely what happened. Everything.''

Clara did, from the moment the man knocked on her kitchen door to her escape. When she finished, the man was silent. Clara dared a quick look over her shoulder. The moon cast an odd silvery light over his face. In that split second she saw that he wasn't handsome at all. His face was broad-jawed and pugnacious, with a crooked nose and thin lips quirked now in what was almost a smile. Black hair that was too short for her taste gleamed blue in the moonlight. But what caught her attention was the extraordinary color of his eyes. In the moonlight, they glittered as brightly green as emeralds.

"So Rostov drove all the way down here on the strength of a dedication in a book, did he?" Although she was no longer looking at him, she could swear he was grinning. "He must have found it in my apartment. My girlfriend reads that romantic trash all the time. She must be a fan of yours. What did you say your name is?"

"Clara. Clara Winston. But I write under the name of Claire Winston." She was willing to disregard his slander to her profession under the circumstances.

He shook his head. "So you wrote a book about a spy and called it *The Magic Dragon*, huh? And dedicated it to the real Magic Dragon, with love?" There was no mistake this time. He actually chuckled. "Well, you certainly succeeded in laying a false scent, I'll give you that."

He straightened suddenly, standing up and thrusting the gun into his belt. Looking up at him, Clara saw that his shoulders were very broad while his waist was narrow and his legs were long and muscular. He was clad in a black sweatshirt and jeans, and towering over her like that he looked very menacing, despite the fact that he'd put the gun away.

"Let me give you some advice, Miss Winston," he said softly. "Find someplace to go for a couple of weeks. Rostov thinks you know where I am, and he wants to find me very, very badly. And he is not the type to take no for an answer. So take a vacation. He's gone for now—he and his men drove off shortly after you ran into the fields. But believe me, if he doesn't find what he's looking for soon, he'll be back. And I mean to see that he doesn't find what he's looking for."

"Who are you?" The whispered question was involuntary. She didn't really expect a reply, which was just as well, because she didn't get one.

Instead, he turned and melted away through the tobacco. Only the rustling of the tall stalks as he passed told her that he was real, that she hadn't just imagined the whole thing. Shaken, she continued to crouch in the mud without moving for a long time. But gradually it began to dawn on her that she was alone, and safe—for now at least—and the rain was starting up again. Standing, she peered warily between the rows of tobacco toward her little house. The kitchen door swung wide, and every window blazed with light. No one was about. Could she really take that man's word that Rostov and his thugs were gone? Who was he, anyway? He'd said Rostov wanted him. Could he have some connection with the mysterious dragon Rostov was searching for? From his reaction to her story, she rather thought he did. What in the world had she gotten involved in?

A familiar round gray shape stalked into view, framed by the light spilling from the kitchen door. Seating himself on the stoop, Puff began to wash his face. That settled one question, Clara thought, stepping shakily forward. There was no one in or near the house. Puff was better than any watchdog at detecting intruders. He would never behave so calmly if a stranger were near. Walking first slowly, then quickly, and finally running, bare feet squelching through the mud, Clara made it across the road and lawn and up the steps. Puff watched her galloping approach slit-eyed, then stalked down the steps as she leapt past him. His dignity was unimpeached by what had happened. Hers was nonexistent.

Once in the house, Clara quickly slammed and locked the door. Not that it would do any good if that man—any of them—came back, she thought. The second man—the good man, she labeled him for want of a better tag, though he was "good" only in comparison with the first, who had been brutal—had advised her to take a vacation, and that was precisely what she intended to do. As soon as she called Mitch. Damn it, he was the sheriff, it was his job to protect innocent citizens like herself. She had even voted for him in the last election. So where was he when she needed him?

Picking up the phone, she started punching out the number before she even had the receiver to her ear. It was all she could do to stand there and calmly make a phone call. Her every nerve ending wanted to send her screaming into the night.

The phone was dead. That information filtered through slowly, and when it did she wasted a precious few seconds staring blankly at the receiver. Then, as the horrifying implications of how alone and helpless she really was came over her, she dropped the phone as if it had suddenly turned into a warty toad. Oh Lord, she had to get out of the house, now, before Rostov and his men returned!

Running through to her bedroom, Clara shed her robe, snatching some jeans and a shirt out of the drawer and throwing them on over her mud-smeared body and the lacey white teddy that she was wearing for sleep. She was filthy, covered with mud from her head to her feet, but she didn't care. She didn't even care that her full breasts jiggled indecently beneath the shirt without the support of a bra. She could change into a proper bra and panties later, when she was safe. She tossed them into a small case. Dragging a pair of battered boat shoes and a rain jacket from her closet, she pulled them on and headed for the door. All she wanted to do was get out of the house. Immediately.

She needed her purse. Her car keys were in there. Looking wildly around, she had to bite back a terrified sob. She could never find her purse when she needed it . . . Thank God, there it was on the floor. The thugs had apparently searched it and thrown it aside. Its contents were spilling out onto the rug. Scooping them back inside with a single sweep of her hands, she grabbed her keys and purse and headed for the front door. Not for anything would she go through the kitchen door again. Just the memory of a black-gloved hand coming through the pane was enough to give her the shakes.

The cats. She couldn't leave the cats. Swearing under her breath, she ran back into the kitchen. Amy and Iris were under the table. She called them, and they came to her, hesitant but obedient. Snatching them up, she hurried out the door. Puff was outside. She called him as she ran down the steps. But of course he didn't appear. Clara whistled for him—he usually came to a whistle just like a dog—but got no response.

"Come on, Puff!" she muttered as she dropped Iris and Amy onto the back seat of her Honda Civic. Stowing the

suitcase in the trunk, she kept a wary eye out as she tried
another whistle. "On your head be it, then," she muttered,
and got into the car. Not even for Puff would she risk
another encounter with Rostov and his hooligans. She could
send Mitch back for Puff, because Mitch was the first
person she expected to see. Not that Mitch, for all he was
the sheriff and carried a gun, was a match for the thugs who
had just left. But she would feel a thousand times safer with
him than on her own.

Just as she started the car Puff came sauntering into view.
Cursing, sweating, Clara swung open her door after a
hunted look around assured her that she was still alone.

"Come on, Puff!" He sat on his fat behind and stared
unwinkingly at her. Clara would have left him then, except
that he happened to be blocking the driveway. Cursing some
more, she got out of the car and ran to snatch him up. He
purred as she touched him and rubbed his head against her
shoulder.

"I ought to strangle you," Clara muttered as she deposited
him on the passenger seat. Jumping in herself, she slammed
and locked the door and burned rubber on her way out the
driveway.

IV

By suppertime that day Clara was feeling very much better. She had spent what was left of the night at Mitch's house, under the eagle-eyed chaperonage of his disapproving mother. After consuming a hearty breakfast, Mitch had driven out to her house to check out her story. The window was broken on the kitchen door, all right, he reported, but nothing seemed to be missing from the house. He appeared to think that her encounter had been with a burglar—all right, a team of burglars, if there had been four of them—who knew that she was a writer and erroneously supposed that she was rich. They hadn't gotten much, and Mitch doubted that they would be back. Still, Clara was welcome to stay with him and his mother until her own mother got back from that cruise she was on. Or until she could make other arrangements, if she was scared to stay at her house on her own.

Despite Clara's insistence that the "burglar's" name was Rostov and that he was a KGB agent, it was clear that both Mitch and his mother thought her vivid writer's imagination was turning a rather ordinary situation into the extraordinary. Being an author of juicy romances was not exactly a respectable profession as far as Mitch and his mother and most of the other residents of Clarke County were concerned. This latest incident only served to confirm their opinion that she had to be slightly dotty. Fuming, Clara swallowed her protestations and allowed them to think they had convinced her that she had been the victim of a burglar. Although she knew better.

The cats were not exactly welcome at Mitch's house. Clara supposed she would have to take them over to Lena's after supper. Lena Kennary was her best friend, had been since the two had started first grade together. The friendship had lasted all through school, through Lena's procession of boyfriends (Clara had had just one in high school, and even then she had gotten him by default; Lena had dumped him and he had turned to plain but nice Clara for comfort). It had survived both Lena's marriages, the birth of her three children, and the financial difficulties that had prompted Clara to employ Lena as a part-time secretary. The two of them had celebrated their almost joint (Clara's birthday was in early September, Lena's in early August) thirtieth birthday together just a month previously. During their school years, Lena had been the popular one and Clara had been the plump, stringy-haired best friend. Now the situation had changed. Lena was slightly plump and Clara had dieted, so that Clara was the more slender of the two, and Clara was financially comfortable while Lena was constantly having to juggle her bills despite alimony from husband number two and child support for three children, and her part-time job with Clara. Their situations had changed, but their friendship hadn't. Clara knew that Lena would unhesitatingly care for the cats. Of course, she would insist on paying a reasonable boarding fee, because there was no way she was staying anywhere but under the protection of Mitch's gun until her mother was home and/or she felt a whole lot safer. . . .

"That sure was good pie, Ma." Mitch wiped his mouth with one of the linen napkins that his mother washed and starched religiously (she insisted that paper napkins were for "trash"). His mother beamed at him, cut another huge wedge from the remaining half of the pie, and slid it onto his plate.

"Don't you like the pie, Clara?" she asked with a disapproving glance at Clara's barely tasted piece.

"It's wonderful, Mrs. Potter, but I just can't eat another bite. I'm so full from the rest of your delicious meal I can barely breathe as it is." This was not strictly true—Clara had been too edgy to do justice to Mrs. Potter's dinner of country fried pork chops and mashed potatoes with accompanying side dishes—but Mrs. Potter was a notable cook and the compliment mollified her. She smiled slightly at Clara. She was convinced that the younger woman was scheming to marry Mitch, who she was equally convinced was the catch of the county, so she was on guard against being too friendly. Clara smiled back.

"Can you believe this?" Mitch had just opened the evening paper, and one of the headlines caught his eye. Clara and his mother looked at him inquiringly. He glanced up, caught their eyes on him, and shook his head. "Some fruitcake shot up Bethesda Naval Hospital's emergency room last night. Killed a bunch of people, nurses, doctors, an ambulance crew, people just sitting in the waiting room minding their own business. For no reason at all."

"Isn't that awful?" Mrs. Potter marveled, shaking her head. "Now who would do something like that? I declare, a body's not safe anywhere anymore!"

"It says here some guy they brought in just went nuts. What can you do against something like that?" Mitch consulted the paper again. Mrs. Potter tsk-tsked and shook her head.

"May I please be excused?" Southern manners had been drummed into her from the time of her first breath. Clara supposed that if she were scheduled to be executed she would first thank the executioner. Now, though she could suddenly hardly bear the sight of Mitch stuffing that second huge piece of pie down his stolid face, she waited politely until Mrs. Potter nodded. Clara rose, dropped her napkin on the table, and crossed into the parlor (really the living room, but Mrs. Potter had insisted on calling it the parlor ever since Clara had known her, and the name had stuck).

"I'll run over to your house again after supper, Clara. Just make a list of the things you want me to pick up," Mitch called after her.

"Thanks, Mitch. Just clothes and things, basically. And my book. It needs to go in the mail." It was nice of Mitch to make a second trip back over to her house to pick up her clothes, Clara knew. He was really a very nice man. It wasn't his fault that she was so edgy.

From the large front window, framed in stiff gold satin draperies from a Sears catalogue, she watched the antics of a trio of squirrels, wondering all the while if there was any chance of joining her mother on that cruise. It had stops in Acapulco and Cancun, she remembered. The good man had said she should take a vacation; maybe she should. She hadn't had a vacation for years, hadn't really wanted to take one. She liked being at home, was a home-loving type of person, something her social butterfly of a mother had never been able to understand. But she didn't much like her mother's new boyfriend; on a ship she'd be stuck. Besides, surely there was no longer any danger. Even a lunatic like Rostov must by now have figured out that he had made a mistake where she was concerned.

Dusk was creeping up over the countryside. The last golden rays of the sun touched the orange-red leaves of the two large oaks in the front yard, making them glow crimson. The squirrels were working busily, storing up acorns for the coming winter. Clara had always loved to watch them.

Out of the corner of her eye she saw a fat gray shadow slinking closer and closer to the gamboling squirrels.

"No, Puff!" she cried, but of course he paid not the slightest attention, if he even heard her, which was doubtful. Puff was a formidable hunter, and allowed nothing to distract him from the pursuit of his prey. Not even the tiny silver bell which she had suspended from his collar years before slowed him down. It had taken him all of a week to learn how to move without making it jingle. Since then, Clara had spent a considerable amount of time scooping him up in the very act of pouncing on an unsuspecting small creature.

"Puff, stop it!" She hurried out the front door and crossed to the big hyacinth bush near the driveway. Puff was staring fixedly at the nearest squirrel, his golden eyes agleam and his huge tail aswish. "I said stop it!"

Clapping her hands, she tried scaring away the squirrels, but they were used to people and only ran as far as the base of the nearest tree. Knowing that they would immediately return to work as soon as she left, and would shortly thereafter very likely become Puff's pre-dinner appetizer, she muttered "Drat!" under her breath and dropped to her knees. Grass stains on the knees of the one pair of jeans she had with her were just what she needed.

"Come out here, Puff!" she grunted, stretching one arm beneath the bush and grabbing him by his collar to drag him out. He growled, his golden eyes regarding her balefully. Clara paid no attention as she gathered him into her arms. She and only she knew his closely guarded secret: that ferocious growl masked the heart of a real pussycat. He would not dream of scratching or biting her. Although he had been known to attack strangers who were doing something to him which he found offensive, like Lena's youngest son who had been trying to take a pair of safety scissors to his tail.

She was just getting up off her knees when a faint rustling sound alerted her that someone was nearby. She glanced up, her muscles tightening. A hand holding a can was thrust into her face; icy cold mist shot into her nose and mouth. Clara opened her mouth to scream, but just succeeded in swallowing more of the mist. Her eyes closed in instinctive defense against the spray as the world began to swim around her in sickening swirls. She was falling . . . Her arms tightened around Puff as she felt something being thrust down over her head, smothering her. . . .

♦

V

♦

She was going to throw up. Clara felt bile rise in her throat before she was even aware of where she was. When she realized that she was enclosed in musty smelling folds of dark canvas, and that her arms were bound tightly to her sides by means of something on the outside of the canvas, she swallowed hard. She could not throw up, nearly suffocated as she was. She might suffocate for certain.

She was lying on her back on something hard, something that bounced and joggled her. Her face, and as far as she could tell her whole body, were enveloped in the smothering, rancid smelling canvas. An unfamiliar weight rested on her chest. Her stomach churned, her head hurt, and she was totally disoriented. And every barely functioning brain cell she possessed screamed that she was in big trouble.

Impressions began to sort themselves out. She realized that she was lying trussed up on the cold metal floor of a van or truck, and that someone, or several someones, were nearby. Of course, the vehicle had to have a driver, but she sensed an even closer presence, possibly someone crouched next to her in case she should wake up. What he or they

would do to her in that case she shuddered to think—
probably administer more of that knock-out spray. Or maybe
worse. It did not require genius intelligence to figure out
that she had fallen prey to Rostov and his men again. Cold
terror started to creep over her at the thought. What would
they do to her? Kill her, came the answer from the pragmat-
ic part of her mind that she tried desperately to stifle. What
else would they do with her? She couldn't give them any
information even if she wanted to.

A sharp stabbing connected with the weight on her chest
made her stir uncomfortably before she remembered the
unseen presence beside her and forced herself to lie still.
With her arms bound to her sides it was impossible to move
the object that was causing her discomfort, but suddenly she
didn't want to. With a completely ridiculous sense of
comfort, she realized that the weight was Puff, that he was
trapped in the enshrouding folds of canvas with her and was
even now crouched on her chest. The stabbing sensation
was caused by his claws as he dug them into her sensitive
flesh. Under the circumstances, she welcomed that small
pain. If she had had the use of her arms she would have
hugged him.

The vehicle slowed and veered left. There was more
jolting as it left the pavement to grind over what sounded
like gravel. Clara felt her stomach sink clear to her toes.
Obviously they were taking her to an isolated spot, where
they would do their worst to her. Bound, blinded, and half
suffocated as she was, there didn't seem much she could do
to save herself from whatever fate they intended for her. At
the moment, all she could do was continue to feign unconsciousness and wait for whatever opening God might see fit
to send her.

As the road grew rougher, Puff's claws sank deeper. Clara

winced at the pain, but there was nothing she could do to alleviate her discomfort without announcing to her captors that she was conscious. So she lay, gritting her teeth, willing her churning stomach to be still, and endured.

At last the vehicle jerked to a halt. Clara's first reaction was relief, followed by an immediate stab of fear. Whatever they intended to do to her, they would probably do now.

"She still out?" The voice was thick, gutteral—and not Rostov's. Clara knew that she would recognize the KGB man's distinctive accent anywhere.

"Yeah."

Ridiculously, the knowledge that neither of her captors was Rostov comforted her. Although she knew perfectly well that they were almost certainly his henchmen, told to bring her to him. Still, it was likely that she would not be harmed until he appeared.

Clara felt hands grab onto her shoulders, and other hands take her feet, which from the feel of them on her bare ankles were clear of the canvas. Then she was lifted and carried clumsily from the van. Concentrating on being a dead weight—no easy task with a twenty pound cat digging its claws into her chest—Clara tried to project the muscle tone of a limp noodle.

"Heavy, ain't she?"

This grunt, as they descended what felt like a steep flight of steps, piqued her pride. Which was ridiculous under the circumstances, she knew. Still, she'd always been sensitive about her weight, and it was some comfort to her to reflect that Puff was responsible for an additional twenty-odd pounds.

"God, I'm going to drop her!"

He did, before his gasping announcement even registered. Luckily, it was the man holding her feet who had fallen victim to butter fingers. Still, her leg crashed into what felt like the corner of a table, and the ensuing sharp pain did not quite cancel out the ripping of claws in flesh as Puff, dislodged from his perch, skidded protesting to where the rope binding her arms to her hips made it impossible for him to skid any further. Despite her best efforts to fall like a dead weight, she could not help trying to protect herself as much as possible. Perhaps they hadn't noticed how she'd cringed?

"What was that?"

The question was clearly in response to Puff's menacing growl.

"The damn cat."

"You didn't get rid of it?"

"How the hell was I supposed to get rid of it? The thing's a monster. You stick your hand up inside that bag and get rid of it."

"I don't suppose it makes that much difference. Come on, pick her up again and let's get this over with. The colonel will be here soon."

Clara's feet were lifted again. She was carried through a door and then put down on what felt like a cold stone floor. The scent of dampness wafted through the stiff folds of canvas. She was in a cellar of some kind.

There was a sharp rapping on a door a few feet away.

"What?" The question came from inside the door.

"Open up." It was one of her captors. "We've got the merchandise."

Clara heard the unmistakeable sound of a lock clicking open. Then she was picked up again and lugged through a narrow doorway. Her shoulders scraped the jam, but the canvas protected her flesh. Once inside, they set her on her feet, one of them holding her upright while the other seemed to be working at the rope. Conscientiously maintaining her pose of unconsciousness, Clara sagged at the knees. A ringing blow to the side of her head made her cry out, and straighten up fast.

"We know you're awake, Blondie. If you know what's good for you you won't give us any trouble."

The blow and the muttered warning came from the man who was still struggling to untie the rope that wound around the canvas. Another voice, one she hadn't heard before, spoke from further in the room.

"Here's the present we've been promising you, McClain."

"What the hell kind of screw up have you done now, asshole?" The rasping, taunting voice belonged to the man in the tobacco field. The one that Rostov had been searching for. Well, apparently they'd found him. But if so, what did they want with her?

"Next time Rostov tells you to talk, you'd better do it. Because I doubt your little girlfriend here will hold up very well to what Rostov will do to her. How do you think she'll like having each finger broken one by one—and how do you think you'll like watching? And if that doesn't work, we can always try cigarettes on soft little titties. Or a cattle prod. I can think of something fun to do with a cattle prod..." And he went on to describe an act so vile that Clara felt sick to her stomach. She had no illusions that the man was just talking, trying to frighten her. She *was* frightened. But no one cared about her. They were going to use her to try to make McClain talk—and he wouldn't talk to save her. She didn't know the man, but she suspected he would let them do anything they wanted to her, even kill her. She moaned.

There was a low chuckle. "See, she's smarter than you are. Are you going to let us do that to your sweetie without doing anything to stop it? All it takes is the right words from you."

"I keep telling you, she's not my girlfriend."

"You keep telling us," he agreed. Then, apparently to the man still trying to work the knots out of the rope, he said, "Cut it, you fool!"

Seconds later, Clara felt the sawing of a knife at the rope. Without warning it gave. Her arms were released from the circulation-stopping restraint—and Puff, with no support for his rotund body, dropped to the floor like a stone just as Clara was freed from what proved to be a large laundry bag.

"What the hell is that?" The startled question came from the man who had originally been in the cellar with McClain.

"It's only a cat," one of her captors tried to assure him. But Puff was not behaving like "only a cat." Thoroughly outraged by the treatment that had been accorded him, he snarled, crouching at Clara's feet, then leaped for the top of a heatlamp that had been directed at McClain. Clara, still blinking in the unexpectedly bright light, barely managed to take in all that happened next. The light pole fell with a crash. Puff, emitting bloodcurdling yowls, was thrown from his chosen perch to land with claws extended on the shoulder of one of her captors. The man screamed and tried to drag Puff from his back. The other two watched goggle-eyed as their buddy danced around the small room trying to dislodge the huge furry ball, and McClain, who had been sitting on a small wooden chair, his face swollen and bloodied from blows, rose to his feet with a sudden surge of power, his hands handcuffed uselessly behind him. Even as the man who had been guarding him turned toward him, one of McClain's feet lashed out and made contact with the other's crotch. Screaming, the man dropped to his knees. The other two men, their attention caught by the scream, turned in time for one of them to be flattened with a flying drop kick that landed right beneath his chin. The third, finally free of Puff, who had leapt for safety to the top of a metal locker, fumbled inside his jacket for a gun. McClain ran toward him, butting him in the stomach with his head before the gun could be drawn. The man doubled over with a whoosh of escaping air.

"Let's get the hell out of here!" McClain roared, hardly looking over his shoulder at her as he bolted through the open door. Clara, who was still somewhat dazed but not stupid, ran after him. The three thugs were already recovering.

McClain ran up the basement stairs, through a pantry and then a kitchen of what seemed to be a large, elegantly furnished house, and out onto the paved patio, where numerous vehicles were parked.

"Check for keys," he yelled at her. Clara ran to look in the window of the vehicle closest to her. It was a van, and the keys were in the ignition.

"Here!"

He was beside her even as she got the door open, shouldering her inside then dropping into the passenger seat.

"Get us the hell out of here!"

"But—"

"Drive!" he bellowed. Clara turned the key over and started to pull away just as a gray furry ball erupted from the open door of the house, followed by three men.

"Puff!" she screamed, barreling toward them. One of them was taking aim . . . She ducked, the bullet shattered the windshield, McClain yelled the foulest curses she had ever heard, the men leapt out of the way, and then Clara hit the brakes so hard that the van slid sideways to a screeching halt.

"What the—" She barely registered McClain's protest. Swearing under her breath, she jumped out of the van, ran to scoop Puff out of the driveway where he crouched, apparently frozen with fear, and jumped back into the van just as another bullet whistled over her head. Dumping Puff unceremoniously into the back, she put the van in gear and stepped on the gas so hard that the vehicle shot forward like a rock out of a slingshot.

VI

"You almost got us killed over a damn cat?" McClain's voice was a barely subdued roar.

"He was sitting in the middle of the drive. I couldn't just run over him."

"Those aren't play bullets, you know. Those are real bad guys and they really would like to kill us."

"There's no need to be sarcastic."

"I can't believe any rational human being would stop for a damn cat. . . ."

Clara ignored this mutter and concentrated on driving. The twisty road opened out onto a two-lane blacktop. She barely paused at the stop sign; the van's wheels spun as she pulled out. Every few seconds she glanced in the rearview mirror. McClain had said that they would be followed. What was taking them so long?

"Where do you think you're going, anyway?"

Clara looked over at him, surprised. The darkness was kind to his bruised and battered face, but he was certainly no better looking than she had thought him at first meeting. With his square, pugnacious jaw distorted, a swelling the size of one of her fists just below his ear and an ugly looking gash the size of her middle finger behind it, a smear of blood at the corner of his mouth and a dark purple circle surrounding one bright green eye, he looked like he had been made up for Halloween. Only Clara knew that the marks were not makeup.

"Home," she said, surprised that he should even ask. Then, thinking about it, she was surprised again at her own slow-wittedness. The drug they had sprayed her with must be having some residual effect. Of course she could not go home. If Rostov had sought her out twice, once at the home of the county sheriff, she was not safe anywhere. The thought was frightening.

"Dumb idea, huh?"

He nodded. "They'll be looking for us. We'll have to hide."

"Explain something to me. If they had you, why did they want me?"

"The only thing that was keeping me alive was the idea that I might have passed on to a few people some information I have. Rostov didn't dare kill me until he found out who I might have talked to. They tried to torture the information out of me. When that didn't work, they decided to bring you in and see if I could stomach watching them kill my girlfriend by degrees. They were gambling that I couldn't. But either way they would have killed us both."

"I'm not your girlfriend."

"No."

"It doesn't matter, does it?" Her voice and the eyes she turned to him were suddenly despairing. "It doesn't matter that I never saw you before in my life until you popped up in that field and scared the life out of me. It doesn't matter that I have absolutely nothing to do with whatever you're involved in. It doesn't matter that I don't know anything about anything. They want to kill me anyway, because of you. It isn't fair!"

"Life isn't fair." His calm rejoinder set her temper to sizzling. She glowered at him, then switched her attention back to the road. He was right: life wasn't fair. If it was, Rostov would have made hamburger of him long before she'd become involved in this nonsense.

"What's that?"

A dull roar prompted her question. McClain frowned, then his eyes widened and he looked out the van window.

"Holy shit," he said. "They've got a helicopter. Hit it, would you?"

Even as Clara took a quick, instinctive look out her window, the spotlight picked them out of the darkness and the copter swooped until it was flying just above and behind the van. Stepping on the gas for all she was worth, Clara concentrated on keeping the van on the twisting road. Driving at such speed under the conditions was suicide—but so was doing anything else.

The spotlight beaming down on them made it impossible for her to see the helicopter's occupants, but from her recent experience with Rostov and his thugs Clara did not doubt that they had guns. She was right, and ducked reflexively as a hail of bullets strafed the van.

"Oh my God!"

Head still lowered so that her eyes just peeped over the steering wheel, she stood on the accelerator. The van tore down the road. McClain, hampered by his handcuffs, was practically thrown out of the seat. Cursing a blue streak, he kept his head down and watched the helicopter's progress through the passenger side mirror.

"Turn right!"

"Where?"

"Here!"

Clara barely saw the narrow road that cut through a swathe of trees. But she swung the wheel for all she was worth. The van stood on two wheels as it obeyed her. Then they were passing safely under the overhanging branches, protected from the helicopter—for the moment. Clara barely had time to breathe a sigh of relief before the van was shooting out into the open again.

The helicopter's spotlight found them. Clara had to fight the urge to close her eyes as it dived around them like a demented seagull. It was swooping after them, bullets smacking into the pavement and the dirt on either side of the road. A bullet smashed through the roof to ricochet through the interior. Clara and McClain ducked simultaneously. The bullet whined over McClain's head to smash through the window on his side.

"Oh my God!"

For just a moment they were safe beneath another group of trees. But then they were in the open again. This time the helicopter swooped and dived at the van's roof. Its runners scraped against the metal over Clara's head. She cringed, stomping down on the accelerator so hard that the van's wheels were barely touching the narrow, dark road. The speedometer needle climbed past seventy. The left rear wheel hit gravel at the side of the road, and for a moment Clara thought that it was all over. But with a desperate swing of the wheel she managed to right the van, although her correction sent it careening amidst a spray of gravel down the wrong side of the road.

"The object of this is for us to end up alive," McClain said through clenched teeth when Clara finally had the van in the right lane again. "The KGB doesn't want us dead at this point, remember. They want to take us alive so they can find out if I've told anyone what I know. Just keep calm, and try not to run off the road. Wrecking the van is the worst thing we can do."

"Keep calm!" Clara wanted to laugh hysterically, but she was too busy trying to get away from the swooping helicopter. It dove in front of the van, its runners nearly touching the pavement. Clara stood on the brakes, then at a shout from McClain tromped on the accelerator again and headed straight toward it through a hail of gunfire.

For a moment it looked as though the copter and the van would collide. Clara shut her eyes and kept the gas pedal pressed to the floor. There was a curse from McClain, a whooshing sound, and then she opened her eyes to find that they were safe under more overhanging trees. At the last minute, the helicopter had lifted out of the way.

"Do me a favor," he said, sounding as though his calm tone was costing him an effort. "Next time we play chicken, keep your eyes open, will you?"

Then they were out in the open again, briefly, so that the helicopter only had time to swoop once before the van shot under the protection of more trees. This time there seemed to be a lot of them. Clara felt some of the tension ease from her body. They were safe for the next couple of minutes, at least.

As far as she could tell through the enveloping darkness, the road wound up the side of a wooded hill. It was a two-lane blacktop. She only hoped that they didn't meet anything coming the other way.

"Cut the lights."

McClain sounded tense, but in control. Clara looked at him. Surely he didn't expect her to drive this unfamiliar narrow country road in pitch darkness? His expression was unreadable, but his green eyes glittered as they met hers. He looked vibrantly alive, she thought. With a sense of shock she realized he was enjoying this! The knowledge scared her even more than she had been.

"Did you hear me? I said cut the lights!"

There was an edge to his voice this time. She thought, this is a dangerous man.

Then, on the verge of an acute attack of hysteria, she doused the lights. Immediately the darkness enshrouded them. Clara could no longer see the road. Instinctively she hit the brakes. The van slowed its precipitous rush with a squeal and a sideways skid. By the time it straightened out, she was—just barely—able to see the road again. Keeping the van at a crawl, she cast a quick, shaken look at him.

"Who are you anyway—James Bond?"

Despite the bravado she tried to inject into it, the question had a squeaky note. He looked over at her, unsmiling. Funny, she was getting to know him better than she wanted to. She was able to recognize that unrelenting look. It was the one he had worn the night before in the tobacco field. When he had held the gun to her head.

"Something like that."

"You're telling me you're a spy?" Her voice rose two octaves on the last word. James Bond existed only in the movies. Even real life spies—and she knew that they existed—she read the newspapers, but not in Virginia, for God's sake!—were sort of glorified gossipmongers and pencil pushers. All that James Bond stuff was so much fiction. She knew that. Didn't she?

"Agent."

"Oh my God." That seemed to be all she could say. Driving along the dark, twisty road with a man who scared the daylights out of her when she thought about it, praying

that the overhead branches would shield them from the
helicopter, Clara felt she was caught up in a nightmare. Real
life wasn't like this. At least, not in Virginia.

"Look, suppose I get out here and let you go on by
yourself? I really don't want to be involved in this."

His eyes gleamed catlike through the darkness as he
looked at her.

"You *are* involved in it. And you can't get out of it just
by walking away. Rostov will never let up until he has both
of us, and as we've both learned, he's good at finding
people. Besides, I can't drive with these damned handcuffs
on."

"That's hardly my problem." She was short on sympathy
at the moment. This man was likely to get her killed, and
she didn't even know him. Didn't know anything about him.
Didn't *want* to know anything about him. She took a deep
breath. "I'm sorry if it puts you out, but I'm driving
straight to the nearest police station. After that, you're on
your own. Tell them anything you like, I won't say anything
about you being a spy, but I'm not going to be involved in
this any longer. It's dangerous."

"Look, lady—Cora, whatever your name is—"

"Clara!"

"Clara. Whether you like it or not, you *are* involved in
this. Going to the police is out. There is no one you can
trust. No one. Do you understand?"

"No, I do not." Clara felt better now that she had made a
decision. "The Virginia State Police are in no way involved
with the KGB, if it's even the KGB who's after us and not
some sort of crooks you ripped off in some sort of dope deal
or something. Not that I care," she added hastily, not
wanting him to get the idea that he had to kill her to silence

her. "You do what you want, but that's where this van and I are headed. To the police."

"Oh no you're not."

"You can't stop me! I saved your life! Besides, you can't drive. Remember the handcuffs?"

Fear made her voice shrill. He looked at her for a moment through the darkness, his eyes glittering. Then she heard him take a breath. When he spoke, his voice was low and harsh.

"You don't trust me. Fair enough. I probably wouldn't believe this myself. Let's take it point by point, shall we? Reach into my pocket and pull out my wallet. My agency ID is in there."

Hesitating, casting a long, considering look at him, Clara finally did as she was told. Her hand touched the hard muscle of his lower back—he had gestured to the left rear pocket of the faded jeans that fit him like a second skin—and drew back instinctively. She did not like touching him, even for so straightforward a reason. There was something . . . sexual about it. He was too male. Primitive male force seemed to emanate from his pores. And she had reason to know that he could be violently aggressive. No, touching him wasn't a safe thing to do. But she wanted very much to look at his ID to see if he was telling the truth about this whole misadventure being tied up with the government, at least. So she forced her hand to slide inside his pocket and extract the flat leather wallet she found there.

"Flip on the overhead light," he directed. She did. Keeping one eye on the road, she nevertheless managed a thorough look at the wallet's contents: a reasonable amount of cash, a MasterCard, American Express and a Sears charge card, a picture of a very pretty blonde woman slightly thinner than herself, his Maryland driver's license, and the ID card that proclaimed him one John Thomas McClain, employee of the Central Intelligence Agency. Both the driver's license and the CIA card bore identical photos of the man sitting beside her. There was no mistake. She flipped the wallet shut, tucked it back inside the breast pocket of his black sweatshirt, and turned off the overhead light, all without a word. She could feel him looking at her, but she steadfastly refused to look at him again. Funny, the knowledge that he worked for her own government should have made her feel safer, but it didn't.

"Look, Clara. I know you're scared, and you're right to be scared. The people who are after us—us, not just me—are killers. You think you'll be safe with the police. And you'd be right, if it were only the KGB we were dealing with. The chances of a state police trooper being a mole are remote. But ask yourself this: would the police turn you over to the FBI or the CIA or any one of the other federal agencies? Yes, they would. In a minute. And in due course you would find yourself facing exactly the same situation we just escaped from. Because there is a Soviet mole at a high level in the U.S. Intelligence service, and until he's identified and exposed he will be using every bit of his considerable muscle to have us found and eliminated. To the agency we are very likely already the bad guys on the mole's say-so. We could be killed by our own side just as easily as by Rostov. Do you understand now?"

There was a pause. Then Clara said, "You're exaggerating."

"Am I? Do you really want to risk your life to find out?"

He had a point. Clara, glaring impotently out the window into the shifting darkness through which they were driving, conceded it.

"What exactly did you do to make everyone want to kill

you, anyway? If I'm going to die with you, don't I have a right to know?"

"I know about the mole, and they mean to see that I don't have a chance to get the word out. For all they know, I may even have told you." He was silent for a moment, then, speaking slowly as if he were thinking, he added, "In fact, I will tell you, in case they catch me and you escape."

"I don't want to know!"

Her horrified protests had no effect. In concise sentences he told her everything that Yuropov had told him. About Bigfoot, and how important it was that this high-level Soviet spy be neutralized. About some kind of plot to murder the secretary of state. About a defector who was being taken back to Russia to be tortured and killed. . . .

"If they get me but not you, go to Tim Hammersmith with this," he concluded. "Tell him what I've told you, and also tell him that Natalia didn't die in Budapest. Don't forget that part. That's how he'll know that what you're telling him comes from me."

"Now they really will kill me!" Clara wailed.

He half smiled. His voice sounded soothing. "They would have killed you anyway. Now, if you get away and I don't, at least you'll be of some use."

"Oh my God!"

"We're going to have to ditch the van. They've probably got a car behind us now. It won't take them long, now that the chopper has given them our general position. And if we come out of the woods the chopper will be on top of us in a minute."

"All right." There didn't seem to be anything she could do for the moment but agree. He was calling the shots, and she was stuck with him until she figured out some way to extricate herself from the whole mess. But how? She couldn't even flee to her mother—what if she brought the thugs down on her? As she knew to her own cost, innocence was no defense.

"Head up through those trees up there. As far as this thing will go. At least it will be hidden until morning."

Not seeing anything else she could do, Clara obeyed. The van bumped and thumped its way over the ground until the trees got too thick for it to pass. She put on the brakes, stopped the motor, and turned to look at him.

"Now what?"

"Now we walk. But first I want to take a quick look through this thing to see if there's anything we can use. Like a pistol."

"Oh my God!"

He gave her a disgusted look.

"Can't you say anything besides 'Oh my God'? You're beginning to annoy me."

"Well, excu-u-u-use me."

"That's better." He was on his feet before she could turn the full force of her glare on him. Bent almost double, he made his way back through the van. The rear had been stripped of its seats. Only a few tools and a dirty blanket were crumpled together in one corner. As McClain crouched in front of the heap, Clara heard a low, ominous sounding growl. McClain straightened so fast he bumped his head on the roof.

"Damn cat!" He identified the source of the growl from two glowing golden eyes before Clara had a chance to tell him. Puff had evidently taken refuge under the blanket. Even as she moved back to rescue him another growl sounded.

"Move it, would you?"

Clara needed no second bidding to reach down and gather

Puff into her arms. Still nervous from the treatment he had received, he snarled as she picked him up. She paid no attention, nuzzling her face into his fluffy fur and murmuring reassurances to him.

"Throw it out the door, will you? And grab some of this stuff. Never know what we might be able to use."

"Throw him out the door?" Her voice was indignant.

He looked at her impatiently. "What else are you going to do with it? We can't take a cat with us. It'll be fine, believe me. Rostov's not after the damned cat."

"We most certainly *can* take him with us. And we are going to. I'm not leaving him. So there." She meant what she said and it showed in her voice. He looked at her for a moment, then shrugged.

"Have it your own way. You're the one who's going to be lugging it. If it slows you down you're on your own. I'm not going to get my ass nailed over some stupid bleeding heart who can't bring herself to leave her sweet little kitty cat." The mincing falsetto in which he uttered the last four words set Clara's teeth on edge.

"This sweet little kitty cat saved your life, if you recall."

A shrug was his only answer to that. He was crouching in front of the tools again, staring down at the jumble with concentration.

"Grab the screwdriver and the hammer," he directed. "And the blanket. Nothing else we can use."

At Clara's look he said, "The handcuffs, remember?"

Annoyed, Clara picked up the tools and bundled them awkwardly in the blanket, juggling a growling Puff all the while. Finally she managed to tuck the bundle under one arm, while holding Puff, who was squirming like a landed fish, beneath the other.

"Sure you don't want to leave it?"

He sounded as if he was on the verge of laughing. Clara glared at him. If she'd seen the merest hint of a grin she would have stomped on his foot. But his face was expressionless as usual. There was just something about the glint in those green eyes. . . .

McClain exited through the rear of the van. Clara followed, her movements awkward because of her twin burdens. Puff never liked being carried at the best of times, and he squirmed and growled threateningly as she lugged him up the hill. Getting crosser by the second, Clara wished she had a free hand to konk the head of the man who was striding so effortlessly ahead of her. Handcuffed or not, he didn't seem to have any trouble walking.

"Hurry up, can't you?" He was waiting for her beneath a tall pine tree near the crest of the hill. In the darkness, with his dark clothing, he was practically indistinguishable from the trees. Clara, puffing as she came up to him, was annoyed to note that he was not even breathing hard. But she refused to complain about being weighed down, because Puff was the major part of the burden.

"Do you have any kind of plan? Or are we just going to walk until they find us?"

Sarcasm laced her voice. He started walking again, with long, seemingly effortless strides that made no concessions to the unevenness of the ground beneath his feet or the shadowy darkness of the woods that could have hidden anything in their path. Clara followed, glaring at his back. She had no choice but to keep up with him. In this cold, dark world gone mad, he was the only security she had.

As the night went on the woods grew denser, the temperature colder, the night darker—and Puff heavier, until she felt as if she were packing an anvil under her arm. Clad in her jeans and tan and brown plaid flannel shirt with only her teddy beneath and boat shoes on her bare feet, she was less than adequately dressed for hiking through a forest on a cold October night. If she had had a free hand or an extra second she would have wrapped the blanket around herself. But in front of her, McClain kept relentlessly going, climbing over the hilly woodside as if he were some kind of machine. If she stopped for an instant she feared losing sight of him. And she definitely didn't want to be left on her own in the woods in the middle of the night with Rostov and his goons on her tail and God knew what in the undergrowth all around her.

"Wait, please!" They had been walking for what seemed like hours. Clara couldn't be sure, because she had thoughtlessly not been wearing her watch when she was abducted. But she knew that she was chilled to the bone and thoroughly exhausted. If he had a plan, she wanted to know what it was.

"The cat's slowing you down. You'll have to leave it."

She was cold, tired, and fed up. Her normally gentle blue eyes shot sparks as she caught up to him. Even through the darkness she could see his eyes widen at the fury in hers.

"Listen, James Bond, I am not leaving the cat! Is that clear?" she roared, her very stance challenging him to disagree. To her surprise, he didn't. Instead he turned away to walk on with no more than a shrug.

"Wait!" She wailed the word. He stopped, frowning at her over a shoulder.

"Can't we rest for a few minutes? My legs are killing me."

"All right. Two minutes."

He didn't seem tired at all, she noted bitterly as she sank to the ground where she stood. Puff, released, shot off to cower under a bush. Clara didn't even care. Puff weighed about as much as a small elephant, and if she didn't love the dratted animal so much she would leave him. But he would never find his way home from there . . . Shivering, she drew her legs up to her chest and, grabbing the blanket, wrapped herself in it. She was freezing.

"Think you can get these handcuffs off?"

Clara just looked at him as he crouched beside her. Her dislike for him was intensifying with each passing second. She had not asked to be involved in this mess. It was all his fault!

"With the screwdriver and hammer," he explained patiently, as if she were dim-witted. Clara narrowed her eyes at him. Dislike was a mild word for what he made her feel.

"Hey, are you alive?" The question was impatient.

Clara, her eyes narrowing still further, shook her head. "No."

"If you can help me get these handcuffs off I can carry something."

At this blatant bribe, Clara pursed her lips. If he would only carry Puff for a while, she might make it a little further after all.

"How?"

"Grab the screwdriver and the hammer."

She had to get out of the blanket to obey, but she did it. The prospect of having him carry Puff was too alluring. He found a rock and dragged it over, placed his wrists on it. His back was to her, and Clara had to fight an urge to crack him over the head with the flat of her hand. This whole mess was all his fault.

"Wedge the screwdriver in where the chain meets the cuff."

She did.

"Now whack it a good one with the hammer."

She brought the hammer down as hard as she could.

"Shi-it!" He leaped to his feet, dancing sideways, swearing furiously. Clara watched him. So she had missed with the hammer—big deal. A smashed finger was a small price to pay for the mess he had involved her in.

He stalked back toward her, still swearing, his eyes narrowed threateningly. To her own surprise, Clara felt no fear.

"Sorry," she offered.

"Yeah," he said sourly, kneeling and presenting his back again. After his wrists were once again positioned on the rock, and the screwdriver was once again in place, Clara lifted the hammer for another try. His shoulders tightened in anticipation. Clara noted that and brought the hammer down carefully. She didn't so much as scratch the metal.

"Try again."

She tried again. And again. And finally, on what must have been the twelfth try, she was so tired of trying that she brought the hammer down as though it was going to make contact with his thick skull. And, lo and behold, the link connecting the chain to one of the cuffs split.

"Good job!" He turned, raising his arms wide and then rubbing the wrist where the handcuff with the chain was still securely fastened. The other wrist was also adorned with a metal cuff, but at least now the chain was broken and he had free use of his hands.

"What time is it?" He had his watch, she saw.

"Twenty after eleven. Why?"

"It seems later. Six hours ago I was finishing supper at Mitch's house."

"Mitch?"

"The sheriff. I went there last night."

"Wasn't much help, was he?"

"No."

McClain grunted, turning away to gather up blanket, screwdriver, and hammer.

"How'd they catch you, anyway?" She was curious.

He looked at her. "They were waiting down the road from your house. I drove right past them. They shot out my tires, my car went off the road, and they had me. Easy."

"That would never have happened to James Bond," she said with a sniff. His eyebrows snapped together.

"Here, wrap this around you and let's get going," he said, thrusting the blanket at her. Clara stared at him for a moment, silently resisting. She couldn't move; she, who never walked when she could drive, had already hiked at least seven or eight miles, she guessed. Her legs were aching. She couldn't go any further.

"Rostov and his men are on our tail, believe me," he said. "They may even have found the van by now. They may wait until daylight to trail us through these woods. Or they may not."

Clara stood up without a word, taking the blanket and wrapping it squaw fashion around her shoulders. McClain was dressed no warmer than she—even his ankles were sockless in their white sneakers—but if he wanted to be a gentleman and give her the blanket she wasn't going to object.

McClain stuck the tools in the waistband of his pants as she walked over to the bush to retrieve Puff. Puff resisted with a miserable snarl, but Clara dragged him out by his collar and picked him up.

"Hush," she told him irritably, then rubbed between his ears to make up for her hostile tone. He growled again, and Clara sighed.

McClain was already walking away as she straightened. She hurried after him.

"Hey, you promised you'd carry something if I got the handcuffs off you."

"I am carrying something. The tools."

"That doesn't count. They don't weigh anything! It's your turn to carry Puff."

"I am not carrying that damn cat. I hate cats."

"You hate cats?" Clara was shocked to her bone marrow. She withdrew from him as if he had suddenly grown horns. "How on earth can anyone hate cats?"

"It's easy, believe me. Especially that thing. It acts more like a saber-toothed tiger than a cat."

"Puff doesn't like you either."

Indeed, Puff was growling, but Clara wasn't sure whether it was from being held, which he disliked except when he requested to be picked up, or from not having had his dinner, which she decided was more likely. His opinion of McClain was probably a very distant cause of his bad temper.

"Breaks my heart."

"You're not a very nice man." This was such an inadequate reply that even Clara was ashamed of it, but McClain marched on without even bothering to acknowledge it. She trailed him, doing her best to keep up, casting silent aspersions on every aspect of his person. It made her feel better, at least for a while.

As another hour or so passed, Puff lapsed into sullen silence—and seemed to gain about a hundred pounds. Clara, arms aching, legs aching, back aching, almost wished that Rostov would hurry up and catch them. At least then she could sit down. Then, with a look of glimmering hatred at McClain's disappearing back, she changed that to catch *him*. She would like to be a fly on the wall the next time they tortured him. She would cheer them on.

The neat little copse of trees in which they had started out had grown into a full-fledged forest. A real forest with trees so thick that it was hard to thread through them and vines hanging to catch at one's face and clothes and scare one to death and animals skittering and occasionally screamed, but she no longer even heard them. Every bit of her mind was concentrated on putting one foot in front of the other. *Clara shivered as she enumerated the hazards. The near total darkness made the going even harder. More than once Clara tripped over a protruding branch that she couldn't see because of the shadows. Owls hooted and small furry creatures scurried and leaves littering the ground and undergrowth trying to trip one up . . .*

She bumped into McClain. Literally bumped into him. In his dark clothing he was hard to discern from the shadows, and her mind had been so attuned to the left right, left right litany she had been repeating over and over that she hadn't even realized he had stopped. So she bounced right off his chest, and he had to catch her by her arms or she would have fallen. Puff growled and took a swipe at him. McClain stepped back, scowling.

"I think we should grab a couple of hours of sleep."

"Hallelujah."

"There's a hollow log beside the trail. If we crawl inside they could pass right by us without even knowing we're there."

"Do you think—"

He shook his head. "No, I don't think they could have followed us very well through the forest in the dark. Tomorrow may be a different story. That's why we should sleep while we can. I don't want you dropping on your feet."

Clara wasn't about to argue, or point out that he could very well be dropping on his feet too. The notion of sleep was so irresistibly attractive that she would have agreed to anything in exchange.

"Put the damn cat down and follow me."

"No!" Anything but that. She was not abandoning Puff.

"I sure as hell am not sharing a log with a cat."

"And I sure as hell am not leaving him out here. Besides," she added with a cunning born of desperation. "If Rostov's men should happen by and find Puff they'll know we have to be nearby. And there's no way they would forget him. He's very memorable."

That notion appeared to hit home. With a narrowing of his eyes and a furious mutter about damn women and their damn pets, he walked about ten feet forward, then dropped to his knees to disappear inside a huge overturned log. Clara followed, holding Puff tightly against her chest as she felt her way in the darkness. The rotting wood was both crumbly and slick beneath her fingers. Clara shuddered, thinking it was just as well that she couldn't see where she was putting her hand. There were some things that one was better off not knowing.

Puff, not liking this change in position, was growling again. Clara felt the claws of his hind leg dig into her chest.

"Goddamn it!" McClain swore furiously as Puff launched himself away from Clara to swarm over McClain's shoulders and lose himself in the darkness beyond.

"Puff!" Clara cried.

"Don't worry, we couldn't lose the damn animal if we tried," McClain said bitterly. "The back of this thing is wedged against another tree. He can't get out back there."

"Oh, good." Clara collapsed, resting her head on her bent arms and closing her eyes. She would be asleep in an instant . . .

"Come here."

That roused her. Her head lifted, and her eyes peered suspiciously through the darkness toward where McClain lay with his back pressed against the curving log and his legs drawn up to his chest.

"Why?" She had almost forgotten that he was a man, for God's sake. As a species, they were dangerous in many ways.

"What do you mean, why? When I say come here, you do it. I'm in charge of this little comedy."

"Oh, is that so?" Sparked by indignation, she glared at him.

"Yes, it is. Now come here."

"No."

She could almost hear him gnashing his teeth. For a moment the issue hung in the balance. Then he reached forward and grabbed one of her arms, dragging her toward him. Clara gasped.

"I am in charge. You do what I tell you, when I tell you, with no more damn arguments," he said through his teeth, practically spitting the words in her face. Both his hands were on her upper arms now. He had dragged her forward until her face was mere inches from his. "We are in a desperate situation here. All these little arguments of yours could get both of us killed. From now on, when I say jump, you ask how high? Got it?"

"No, I do not!" His brutal assumption of command set Clara's temper to boiling. Ordinarily she was the most mild mannered of creatures, but she hated being manhandled. She met his eyes with fire in her own. His narrowed; she didn't give an inch.

"What did you say?" The question was ominous in its quietness.

"I said no!" Clara stared at him eyeball to eyeball. "Either we operate as a team or we don't operate. I'd rather take my chances with Rostov and the state police than take this kind of abuse from you!"

There was a moment of silence.

"You've got the brains of a cockroach," he said finally, releasing her arms. "If you get killed, on your own head be it. I'm not risking my life for a bad tempered, stubborn, stupid—"

"Fine!" Clara said, scooting backwards.

"Fine," McClain echoed, catching the end of the blanket and pulling it from her to wrap it around himself.

"Give that back!"

"No way. You want equality, you've got equality. I was going to share it with you, but since you're so damn tough, freeze."

Clara stared at him through the darkness. If looks could have killed he would have been a corpse.

"Oh, for Christ's sake, this is ridiculous," he said suddenly. Before Clara knew what was happening he had grabbed her arms and hauled her to him again. Twisting her sideways, he had her lying on her side facing the curving side of the log before she had even gathered her wits enough to protest. Then he was lying down behind her, drawing the blanket over them both and putting a hard arm over her to hold her still.

"We're in this together, damn it, whether either one of us likes it or not. Now, if you've got any damn sense at all, you'll shut up and go to sleep," he growled in her ear. Clara was rigid for a few moments. Then, feeling the welcome warmth of his body behind her and the comfort of the

blanket over her, and hearing a decided snore that told her
he was already fast asleep, she slowly relaxed. He was
right, blast him. They were in this mess together, for better
or worse, at least until she could figure out how to get
herself out of it. . . . Before she could come up with anything that offered the least hope of success, her lids dropped
and she was asleep.

VII

An explosive sneeze right beside her ear woke her. It was followed by another one, then viciously muttered curses. Clara turned to look at the man behind her. His battered face was even more painful looking in the weak dawn light. Purple and yellow bruises adorned most of his features. The large cut behind his ear looked raw. The swelling in his jaw had subsided, but the bruise that accompanied it had spread from his neck all the way up to his temple. Appalled, she stared. He had two black eyes, she saw as he met her horrified gaze. He glared at her fiercely. Clara blinked at him. He looked as mean tempered as a snake. She became aware that her body was pressed tightly against his from shoulders to feet. She could feel every solid muscle, every bulge and hollow, his heat. His arm was wrapped around her waist, its weight warm and heavy. His other arm was beneath her head. They had instinctively curled together beneath the blanket in mutual defense against the chill of the night.

He sneezed again, violently. Clara recoiled.

"That damn cat," he said with loathing, directing a

77

killing glare to where Puff was sitting with twitching tale at the blocked end of the log, watching them. Clara, understanding at last, felt a grin form on her lips. It broadened into a chuckle.

"You're allergic to cats," she said with delight. He glared at her, removing his arm from her waist and his body from the intimate contact with hers as he sat up as well as he could in the small space.

"I hate cats," he corrected coldly. And sneezed again.

Clara grinned. James Bond had never been allergic to cats. It made McClain seem much more human.

"Quit giggling," he said sourly. "We have to get moving."

"Yes, sir," she agreed, snapping a mock salute as she wriggled past him. Discovering that he was allergic to cats put her in a much better frame of mind. "Come on, Puff," she coaxed, one eye on McClain to watch for his reaction. His face was a study in revulsion. Clara grinned again. Puff stood up with immense dignity and approached her outstretched hand, his tail waving gently back and forth. Clara scooped him up and cuddled him against her. McClain sneezed.

They crawled out of the log. Clara's sore muscles protested every movement. But when they were outside and standing upright, Clara realized that McClain must be in much worse pain than she. Her body was sore from unaccustomed exercise. Every inch of his body that she could see was swollen or bruised. In the brighter daylight she saw damage that the dimness of the log had concealed. His lower lip was swollen to about three times its normal size and sported a jagged cut on the right corner, another bruise decorated his right cheekbone, and a slash that looked as if it might have been inflicted with a knife slanted across his throat from beneath his left ear to disappear beneath the grubby sweatshirt. From the way he was rubbing his ribs and wincing, Clara guessed that the bruises on his face were not the worst that he had suffered.

"Are you badly hurt?" she asked with the first real sympathy she had felt for him.

His blue-ringed green eyes met hers. "I'll live," he said, dropping his hand. The chain attached to his right wrist jingled, making Clara jump before she realized the source of the noise. It was only then that she realized how scared she truly was. Rostov could be anywhere, a few feet or many miles away, but wherever he was he was searching for them. If he found them . . . She shivered and forced the thought from her mind. She would go crazy if she let herself think about it.

He was carrying the blanket, and he reached into his waistband and pulled out the screwdriver. Using it to make a hole in the tightly woven material, he ripped the blanket in half. Then he poked a hole in the center of both halves, tearing it into a foot-long rip. Finally he stuck the screwdriver back in his waistband and pulled one of the blanket halves over his head. He'd made a crude poncho, Clara saw, and when he tossed the other one to her she pulled it over her head without a word. It provided welcome protection against the misty chill of the dawn.

"Come on," he said, heading out.

Clara, wincing as her muscles protested the stretching they had to do to keep up, fell in beside him. McClain cast a look of dislike at Puff, who was purring like a motor, probably in hopes of cajoling a meal out of his mistress.

"Where are we going?" she asked, trying to match her stride to his.

"To Maryland."

"We're walking to Maryland?" Virginia was right next to Maryland, true, but she was sure they must be at least fifty miles from the border. If not more. There was no way she could walk that far.

"I did some thinking last night. I've worked for Tim Hammersmith for a lot of years, and if we can trust anybody we can trust him. This is Sunday, so he'll be at home. We're going to lay all this on him. Once the word's out, Rostov loses a lot of his motivation to kill us."

"Oh." Clara felt an overpowering sense of relief. There was a way out of this mess after all. She'd known there had to be. "Why didn't you call your boss sooner?"

"Because when I called him to tell him that Yuropov had dropped a bombshell and I was bringing him over to talk to him, somebody picked it up. That led to several possibilities. Number one, Hammersmith's in league with the mole. Not very likely, but possible. Number two, someone had overheard our conversation at the restaurant. Again, not very likely. Number three, Hammersmith's phone is tapped. Likely. Hammersmith's phone is tapped, I told him where I was and that Yuropov and I were on our way. They sent someone out to make sure we didn't make it. But I had to work it out. No sense in jumping out of the frying pan into the fire for want of a little forethought."

Clara thought about that. "You're sure Hammersmith is one of the good guys?"

He grinned suddenly. "Reasonably sure. I think."

"Great."

McClain looked at her. "I don't want to die any more than you do."

And that was the most reassuring thing he could have said.

They walked for hours, until the sun had dispelled the mist and the air had warmed considerably. It was an Indian summer day. Falling leaves drifted past her face and the foliage overhead was beautiful in shades of crimson and orange and gold. A thick pile of leaves crunched beneath her feet. Squirrels and birds chattered and called in the trees. The setting was idyllic. It was hard to accept that in the midst of such peace and beauty evil men were searching for them, wanting them dead.

Clara shivered at the thought and edged closer to McClain. Determinedly forcing her thoughts from Rostov and his men, they turned instead to him. He was taller than she had first thought, she noted as she walked behind him. His broad shoulders in the dark that first night had made him seem deceptively stocky. She was tall herself, and the top of her head did not quite reach the bottom of his ear. His shoulders were wide beneath the scruffy blue poncho. He had belted it around his waist to keep the ends out of his way, and she observed with interest that his waist was narrow compared to the width of his shoulders. The trailing ends of the poncho obscured his rear, but his legs were long and powerful looking in the faded blue denim as they moved effortlessly over the ground. He was muscular all over, she thought, and then surprised herself by blushing as she remembered how he'd felt lying against her when she awoke. Hard and warm and very, very male. . . .

He stopped, and again she almost cannoned into him. He was standing at the top of a hill looking down. Clara stepped up beside him. Directly below where they stood was a section of winding country road with a mom-and-pop gas station–grocery store nestled into its curve. One car, a battered white Chevy, was in the gravel parking lot. An ancient looking pay phone hung on the cement block wall.

"How about some breakfast?" McClain asked.

"That sounds wonderful," Clara said fervently. She'd been wondering when they were going to get to eat for some time. She had feared they would have to trudge all the way to Maryland first. Beneath her arm, Puff squirmed and meowed as if he understood. "Puff thinks so, too."

But he made no immediate move to descend. His eyes were hard as he surveyed the terrain below. Everything seemed peaceful enough.

"These cuffs have to go before I go down there. Think you can do the job without maiming me?" He rattled the chain on his hand as he spoke.

"I'll do my best." The night before she had thought that breaking a pair of handcuffs was totally beyond her. Today she was a lot more confident of her ability to do the job. He found a large flat rock, placed his left wrist across it, and positioned the screwdriver for her. All she had to do was hit the screwdriver with the hammer. She put Puff down, took the hammer, held her breath, and banged it down with all her might. He yelped, jumping back, but the handcuff opened and he was able to pull it off his wrist.

"Christ, you're a menace," he said, rubbing his newly freed wrist and eyeing her with disfavor. "Hit the screwdriver squarely on the head, damn it. You almost broke my wrist."

"Sorry," Clara said meekly. With another hard look at her he placed his other wrist across the rock and the operation was repeated. This time Clara held the screwdriver, and was more successful. It took her only two tries to crack the latch, and best of all she didn't dent McClain's person a bit.

"Better," he said, when the cuffs were off. "Now you get fed." They were standing on top of the hill looking down at the little store again. Puff, once again cradled in Clara's arms, let out a meow of appreciation. McClain scowled down at him.

"I didn't mean you, furball."

Clara looked up at him pleadingly. "You have to get him something too. He's hungry."

"Meow!"

"I don't believe this," McClain muttered. Two pairs of eyes, one golden and one soft blue, beseeched him. "All right, all right. I'll spend my last few dollars to buy breakfast for the three of us." He shook his head. "You wait here. I'll be as quick as I can." With another shake of his head he started down the hill.

"McClain!"

"What?"

"Be careful!"

"Yeah."

He kept going, striding easily through the undergrowth. Clara watched him for a moment. Then it occurred to her that now would be a good time to attend to a rather pressing need that she had been ignoring for quite some time. Setting Puff down—she was pretty confident that he wouldn't wander off by this time—she went behind a bush and felt immediately better. When she came out and took up her vantage point on the hill again, McClain was nowhere to be seen. The white car was pulling out of the parking lot. Clara watched it, frowning. Of course, McClain could be inside the store or. . . .

A lean brown hand attached to an arm clad in black sweatshirt material waved impatiently from the driver's window. Clara's eyes popped. McClain was stealing the car! Snatching up Puff, she ran down the hill, nearly tripping several times but managing not to fall flat on her face.

"You're stealing a car!" she accused breathlessly as she dropped into the seat beside him. Puff went swarming into the backseat.

"You want to walk to Gaithersberg?" He was as calm as if stealing a car were an everyday occurrence.

"But to steal a car! That's a crime!"

"Needs must." He was strangely terse. Looking at him, Clara saw that his brows had drawn together to form a straight black line over his eyes.

"Is something the matter?"

McClain snorted. "Something new, you mean? Look at that." He nodded toward the middle of the bench seat. Clara noticed the thick Sunday paper lying there for the first time. She picked it up, frowning. Then she gasped. A head and shoulders shot of McClain was on the front page. Under the headline Massacre Suspect Identified she read, "A nationwide search is underway for John Thomas McClain, an employee of the Central Intelligence Agency and a former mental patient, who has been identified as the prime suspect in the Bethesda Naval Hospital massacre Friday night."

"Oh my God!" Clara said, looking over at McClain in horror. For one terrible minute she believed it. Then her mind began to work.

"Did Rostov do this?" she gasped.

"Rostov's thugs did the killings. I was in that emergency room Friday night after I got away from Rostov the first time. He's a careful man, Rostov. He doesn't take chances. He had all those people slaughtered on the off chance that I told one of them what I knew. But Rostov wouldn't think of using his goons' bloodbath to trap me. He's a straightforward bastard. Just kill, kill, kill. I figure Bigfoot himself set me up to take the fall." McClain's mouth twisted humorlessly. "It's brilliant, I'll give him that. Every lawman in the country will be after me, liable as not to shoot first and ask questions later. They've got me down as a crazy, a mass murderer. I'll be lucky to last a week."

"Does it say anything about me?" A tiny hope raised its head. Perhaps, if they were to concentrate on McClain, she might be forgotten. Maybe she could even go home.

McClain shot her a look. "Read the article. It says I'm suspected to be traveling with a woman. A blonde. Although they don't identify you by name. Rostov must not have told them that part."

Clara was silent for a moment. The tiny hope flickered and died. There seemed to be no escape from this mess.

"What are we going to do?" She whispered the question, her eyes already moving to read the rest of the story. She remembered Mitch talking about it and his mother saying that a body was not safe anywhere these days. All those people had been brutally slain because of the man beside her. The extremity of her own danger hit her like a slap in the face. She might very well die because of him too.

He threw a quick look at her. It was impossible to read the feelings hidden behind those emerald eyes.

"We're going to go see Hammersmith. Then we'll take it from there."

Clara looked at him helplessly. His attention was on the road in front of him, his hands locked over the wheel. The bruises stood out lividly against his swarthy skin, reminding her that he was in mortal danger, too. They were in it together, she repeated grimly. And tried not to think how much she wished that wasn't true.

VIII

She had finished the article and was folding the paper when the headline caught her eye: CIA Employee Shot by Wife. It was a small story, just a few paragraphs, but her heart began to pound as she read it.

"McClain," she said, her voice croaking because her throat was suddenly as dry as dust. "Was Hammersmith's wife named Mary?"

He looked over at her. "How'd you know?"

Clara swallowed, wetting her lips with her tongue. "She killed him. Yesterday afternoon. The paper says that she suspected he was going to leave her for another woman and she shot him."

"What?" McClain almost drove off the road.

"Be careful!"

He swore under his breath, pulled the car over to the side of the road, slammed it into park and then reached for the paper. "Let me see that!"

She handed it to him wordlessly, watching him as he read. He sat staring down at the paper for long moments after she knew that he must have finished the small story.

"McClain, are you all right?" she ventured to ask at last. His head lifted and he looked at her. His green eyes glittered brightly. Too brightly.

"May God damn the filthy bastards to hell," he said bitterly. Her eyes widened as she searched his face.

"What do you mean?"

McClain snorted. "They got to him. Somehow. I know it, just like I know the sun came up this morning."

"Who?" But Clara knew what McClain suspected even before she asked it. "Rostov?"

"Yeah. Or someone like him. Because of me. What I know."

"Oh my God!"

"They knew I'd go to him. Sooner or later. So they took him out. Those bastards."

"But McClain, couldn't the story in the paper be true? I read somewhere that there's always a motive for murder between husband and wife. Maybe she did find out that he had someone else. Maybe it happening right at this time is sheer coincidence."

He looked over at her again, then reached down to put the car in gear, driving back onto the road.

"In this business there's no such thing as coincidence," he said, swinging the car into a tight U-turn. Then he drove silently south until Clara could stand the silence no longer. But she didn't know how to break it.

Looking helplessly over at McClain's hard profile, she saw that his lips were clamped together and his jaw jutted forward. Hammersmith had been his friend as well as his boss, she gathered from what he had said. He must be grieving.

She reached out and put a timid hand on his sleeve. His arm felt iron-hard beneath the sweatshirt.

"I'm so sorry," she said. He looked down at her hand and then up at her face. His green eyes glittered like gems.

"He was a pro; he knew the risks," he said brusquely, and shook her hand off his sleeve. Clara sank back in her seat, not knowing what else to do. He was hurting, she could tell, but he could not stand the hurt to be touched. Biting her lower lip, she turned her attention out the window to the passing countryside. The best thing she could do for him was leave him alone.

They drove without speaking for nearly two hours, the car slicing through the maze of twisty roads that criss-crossed the Virginia countryside. They seemed to be moving both west and south, Clara noted. Finally she got up the courage to ask him about it.

"We're taking the Blue Ridge Parkway to Florida," he answered in response to her request to know where they were going.

"Florida!"

He nodded. "With Hammersmith gone there aren't a lot of people I can trust. I wasn't exactly Mr. Congeniality at the agency. But there's somebody, Michael Ball. He was head of covert operations for twenty years. In fact, he hired me. He's got a place down in the Florida Keys. We'll take this to him. He can't be involved in it. I don't think."

"McClain." Clara's voice was barely audible.

"What?"

"There's a helicopter up there." There was no way of knowing if it was the same helicopter that had chased them the night before, but Clara felt a sinking sensation in the pit of her stomach as she looked up at its shiny blue belly. It was flying over the wooded area parallel to the road.

"I see it."

His voice sounded calm. But the knuckles of his hands

were white as they clutched the steering wheel. His bruised jaw was set.

"Do you think it's the same helicopter that was chasing us last night?"

"Probably not. There are a lot of them around like that. It's a police chopper."

"Oh my God!"

He threw her an exasperated look.

"There's no way they can know it's us down here. So just stay calm. If they're even looking for us, they're looking for two people on foot, remember?"

Clara was hardly listening. "They'll shoot us on sight, like Bonnie and Clyde!"

McClain sighed again. Then he tensed.

"Put your head down on my lap. Now!"

"What?"

"Do it!" His words were so fierce that she did as he said. She lay stiffly, her body stretched across the seat, her head resting against his hard thigh. Her face was uncomfortably close to the steering wheel, but she would let her nose be crushed before she'd turn it in the opposite direction. He was too potently male.

He leaned forward, squashing her head between his thigh and upper abdomen, to fiddle with the radio, which didn't work. Clara jerked as she felt his body all around her face. He smelled of man. . . .

"There's a cop car behind us," he whispered savagely. "If they're looking for us, they're looking for a man and a woman. I want them to think I'm alone. Stay down, and stay still."

Clara froze. McClain pretended to adjust the radio. "Please, God, please, please, please," she prayed. There was a whoosh as another car passed them. McClain straightened. She felt his tense muscles relax.

"See? Nothing to worry about," he said as she returned to her seat. "How about something to eat? I got some ham sandwiches and some Cokes back at that little store this morning. They're in the back."

Clara turned around to get them. What she saw made her eyes widen with alarm. Puff was sitting in the middle of the backseat, an open bag beside him. A solitary crust of bread with a trace of mustard still clinging to it lay just inside the bag, which except for two cans of Coke was otherwise empty. Puff was washing himself contentedly, a big feline smile on his face. Crumbs littered the backseat.

"Oh, dear," she said.

"What's the matter?" McClain shot a look at her. Then, seeing where her eyes rested, he looked over his shoulder into the backseat. When he met her eyes again his look was murderous. "That damn cat, I'll wring his fat neck. I'll—"

"We can drink the Coke," Clara interrupted nervously.

"I don't want Coke. I want my ham sandwich!" he gritted.

Puff emitted a delicate burp. McClain cursed. Clara closed her eyes. And then opened them again in a hurry as a siren shrieked behind them.

IX

"Holy mother," McClain growled. Clara looked over her shoulder, past Puff, who was still washing himself contentedly, and out the rear window. Right behind them was a blue and white patrol car from the Virginia State Police.

"What are we going to do?" Clara felt numb.

"Stop," McClain was already slowing and pulling to the side of the road.

"Stop?" Clara couldn't believe that he would just give up so easily. *She* wouldn't surrender without a fight. Why, if everything he'd told her were true they were going to their deaths.

"Let's make a run for it!" she said urgently. "There's only one of him—maybe we can get away. It's better than not even trying!"

"Shut up and pay attention." McClain's voice was fierce. He finished pulling the car onto the rocky shoulder and shoved the transmission into park. "Don't say or do anything, do you understand? Just sit there."

She started to argue, but he was already rolling down the window. Puff, attracted by the fresh air, jumped up on the vinyl headrest behind him, tail waving. McClain cursed under his breath as the furry appendage hit him in the face.

"Is something—" McClain sneezed violently, throwing Puff an evil look as Clara quickly pulled him into her arms. "The matter, officer?"

"Step out of the car, please."

McClain sneezed again. "Is there some problem?"

"Please step out of the car."

"Certainly. Certainly. Just let me get my wallet." McClain sneezed twice more as he reached into his pants pocket for his wallet, his movements slow and easy. The officer, who was young and worried looking, watched carefully.

"Step out of the car!"

"I'm going to . . . (sneeze) . . . Oops!" The wallet dropped from his hand to land with a tiny smack on the pavement. The officer automatically bent to retrieve it. McClain's hand shot to the door handle. Throwing the full weight of his body behind the movement, he shoved the door open. There was a sickening thud as it made contact with the young man's head. Then McClain was out of the car, standing over the policeman who lay sprawled on the pavement, moaning and clutching his head. Quickly he jerked the officer's gun from his holster and cocked it, pointing it at the writhing man as if he meant to blow him into next week.

"No, don't!" Clara shrieked. She'd been craning her neck to follow McClain's movements. She practically had a heart attack, horrified at the idea that he might actually be going to shoot the man. Scrambling out of the car, still clutching Puff whom she'd forgotten in her agitation, she ran around to McClain's side. "Don't do it!"

"Don't be more of an idiot than you can help," he

growled. "Get back in the car and drive it over there behind those bushes."

When Clara hesitated he gave her a look that should by rights have made her quail and barked, "Do it!"

She did it, dumping Puff in the back seat and squealing the tires as she reversed. The spot he had chosen was off the road, partially concealed from it by an abundance of evergreens. Bumping through a shallow ditch, she managed not to get the car stuck in the mud. Her feeling of mild triumph was completely overlayed by anxiety. What was McClain going to do to the cop?

"Don't shoot me!" The young man was lying still, watching McClain warily. In response to a gesture from the gun, he clambered slowly to his feet. Cold-eyed, McClain watched his every move. The man was careful to keep his hands above his head. Clara saw that he was starting to sweat. Tiny beads of perspiration were forming under his nose. His face was very pale, too. Probably about as pale as her own, Clara thought as she rejoined McClain. He couldn't be any more frightened than she was.

"Not unless you make me, pal," McClain replied. Then, to Clara, "Get his handcuffs."

The order was clearly nonnegotiable. Clara, blanching, reached over to do as she was told. She fumbled at the man's belt, feeling sorry for him and herself as well. How had either one of them gotten into this mess?

"Now I want you to get on the radio and tell the dispatcher that you're not feeling well and you're going to take an early lunch break. Say anything else and I'll blow you straight to hell. Understand?"

"Yes, sir," stuttered the young man. Clara cringed as McClain reached inside the car and pulled out the transmitter. If they weren't already, the entire Virginia State Highway patrol would soon be after them with a vengeance.

"Now talk," he ordered, handing the officer the mike and pressing the gun right below his ear. Gulping, the officer did as he was ordered.

"Smart man," McClain approved as he replaced the mike and removed the gun to a distance of about a foot from the officer's head. "Now I want you to walk over to that car. Carefully, now. Don't make me shoot you."

"McClain," Clara said urgently, her voice not much more than a whisper. If he was actually going to commit cold-blooded murder, she wanted no part of it. But he wouldn't, would he? He couldn't just kill someone for no reason, much less a cop. Could he? What did she really know about him? Except that he was silent and ruthless and hated cats and had grieved for his friend . . . Maybe he could kill a man in cold blood. Anyone who hated cats was certainly not all good.

"Can it, would you?" he answered in a snarling whisper. "Get into the police car and sit! Don't touch a thing. And don't say another word!"

But Clara was too worried about what he might do to the cop to obey. She wasn't letting McClain out of her sight, not while he had that gun. Besides, Puff was still in the white car. She had to rescue him. It was a cinch that McClain would leave him behind. Or shoot him if he was feeling murderous. Clara trailed behind as he forced the young man through the muddy ditch to the car. If McClain had a notion to shoot him, she didn't know what she could do to stop him. But there had to be something. A cop killer! The very idea made her shudder. He would be hunted like a rabid dog—and herself with him. She thought she was going to throw up.

The pair stopped beside the car. Clara, hurrying anxiously up behind them, got a narrow-eyed look from McClain for her pains. It practically dared her to say a word. Biting her lip, she was silent. The policeman sent her an imploring look. She looked nervously at McClain, who glared at her.

"Get inside," McClain ordered the officer. Swallowing nervously, the young man slid into the driver's seat.

"Put your hands on the wheel."

The officer did, and McClain neatly cuffed his wrists to the steering wheel. Immediately his manner became less threatening.

"Just sit there, pal, and you'll be found before too long. There's a chopper flying around with your name on it."

With that, he walked around to the front of the car and opened the hood. Clara, following him, watched curiously as he pulled the screwdriver from his waistband and in a matter of perhaps two minutes had the battery out of the car. Then he heaved the battery into the bushes. Clara frowned as he slammed the hood again.

"So he can't lean on the horn," McClain said in response to her questioning look. Then he was headed back toward the police car.

"Oh, wait, I forgot Puff!" Clara ran back around the side of the car. The officer looked frightened as she returned.

"I forgot my cat," she explained, opening the rear door and reaching in for Puff, who was busily licking the last of the crumbs from the seat. He purred as she picked him up. When he had a full belly, Puff was a pussycat.

"I'm really sorry about this," she offered in tentative apology to the cop as she slammed the rear door. "I mean,

about your head being hurt and you being handcuffed
and—"

"Clara!" The roar made her jump. McClain was not
more than six feet away, glaring at her. With a single,
apologetic look at the cop, who was looking nervous again,
she hurried to join him.

"Can't you keep your big mouth shut?" he hissed,
turning away and striding toward where the police car
waited. "The whole idea is to make the other guy afraid of
you. If he's scared enough he's a lot less likely to do
something dumb. If that guy had tried to be a hero, I might
really have had to shoot him. Try to keep this idea in your
head: it's us or them. Think you can remember that?"

"Oh, shut up," Clara said to his back. Such rudeness
was as foreign to her nature as soap was to a sweathog, but
it felt good. She lifted her chin and glared at his back,
daring him to turn around and say something rude in return.
To her disappointment, he acted as if he hadn't even
heard.

When she reached the police car, he was already in the
driver's seat. As she hurried around the hood to get in
beside him, he turned the ignition over. The motor roared.
Clara barely had the door shut when he pulled out with a
spray of gravel. The force of it threw her back against the
seat. Puff scrambled out of her arms and swarmed to perch
on the headrest right behind McClain's head. McClain gave
her a demonic look and reached behind him to sweep Puff
off with a blind push. He received a smack on the wrist
from a razor-clawed paw for his pains.

"Ouch!" McClain put his damaged wrist to his mouth,
sucking on it. The look he turned on Clara was positively
evil.

"I hate that damn cat," he ground out.

Clara could not repress a grin, which made McClain look more furious than ever. Puff settled himself firmly on his new perch, purring like a lawn mower, tail twitching against McClain's neck. Even as Clara reached for Puff, McClain let loose with a sneeze that almost shook the steering wheel with its violence. Clara grinned again, but nonetheless pulled Puff away from his perch and into her lap, where he settled down with a sigh for his after lunch nap. McClain sneezed, swore, and sneezed once again. Clara giggled. And Puff purred.

McClain drove for about an hour in glowering silence, directing the car along twisting country roads in a westerly direction. Clara jumped every time a car came into sight, which fortunately happened with less and less frequency. Puff had curled up into a contented ball in her lap and was fast asleep.

"McClain," Clara finally ventured, "do you think they've found that cop yet?"

"Probably."

"Won't they be looking for us? They must know we're in his car."

"Which is why we're going to dump it. Soon now."

Clara was silent for a moment as she digested that.

"Then what?"

"Then we walk until we find another form of transportation. Something not so conspicuous."

"Couldn't we just take a bus? You have some money, don't you?"

"Every airport, train station and bus depot on the entire Eastern seaboard is being watched right now, I guarantee you. That would be the easiest way I can think of of giving them what they want. Which is us.''

Clara was silent again. Then she said in a small voice, ''What do you really think our chances are of getting out of this mess?''

McClain looked at her. His eyes were grim in his battered face.

''*If* we make it to Michael Ball, and *if* he is not involved in this, and *if* he believes me and manages to convince the powers that be that this is not just a bag of moonshine from a flipped-out agent, and *if* they are then able to quickly identify and neutralize Bigfoot, then our chances are pretty good.''

''That's an awful lot of ifs.''

''Yeah.''

''McClain, what would happen if we just drove away? To California or Mexico or somewhere? Just left Bigfoot alone? Would he leave us alone?''

McClain's eyes flickered in her direction again. ''Never in a million years. There's too much at stake here. Having a high-level operative in our intelligence service is too valuable to the Reds to leave him vulnerable. They'll never rest until we're neutralized. Believe me.''

''Neutralized? That's a nice word for it. Why don't you say what you mean—dead.''

''All right, dead.''

McClain was silent for a moment, and then he added, ''And don't forget the cops. They think I shot up that emergency room. And you're probably pegged as some sort of accessory. They'll never let us alone, either.''

Clara sighed. She'd known there wasn't an easy way out of this. McClain continued softly, ''Even if I could, I wouldn't turn tail at this stage. I owe Bigfoot a debt.''

"What are you talking about?"

He turned to look at her, his eyes emerald green. "Tim Hammersmith was a friend of mine. I mean to do my best to see that the men responsible for his death pay the price."

Clara shivered. He sounded cold and hard and capable of anything—including murder. She wouldn't want to be on the receiving end of that icy rage.

"So what happens after we get to Michael Ball? Assuming he believes us?"

"We try to identify Bigfoot."

"Do you have any ideas?"

"About who Bigfoot might be? I can probably narrow it down to a dozen or so, if I work on it a while."

"Great."

McClain grinned suddenly, his black mood fading. He looked over at Clara, a decided twinkle in his eyes at her acerbic tone. "But I do know who can help us figure it out."

"Who?"

"Big Floyd."

Clara snorted. "That's very helpful. Just who is Big Floyd? A pop star? A clown?"

"A super-computer. Big Floyd can do things you wouldn't believe. To begin with, he can access the agency's files and find out who had access to the information that Bigfoot has passed on. That should narrow the field somewhat. Then he can give us background on the short list of candidates: childhood, education, affiliations, family, bad habits such as gambling or women, that kind of thing. We should be able to narrow it down even more from that. Then he can give us a profile of the kind of guy our mole would most likely be."

"Then what?"

"Then we use the computers we were provided with at birth: our brains. And we pray a lot."

"Fantastic."

"You got any better ideas?"

Clara had to admit that she didn't.

"There's just one thing," she said after a moment, looking over at McClain suspiciously. "How are we going to get to use Big Floyd? I doubt that anyone is just going to let us."

McClain grinned an evil grin. His green eyes were glowing. Clara thought again that he was enjoying himself, and felt a little frisson of fear. A man who enjoyed such a life-and-death predicament was not a man to trust to get one out of it in one piece.

"We're going to break into it, of course. All we need is a PC with a modem."

"Is that all? Just a minute, let me check my pockets. Oh darn, I seem to have left my PC and modem at home." Her tone was definitely sarcastic. His grin broadened.

"Michael Ball has a PC and modem. He gets briefed on all the agency's doings that way. That's another reason we're going to Florida."

"How do you know Michael Ball isn't Bigfoot?" Clara was getting so she didn't think it was safe to rely on anybody.

"I don't."

"You *don't*?"

He shook his head. "How could I? But I don't think so. My gut instinct tells me he's clean. You trust my gut instinct, don't you?"

"Like hell," Clara said. Under stress, it was amazing how years of careful upbringing fell away. Sometimes a swear word was all that would do to express the way she felt. Like now. Trust his gut instinct, indeed! Not when her life was at stake!

"You're hurting my feelings." He looked anything but hurt. In fact, he was laughing at her. Clara gritted her teeth. It was his fault she was in this mess; it was his fault that everything kept getting more and more complicated; it was his fault that umpteen people had been murdered, and the two of them might be next. And he was laughing at her?

"I want to go home," she muttered distinctly. He grinned. And started whistling a tuneless song that sounded vaguely like "Ghostbusters!"

They were climbing now, high into the mountains. Despite the bright beauty of the day it was cold out. The thick forest of trees boasted foliage of scarlet and gold and every shade in between. The scenery was absolutely magnificent. Looking out at it, it was almost impossible for Clara to believe that she was riding in a stolen police car with a renegade secret agent beside her and every police and federal officer in the vicinity—not to mention Rostov and his KGB thugs—on their trail. She kept having the feeling that she was trapped in some kind of nightmare.

Puff, curling up into a tighter ball in her lap, kneaded her thighs with contentment. She yelped as his needlelike claws penetrated the denim jeans, and disengaged the offending paws with a reproving tap. He purred, McClain looked disgusted, and Clara gave up hoping that she would awaken soon. This was no dream. Incredibly, it was her life.

A small roadside sign bore the legend Blue Ridge Parkway, 2 miles. McClain pulled off just past it, idling the car on the side of the road. Clara looked nervously around.

"Why are we stopping?" She didn't even like to ask. Every time they stopped there seemed to be more trouble.

"It's time to ditch the car. Get out."

With a sigh, Clara got out, clutching Puff to her. He ordinarily didn't like being awakened, but he was apparently still feeling good from his purloined lunch. He purred, stretching. Clara scratched his head, watching as McClain backed down the road. She frowned. What was he doing? The thought occurred that he might just leave her there, only to be immediately dismissed. She was sure he wouldn't do that. Strangely enough, in that particular way she did trust him. . . .

The police car with McClain at the wheel went whizzing by her with a screech of tires. Openmouthed, Clara whirled to stare after it as it disappeared around the bend in the road that was some little way ahead. Seconds later, the sound of crunching undergrowth was followed by a tremendous crash. For a moment longer Clara just stared in the direction of the noise. Then she began to run. The sounds of an auto accident were unmistakable.

She was half walking by the time she got around the bend. A stitch in her side had slowed her, and she was clutching that and Puff as she limp-trotted over to where a bare spot in the undergrowth lining the road indicated that something had recently passed through it. Something like a car. With dawning horror, Clara made it to the bare spot and stared down into a leafy ravine. At its bottom, some twenty feet below the road, the police car rested on its top. Its wheels were still spinning.

"You'll catch flies," said a voice behind her. A square, blunt-fingered hand reached around her to gently tap her sagging jaw. Clara's mouth shut with a snap as a wave of relief washed over her. Of course she had known he hadn't gone down with the car, but. . . .

"Here, you carry Puff," she said, thrusting the cat at him in the best revenge for her momentary fright she could devise on an instant's notice. Instinctively he accepted her hand-off. She didn't wait for his sputtered protest before turning on her heel and marching off down the road. A mighty sneeze followed by a series of curses told her that he followed, but she didn't even much care. He had scared her to death, the—

"What the hell's the matter with you?" he demanded, catching up and thrusting a growling Puff at her. Clara crossed her arms over her chest and marched on. McClain sneezed again, cursed, and followed.

"Damn razor-clawed fiend!" This was a shout, followed by a truly tremendous sneeze. Clara halted her march, and looked back over her shoulder to see McClain rubbing at his shoulder while Puff, every bristling bit of fur indicating his outrage, disappeared into the undergrowth beside the road.

"Now just look what you've done!" Thoughts of murder and mayhem flashed through her mind as she marched back toward where McClain alternately sneezed and glared. "You can just catch him!"

"I'll be damned if I will! That thing's meaner than a sewer rat! I don't think he's a cat at all! He's some kind of fiend in cat clothing!"

"Don't you say that about Puff!"

"I'll say anything I damn well please about anything I damn well please!"

"Oh, you will?"

"Yes, I will!"

They were standing nose to nose, shouting at each other, when all of a sudden a frighteningly familiar sound caused them to look up simultaneously.

"Helicopters!"

"Get into the bushes!"

McClain grabbed her arm and shoved her into the small

forest of scrublike shrubs at the side of the road. His hand on the top of her head to force it down was needless. Clara was already crouching, cowering from the threat that whirled from the sky. McClain crouched beside her. Both of them stared up. They could see only the narrow patch of sky above the roadway; everywhere else the trees were too dense to permit them to see the sky. But from the sound of it the helicopters were close—there were definitely more than one.

"Do you think they'll see us?" Clara's question was whispered. Which was silly, when she thought about it, because certainly whoever was in that helicopter was not going to be able to hear them. She could barely hear her own words over the blasted thing's roar.

"No." But she detected a note of worry in his voice. Then Clara realized that, while the helicopter's occupants were unlikely to be able to pick out two individuals cowering in the bushes, there was a far greater chance that they would be able to see an overturned police car.

A helicopter came into view. It was the familiar blue and white of the Virginia State Police, and it was following the road. Behind and slightly to the north of it trailed another one. From the volume of the droning beating down on Clara's ears, the two that she could see were not alone. It sounded as if there was a veritable air force of helicopters searching the forest.

"Apparently they found our cop friend." McClain was whispering too. Clara was both glad and sorry that the situation unnerved him as much as it did herself. She didn't feel like such a coward, but on the other hand, would James Bond whisper in a situation like this? Her stomach sank even further as it occurred to her that her secret agent just might be fresh out of secret agent tricks.

"Good thing we got rid of the car."

"Yeah. If they don't spot it."

"They would have spotted it for sure if we'd been driving it down the road."

"True. Hide your face. It'll reflect the light."

The first helicopter was flying almost directly above them now. Clara was on her knees, her back bent so that her face was parallel to the ground. McClain's hand was on her head, presumably so that she wouldn't forget and look up at the wrong moment. He was in a similar position by her side. Clara pressed against him, feeling the strength of him, the warmth of his body. Despite the fact that he was the reason she was in this mess, she found his presence comforting.

Moments later both helicopters had disappeared from view. Clara straightened cautiously and looked up at the sky to make sure it was really all clear. When she looked back down, McClain was frowning. The helicopters' drone was still clearly audible.

"Do you think they saw us?"

"I don't know. I hope not."

"Wouldn't they have done something if they had?"

"Called for ground support. Which we would have no way of knowing they had done."

"Do you think they did?"

McClain got to his feet abruptly, his hand ungentle on her arm as he hauled her up beside him.

"I sure as hell don't mean to find out the hard way. Grab the furball and let's go."

Mildly surprised that he would even remember Puff, she stared at him.

"Hurry up!"

Clara called, but Puff remained stubbornly absent. Bending over, she spied him crouched beneath a tangle of bushes. She dropped to her knees, reaching for him, but Puff backed up, eluding her stretching fingers by inches. Apparently he hadn't forgiven her for passing him to McClain.

"May God damn all cats and all women who own them," McClain said bitterly, and dropped to his knees beside her to haul a hissing, spitting Puff out from under the bush. "Ouch!"

He got to his feet, glowering as he thrust Puff at her, sneezed, and stuck the side of his hand where tiny beads of blood were beginning to form in his mouth.

"Thank you," Clara said. He responded with a glare, still sucking on his hand, then turned on his heel and marched off through the undergrowth. Clara, clutching Puff to her breast, followed.

The makeshift ponchos were little protection from the cold as the afternoon progressed. Despite the brisk pace that McClain was setting, Clara was shivering. Puff was a welcome source of warmth, and she held him tightly as she stumbled through layers of leaves and vines so thick they must have lain undisturbed for years. If only Puff weren't so heavy. . . .

"McClain, wait!" Clara finally reached the point where she could walk no further. They had come at least ten miles, she knew it had to be that far or close anyway, without so much as a break. Her legs felt as if they were about to fall off, she was freezing to death, her arms were breaking from lugging Puff, and to top all that she was starving. Which last point she would not mention even if she starved to death. To do so would be sure to bring more recriminations about Puff down on her head.

"We need to keep moving." He came back to where she had collapsed on a half rotted log. The fresh air showed up his bruises vividly, but there was an alive look to his face that made him look almost handsome. He was at his best when facing danger, Clara realized, and scowled at him. Now *she* was at her best in her own mauve-toned home— where she would be right this minute if it weren't for him.

"I am taking a break." She said the words distinctly, with immense dignity. For punctuation Puff meowed. McClain frowned down at Puff, his arms crossing over his chest.

"That's the meanest, fattest cat I ever saw. He's as big as a pony. What do you feed him, cat Wheaties?"

"Oh, ha, ha."

"He ate our lunch. I don't know about you, but I'm starving. How about if we skin him and roast him? There's enough meat on him to feed us for a week."

"That's not funny."

"I wasn't trying to be funny."

"Look, just because you're an animal hater—"

"I am not an animal hater. I like dogs. I have a dog, as a matter-of-fact. I keep him on a farm and see him on weekends. He's a nice dog, a collie."

"Seeing him on weekends does not count as having a dog."

"It does too. I'm sensible about animals. They're not kids, after all. Woofer needed a place where he could run, and more attention than I could give him when I'm gone as much as I am. So I leave him with one of my sisters."

"Woofer?" Clara hooted. "That's some name."

"It's no dumber than Puff."

"Puff's not dumb!"

"Oh, yeah? If that cat was very smart he'd run a mile from me, because I'm likely to turn him into a catskin cap. Any minute now."

"You just don't like him because he makes you sneeze. It must be embarrassing for such a tough guy to be allergic to cats. Tell me, did the other boys used to tease you about it when you were growing up?''

McClain's scowl deepened. "I'm surprised somebody hasn't strangled you before now. But maybe I can rectify that.''

''You don't scare me, Mr. Secret Agent Man.'' And, surprisingly enough, he didn't.

McClain's eyes narrowed. "You know, I don't think you've thought the situation through. What would you do if I just walked off and left you and that damned furball to face Rostov or the cops or whoever on your own?''

Clara smiled seraphically. ''Tell them every detail of your plan, of course. How you plan to access Big Floyd and see Michael Ball in Florida and—''

''Bitch.''

''So you're stuck with us, McClain, just like we're stuck with you. Believe me, we don't like it any better than you do.''

''Oh, yeah?''

''Yeah!''

McClain's eyes narrowed. His lips compressed. His arms uncrossed and his fists settled into twin balls on his hips. He leaned forward and down until his face was inches from Clara's and gritted, ''I've had about as much of your smart mouth as I'm going to take, lady. I thought we settled all this last night. I give the orders, and you take them!''

''Pooh!''

She stared back at him with a narrow-eyed defiance of her own. She was tired, hungry, and scared silly, and he was the least of her worries. She stuck out her tongue at him.

''You know what your problem is?'' he said through clenched teeth. ''You're a man hater. I bet you've never had a boyfriend in your life!''

That hit home. Clara was sensitive about the lack of men in her life. Not that she wasn't attractive. She was. She knew she was, and her mother and Lena assured her of it several times a month. She had just never had the knack of attracting men. Not like Lena.

"Have you ever been laid, Miss Man Hater? Or even kissed?"

Clara's face reddened at the jeer. While she sputtered, he continued in a singsongy taunt, "Old maid, never been kissed; old maid, never been kissed—"

She slapped him. Right on his bruised cheek. So hard her hand stung. So hard his head snapped back. So hard he yelped. Then his green eyes darkened to emerald and shot sparks. He reached out and grabbed her by her upper arms, hurting her as he yanked her up and against him, dislodging Puff who leaped for safety with a yowl. Then in the same rough movement he was bending his mouth to hers and kissing her with a bruising force that hurt her mouth.

Clara felt the greedy heat of his mouth all the way down to her toes. Her stomach churned; her loins tightened; her toes curled. Her arms went up around his neck. She melted against him like superheated plastic. More than she had ever wanted anything in her life, she wanted his kiss.

His tongue was in her mouth. She thought she would die with the wonder of it. Quivers started at the base of her spine to race along her nerve endings. She touched his tongue with hers, caressed it, felt his heart begin to slam against his ribs. His arms went around her, straining her to him. His hands slid down to cup the round cheeks of her behind. He pulled her up against him, and she felt the size and hardness of him pressing against that part of her that suddenly ached with need. Her knees went weak. Her head rested on his shoulder as he bent her over his arm and slanted his mouth across hers like a man who was suddenly starving. . . .

Then, just as suddenly as he had grabbed her, he straightened and thrust her away from him so that she sat down hard on the log, hard enough to hurt her behind if she had been noticing such things but she wasn't. She could only stare bemusedly into green eyes that were the mysterious dark hue of pine forests now.

"McClain," she breathed. He sucked in a breath and his jaw clenched.

"If there's one thing we don't need at this point it's that kind of complication," he bit out. "So control yourself, for God's sake!"

Then he turned on his heel and marched away into the forest. Clara stared after him, her emotions slowly crystallizing into anger. He was nearly out of sight before she regained the presence of mind to retrieve Puff and scramble after him.

XI

Puff picked up the sound first. The sun was hanging low in the sky; beneath the trees, the world was already verging on dusk. It had been about four hours since they had abandoned the police car. Most of that time had been spent in fuming silence as each made a conscious effort to ignore the other. Clara had finally had to put Puff down; her arms were simply too tired to carry him. To her pride—which she communicated with a superior look at McClain—the cat had the good sense to follow along behind. He was smarter than any dog, as she had known for years. Now, when she looked behind her to make sure that he was keeping up, she found him unmoving some twenty feet behind, ears pricked and tail moving as he stared unblinkingly back down the trail.

"He hears something." They were the first words she had spoken to McClain since that soul shattering kiss.

Even without Puff's weight to slow Clara down, McClain still managed to stay some little way ahead of her. Now he threw an impatient look over his shoulder without stopping.

"Dumb cat probably sees a bird. Keep moving."

"No, he hears something," Clara insisted, stopping and walking back to where Puff was still staring alertly back the way they had come. The urgency of her tone must have gotten through to McClain, because he turned and walked back to join her, muttering a curse under his breath.

"Goddamn!" The drawn out profanity signaled a calamity of the highest order. Clara's eyes widened as she stared up at McClain, who had stopped to listen. She too heard something, strange high-pitched sounds she could not identify.

"What is it?"

"Dogs." The terse monosyllable was alarming in the extreme.

"What?"

He threw her an impatient glance and bent to scoop up Puff. Watching him, Clara was frightened to death. Only a disaster of apocalyptic proportions would move him to pick up Puff.

"Dogs. You know, the opposite of furball here. Get your ass in gear, we've got to make tracks."

Sneeze!

He was already moving at a steady jogger's trot, his sneakered feet kicking up the top layer of the leaves underfoot, sneezing and cursing periodically as he ran. Clara was no jogger, but fear inspired her: she managed a very creditable skip-run that kept her just behind him.

"What do you mean, dogs?" she called to him. He had Puff tucked under one arm like a football, to her amazement. Despite the sneezing that was violent enough to throw him off stride when it came, he showed no indication of abandoning the animal or leaving him to her to carry. Her opinion of him, after sinking lower than a snake's belly after that unforgivable order to control herself, inched back up a little. But only a little.

"A dog pack. Trackers. And who do you suppose they're tracking?"

Sneeze!

"Us?" Clara felt her heart lurch. She had seen those prison escape movies where the baying hellhounds chased down and chewed up their prey.

"Right."

"What are we going to do?"

He spared a quick glance over his shoulder. "Run like hell. And pray."

Sneeze!

Clara was already praying. And thinking. The helicopter must have seen the police car. They had, as McClain had thought they might, summoned ground support. The ground support had, in turn, summoned the owner of a pack of dogs. And the dogs were on their trail. Clara thought about their slow trudge through the forest that afternoon and groaned. They should have run like rabbits before the hunters. But recriminations wouldn't help now. Only prayer would. And quick thinking. And quicker feet.

The sound of the dogs was growing more distinct. Clara didn't know if it was because she was aware of it or because the pack was getting closer. Would they be torn to shreds or forced to climb a tree for safety, to be held at bay until the equally fearsome humans with the animals brought them down at gunpoint? Maybe they could make somebody believe their story before it was too late. . . .

"McClain!" All those hours when she had coddled her writer's block by watching old movies suddenly repaid her. "McClain!"

"What?"

"Water! We've got to run through water! Dogs can't track through water!"

"Seen any bathtubs lately?"

Sneeze!

He would be nasty on the way to a firing squad, she thought resentfully, but it took all her breath just to yell her thoughts at his retreating back. She didn't have any to spare for arguing with him.

"We've got to find a creek! We can run through it and the dogs will lose our scent. Would you wait for me?"

This last was as close to a screech as she felt safe to coming with the dogs and their handlers on their trail. A stitch was stabbing through her side and she did not think she could continue to yell after a retreating McClain. It was all she could do to keep running.

"Come on, then." He came back for her, grabbing her hand and hauling her after him. The pace he set was murderous given the stitch in her side. She set her jaw, narrowed her eyes, and resolved to keep running until she fell over dead. Stitch or no stitch.

Sneeze!

"If we run parallel to the hilltop we're bound to come across a stream. Water runs downhill, and there has to be some on this mountain."

"Stop talking and run. Where do you think I'm going, anyway?"

He was, indeed, running sideways across the mountain instead of up it. He must have watched the same old movies she had, she thought. If only they could come across a stream soon. . . .

Clutching his hand for all she was worth, she forced her protesting body to move like it had never moved before.

Even Puff seemed to realize the urgency of the situation. He was making no protest at being carried in such an undignified way by a man he loathed.

The baying of the dogs was getting louder; throwing a scared glance over her shoulder, Clara was relieved to see that at least they were not yet in sight. But from the sound of them they were closing fast, much faster than she and McClain were escaping. The animals would catch them soon unless they found a stream.

In the end, just as the dogs' yelping was so distinct that Clara feared they would burst into view at any second, they nearly fell into their savior. McClain yanked on her hand, stepping up his pace, and as Clara looked up despairingly she saw it too: a broad, shallow stream meandering down through a leaf-filled basin. It was an ordinary little mountain stream, which at the moment was the most beautiful thing she had ever seen in her life.

McClain didn't slacken his pace as he ran into the water, turning downstream. This didn't make sense to Clara, as the dogs were coming uphill and they would therefore be running past them. But she didn't have the breath to protest. Sneezing with every other step, McClain was towing her through the creek like a minnow on a line. The stream bed seemed to be made of slippery pebbles and sand. It was all she could do not to stumble on the uneven bottom and fall. The water barely came past her ankles, but with all the splashing they were doing her jeans were soon wet to the thighs. And it was cold. As cold as the ice water in the refrigerator.

The baying of the dogs grew briefly louder. Clara could hear a human voice urging the animals on. Puff's fur stood on end, and then the sounds were behind them, gradually growing fainter as they continued to run through the stream.

At last they could no longer hear the dogs. McClain, sneezing only sporadically now, slowed to a walk. Clara felt like dropping flat on her face with the agony of the stitch in her side, but of course if she did she would drown. Besides, McClain would very likely leave her.

"I think we've lost them." He didn't even sound out of breath, Clara thought, eyeing him with exhausted resentment. She was willing to bet he was one of those fitness freaks who ran miles every day and spent their non-running time smirking sanctimoniously at saner folk. She despised fitness freaks—but her side was aching too much to allow her to throw the kind of putdown at him that he deserved.

"Kind of out of shape, aren't you?" he observed next, apparently having noticed her bug-eyed, crimson faced, half stooped form of locomotion.

If looks could have killed, he would have died on the spot. Unfortunately, she did not yet feel capable of words.

"All right, we'll take a break. For one minute, no more. Here, lean against this rock. We can't get out of the water yet."

Clara staggered up to a thigh-high boulder that protruded from the middle of the stream. Greenish water split into a V of white ripples on either side of the rock as it flowed past. Collapsing stomach down across the boulder's curved top, she let her hot face rest against the cool stone as her fingers curled down into the icy water. Maybe, just maybe she was not going to die. Puff, who was as wet as her jeans, was parked near her head. He growled direly.

"Not having a heart attack, are you?" He sounded

cheerfully unconcerned as he leaned against the boulder near where her face flopped.

"Go . . . to . . . hell," she managed, trying to glare at him. But she was just too tired.

Then he sneezed again and she felt vaguely revenged.

"We'll follow this creek for as long as we can. If we're lucky they'll figure we went the other way. It'll take them quite a while to run the dogs along both sides of the creek upstream. Of course, if they're smart, they'll also send a foot patrol downstream. Just in case we did what we did."

"Let's get moving," Clara groaned, pushing herself up and away from the boulder despite the effort it cost her. The vision of the foot patrol that he suggested transcended physical agony. McClain clapped her on the shoulder and straightened, grabbing her hand before trudging off again through the water, Puff once again tucked under his arm.

Nearly an hour later the creek ran into a river.

"Now what?" Clara stopped to stare at the rushing expanse in dismay.

"Good question." McClain, too, was staring at the swiftly moving brown water. He had stopped sneezing, finally. Clara supposed it was because Puff was wet and the fur that brought on the symptoms was no longer irritating McClain's nose.

"We certainly can't wade through that."

"No."

Clara started to slog toward the bank. McClain tugged on her hand.

"Wait a minute. Look over there."

"Over there" was a clump of trees, a tangle of weeds,

and an orange and black rubber raft overturned on the bank.

"Probably belongs to some hunters," McClain observed, thrusting Puff at her before moving toward it. He had dropped Clara's hand when they had stopped. She vaguely missed the comforting warmth of his grip. Holding Puff, who seemed to have resigned himself to being hauled about, she splashed after McClain.

"You don't mean for us to take that thing," her nod indicated the flimsy looking raft, "out there, do you? It looks like some kid's toy!"

McClain looked briefly at the swollen river, then back at Clara. "It's the best I can come up with. Unless you want to go on walking through the woods until we come across the dogs again."

That silenced Clara. She watched as he leaned over to pull the raft into the water after a wary look around. Whoever belonged to the raft was nowhere in sight. Beneath the octagon shaped vessel was a pair of aluminum oars, neatly placed. Careful that his feet never left the water, McClain grabbed those too and threw them with a clatter of metal on metal into the raft, which was already beside him in the creek. The thing appeared to float, or at least its back side did. The front end was resting on the pebbly creek bottom beside McClain's foot. Clara could see at least two black rubber patches from where she stood. There was no way the thing would carry McClain, herself and Puff down the swollen river.

"Hop in," he said, pulling the ridiculously small raft out into the middle of the creek. Clara was relieved to see that the front end floated as well. Temporarily, anyway.

"It doesn't look very river worthy," she protested nervously, eyeing the sausage-roll sides and black rubber bottom that was streaked with mud and littered with leaves. The chubby, patched sides reminded her of innertubes she swam with as a child. Fun then, maybe, but nothing she cared to attempt now. Not on a river, when her life was at stake.

"What do you want, the *Pacific Princess*?" he asked, naming a well-known cruise ship as he waded around beside her. Before she knew what he was about, one arm slid around her shoulder and the other around her knees. She was lifted and deposited willy-nilly on the floor of the raft before she could do more than squeal. Puff yowled and leaped for safety at this unexpected occurrence. Fortunately he too landed in the raft. Clara's bottom was immediately as wet as the rest of her from the inch or so of ice cold water that had settled in the raft's bottom. Puff, feeling water, that most dreaded of all substances, on his feet, yowled like a banshee and leaped up into the air, only to land again in the same puddle. He looked wildly around, then appeared to realize that there was no dry place on which to rest. With a moan, he lifted a paw, shook the water from it, washed it—then had to set it down again into the mess. He moaned again and repeated the process.

"Listen, can the he-man stuff," Clara said furiously, sitting upright and glaring at McClain as she clutched both sides of the furiously rocking raft. He was already behind it, pushing it out toward the river. The water swirled up past his knees to his thighs.

"I'm perfectly willing to plant my ass in the raft while you push it out," he said, pulling his poncho over his head and tossing it to her for safekeeping as he spoke. The words were matter-of-fact, but there was a glint in his green eyes that Clara disliked. She made no reply, just clutched the poncho to her chest and eyed him resentfully. If she argued with him at this particular point she feared she just might find herself waist-deep in the muddy water. Which, when she thought about it, she was perfectly willing to leave to him.

"Move to the rear, would you? It'll make it easier to push."

Not being blessed with Puff's coordination, Clara had problems getting her bottom off the bottom of the raft. The rubber gave with every movement she made, and in the end she was forced to scoot backwards to the spot McClain indicated in the stern. Puff she set in the middle. He moaned and repeated his attempts at drying his paws.

"At least most of you can dry off," she told him, draping McClain's poncho around her neck and trying her best to brush the water off her soaked jeans. It was impossible, of course, with water sloshing in the bottom of the raft. After a few minutes she resigned herself to freezing.

In minutes they were beyond the protective banks of the creek. The current was much swifter in the river. The water was up to McClain's chest when he hauled himself up over the side. The raft heeled precariously. Clara threw herself as far to the opposite side as she could, leaning out over the swirling water at a ninety degree angle. Puff climbed her arm with a yowl to sit perched on her shoulder as water sloshed into the raft in McClain's wake.

"I knew I'd find a use for you two sooner or later," he said with evident satisfaction, sitting up and then kneeling as he retrieved the oars from where they had rolled beneath the sides.

"What's that?" Clara asked suspiciously, straightening but still holding tightly to the side with one hand as she dislodged Puff with the other.

"Ballast," he answered with a grin, pulling his poncho

from around her neck and yanking it over his head before thrusting an oar at her. Then he crawled forward before she could brain him with her oar.

Fortunately, since Clara had never maneuvered a raft in her life (outdoor pursuits were not much in her line) the thing floated downriver with the minimum of assistance, drawn along by the rain swollen current. All kinds of debris swirled in the water around them, branches and even whole trees, rubber tires, a grocery cart, aluminum cans, cardboard boxes. At one point the bloated carcass of a cow floated past, swirling in slow circles, accompanied by the sickening stench of rotting flesh; McClain speculated aloud that it must have fallen in from some slippery bank and had been unable to get out before it drowned. On either side of the river, which was perhaps a quarter of a mile across, tall trees in their autumn foliage lined the banks. That the water rose partway up the trunks of some of them was evidence of the river's recent rise.

"Do you have any idea where we are?" Clara had lost all sense of direction during that wild run from the tracking dogs. McClain was paddling in a desultory manner, not so much to propel the raft but to keep it on course and away from both the banks with their hidden obstacles and the swiftly running center of the river.

"Well, we ditched the car just to the south of Pipers Gap. Since then we've been moving in a sort of southwesterly direction. We may even be in North Carolina by this time. We're certainly headed that way."

"What river is this, do you know?"

McClain pursed his lips. "The New? It's just a guess, but if this isn't it we're near it. Geography was never my best subject."

It hadn't been Clara's, either. The only rivers she knew

were the Mississippi, the Ohio, and of course the Potomac. None of which this one was. The New River seemed as likely as any.

"McClain—"

He sighed. "Why don't you call me Jack? The way you say 'McClain' reminds me of my old drill sergeant, the terror of Parris Island. I hate being reminded of Sergeant Jackson. He cussed me out a minimum of ten times a day."

"What for?" Clara thought the name Jack suited him much better than the John he had been christened, but she felt a little awkward at the idea of calling him by his first name. When she called him McClain it served to set a distance between them, a distance that she wasn't sure she wanted to eliminate. Her thoughts were momentarily diverted by the idea of him as a green young recruit blanching before a tough drill sergeant.

"Fun. He liked watching people squirm. He was a real asshole. He finally bought the farm in Nam. Nailed by his own troops, I heard."

"You're kidding."

"Nope."

"Were you there?"

"When old Iron Balls bought it? Nope. Too bad, too."

"I meant in Vietnam."

"Yeah."

Clara shook her head. He had his back to her so he didn't see the exasperation evident in her gesture. Getting information out of him was about as easy as keeping Puff out of the refrigerator.

"You were in the marines?"

"Yeah."

"How old were you?"

"Twenty, twenty-one. I dropped out of college to join up. More fool me."

"When was that? The late sixties?"

"Sixty-eight and nine. Which makes me thirty-eight, if that's what you're getting at. Not that much older than you, I'd guess."

"I only just turned thirty," replied Clara, stung.

"That's what I said," he answered smugly, and again Clara had to fight the urge to bop him with her oar. There was a moment's silence as she struggled with an acute case of piqued pride.

"So what was it like, Vietnam?"

"What is this, twenty questions?" He finally turned to look at her. His eyes were narrowed, his jaw hard. There was tension in the set of his broad shoulders.

"I was just curious. Curiosity is a writer's stock in trade, you know. You never know. If you tell me all about it your life story might end up in one of my books."

"God forbid."

Clara was affronted. "They're very good books."

"I'll take your word for it."

"They are!"

"Okay, they are. Gloria's a big fan of romance novels. That's her biggest problem. She keeps expecting Mr. Wonderful to come charging up on a white horse and carry her off with him."

Clara's eyes narrowed. "Poor woman. Her life must be rife with disappointment."

McClain looked suspiciously at her over his shoulder. "Is that some kind of dig at me?"

"Certainly not. But to a woman who's waiting for a

knight in shining armor you must certainly seem like the booby prize of the century.''

"You know, you've got a damned nasty tongue. No wonder you're not married.''

Clara glared at his broad back. He hadn't even bothered to turn around to deliver the insult, which added it to injury.

"How do you know I'm not? Maybe my husband is traveling on business or something.''

"You don't wear a wedding ring.''

"So? A lot of women don't anymore, Mr. Dark Ages.''

"You don't kiss like a married woman.''

"Maybe it depends on whom I am kissing.'' She thought she injected a nice scathing note into that. *He* couldn't see how her cheeks burned at the memory of their kiss.

"Besides,'' he added softly, still without looking around, "I read the bio inside the back cover of your book. 'Miss Claire Winston, who has vowed never to marry until a man as irresistible as her fictional heroes comes along, resides with her mother on her family's antebellum estate, Jollymead, in the horse country of Virginia.' ''

He quoted the last in a mocking falsetto that made Clara grit her teeth and flush to her hairline. She had hated the way the blurb writers worded that bio from the first time she had seen it. Which had been much too late to keep it out of her book.

"Oh shut up,'' she said. "It's not a disgrace to be unmarried, you know. Not in this day and age.''

"Then why does it embarrass you so much?'' That soft taunt hit home. Clara glared impotently at the back of that close-cropped black head, imagined with a moment of real pleasure what it would be like to send her oar arching into intimate contact with it, and dropped the idea with deep reluctance. She had no doubt that his retaliation would be immediate and extremely unpleasant.

"You shouldn't have too much trouble landing a man, you know," the ape with the paddle continued in a soft, goading voice. "You're not unattractive, exactly. You could use a little makeup and a trip to a good hairdresser, and you could maybe stand to lose about ten pounds, but on the whole I'd say you're as good looking as a lot of the gals with husbands."

"Well, thank you very much," Clara spat. She had gone rigid at his catalogue of her "virtues," and now sat clenching her fists as she glared daggers at his back. "Coming from a box-faced, squash-nosed Neanderthal I'll take that as a compliment."

"Maybe it's your kissing technique," her tormentor continued musingly. "It certainly could use improvement. I'd liken kissing you to sucking on an overripe tomato. Lots of mush, but no texture or bite."

"Why, you . . ." That did it. Retaliation or not, she was going to brain him. She surged to her feet, swinging the oar. The raft bucked wildly, the oar missed its mark by a mile, he cursed and looked over his shoulder—and she fell into the river with a splash that rivaled any ever made by Moby Dick.

When she surfaced seconds later, sputtering and choking on the muddy water, Puff was staring at her over the side of the raft and McClain was laughing so hard that she hoped for a minute that he would fall into the river, too. But he didn't, of course. Instead, he obligingly stretched his oar toward her, and when she caught it hauled her close to the side. Of course, with her clothes soaking wet and her natural athletic ineptitude, she could not heave herself aboard. He had to reach down, grab the waistband of her jeans, and haul her over the side. For a moment Clara flopped around the bottom of the raft like a landed fish, glaring at his soggy sneakers which were all of him that she could see. Then she scrambled to her hands and knees, crawling precariously through the two inches of water she had brought to huddle in the stern, wrapping her arms around her body in a vain effort to stop herself from shivering. Puff took one look at her and turned tail, marching with great dignity as close to McClain as he could get before turning to glare at her. McClain guffawed loudly as she scowled right back at him. Her attention shifted to McClain; thoughts of murder ran rampant in her head.

"I hate you," she said with conviction.

"Oh, and I was hoping you'd think I was irresistible," he said with a simper, then roared again at the picture she made clenching her fists and glaring at him, soaked from head to toe in muddy water, drenched hair straggling over her face, each matted strand sending its own individual rivulet over the soaked poncho, smears of mud marking her left cheek, and an enormous puddle of water forming around her bottom.

"You are a—" she started furiously. He shook a finger at her.

"Uh—uh," he said. "Any more insults out of you and I won't let you wear my blanket. You'll just have to sit around in those soaking wet clothes until you freeze."

His warning effectively silenced her. She glared at him as he pulled his poncho over his head and passed it to her. If she hadn't been absolutely freezing she would have told him to take it and stick it where the sun don't shine. As things were, she accepted it with poor grace.

The idea of undressing with him sitting two feet away, even though he had his back turned as he guided the raft,

made her grit her teeth. He was the most loathsome man she
had ever met; she hated him; she despised him; she hoped
Rostov caught him and tortured him to death. It was what
she would like to do herself if she could. But if she did not
get her clothes off soon and get into something dry and
warm, she thought she would die. So, fixing him with a
killing stare that his occasionally heaving shoulders only
sharpened, she kicked off her soggy boat shoes, rolled down
her dripping jeans, and pulled the soaked poncho and flannel
shirt over her head. She hesitated for a moment over her
teddy, which when wet was nearly transparent, throwing
him a suspicious look. But his attention seemed fixed on the
upcoming curve in the river—and the teddy was as clammy
as the rest. Sliding the spaghetti straps down her shoulders,
she quickly stepped out of it and pulled his relatively dry
poncho over her head. Oh, blissful warmth! She had not
realized how bone cold she was until she experienced the
rough comfort of that blanket, still warm from his body.
Shivering, she sat on the back roll of the raft, careful to
hang on so as not to fall off backwards but unable to sit
any longer in that puddle of freezing water on the bottom.
Her feet could not escape, however. She leaned forward,
careful to keep the tails of the poncho out of the water,
wrapped her legs with her arms, and watched her feet turn
blue.

"I take that back about you needing to lose ten pounds,"
the fiend said softly. "Five would do it."

As he had no doubt intended, the mocking revelation that
he had watched her undress sent her temper soaring again.
But she was too cold and too miserable to attempt any
further overt action. Seething impotently, she gritted her
teeth and clenched her fists. One day . . . one day she would
make him pay.

"You are undoubtedly the most insufferable man I have ever met in my life," she said with conviction. Then, setting her jaw resolutely, she pretended he didn't exist as she wrung out her soaking clothes and arranged them along the sausage rolls at her side as best she could in hopes that they would dry.

✦ XII ✦

Half an hour later it was dark. Clara was shivering uncontrollably as she bailed water from the bottom of the raft with her shoe, a task that the heartless beast in the bow had set her to, telling her that if she didn't want them to swamp she would bail. As her shoes didn't hold much, and her sojourn overboard had brought in quite a bit, the task promised to take a long time. And she was freezing in the meantime. Between the chill of the night and her nakedness, the blanket that had seemed so warm when she had first donned it now was little protection.

"McClain, I'm freezing," she said finally. He shrugged and kept paddling.

"I'm also starving."

"It was your cat that ate our lunch."

"So? I'm still starving. And I have to go to the bathroom."

"Go over the side."

Clara gave up. He was the most unfeeling man she had ever met. She was probably going to die in the miserable little rubber boat and he wouldn't care a snap. He would just toss her body into the river.

She alternately bailed and fumed silently, shivering all the while. The river at night was an eerie place, not as dark as the shrouded forest on either side but a glistening black swath cut through the shifting shadows. Strange rustlings came from the bushes along the bank. McClain was careful to stick fairly close to shore, both to avoid the possible sweep of a helicopter down the river and the treacherous plethora of objects that littered the river toward the middle. Thus Clara was able to make out slinking shapes of animals as they crept from the trees to drink at the river's edge. Once she even thought she saw a bear and its cubs, but they were far ahead so she couldn't be sure. Just the thought of walking through a forest where bears lived made her shiver more than she was already.

The moon came up, a glimmering white sickle occasionally obscured by the dark clouds that blew across the sky. Stars twinkled in the narrow overhead path that was visible from the river. The wind picked up and grew colder, carrying with it the scent of pine needles and rotting worms in equal proportions. Huddled in the poncho which was too narrow and reached to perhaps her knees when she stood up (which she now knew better than to do), Clara thought she had never been more miserable in her life.

McClain seemed tireless, right at home under such adverse conditions, she thought, eyeing him with dislike. Of course, he wasn't sitting around nearly naked with damp hair, either. Only Puff seemed to echo her discomfort. He was pacing up and down between the two of them, staring toward shore, and now and then uttering a piercing yowl.

"What ails the hairy monster now?"

Correctly interpreting McClain's reference to mean Puff, Clara glared at his back.

"At a guess, I'd say A: he's hungry, and B: he probably has to go to the bathroom."

"He's not nearly as hungry as I am, thanks to him. And as for the other, tough. He can hold it."

"He can only hold it so long," Clara warned with malicious enjoyment. "He has a bladder problem. He's a very old cat, you know."

"Great."

McClain sounded about as cheerful as she felt, which paradoxically improved her mood. She hoped he *was* miserable. He deserved to be miserable. . . .

Puff yowled again, the sound more piercing than ever.

"You keep that thing as a pet?" McClain demanded with apparent disbelief. "I'd sooner keep a vampire bat."

"I'm sure you would," Clara responded sweetly. Puff yowled again.

"All right, all right." There was some hope for McClain after all, Clara decided with surprise. This remark had been addressed directly to Puff. "Hold on, will you? We need to stop for the night anyway."

Unmollified, Puff yowled piercingly and resumed his pacing.

"You'd better hurry," Clara informed McClain with unalloyed joy. "He's really got to go. I don't know if you're familiar with male cats, but—"

"I'm not, and I don't want to be," McClain replied shortly, and began to maneuver the raft toward the left bank. When they were perhaps two feet away, he jumped out and dragged it the rest of the way in. Puff leaped out before the raft had even reached the shore and disappeared into the shadows beneath the trees.

"If we're lucky he won't come back," McClain said as Clara slid her clammy shoes onto her feet before inadvertently stepping out into about six inches of icy river water. Swearing under her breath, she sloshed up on the bank. She was so cold she didn't think it was possible to get any colder.

"Or maybe a bear will have him for dinner," McClain continued on the same hopeful note. Clara ignored him. She was too miserable for arguments. She was too miserable even to worry about Puff. She was too miserable for anything except being miserable. To top it off, she too had to go to the bathroom. With a sour look at McClain, she tromped off behind the same bushes Puff had favored. There were some advantages to being next door to naked, she reflected.

"What now?" she demanded when she returned to see McClain pulling the raft up into the trees and, placing the oars beneath it, overturn it under some bushes. Her still wet clothes tumbled into the litter of leaves. Clara scarcely noticed.

"I thought I saw a cabin up through the trees. If we're lucky it's empty."

"Wh—where?" Clara was so cold she could barely talk. McClain took a look at her, frowned, and headed in a southerly direction through the trees. After perhaps a hundred feet she saw it too, a small log cabin, not much more than a shack, actually, perched crookedly beneath a tall pine. The windows were boarded up and the place had the forlorn air of having been deserted for years. It also looked as though it might collapse at any second, but at least it was shelter from the rising wind and that was all that Clara cared about for the moment.

"Do you think you can break in?"

McClain snorted. "I don't imagine much breaking will be required."

He walked up to the door, which was a foot or so off the ground as though a step had once stood before it. When he pushed on the door, it moved inward with a rusty creak for about three inches before stopping. After another gentle shove, which produced no progress, McClain put his shoulder to it and pushed. With a piercing shriek of outraged hinges, the door swung open.

Inside the cabin was as dark as a cave except for the slightly grayer rectangle cut by the open door. It smelled of mildew, but Clara didn't care. She was right on McClain's heels as he stepped up and in. She would face anything just to get out of the cold.

"Umph!" She was concentrating on not putting her feet through any of the holes in the floor when she bumped into McClain's back and stopped, standing as close to him as she could. She was really freezing, and the warmth his body emanated was as welcome as a furnace.

"Graceful as ever, I see," he remarked sourly over his shoulder. But he drew her beside him and put his arm around her, all with such an unpleasant expression on his face that Clara knew better than to get the wrong idea. He was simply trying to warm her.

"I don't suppose you've got any matches?" Given the state of her undress, McClain's little joke didn't even drag forth a reply. She stood, shivering, pressed up against him even though he had removed his arm, feeling his movements as he fished in his pockets. There was a clatter of change, a rattle of crumpled paper, and then a pleased grunt.

"Matches?" she asked.

"Better. A cigarette lighter. Wait here."

"Where are you going?" But it was too late. He had already headed out the door, withdrawing his precious warmth. When he reappeared seconds later, he was carrying a flaming torch made out of something that looked like a pine cone. As McClain held it high, they both surveyed the interior of the cabin.

The inside was as rickety looking as the outside. The walls were made of rough slabs of wood haphazardly fitted together so that chinks of the darkness outside showed through the joinings. The two boarded windows had once had glass in them. A few shards were left clinging to rusty metal frames. The far wall was lined with shelves, on which several ancient looking canned goods still rested. A rusty potbellied stove sat in one corner, the stovepipe slanting up at a crazy angle through a jagged hole in the roof. The floor was rotting linoleum over equally rotting wood, mined with holes. The roof appeared to be tin. The cabin itself was only one room, and it was bare of furniture of any description.

"It's not the Sheraton, but it's better than nothing," McClain said, then yelped as the torch burned down to his fingers. Dropping the thing with a curse, he stepped on it to make sure that it was out. Then he turned and went back outside, leaving Clara standing, shivering, in the middle of the cold, dark room.

When he returned some five interminable minutes later, he was carrying a small armload of branches and was accompanied by Puff, who meowed imperiously when he saw Clara.

"I knew we wouldn't lose him. My luck's been running this way all week."

Clara ignored that, kneeling and holding out her arms to Puff, who swarmed into them. She gathered him against her chest, murmuring soothing endearments into his ear. At least he was fairly dry, she was glad to note. Only his feet were still wet. He purred furiously at her attentions, butting his head against her chin. After a moment she put him down. He stared up at her, rubbed himself against her bare, frozen ankles, and meowed ingratiatingly. When she did not immediately respond, being too busy shivering, he meowed again.

"What's he squalling about now?" McClain was piling branches into the stove as he spoke.

"He's hungry." Clara was, too. She had a feeling that if she ever got over being on the verge of dying from the cold she would expire from hunger.

"Oh, is he? Listen, you mangy furball, I have not eaten for almost thirty-six hours, thanks to you. Keep on yowling and you may be my next meal."

Puff merely looked at him and yowled harder, while Clara watched with greedy anticipation as McClain applied the small flame of the lighter to the tangle of branches in the stove. After a moment, a larger flame appeared, then flickered and grew.

"A fire," Clara breathed, enraptured, rushing to stand near it, shivering harder in blissful anticipation of waves of warmth. Puff followed, still complaining. Clara ignored him with the ease of long practice. McClain fixed him with a baleful glare, then turned his attention back to the stove. For some moments he watched the slowly building blaze with a critical eye, then shut the door to the small stove. The stovepipe swayed precariously. Clara crowded nearer to the rusty black object.

"Don't touch it. I imagine it'll get pretty hot in a few minutes," McClain warned, moving away. Clara paid no attention. The scant wafts of heat that were emanating from the squat thing were pure Nirvana. She could have embraced it.

"Corn, corn, corn and carrots."

Clara looked around to find that McClain was using his lighter to read the dusty labels of the cans still left on the shelves.

"Do you suppose that stuff's still any good?" she asked through chattering teeth.

McClain shrugged. "The cans appear to be intact. We can open them and see if they look all right. I don't know about you, but I could eat a—cat." He added this last as his eyes fixed on Puff, who, seeing him holding a can, was staring avidly up at him and yowling with the vigor of a cheerleader at a pep rally.

"Sorry, pal," he said to Puff with what sounded like malicious enjoyment. "Nothing here for you. Just veggies. Better luck next time."

"Oh, he'll eat anything," Clara assured him. McClain had set the can down and was fishing in his pockets for something. The screwdriver. He brought it out with a triumphant flourish and proceeded to attack the can, making a good sized hole in the lid after a series of whacks and jerks. After inspecting the contents, he set the can down on top of the stove and proceeded to open another and do the same. Finally all four cans were opened and warming on the stove. The smell of food—even corn and carrots, neither one of which had ever been high on Clara's list of favorites— was enough to make her dizzy. She hadn't eaten since her meal at Mitch's house more than twenty-four hours before, she realized. Then she remembered he'd said that he had not eaten for thirty-six hours, and almost felt sorry for him. Almost.

Puff yowled pitifully, staring up at the open cans. Clara's stomach growled in concert. She heard another rumbling sound and frowned. It took her a moment to realize that McClain's stomach was growling as well. This shared human weakness softened her toward him just a little. It was good to know that at least some of her misery was shared, even by so loathsome a creature as he.

"Soup's on," McClain said, gingerly picking up the cans and setting them on the floor. Puff rushed over to them immediately; McClain swatted him away with a foot. Puff yowled piteously as McClain dropped to sit cross-legged, guarding his prize. Clara sat too, careful to keep the makeshift poncho about her. Even with McClain's belt holding it in place at the waist it was not the most reliable of garments.

"Oh, give him some, please," Clara said impatiently as Puff continued to yowl.

"We only have four cans."

"He can have some of my share. There's no way we're going to eat four cans of vegetables, anyway."

"The way I feel now I could eat four grocery stores full of vegetables, much less four cans. And he, if you recall, had two ham sandwiches. *My* ham sandwiches. The . . ." His words lapsed off into indecipherable muttering, accompanied by a dark look at Puff.

"Please . . ."

Yowl! Puff yowled again.

"Oh for God's sake." McClain picked up one of the cans of corn and, turning, dumped about a tenth of its contents on the dirty linoleum behind him. Puff was on it with the avidity of the starving. McClain watched him in narrow-eyed disbelief.

"That cat's unnatural."

"No he isn't. He's hungry. And so am I."

That brought McClain's attention back to her. He looked her up and down with that same narrow-eyed stare he usually reserved for Puff, reached down into the jagged hole he had made in the top of the can of corn with two fingers, scooped up some corn, popped it into his mouth, and chewed with evident enjoyment.

"So eat," he said. Clara, giving him a look of disgust, nevertheless picked up another can of corn and proceeded to consume its contents in the same uncivilized fashion. It was surprising how delicious vegetables could be when one was hungry.

After the meal, McClain wiped his hands on his jeans and disposed of the cans by the simple act of tossing them out the cabin door. Then he went outside. When he came back some ten minutes later he was carrying the raft upside down on top of his head. Clara's half frozen clothes were perched up on top. Clara watched with interest as McClain struggled to maneuver the unwieldy raft in through the narrow door. When he finally forced it through, to send it shooting and slithering to land almost at her feet, Puff leapt up from the nap he had succumbed to after his meal, hissing and spitting at the unexpected arrival. Clara stayed where she was, eyeing first McClain and then the raft. Bringing the raft inside for the night seemed a little strange, but doubtless he had his reasons, and she was too tired to worry about them.

"Here." He tossed her clammy clothes at her. Clara had been half asleep, leaning back against the wall with her entire body drawn up under the poncho. His action caught her by surprise; before she could react she was slapped in the face by icy cloth. More rained around her.

"Why did you do that?" Clawing her way out from beneath her stiffened jeans, which had landed on her head, she glared at McClain.

"If you want those things to be dry in the morning you'd better rig them up in front of the stove tonight."

Acknowledging the truth of that, Clara groaned as she got

to her feet and gathered up her garments. She was so tired it was all she could do to breathe.

"Here." McClain untied the rope that surrounded the raft's perimeter and attached one end of it to a nail protruding from a wall. The other he affixed to a rusty cup hook at one end of the middle shelf, creating a crude clothes line.

"Thank you." She was surprised, and not a little touched, at his effort, which was solely on her behalf. Now that she came to think of it, it was the first thing he had done that had not benefitted him as well. Of course, it could just be that he didn't fancy traveling with a damp companion in the morning.

As she draped her clothes carefully over the line so that they would get the maximum heat, he went out again. When he came back, he set two of the empty cans he had apparently retrieved from outside on the stove.

"Present for you," he said briefly in response to her inquiring look. When she frowned, he gestured at the cans. "Water. To wash with. I don't know about you, but I feel grubby as hell."

Clara did too. She looked at him for a moment with real gratitude. Of course, she wouldn't be able to get very clean with the small amount of muddy river water he'd been able to fetch, but still it was better than nothing. And a very nice thought.

"Thank you," she said again. And meant it.

She was draping her teddy over the line when she heard the unmistakable sound of a zipper being lowered behind her. Turning around, she was aghast to see McClain calmly sliding out of his jeans.

"What are you doing?" Her voice held just the tiniest edge of hysteria. Seeing McClain standing before her in nothing but a sweatshirt and a pair of maroon cotton jockey briefs was unnerving, to say the least. His legs were long and hard muscled and covered with dark hair. The sweatshirt ended just below his waist, providing no coverage for what lay below it. His underwear provided little more. They clung to his narrow hips like a second skin. The little placket in the front of the briefs bulged with silent proof of his maleness. Then he crossed the room to hang his jeans on the line beside her clothes. His soaked sneakers he placed carefully beside her shoes in front of the stove. She had an excellent view of a tight, well-muscled rear in motion. Dazzled, she stared.

"I was hanging up my clothes to dry. Now I'm going to wash and then I'm going to go to sleep."

She had been so lost in contemplating the view that his words made her start. Guiltily, she looked at him, to discover him watching her, his eyes narrowed. His green eyes were as bright as emeralds. Clara hastily busied herself with straightening her clothes on the line. A totally unnecessary action, since she had done it once already. But she didn't want him to think that she was watching him.

With all her good intentions, she couldn't help herself. As he poured water from one of the cans into his palm and splashed it over his face, she stared. She stared even harder when he casually grasped the edge of the sweatshirt and pulled it up over his head in a fluid movement, leaving him bare except for the clinging maroon briefs. His back was magnificent, she saw as he splashed more water under his arms and on his chest. Deeply tanned and broad-shouldered with a deep cleft running down the center to disappear beneath the white elastic waistband of his briefs. His muscles rippled as he moved. Clara watched, feeling a quickening of her senses. He had the most beautiful back she had ever

seen; she had to fight an urge to go over and run her hands
along that satin over steel flesh. . . .

He pulled the sweatshirt back on and turned so fast that
Clara barely had time to switch her eyes back to her jeans.
She would die of mortification if he guessed she had been
watching him like a starving man at a feast. Nervously she
moved over to the stove and stared down at her can of
water. She needed some kind of cloth to wash her face. The
poncho that she had been wearing when she fell in the river
was hanging on the line with her other clothes. She took
that from the line, dipped its end in the can, and proceeded
to wash her face and neck.

With another of those narrow-eyed looks in her direction,
McClain crossed to where the raft sat in the middle of the
floor. She took advantage of his inattention to scrub hastily
at her body beneath the covering poncho. As a bath it
wasn't much, but it was the best she could do. Warily she
looked over her shoulder to see if he was watching her. To
her astonishment he was stretched out at full length in the
middle of the raft. He just fit, using the rolled side as a
pillow to support his head. Clara blinked at him. He
returned her look, unsmiling.

"You're going to sleep in the boat?"

"You have any better suggestions?"

Looking around at the empty cabin, Clara had to admit
she didn't.

"But what about me?"

"If you have the sense God gave a flea, you'll join me."

Clara stared down at him. He looked perfectly serious—if
one didn't count those outrageously sexy legs that were
stretched at full length and crossed at the ankles.

"I can't sleep in that ridiculous boat with you. There's
not enough room, for one thing."

He shrugged, stretched, and crossed his arms under his head. His green eyes narrowed as they looked up at her.

"The less room, the better. It's cold out there tonight and getting colder. That stove doesn't put out much heat. And you are probably well on the way to pneumonia already from the asinine stunt you pulled earlier."

What he said made perfect sense, she had to admit. It was ridiculous under the circumstances for them not to curl up together and share their body heat. Only that was the problem, she discovered as she turned the possibility over in her mind: Just thinking about sleeping next to McClain in his underpants made her body heat.

"You're going to have to shed the blanket, by the way. It's the only cover we have."

He said it so negligently that it was a moment before Clara caught the full meaning of the words. Then, as she pictured herself lying without the blanket—naked—in his arms, she felt her blood heat to scalding. Whatever else he was—and she generally felt he was three separate kinds of sons of female dogs—he was every inch a man. And sexy. So sexy that she had to bite her tongue just to keep from staring at those sinewy legs. To say nothing of the tantalizing cling of claret cotton. . . .

"There is no way we are sharing this blanket. I am wearing it."

McClain's eyes narrowed even more. "So?"

"I am not wearing anything else," she clarified, her eyes still having to struggle to look only at his face.

"So what? Believe me, I'm too tired to do anything about it. If it makes you feel better, I'll shut my eyes."

This did not make her feel any better. "No!"

"Don't be any stupider than you can help, Clara."

This weary statement sent her eyes flying to his. He was

looking at her with the kind of exasperated patience a man might show to a slightly thickheaded dog.

"I am not sleeping naked with you!" Clara blushed even as she said the words. She felt the hot color wash up over her neck and chin and cheeks to the roots of her hair. Blushing was the bain of her existence when she was a teenager; she had thought she'd gotten over it by now. In more ways than one, it seemed, McClain brought out the worst in her.

"All right, so you're not sleeping naked with me." These unexpectedly reasonable words made Clara look at him suspiciously. He was sitting up, pulling the sweatshirt over his head and tossing it at her. She fumbled for it, dropped it, and bent to pick it up, all the while trying to look every-where but at his magnificently muscled torso. Bare except for his briefs, his body was gorgeous. His front looked even better to her than his back. His shoulders were bronzed and thickly muscled and broad; his arms too were well-muscled. His chest was wide and tapered and covered with a thick wedge of coal black, curling hair. His abdomen was ridged with muscle, looking impossibly hard and enticing above the clingy cotton of his briefs. And the part covered by the briefs was dazzlingly tantalizing . . . Clara felt her mouth go dry and hastily averted her eyes. The quickening she felt from just looking at him was embarrassing.

"So put on my sweatshirt and get in here. Now."

"No."

"Do it!"

Clara was so befuddled by the totally unprecedented feelings his mere physical presence was evoking in her that she couldn't even summon up the strength to argue. If truth were told, she wanted to cuddle up to that strong, hairy chest. . . . If she pretended he wasn't McClain, he could almost be her fantasy man, she thought, gazing at him distractedly. The hero she wrote about—

"Goddamn it!" he roared, jackknifing into a sitting position. The shouted profanity effectively quelled her too vivid imagination. This was nobody but McClain, nasty, unprincipled, overly aggressive McClain, no matter how attractive the package. Muscles and chest hair were no proof against a rotten personality.

"All right," she capitulated suddenly, relieved to have gotten over that sudden attack of the hots for him. "Just shut your eyes."

"Oh, for God's sake," he muttered, but shut his eyes he did. Keeping a wary eye on him, Clara pulled the sweatshirt over her head without removing the poncho, managing to get it on without revealing anything that shouldn't have been revealed. The sweatshirt, thankfully, hung halfway down her thighs.

"I could have kept my eyes open," he said with disgust, opening them.

"You were peeking," Clara accused, still clinging to the blanket that she had just pulled over her head.

"Would you please get over here with that blanket? Now that you're wearing my shirt, I'm the one who's freezing to death."

Clara tossed him the blanket, relieved when he covered himself with it and lay down. Intellectually she knew he was a real stinker, but when faced with all that sinewy bronzed flesh her body reacted with a mind of its own. It went all tingly and soft, female to his male. A reaction she didn't like at all.

"Well, come on," he said impatiently, throwing back a corner of the blanket, which, when stretched out, was just sufficient to cover the raft. The hole in the middle McClain had cut for his head would undoubtedly let in a draft, but that couldn't be helped. Swallowing, avoiding his eyes, Clara took the three steps that brought her to the raft's side and climbed gingerly in. Once she was sitting he pulled her down beside him. Before they were settled comfortably, her head was on his shoulder and his arms were around her. For warmth, she told herself fiercely as her blood started to heat again at the feel of the satiny smooth shoulder beneath her cheek. The smell of man enveloped her, making her spine tingle. Her breasts were pressed into his side, her smooth bare legs brushed his hair-roughened thighs. She had never, in her life, been so aware of a man as a man.

Her hands she kept tucked firmly between them; she had already had an accidental encounter with the soft hair on his chest when she had first lain down, and it had unsettled her to such an extent that she dared not risk another. But her fingers, with a mind of their own, ached to touch him. . . .

The inside of the cabin was dark and alive with shifting shadows. The glow from the stove provided a red tinged illumination for a few feet in either direction. The air was not warm by any means, but compared to the chill of the outdoors it was warm enough. Outside the four tumbledown walls that were all that stood between them and the freezing night, Clara could hear an occasional muffled hoot of an owl, or the cry of a small creature captured by a hunter. She tried not to think of what—or who—might be in the forest hunting at night. Bears or wildcats or even horrible, deadly men.

''McClain.''

''Mmm.'' He sounded sleepy. Indeed, when she finally dared to look over at him his eyes were closed. His eyelashes were short and spikey and incredibly black as they rested against his cheeks. She relaxed a little. She would feel far, far safer if he would just go to sleep.

"Do you suppose they're still looking for us?"

His eyes opened a slit to meet hers.

"Without a doubt."

"Then—"

"I just don't think they'll look for us here. I think we lost them pretty thoroughly today. If I didn't I wouldn't have stopped. Now go to sleep."

"All right."

He had already closed his eyes again. Clara felt the tension slowly draining from her body as she studied his face. Seen in profile, with the flickering light from the stove casting strange shadows over everything and softening the healing bruises, she thought again that he was not a handsome man. His face was too square, too aggressive for that. His forehead was broad and high beneath the ruthlessly short black hair; his cheekbones were high, too, and flat. His nose had been broken in more than one place. It had probably been a good looking nose at one time, but now it gave him the look of a battered prize fighter. His jaw was square and uncompromisingly pugnacious, covered now with two days growth of bristly black beard, but the lips above it were well shaped. Funny, she could still remember the feel of them against hers; they had been scaldingly hot, and soft at first before they hardened with desire.

But she wasn't going to think about that. That was a stupid, stupid pastime. Fantasizing about McClain under the circumstances was likely to get her into more trouble than she was in already. And if there was one thing she didn't need it was more trouble.

Their makeshift bed was toasty warm. It was the warmest she had felt for a day and a half. Clara stretched her legs luxuriously, no longer alarmed by the hard feel of McClain's legs next to hers or the soft abrasion of his hairs against her own silky smoothness. Lying on her side, tucked against his ribcage as if she belonged there, felt like the most natural position in the world. Despite the cabin and the forest and Rostov and the police and everything else she felt ridiculously safe. And happy.

Her eyes were closing and she sighed once with warm contentment. Then she was asleep.

XIII

The air she was breathing was cold, so cold that she burrowed against the warmth beside her like a rabbit seeking its nest. Her nose was flattened against a soft, furry pillow. Heat and a peculiar pungent scent were all around her, enfolding her. Her arms were clutching a warm, tensile object; her legs splayed across twin tree trunks cloaked in a rough velvet. . . .

Her eyes opened to encounter a broad expanse of hairy chest. Her nose was buried in it. Its fragrance was in her nostrils; its warmth pillowed her head. Her arms, she discovered, were wrapped around a powerful neck. Her legs were sprawled over sinewy legs. McClain! She was lying right on top of him.

"Good morning, angel." The husky drawl sounded like nothing she had ever heard come out of his mouth before. Raising her eyes from their mortified contemplation of his chest, she encountered warm, gleaming slits of green and blushed to her little toes. Hurriedly she tried to slide her hands down from his neck. Those sexy lips smiled a little.

His hands caught her wrists and held them against his chest.

"I'm sorry," Clara muttered, embarrassed, as she tried to roll off him. He prevented her with an agile movement of his leg. Her legs slipped down until they were on either side of one of his. His hair-roughened thigh lifted slightly until it was pressed against the juncture of her legs. Clara remembered with a sense of shock that she was not wearing any underwear. Her body was completely bare beneath his sweatshirt, and the sweatshirt had ridden up somewhere around her hips. His thigh pressed against naked skin. Clara flushed as she felt the heat and pressure of it, and squirmed in an effort to escape without making him aware of how very intimate the posture was. Squirming was a mistake. She felt a jolt of electricity that sent pleasurable tremors coursing down the insides of her thighs.

"I'm not," he murmured, tugging on her hands. Helplessly, knowing she would regret this but unable to resist the marvelous quivering that was radiating out from the place where his thigh, so warm and hard, pressed against her, she subsided against his chest, her fingers curling convulsively in the nest of hair. His thigh between her legs pressed her upwards until her mouth was level with his neck. Then he bent his head and kissed her.

His kiss was every bit as devastating as she remembered. Clara closed her eyes and was lost. When he stroked her lips with his tongue she parted them helplessly. She remembered too well the abortive fire he had engendered before.

He tasted faintly musky. His tongue was hot, soft, barely demanding at first as it explored her mouth. She touched it with her own tongue, stroked it, caressed his lips as he had hers; his skin tasted of salt. Then her tongue was in his mouth as his tongue was in hers, and she was wrapping her arms around his neck, pressing herself against him, catching fire.

She clung to him, kissing him as devouringly as he kissed her, hardly noticing as his hands slid beneath the oversized sweatshirt to caress first the silky skin of her back, and then her shoulders, and finally her bottom. When a large warm hand closed on each separate cheek, she jumped a little, her mouth striving for an instant to separate from his. But his hands held her, squeezing, easing her back down onto that pleasure giving thigh, and she allowed herself to settle back, to be pleasured. The exquisite feelings that were radiating through her flesh were not to be denied.

"Gently, baby."

Until he whispered the words she hadn't realized how she was straining against him, instinctively searching for the ultimate pleasure. Before she could assimilate the knowledge he was turning with her, holding her to him as he eased her onto her back, lifting the sweatshirt clear of her breasts at the same time. An icy finger of air creeping beneath the blanket as he turned gave her another moment's awareness. But then he was pulling the blanket over both their heads, settling her down in their cozy world of blanket covered raft, protected from the cold by the sausagelike sides. And he was looking at her breasts. Clara felt her breath catch at the look in his eyes as he studied her.

"You've got great tits, baby," he murmured. The words, which she would have found offensive from anyone else at any other time, excited her almost unbearably. Her hands came up to clutch at his shoulders. She pulled him down to her, quivering as she guided his mouth to her nipple. . . .

Oh, the pleasure of it! The exquisite wonder of his hot

wet mouth moving over the tip of her breast, drawing in the distended nipple, suckling it like a babe. She felt a shaft of excitement shoot down between her thighs, where his thigh had taken up residence once again. As he kissed and suckled and nibbled she arched her back, pressing her breasts against him with wanton abandon, clutching his head with both hands in his hair as she rubbed herself against that marvelous thigh. . . .

Then one of his hands was sliding down from its play with her breasts, stroking her stomach, a finger burrowing playfully into her navel before moving lower, hovering just above the soft triangle of hair that ached for his touch.

When still he hesitated her hips lifted in instinctive supplication, inviting his touch in a wordless gesture that was as old as woman. Still his fingers continued to trace tantalizing circles just above and around the sides, tickling her thighs, darting playfully close and then retreating.

"Please, Jack!" The words were gasped against his neck. She thought she would die, just die, if he didn't touch her there, now. She felt his teeth close on her nipple with a force that would have hurt if she had not been so far gone in pleasure, felt his hand clutch her other breast in a grip that was bruising in its power. Then that craved-for hand was homing in between her thighs, finding the tiny bud that quivered desperately beneath his caress, then sliding lower and inside. . . .

"God, you're hot," she thought she heard him mutter as she gasped and shuddered and sighed at what he was doing to her. Then his hand was withdrawing, and she was whimpering protests, her hands leaving his head to tug beggingly at that deserting hand. But instead of yielding to her entreaties, the hand she was clutching led her to his body, where she encountered first the hard skin of his abdomen and then the elastic waistband of his briefs. Her knuckles brushed the hard bulge below it and her knees turned to cream cheese.

"Now you touch me," he murmured, and she did, her hands greedy for him, caressing the muscle-ridged abdomen, tugging at the curling tufts of hair, then suddenly starving for the feel of him and yanking down the briefs with fingers that were unsteady until he was in her hands, huge and hot and pulsing, and he was groaning and sighing with her hungry caresses.

Both his thighs were between hers now as he loomed over her, supporting his weight with his knees and one hand. His other hand was caressing her breasts. His eyes were a hot, smoldering emerald as he watched her play with him, watched her face as she took in the size and heat of him, watched her body as it lay spread open beneath him, ready for his taking. And yet still he held himself from her, not giving her what she craved. Clara felt that she would go insane if he didn't come into her soon. She lifted her hips to encourage him. He bent and kissed her swiftly on the lips, but that wasn't what her body wanted. She pulled on him, trying to guide him to the burning center of her, but still he resisted. She whimpered enticingly, trying to maneuver him on top of her with squirming movements of her own, trying to seduce him with a tiny line of biting kisses traced up the muscular arm nearest her lips, but to no avail. He was hard and hot and pulsing in her hands, and she was going crazy beneath him, but he still would not give her what she wanted.

"Love me, Jack," she whispered at last, ashamed at having to beg but wanting him desperately, needing him so enormously that her shame was a tiny thing compared to it. But still he wouldn't come inside her. Instead he caught each knee in his hand, lifting them over his shoulders so that her feet rested halfway down his back. Her hips were in the air and her body was spread open for him to see, or smell, or kiss . . . She didn't know whether to die of delight or horror.

"Jack, no!" Horror won out.

"Yes," he corrected softly. Then he kissed her, his mouth and tongue wet and scalding hot against her. And her world exploded into a million brightly colored starbursts of delight.

When at last he lifted his head she was gasping, quivering from head to toe, tingling in places she hadn't even known existed. He put her down and she lay supine beneath him, her head thrown back, body pulsing with random tremors, feeling as though she had died and gone to some place far more marvelous than heaven.

Then it started up again.

He slid inside her, enormous and as hot as a poker just off the fire, filling her to capacity and then some, not even giving her time to come down off the high she was floating on before he was thrusting, caressing, taking, giving, making her feel more and more and more until she was crying her ecstasy into his mouth, tasting herself on his lips and knowing that it was the most erotic sensation she had ever experienced, gouging his back with her nails and moaning his name, "Jack, Jack, Jack, Jack, Jack, Jack, *Jack!*" until at last he took pity on her and found his own release, groaning his pleasure into her throat as he ground himself into her shaking body.

Afterwards, she lay there for long moments, eyes closed, body limp except for the random tremors that still racked it. She had never felt so utterly replete, so totally a woman. His woman. Jack McClain's.

Slowly her eyes opened. He was still on top of her, sprawled deadweight across her, his sweat dripping onto her body, his breathing stertorous in her ear. Slowly what she had just said to herself replayed in her mind: His woman. Jack McClain's. Just who the hell *was* Jack McClain? She didn't know, not with any certainty. She doubted if anybody did. He was a stranger, a dangerous stranger from a shadowy world she wanted no part of. How could she have been such a fool?

"Get off me," she said, pushing at his shoulder with both arms. She might as well have pushed at Mount Rushmore. He didn't budge.

"I said get *off* me!" This time her voice was loud, and her push meant business. He lifted himself up on one elbow so that he could see her face. The rest of his body still skewered hers to the rubber bottom of the raft and the hard floor beneath.

"Are you *deaf? I said get off me!*" She was shrieking now. His eyes narrowed and he obligingly rolled off her. She immediately leaped to her feet, pulling the blanket with her to shield her body from his eyes. The icy cold air in the room acted like a douche of equally cold water. Self-disgust at what she had done rose like bile in her throat. She felt physically nauseated. For a moment she feared she might be sick.

"What's your problem, anyway?" His voice was a low-timbered growl. He was sitting cross-legged in the middle of

the raft, as naked as the day he was born and not one whit
bothered by it. Clara thought of the things he had done to
her and felt nausea churn again. How could she have
behaved like that, with McClain of all people? Like a sailor,
a spy probably had a woman in every port. James Bond
made it with all the ladies in his movies. McClain was
clearly bent on carrying on the lofty tradition. At her
expense.

"You make me sick," she said clearly, wrapping the
blanket around her like a sarong as she backed toward where
her clothes hung before the cold stove.

"God in heaven!" He sounded thoroughly fed up, and as
she watched with a kind of fascinated fury he stood up with
magnificent unconcern for his nakedness and glared at her.
"I didn't make you sick. You *are* sick. Crazy sick! What in
God's name are you getting so bent out of shape about? It
was only sex, after all."

"Only sex!" Her voice failed her. She'd known it, just
known it. She'd made an utter ass out of herself only to be
marked down as number 6,849 on his bedpost. He probably
had experiences like that all the time. Horny women throwing themselves at him—

"Yeah. Sex. You know, something normal men and
women enjoy doing together sometimes. Like when a man
wakes up with a hard-on and a naked woman draped all over
him and takes care of it? Sex!"

"You *bastard*." In her fury she could barely talk. That
she should live to be so humiliated—and she had brought it
on herself, through her own lack of control.

"I'd rather be a bastard than a repressed, sex-starved old
maid," he said through clenched teeth. Then, brushing past
her, he yanked his jeans off the line, scooped up his

shoes and stalked outside, still buck naked and sublimely unashamed.

Clara stared furiously after that magnificent bare backside and then, as the door banged behind him, threw the blanket in his wake in a paroxysm of frustrated rage.

XIV

Yowl!

Clara scowled at Puff fiercely. He was stalking back and forth across the limited space in the middle of the raft for all the world like an expectant father. They had been on the river for some forty-five minutes; Puff had howled at least twice a minute. That made some ninety yowls in under an hour.

"Can't you shut that damn furball up?"

Yowl!

Clara's glare transferred from Puff to McClain and intensified along the way. These were the first words he had spoken to her since stalking out of the cabin. Her first inclination was not to even bother to reply to what was clearly a rhetorical question—after forty-eight hours of Puff's company he must know that shutting Puff up was next to impossible—but the temptation to say something nasty was irresistible.

"I could throw him in."

Yowl!

The look he threw at her over his shoulder was deadly. "Let me."

"Or you could use that gun in your belt for something besides looking macho. There are squirrels and rabbits and things like that in the woods, you know. If you were any good with it, you could shoot us something to eat. He's hungry. And so am I."

Yowl!

He turned his attention back to the river. The morning was sunny and clear, but the wind was cold and his shoulders were hunched under the poncho which she had returned to him since her own clothes were dry. Unless he was much more warm-blooded than she, he was already freezing. And the occasional spray of water that blew up around the raft was no help.

Yowl!

"I don't like shooting helpless animals."

Clara thought for a moment that she hadn't heard that correctly. "What?"

He cast another of those malevolent looks back over his shoulder. "I said I don't like shooting helpless animals!"

Clara hooted. "You, the big secret agent men, don't like shooting animals? Ha, ha! You go around shooting people, don't you? Isn't that what spies do? How can you shoot a person and not a squirrel when we're starving? You don't even like animals!"

Yowl!

"I do like animals—except for huge furballs with claws like razors and a howl that could be heard on the back forty. And for your information, I would much rather shoot a man in the line of duty than a squirrel to fill your gut. The few men I have had occasion to shoot deserved it; a helpless squirrel does not."

Yowl!

"So sensitive!" she marveled mockingly.

He half turned to give her the full force of an inimical glare. "If you don't shut up I'm going to throw you *and* the furball overboard. I've had about as much of both of you as I'm going to take."

Yowl!

"Oh, yeah?"

"Yeah!"

"Try it, big man." Clara's hands tightened on her oar. If he made a move in her direction she would do her best to brain him. She hated him so much this morning that her nerve endings vibrated with it. She hated him so much that she could taste it in her mouth. She hated him so much that if he were lying dead at her feet she would laugh and step over his bleeding corpse. She hated him so much—

Yowl!

"Oh, shut up!" Clara said to Puff with all the loathing she had not succeeded in expressing to McClain. McClain laughed jeeringly and turned back to steer the raft. Puff looked at her reproachfully, then stopped his restless pacing long enough to put his front paws on the side and look over into the rushing brown water.

Yoowwlll!

"If we get lucky, maybe he'll fall overboard on his own," McClain muttered as Puff resumed his pacing. Clara glared at McClain's back. If anyone was going to fall overboard, she fervently hoped it would be him. How she would laugh! The very thought dragged a grim smile to her lips.

Two hours later, the day had warmed slightly while the river had swiftened. They were speeding along now; McClain's oar was required only to push them off any objects that happened to get in the way. Puff had finally stopped yowling.

He was huddled in the very center of the raft, hunched on all fours as though ready to take action at any moment, tail twitching furiously, gold eyes angry slits. The bottom of the raft was awash in about half an inch of icy water. Like Clara, Puff had evidently given up the hope of finding any escape from the freezing wetness. He just crouched there looking evil tempered, while she sat cross-legged behind him feeling more evil tempered than he looked. Exchanging a glare with him, Clara felt a momentary spurt of sympathy. Poor cat, he hadn't asked to get caught up in this mess any more than she had. It was all the fault of that insensitive, boorish Neanderthal in the bow.

McClain was frowning as he scanned the banks on either side of the river. Clara watched him sourly. The man was by no stretch of the imagination handsome: his nose looked like it had been run over by a Mack truck, his chin stuck out like Jay Leno's and the rest of his face was nothing to write home about. His hair was cut so short his ears stuck out, and his neck was as thick as a gorilla's. His only good points were a pair of beautiful green eyes and an admittedly gorgeous body. Which were more than offset by his nasty disposition. He was undoubtedly the most hateful man she had ever met in her life. She *despised* him.

"We'd better pull for shore."

"Why?" Something about the too casual way he said it caught her attention.

"I think there may be a dam ahead."

Clara still didn't understand. He must have caught a glimpse of her puzzled look, because he added impatiently, "You know, with a waterfall?"

A waterfall! Clara's eyes widened and she picked up her oar, ready to do her utmost to help McClain pull for shore. Of course that was why the current had speeded up so.

Debris swirled by them at an ever increasing pace, all headed toward the falls. Visions of the enormous roaring drop-off of Niagara Falls, the only waterfall she had ever seen firsthand, danced in her head. They would never survive something like that!

The bank on their side of the river, the west side, was a low, sloping rock wall topped by tall pines that crowded right to the rock's edge. Getting a purchase on that rock wall might be tricky, but then Clara saw where McClain was aiming for. A fallen tree lay top down in the river some twenty feet ahead. Its roots had torn out of the bank to form a web of interconnecting branches. If they could maneuver the raft toward that, it would no doubt catch them and they could climb out along the pine. She hoped.

They were heading straight for the fallen tree when Clara just happened to lift her eyes slightly beyond it. For an instant she could hardly believe what she was seeing. She blinked once, then twice, then let out a yelp.

"McClain, look, stop, go back!"

He looked sharply around at her, then followed her horrified gaze to the small group of armed sheriff's deputies standing under the trees not more than a few hundred feet ahead. A pack of yapping hounds milled at their feet.

The word McClain uttered then was the filthiest one Clara had ever heard. It expressed her sentiments exactly.

"Paddle!" he bit out next, suiting his actions to the words. Clara needed no second bidding. She paddled for her life, imitating McClain's actions as the raft changed directions and headed for the swift current at the center of the river. There was a sharp popping noise, another curse from McClain, and Clara chanced a look at the deputies, who were almost directly across from them now. Three had rifles lifted to their shoulders; a fourth was lowering his.

Pop! Pop! Pop!

"Duck!" ordered McClain, paddling like crazy. A cacophony of pops sounded over her head as Clara threw herself on the floor of the raft, huddling on her knees, arms covering her head. Puff happened to be where she had landed, and she hugged him beneath her, expecting any instant to feel a bullet ripping into her shrinking flesh.

Of course, if a bullet hit the raft they would sink. Clara's head lifted as she thought of that. She got just a glimpse of McClain hunched over the bow, paddling for all he was worth, his bowed back scant inches from her face. Then another series of pops sounded and she covered up her head again.

"You can come up for air. We're out of range, I think."

His less than comforting words sounded breathless. Clara lifted her head cautiously to see McClain frowning back over his shoulder at her.

"You're not hit, are you?" He sounded almost concerned.

"No. I don't think so." She eased herself cautiously back into a semi-kneeling position, looking around as she did so. The raft was rushing along, now caught up in the ever quickening current. The deputies were a barely discernible group of stick figures in the distance.

"What about the furball?"

Puff was crouched in the center of the raft, training those furious golden eyes on McClain, moaning for all he was worth. McClain's mouth twitched.

"*He's* all right," he said, answering his own question as he turned back to guide the raft.

"What about you?" Clara was so shaken that the words were scarcely more than a whisper. She had to repeat them before he heard.

"Me? Not a scratch." But she noticed he sounded worried, and that his face was grim as he stared down the river. Of course, he must be thinking about the falls. But surely they still had time to get ashore, maybe on the other side. . . .

"What's that?" An ominous rumble was just barely audible. As the raft rushed onward, the sound increased in volume until in a matter of just a few minutes it was a full throated roar.

"The falls!" McClain yelled over his shoulder, paddling feverishly for shore without making any noticeable headway against the swooshing water. As Clara absorbed that bad news the raft shot around a bend in the river. What she saw next made her stiffen and grab hold of the sides of the raft with both hands.

Walls of stark rock towered on either side of the river, forming a canyon through which the water rushed. Spray shot up along the rock walls with a hissing sound as the water, its force telescoped, picked up speed and power. Getting off the river would be impossible now, Clara saw. They would have to stay the course, whatever that might be.

"Climb onto the rim and hook your leg over!"

"What?" They were shouting to be heard over the roar, and Clara was not even sure that McClain heard. He was already straddling the rolled side like a rodeo rider mounting a bucking bronc. Clara goggled at him. He had to be joking! As the raft tipped precariously with the shift in his weight, he leaned inward. Clara grabbed the sides again. Puff moaned, his eyes slits of desperation as they scanned the trees far above for succor.

"Hook your leg under like this!" McClain demonstrated how the leg that was still inside the raft was clamped under the rolled side. Clara watched him with growing horror. She couldn't do that. There was no way—

"Do you want to drown?" he bellowed. The roar was getting louder; the current growing swifter. Spumes of icy spray showered the raft, which was bumping along like an airplane in heavy turbulence. They were sluicing through the water at breakneck speed. Puff was moaning in terror, eyes closed, ears flattened, fur beaded by spray as he crouched in the center of the raft. Could cats swim? Could anybody swim in this torrent?

"We're going to drown whether I do it or not!" she wailed. Courage had never been her strong suit, and faced with imminent horrible death she thought she would likely keel over of a heart attack before the water ever got her. Her heart was pumping so hard against the wall of her chest that a heart attack seemed a foregone conclusion.

"Get on the rim!" This time the order was given in a roar to rival the waterfall's. "Over there!"

He gestured with the oar to a spot roughly opposite to where he was stationed. His clothes were soaked already, his black hair glistening like a seal's. Water ran down his face in streams. His teeth chattered. But the look in his eyes was chillingly familiar: a brilliant green glitter that made him seem vibrantly alive.

"You're enjoying this, aren't you, you lunatic?" Clara screeched at him bitterly. Then, realizing she had no choice, she scooted on her bottom to the place he indicated and gingerly lifted one leg over the rim. Immediately the leg dangling in the water protested the icy wetness. But as Clara maneuvered herself upright she forgot all about bodily discomfort. She forgot all about everything as she stared in terror at what was ahead.

The river rushed onward in gushing streams of brown water, each with a current so strong that it was separately visible, leaping and intertwining as if braided by a giant hand before disappearing some two hundred feet away. Just disappearing, with a tremendous roar, beneath a cloud of foggy spray.

"Oh, my God!" she moaned, lying down along the rim and gripping it with both hands in response to McClain's shouted direction. The raft was bucking like a bronco now; its every movement seemed designed to throw her off into the water that boiled like an icy cauldron all about. She clung grimly to the rubber, hardly feeling the cold, so wet she couldn't get any wetter. Her hair streamed over her eyes, practically blinding her. She could just make out Puff's crouched figure in the middle of the raft, ears flat against his head as he stared wildly all around.

"Puff!" she cried. "McClain, what about Puff? He'll drown!"

McClain stared at her from his perch on the opposite side of the crazily spinning raft, then shifted his attention to the soggy, shivering, moaning animal in the center.

"Goddamn it to hell!" she thought she heard him mutter. Then, in the most heroic action Clara had ever seen, he reached out an arm to catch Puff by the collar, dragging him close until he could scoop him up and hold him clamped between his chest and the rubber side.

Clara screamed as the raft bucked wildly over a sea of hissing white froth before shooting straight out into space. For just an instant they hung suspended, a bright orange pellet against an eternity of baby blue sky, then her eyes shut tightly and her stomach jumped into her throat as they plunged down.

Clara clung to the raft with every ounce of her strength, her nails digging into the rubber, her knees gripping it so hard that she could feel them meet even with the air-filled roll between them. The jolt of the landing took them under;

then the raft righted itself, surfacing with a shake like a dog shedding water, only to go under again and then up in the turbulent maelstrom below the dam. Under and up, under and up they went until she lost all sense of where she was and what was happening. All she knew was that she had to hang on despite the river's attempts to tear her free and the icy, numbing water that, with a malevolent will of its own, was trying to drown her.

"Grab the rope! For God's sake, Clara, grab the rope!"

Clara blinked, shaking her head to clear the hair from in front of her eyes so that she could see. McClain was still hanging on, she saw, but barely, clinging to the raft with one arm as the rest of him dangled out of sight in the water.

"Damn it, Clara, grab the rope! You stupid bitch!"

Those words shocked a little fighting spirit back into Clara. She lifted her head to glare at him and then saw the rope that dangled just a few feet from her nose. Following it upward with her eyes she saw that it hung from an army green helicopter that hovered some thirty feet over their heads. The roar of the falls drowned out the roar of the helicopter. It was just there, silently suspended, an angel sent from heaven to save her, all of them . . . Her eyes traveled back down the lifeline that hung from the helicopter's open door. The end of the rope had been made into a loop. It jumped and twitched as the helicopter's pilot fought to keep it within reach of the spinning raft. Without warning, the raft went under again. When it surfaced, bringing her with it, spluttering and gasping for air, she leaped for the dangling loop like the drowning woman she was. It didn't take McClain's shouted instructions to make her pull it over her head and fasten it beneath her arms.

Then with a jerk she was lifted into the air. Her body dangled limply as she was pulled up through the bright blue autumn sky. The rope was cutting into the skin beneath her arms through her clothes, and she felt like she was literally freezing to death as the brisk wind hit her soaked body. But it was such a wonderful relief to be out of reach of the suffocating water! She sucked in great gulps of air and thanked God that she was alive.

Another looped rope dropped past her as she ascended. For McClain, of course. He would be saved, too. Thank you, God, she thought again before exhaustion blanked her mind. Her body swung in an arc like a pendulum as she was hauled upward. Her hands were too numb to allow her to even grip the rope to ease some of the pain beneath her arms. All her life she had had a morbid fear of heights. The disasters that had befallen her in the last forty-eight hours had immunized her against that particular fear, she discovered as she looked down on the tops of bushy pines. Or else her mind was as numb as her body. In any case, she was able to watch with a curious detachment as the raft, swirling and bucking in the murderous basin at the foot of the falls, was sucked under and then shot high into the air. At the very top of its flight, McClain seemed to launch himself through the air from nowhere, grabbing the dangling rope one-handed. He swung from its end, his body still half submerged in water. Apparently he was having trouble getting the loop around his body. Then Clara saw what he had done: instead of saving himself, he had put the loop around the sopping gray bundle that was Puff. Puff was saved! Clara laughed hysterically, then cried as she watched Puff, swatting wildly at the air and spitting for all he was worth, being hauled upward in her wake.

But what about McClain? Even as she thought that, her head hit the bottom of the helicopter with a crack that made her see stars. Then, before she had quite recovered her senses, she was being hauled up and over the side.

"Don't move!" ordered a no-nonsense voice even as hands dragged her forward to sprawl on the floor of the cabin. "You are under arrest! You have the right to remain silent; if you give up that right, anything you say may be used against you in a court of law. . . ."

Half drowned, more than half frozen, still seeing stars from hitting her head, Clara looked up through this spiel to see two uniformed National Guardsmen crouching over her, guns pointed at her head.

"Oh my God!" She subsided with a groan, lying limply in the puddle she had made on the floor, too tired to even think. Out of the river straight into Bigfoot's arms... Suddenly drowning didn't seem like such a bad way to die.

"Look out, he's—" The shout was followed by a scream. Everything happened so fast that Clara received only a jumble of impressions: a wet black head appearing over the side, silhouetted against the dreamy blue sky, a pair of gleaming green eyes meeting hers for the merest instant, a lean brown hand snaking out and hooking into the belt of the nearest guardsman, and then a scream as the man went flying through the air to disappear out the open door. The other one jumped to his feet just as McClain launched himself through the opening like a missile, head butting the guardsman in the stomach as a bullet sang out harmlessly over McClain's diving form. Then, while Clara gaped from her position flat on the floor, the second man was flying through the opening to disappear with a scream. The helicopter jerked as the pilot turned around, fumbling with the gun at his belt.

"Don't be an ass, buddy," McClain said, pointing the rifle he had jerked from the hold of the second guardsman at

the pilot's whitening face. The man subsided back into his
seat while McClain stood behind him, dripping with water,
hair plastered to his skull so that his ears stuck out more
than ever while he grinned his satyr's grin and held the rifle
tight against the base of the pilot's skull. "Just keep this
thing steady and you'll see your next birthday."

Now that bullets had stopped flying, Clara managed to get
up on her knees. Her wits were still a little slow, not having
quite recovered from her near drowning, near freezing and
the bump on her head, but she had no doubt that she had
just seen McClain save their lives—and in the process throw
two men to their deaths. She shuddered. Did they still
electrocute people in Virginia? she wondered. Of course, it
was a moot point. Bigfoot would undoubtedly put a period
to them first.

The radio crackled. "C-193, this is C-204. Chuck, can
you read me? What the hell's going on up there? Chuck—"

The pilot moved his hand sharply. The helicopter heeled
at a ninety degree angle. Clara was almost thrown out the
door. Gasping with terror, she grabbed the legs of the
co-pilot's seat and hung on for dear life. Her legs were
dangling over empty space. Clara threw a scared look down
at the wildly twirling kaleidoscope below her, then shut her
eyes. She could feel her blood vessels pop as she clung to
the metal legs of the seat. The copter righted itself abruptly,
then dove the other way. Clara was jerked violently up into
the air; her body tumbled back inside the cabin. Still she
hung on. McClain had been thrown against the other door,
she saw. Thankfully it had stayed closed. Now he was
pulling himself upright, groping for the rifle which he had
lost.

"Jerry, I'm in trouble here," she heard the pilot say

desperately into the radio. "Tony and Keith are gone. This guy—"

He grunted in pained surprise, then stopped talking abruptly. McClain, holding onto the back of the pilot's seat, had jammed the rifle hard into the small of his back.

"Chuck! Chuck, can you read me?" the radio cackled.

"Say another goddamn word and I'll blow you straight to hell," McClain growled. Even Clara shivered. From his tone she had no doubt that he meant what he said.

"Get over here, Clara."

The words were an order. Clara didn't argue with them. She crawled over next to his feet, then pulled herself up by the pilot's seat, taking care not to let go. She had learned her lesson about that.

"Fly back over the river. At about twenty feet."

The pilot turned the craft. Clara didn't blame him. She wouldn't have dared defy McClain either when he used that tone of voice.

"Clara, you sit over in the co-pilot's seat. See that thing he has his hand on? That's the collective pitch lever. I want you to keep it just like it is for just a moment. And keep both pedals pushed about halfway down. See, just like he has them. Now do it!"

"You want me to fly this thing?" Her voice rose until the last word was a squeak. Her eyes were horrified as she stared at him. There was no way she could—

"Not fly it. Just hold it steady for a minute or two. For Christ's sake, all you have to do is hold onto one lever and keep your feet on two pedals. Even you should be able to do that."

"But, Jack, I—"

"Do it!"

Clara gave up. If they were going to die, the exact

manner of it didn't much matter, she told herself numbly, and did as he directed. The pilot's hand felt cold beneath hers as she took the controls from him; she was sure hers was even colder. She was scared silly. Beneath her hand, the lever vibrated with angry power. The helicopter, now that she was in charge of it, pulsed with malevolent life.

McClain dragged the pilot from his seat, his hand hooked in the man's collar, the rifle pressed to his spine. Clara, frightened at what he meant to do, could not forbear watching. The helicopter bucked; McClain and the pilot nearly went out the door.

"Goddamn it, Clara, keep your mind on your business!" McClain yelled. Clara turned her back on the men silhouetted against the sky. She had to concentrate on keeping the whatever-he-had-called-it lever steady, and not moving her feet on the pedals.

"Jump," she heard McClain say. Her heart pounded. Seconds later her soaking wet spy was sliding into the seat beside her, taking over the controls.

"What did you do to that poor man?" Her voice was shaky as she slumped back in the seat.

"He was trying to kill us, in case you haven't figured it out." McClain worked some sort of voodoo with the lever and peddles that had them turning around and rising at the same time. "But if you want to see what I did to him, look out the door. And haul that damned furball up while you're at it. There's a button overhead that works the pulley."

Clara gasped. She had forgotten about Puff. Poor cat, hanging suspended beneath a jerking, plunging helicopter. She pushed the button, heard the wheezing crank of the gears, and then hurried to the side, taking care to hold on as she looked out. Sure enough Puff was coming up fast. He was fighting the air for all he was worth, swinging wildly in a wide arc as he clawed furiously at space. Beneath and behind them, rapidly receding into the distance, Clara saw the river. Just below the falls floated their raft. It was in peaceful waters now. Another raft was on the river. This one had men in it, and as she watched they fished something over the side: another man. They wrapped him in a blanket as he sat on the raft's bottom and began to paddle downstream.

"You threw them into the river," she said, understanding suddenly.

"I don't murder people in cold blood," McClain returned, concentrating on flying. "Unless, of course, I'm left with no choice."

Clara was left to ponder those chilling words as she hauled a spitting, fighting, furious wet cat into the cabin.

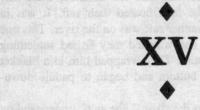

XV

"Jack."

"Hmmm?"

"Thank you. For saving Puff. That was the bravest, most unselfish thing I've ever seen. He would have drowned. Most men would have let him. And you—you're allergic to cats."

"I'm not allergic to cats. I hate them."

Clara smiled slightly. She was sitting in the co-pilot's seat, a soggy Puff huddled on her lap. He was shivering and her teeth were chattering despite the fact that McClain had turned the helicopter's heater up as high as it would go as soon as he had taken over the controls.

"That makes it all the more heroic," she said, and impulsively reached over to plant a soft kiss on his unshaven cheek. Considering his soaked state, his skin felt surprisingly warm against her mouth. His musky smell brought back unexpectedly vivid memories of what they had done together that morning . . . Clara sank back in her seat, feeling her face heat. McClain gave her a quick, glinting look but said

174

nothing. Clara got the impression that tenderness was something of which he was wary.

"You'd better get out of those wet clothes."

His voice was matter-of-fact. Clara smiled at him. His eyes narrowed.

"Just because I didn't let the damned cat drown doesn't make me some kind of hero, you know," he said. His voice was vaguely defensive.

"I know," she agreed, and smiled at him again. He scowled, and switched his attention back out the windshield. Clara stood up to remove her soaked clothes. Unbuttoning her saturated blouse and peeling off her dripping jeans were becoming familiar chores. Clara did them automatically, wringing them out with quick twists of her wrists while she stood shivering in the sopping white silk teddy.

"Why don't you wear a bra and panties like most women?" He sounded disgruntled. Clara cast him a startled look. She had not expected him to be watching her. Despite the thorough introduction he had already had to her body, she felt ridiculously embarrassed about being seen in the nearly transparent teddy. With her hair tangled around her head in a wild wet bush and her white skin splotched with mud and ridged with goosebumps, she doubted that she was the most appealing thing he had ever seen. And she wanted to appeal to him . . . That sudden flare of self-knowledge was as unwelcome as it was shocking.

"I usually do. This is what I wear to sleep in. Usually. But with all the excitement, I forgot to pack my underwear when I ran away from Rostov."

She tried hard to sound matter-of-fact, but she couldn't stop herself from blushing. Automatically, her hands came up in the most casual way possible to hold the wet jeans and blouse between her body and his too-knowing green eyes. Those eyes suddenly lifted to meet hers, glimmered briefly, then were switched to the instruments in front of him.

"You have a great body."

"What?" Clara couldn't believe she'd heard the gruff mutter correctly. His eyes flicked back in her direction. Her hands holding the jeans, which had lowered with his lack of attention, came up again. He switched his eyes forward once more.

"I said you have a great body. You should be proud of it, not hiding it all the time."

Clara stared at the back of his black head. If she remembered correctly, this was the man who'd told her she could stand to lose some weight.

"You said I needed to lose about ten pounds!"

He shook his head. "I hadn't had a real close look at that point. I take it back."

Clara blushed scarlet at the memory of exactly how close that look had been. He cast a quick, glimmering grin over his shoulder at her.

"I've always been a sucker for big tits and a nice round ass," continued the flatterer. Clara recovered from her embarrassment in time to glare at him.

"You sweet talker, you," she said with bite. Though she could see only about a quarter of his face, there was no missing his sudden grin. He was teasing her, she realized, and realized also that she had a lot to learn about men. At least his breed of man. He was all male, and she had no experience with the species at all. Except for Mark, whom she had inherited from Lena in high school, and John Williamson, an earnest law student with whom she had had a rather tepid love affair while she was at Wesleyan and he was at the University of Virginia (they had even been engaged for a while, much to her mother's joy, until John had eloped with another student in his torts class), she had lived in a world of women. Her father had died when she was five; her mother had had lots of husbands since then, but none that she had allowed to get too close to her only daughter. As a result, Clara had always been shy of men. Now she found that she was getting to know this all-male male in a totally new way, as a person, like herself.

"There should be a blanket in the rescue kit in the locker over there."

In fact there were two. Clara pulled one out, wrapped it around herself squaw fashion and, using it as a shield from shifting eyes, wriggled out of her teddy. Then, clutching the blanket close, she draped her wet clothes from the hydraulic lines overhead and returned to the co-pilot's seat. Puff hissed as she picked him up. Poor cat, he'd had a traumatic day. As had they all. And it was barely afternoon yet.

"Think you can hold her steady again while I strip off?"

"I'll give it my best shot." Try as she might to banish the image from her mind, her pulse speeded up at the idea of seeing him in those clingy maroon underpants again. Despite everything, she found him more attractive than any man she had ever met. And when she remembered what he had done to her that morning, how he had made her feel, she felt her toes curl. And then her face turn red. What a fool she had made of herself; he must have women falling all over him.

"Don't crash us," he said. Then her hands and feet were on the controls and he was sliding out of his seat. She heard the thump of his wet sweatshirt hitting the floor, the sound of his zipper being lowered, and had to fight an impulse to look over her shoulder. But beyond the embarrassment she would feel at being caught in such an action, the helicopter demanded all her attention. Even holding it at a steady altitude and pace required all her concentration. For which she was grateful. It kept her from thinking of the man taking off his clothes less than two feet behind her.

In just a few minutes he was sliding back into the pilot's seat, wrapped in a blanket, tossing something into her lap as he took over the controls.

"What . . . ?"

"Peanuts," he said, already ripping open his own bag with his teeth.

"Peanuts!" A steak dinner wouldn't have been more welcome at that point. Clara tore into her own bag, devouring them in a few handfuls.

"Greedy, aren't you?" But McClain had done the same thing to his, so Clara stuck her tongue out at him without rancor. On her lap, Puff sat up and meowed, voice plaintive. Clara looked down at him guiltily.

"Sorry, Puff, but cats can't eat peanuts," she explained.

Meow!

"Oh, no," Clara said, knowing from experience that the mildly demanding meows would soon escalate into a cacophony of yowls, howls, and more yowls.

"No worries, mate," McClain said in a broad parody of a popular Australian phrase. "Here."

And he tossed a packet of dried beef strips into her lap.

"Are there more?" Clara was already tearing open the package and handing one of the strips to Puff, who accepted

it with alacrity. For the first time since being hauled aboard
the helicopter he left her lap, leaping to the floor, prize in
his jaws.

"A few packages of peanuts, a couple of packages of beef
strips, some boxes of raisins and chocolate chips. Survival
rations."

"Oh, yum."

"We have to save some of it. It might be a long time until
we're able to hit a McDonald's."

"I'm *starving*."

"Here, have another bag of peanuts. And there's coffee in
this Thermos. Must have been the pilot's."

"Coffee!" Clara felt like she had died and gone to
heaven. She fell upon the Thermos holding the heavenly
black liquid and poured some into the plastic cup that
screwed onto the top. Taking a sip, she closed her eyes at
the feel of the hot, sweet brew rolling over her tongue.
She usually took hers with cream as well as sugar, but
under the circumstances just getting coffee at all was a
miracle.

"Would you like some?" Guiltily she looked over at
McClain. He was munching his peanuts, fiddling with the
radio that was emitting mostly static. He'd put on the
headphones, so she didn't think he could hear her. She
touched his shoulder, and he looked around inquiringly as
she proffered the cup. He took it from her with a nod of
thanks and drained it, grimacing at its sweetness. Then he
pulled the headphones off one ear and passed the cup back
over at the same time.

"There's not much happening on the airways."

"Oh, really?" Clara was just barely interested. She was
far more concerned with savoring the last of her peanuts and
another cup of coffee.

"Maybe there's interference because of the mountains."

"Could be."

"Or maybe they've ordered radio silence."

Clara swallowed. She tried not to think that they were still being chased, but of course they were. If anything, the search would be intensified. They had stolen a National Guard rescue helicopter, for God's sake. "They can see us on radar." The realization burst on her with a sickening flash.

McClain looked over at her, inclined his head once. "Yeah."

"Will they. . . shoot us down?"

He laughed suddenly, his eyes gleaming a warm green as he looked at her. "Poor Clara, you're not having much fun, are you?"

"Unless you call being faced with a choice of roughly two dozen ways to die fun, then no, I'm not."

"Trust me. I'll get you out of this in one piece. If it's humanly possible." The last words were said under his breath.

Understandably enough, she didn't find that reassurance particularly reassuring. Probably because she was beginning to suspect that it might *not* be humanly possible. She smiled rather hollowly at him, then lifted the cup to her mouth for another drink of coffee as she stared out the windshield at the landscape below.

The helicopter was swooping first low then high, following the contours of the mountains, keeping not far from the tops of the trees. The scenery was breathtaking, golden sunshine beaming down on hillsides covered with a variety of deciduous trees in their autumn finery. Other hillsides were shaded in various hues of greenish blue from the pines and other evergreens, gorgeous blue lakes, ribbonlike rivers and roads, even a range of snow-capped peaks in the distance, the tallest of which McClain identified as Mount Mitchell. In the face of so much beauty it seemed impossible that their lives could be in such danger. Clara embraced the sense of unreality thankfully. It kept her from being scared out of her mind.

"Where did you learn to fly one of these, anyway? In the marines?" She was just making conversation, idle conversation to keep her mind off the chilling possibility of dozens of unfriendly radar screens tracking the tiny blip that represented their helicopter. They seemed so alone, so far away from everything soaring over the mountains. But they were not.

"Yeah. I flew a couple of Med-evacs. Then I got put out of business."

"How?"

"Shot down by the Cong. Haven't flown since. I'm surprised I remember how. I guess it's like riding a bicycle. You never forget."

"Were you a prisoner?" Her eyes were wide as she looked over at him. She'd read what POW's had suffered in Vietnam.

"For a couple of months. Then a buddy and I managed to escape. I made it back to the front lines eventually; I'd been wounded, thought I would be sent home. No such luck. They patched me up then turned me into a LURP."

"A what?"

"A LURP. Recon. The brass figured that since I'd managed to get out of the jungle with a more or less whole skin, I could just as easily survive in it for a while and keep an eye on what the Cong were up to. There were quite a few of us in there. The problem was, we didn't have any contact with each other."

"What happened to your buddy?"

"What buddy?"

"The one you escaped with."

McClain's voice was very even. "He tripped over the wrong wire about two miles from our lines. There weren't even enough pieces of him left to carry out."

Clara felt as though a tremendous fist were crushing her heart. McClain sounded so matter-of-fact about it that she knew he must have suffered terribly. In the brief time she had known him—it had been a little more than two days and yet it felt more like two years—she had learned that he kept his emotions under iron control. The less he showed, the more he felt. It was hard communicating with a man like that, but she was beginning to learn the trick of it.

"I'm sorry," she said as evenly as he had. If she offered him tears and a shoulder to cry on he would turn on her in anger, she knew.

"Yeah. Things like that happen in war. It could just as easily have been me. But it wasn't, so I figured the next one might get me. But nothing did, and I made it home. My mother was real happy about that."

"You have a mother?"

He looked around with that glimmer of a grin. "What'd you think, I was hatched? Of course I have a mother. Everyone has a mother."

"What I meant was, is she still living?"

A crooked smile curved his lips. "Oh, yeah. You couldn't kill my Momma with an axe. She lives on a farm in Tennessee, same one my sisters and I were born and raised on. Since my dad died she's been raising chickens, and does pretty well for herself."

"Tell me about your family." Clara was fascinated.

Somehow this was not the kind of background she had pictured her daredevil spy as having. A mother whom he called Momma with obvious affection, a chicken farm, and sisters? "To start with, how many sisters do you have?"

He grinned, shooting a sideways look at her. "Five. All older, and all bossy as hell. It was like growing up with six mothers. When I joined the marines I thought that if I just had one drill sergeant to boss me around I'd think I'd died and gone to heaven."

"What are they doing now? Your sisters?"

He frowned a little. "Janey, the oldest, she's eleven years older than I am, lives on the farm next to Momma's with her husband, Bill, and four kids. Mary Ann, who's two years younger than Janey, is a travel agent in Casper. She's divorced with three kids. Sue and Sally, the twins, are three years younger than Mary Ann. They have seven kids between them, and they run Powder River Ski Resort with their husbands. And Betty, my youngest sister, is three years older than I am. She has four kids and lives with her husband on the farm next to Momma's."

"My goodness," Clara breathed, a little in awe at the thought of such a family. It had just been herself and her mother almost since she could remember; she'd always secretly wanted a big family, brothers and sisters to squabble with and confide in, lots of noise and chaos. Her childhood seemed so bland in comparison to how she imagined his must have been.

"What about you? Tell me about your family."

Clara shook her head. "There's just Mother and me. Daddy died when I was five. I always wanted brothers and sisters. I used to get lonely, especially at the holidays. Christmas was the worst."

"Christmas with my family is a madhouse," McClain said cheerfully. "I never go anymore. All those kids drive me up a wall."

"Don't you like children?" She was shocked. The only children she'd ever been around were Lena's, and despite their constant peccadilloes she loved them dearly. That was the thing that bothered her most when she considered the growing possibility that she might never marry: she would never have any children of her own. The thought hurt.

"Sure I like them—one or two at a time. When you're talking eighteen strong, the decibel level alone is enough to flatten a marine battalion."

"I'd love it!" She spoke with the sudden conviction that she would. He looked over at her oddly.

"You know, you probably would. So why don't you have kids of your own, then?"

Clara felt her cheeks redden. He had touched on a sensitive area, as he always seemed to. He seemed to have an uncanny knack for zeroing in on her weak spots.

"I know it sounds old-fashioned, but I kind of think I need a husband before I have babies."

"So why don't you have a husband? Oh, that's right, you're looking for Mr. Irresistible, aren't you? I forgot."

Clara shot him a narrow-eyed look. "What's keeping you from getting married?" Determinedly she lobbed the ball into his court. "Or are you?"

He shook his head. "Not hardly. I grew up with a gaggle of women, remember. I'm not in a hurry to saddle myself with another one."

"What about Gloria?" She drew the name out in a way that made it synonymous with Bimbo. As soon as she did it she could have bitten her tongue off, but she couldn't help herself: something about that name made her want to throw up. Or, she told herself in a brief burst of honesty, maybe it wasn't the name at all but the vision it conjured up of a sultry blonde curled up in bed with McClain.

He picked up on the cattiness in her tone. That teasing smile flickered, and the glint in his eyes brightened them to the color of peridots.

"My, my, baby, you sound like you don't like Gloria. You haven't even met the girl. Not jealous, are you?"

"Over you?" Clara felt angry color wash up her neck even as she hooted. "Fat chance."

"No, I wouldn't say that," he mused. "Gloria's not a bit fat. If anything, she's on the thin side. You know, one of those slim, elegant blondes."

Clara silently ground her teeth. He was trying to get a rise out of her, the goat, and he was succeeding. Picturing Gloria as a slim, elegant blonde—something she had always wanted to be, with no luck outside the color of her hair— was almost worse than picturing her in bed with McClain.

"So where is Gloria now? And why didn't Rostov pick on her instead of me?"

McClain looked a bit uncomfortable at that. Then he grinned. "To tell you the truth, Gloria was out that evening. As a matter-of-fact, she'd been out for several evenings prior to that. Gone home to her mother."

Clara hooted. "Couldn't stand you any longer, huh? I don't blame her."

McClain still looked cheerful. "Me neither. But you know something? I was kind of losing my taste for slim, elegant blondes, anyway. I like a little more meat on my women."

It took a minute for that to percolate through Clara's brain. When it did, she looked over at McClain a little uncertainly. What did he mean by that? But he was looking at the instruments and his expression told her nothing.

They were swooping down over a valley, having come across a rolling stretch of mountains. Below were a few farms interspersed with the trees. Clara looked down at them wistfully. How nice to be safe at home. . . .

"Clara." The way he said her name immediately alarmed her.

"What?"

"Look toward the east."

She did. What she saw made her heart jump into her throat. A flotilla of helicopters had materialized on the horizon, flying toward them, skimming over the ground. The helicopters were army green.

"Oh my God!"

McClain manipulated the lever and the pedals, and their helicopter did a sudden swooping turn. Clara felt her stomach fall at the suddenness of it, but her heart remained firmly lodged in her throat.

"McClain." The voice came crackling over the radio. It was the first sound they had heard besides static since hijacking it. Clara felt panic start to build inside her. Beside her, McClain adjusted the earphones and spoke into the mouthpiece.

"McClain here. Who is that?"

"Bill Ramsey. McClain, we have orders to shoot you down."

Clara felt her blood drain toward her toes. Oh God, to die in a flaming ball of wreckage plummeting toward earth. . . .

"General, I have a civilian passenger on board. A woman." His voice was perfectly even.

"I'm aware of that. I also find it hard to believe you're

mad-dog crazy enough to slaughter a hospital full of innocent people, shoot a cop, steal a police car and then a
helicopter without a hell of a good reason. So I'm willing to
give you a chance to tell me your side of it. You will
accompany us to Camp Lejeune, where you will land your
chopper and surrender to me. I trust I make myself clear,
McClain?''

"Clear as a bell, General."

"And McClain," the general's voice had an implacable
note, "I hardly need to warn you that if you appear to be
trying to escape, I will obey my orders immediately."

"Understood, General."

The radio went silent except for the soft crackle of static.
McClain turned the helicopter about. Immediately the flotilla of helicopters resolved themselves into six, and they
positioned themselves in a vee around their prisoner. With
another helicopter leading the way, they flew southeast,
toward, Clara assumed, Camp Lejeune.

"Jack," her voice quavered, "what's going to happen
now?"

McClain's jaw was set. He sent her a look out of eyes
that no longer sparkled, but were hard and cold.

"We've got a chance. General Ramsey was my C.O. in
Nam. We called him Wild Bill. He's a son of a bitch, but
he's a fair son of a bitch. It takes guts to disobey an order,
and his orders were to shoot us down. As long as he remains
in charge of us, we'll be all right."

"But will he turn us over to someone else?"

Clara spoke in a tiny voice. Puff, apparently sensing her
growing fear, roused himself from his nap on the jumpseat
in the rear and walked over to jump in her lap. At his
rumbling question Clara rubbed his head, and he settled
down into a ball on her lap. McClain looked down at him,

seemed about to say something, then changed his mind. They spoke not another word until they were within sight of Camp Lejeune.

"Better get dressed, Clara."

Clara had forgotten that she was clad only in a blanket. Her cheeks flared at the thought of presenting herself in such garb before a bunch of tough marines. Sliding off the seat, she moved to the rear and dressed quickly. Her clothes were still clammy, but she didn't suppose it made a difference that she was immediately chilled to the bone. Pneumonia was way down on her list of things to worry about.

"Your turn." She slid back into her seat, reaching for the controls with only a little trepidation. At this point crashing the helicopter was not one of her major worries either. He threw her a quick, encouraging grin, then stepped back to dress himself. He was back in moments, taking over the controls.

"I feel sort of like a frog in winter."

He was trying to cheer her up, Clara knew. She smiled at him. "Me, too."

The radio crackled, making Clara jump. "Set her down on the helicopter pad behind the terminal, McClain."

"Will do, General." McClain's voice was even. But his knuckles were white on the joystick.

"Oh, Jack, I'm scared!" The words burst involuntarily from Clara as he set the helicopter down on the tarmac. The machine was immediately surrounded by a platoon of marines with rifles at the ready. McClain looked at her, eyes dark, hand still on the lever. Above them, the whirling blades drowned out all outside sound.

"I'll do my best to get you out of this. If they interrogate you, just tell them the truth. That's all we can do now."

"Interrogate me?" Clara didn't like the sound of that. Her eyes were wide and desperate as they met his. He stared at her for just a second, his jaw set, and then he was leaning toward her, his big hand cupping her head as he pulled her toward him. His mouth found hers, kissed her roughly. She twined her arms around his neck and kissed him back with all her might.

"Let's go, McClain!" The shouted command was accompanied by a loud banging on the closed metal door. McClain reached up and pulled her arms from around his neck, kissed her quickly one more time, then moved toward the door.

"Stay back behind me," he said, and then he was sliding back the door. Hands immediately reached in to grab him. He was pulled down onto the tarmac out of sight.

"Be careful of the lady. Like I said, she's a civilian," Clara heard him say to the armed contingent outside the door. Then she was walking forward too, clutching Puff, and to her surprise found that the soldiers were quite respectful as they helped her down, even holding her elbow to steady her descent.

"Sorry, ma'am, we have to search you," someone said, and then hands were run over her, impersonal despite the intimate places they touched.

"She's clean."

"What about the cat?"

"I doubt it's packing a piece."

"I know that. What I meant was what do we do with it?"

"How the hell should I know? Let her keep it for now, I suppose. Hell, ask the general! What do you do with a cat, for God's sake?"

This conversation took place somewhere behind her.

Clara heard it vaguely. She was looking for McClain. Finally she found him. He was lying spread-eagled on the tarmac with half a dozen rifles pointed at his head while his hands were handcuffed behind his back. Those brilliant green eyes met hers for an instant and then he turned his head away. Clara felt tears start in her own eyes. She had the most devastating notion that she would never see him again.

A grizzled officer walked briskly over to the group around McClain and was saluted all around. McClain was hauled to his feet, then turned to face the officer. That was the last she saw of him before she was led away.

XVI

Puff was taken from her at the jail. A uniformed marine lifted him from her arms despite her protests and Puff's growls, and informed her that he would have to be taken to Animal Control on the base. Clara cried then. The tears that she had managed to hold back over McClain came rushing out for Puff. Or maybe she was crying for both of them, and for herself as well. She just didn't know. She did know that she gulped and sobbed and bawled until a doctor was called to give her a sedative. And after that she didn't know anything at all until she woke up on a narrow twin bed in a windowless, green painted room.

"I was just going to wake you. You must get dressed at once."

Clara blinked groggily at the speaker. A dark-haired woman in the uniform of a marine nurse was standing beside the bed looking down at her. The expression on her face was neither friendly nor unfriendly. It was best characterized as efficient.

"Who are you?" Clara struggled up on one elbow, trying to get a handle on exactly where she was and what had

191

happened. She felt faintly woozy and more than a little nauseous.

"Lieutenant Holmes. I've been assigned to you until you leave the base, which will be in approximately ninety minutes. You have time to shower, dress, and eat breakfast if you hurry."

Clara stared at the woman as the events of the previous day came flooding back to her.

"You said I'll be leaving the base in an hour and a half. What about Jack—Jack McClain, the man who—they brought him here with me. And Puff. My cat."

"I don't know anything about either of them. My orders are to get you ready to leave. I've just relieved Lieutenant Moskowitz, who sat with you throughout the night. I understand you were given a sedative. Can you get up?"

"I—I think so." Clara swung her legs over the side of the bed, surprised to find that she was clad in a hospital gown. Her head swam alarmingly, but she gripped the edge of the bed with both hands and after a moment the sensation subsided.

"What happened to my clothes?"

"Prisoners are not allowed to retain any personal property. Your clothes themselves will be brought up shortly, so that you may wear them as you leave. The rest of your property may be reclaimed at the front desk on your way out."

This was more automaton than woman, Clara thought. Then she realized that she was in jail, a criminal, suspected of God knew how many heinous crimes. No wonder the lieutenant was not overly friendly. She wouldn't be either in the lieutenant's shoes.

"Did you say something about a shower?"

Lieutenant Holmes escorted her down the hall to the

shower, provided her with soap and other toiletries, including a meager selection of cosmetics, then stationed herself outside the door. Clara stripped off the gown, turned the silver knobs until the water was coming out in a steaming spray, then stepped beneath it with a blissful sigh. No matter what happened, it was good to be clean again. She scrubbed her skin, lathered her hair, then stood under the spray luxuriating in the warmth.

"You have forty-five minutes left."

The voice from outside the shower recalled her to herself. Turning off the knobs, she wrapped a skimpy white towel around her body and another around her head. Then she stepped out into the large communal bathroom. The tile floor was cold beneath her feet and her skin broke out in goosebumps as she dried herself and dressed again in the gown she had discarded for want of anything better. Ignoring Lieutenant Holmes' eagle eyes, she turned to the mirror and began to blow dry her hair. Looking her best always bolstered her courage, and she had a feeling that today she was going to need all the courage she could get.

The makeup the lieutenant had supplied was minimal. Lipstick, mascara, blush and powder. Clara fell on it with the avidity of a starving man. The blush was a conservative pale pink. She used it everywhere, on her cheeks and her chin and her forehead and even her eyelids, to counteract the sun and windburn that had reddened her normally magnolia white skin. The mascara brought out the pale blue of her eyes so that they sparkled against the pink of her skin. And the lipstick, a soft rose, added just the right amount of color to her mouth. Looking at herself critically in the mirror as she applied it, Clara thought that she had never seen herself look so well. Her hair framed her face in a shining gold bell, her cheekbones

were noticeable for the first time in her life, and she could
even see the bones in her neck and shoulders. Then Clara
understood: she had barely eaten a bite for three days and
had undergone enough physical exertion for a dozen men.
The ten pounds that she never could quite seem to lose had
been taken off with a considerable jolt.

"Half an hour."

Clara turned away from the mirror, handing the toiletries
to Lieutenant Holmes. She accepted everything but the
cosmetics, which she zippered into a small plastic bag and
handed back.

"You can keep these. If you want to eat breakfast, we'll
have to hurry."

In her room there was a tray with eggs, bacon, and toast.
Clara normally did not eat eggs, but remembering how long
it had been since she had had a normal meal she tucked in
with gusto. There was no telling when she might get a
chance to eat again.

Just as she was eating the last morsel of bacon, a knock
sounded at the door. Lieutenant Holmes answered it, then
turned back into the room carrying Clara's own clothes,
washed, ironed and neatly folded.

"Thank you. And please thank whoever washed them for
me."

"All prisoners' clothes are washed as they come in. We
have to store them until they leave, after all."

"Well, I'm glad to have them clean, nevertheless." Still
under Lieutenant Holmes' cold eyes, Clara slid out of the
gown and into her own things. The teddy that had served as
her underwear for almost four days was holding up remarkably well, considering the fragility of the silk and lace.
Clara stepped into it, reminded irresistibly of McClain as
she did so. He liked her teddy, she could tell. Where was

he? What were they doing to him? Would she see him again? Such thoughts were useless, she knew. Whatever was going to happen, she would find out soon enough. She stepped into her newly loose jeans, fastening them over a stomach that was undeniably flatter than it had been four days earlier, then pulled on her flannel shirt. The shirt had a rip in the shoulder. The blanket poncho would hide it, though she hated to wear the ugly thing. She pulled the poncho over her head. It looked exactly like what it was: half of a grungy blue blanket with a hole cut for her head. Oh well, since when had she ever been fashionable, anyway? Lieutenant Holmes saw it and frowned.

"I think we might have a sweater you can wear with that," she said.

"Why, thank you." Clara was surprised at this first evidence of human concern the other woman had shown. She pulled the poncho off as Lieutenant Holmes stepped out into the hall to place a quick call downstairs from the telephone which was right outside. A few minutes later a knock sounded at the door. A dusky rose, bulky knit pullover sweater was the result.

"That's much better."

"It is, isn't it? Thank you." Clara smiled at the woman. Lieutenant Holmes didn't smile back, but her expression lightened slightly.

Another knock sounded at the door. Lieutenant Holmes answered it, then turned back and said, "Time to go." Clara felt butterflies start to turn flips in her stomach.

"Do you know where I'm being taken?" she asked, but the lieutenant just shook her head.

Lieutenant Holmes escorted her to the front lobby, which was indeed enclosed with a barred gate. On the other side two male officers waited to take over. Clara looked at them, swallowed, and lifted her chin. Whatever happened, she would keep her wits about her and deal with it the best she could. They thought she was a criminal; but she was a Winston and a Jolly and a member of one of Virginia's oldest (though slightly impoverished) families. To say nothing of the fact that she was a published author. They could not just railroad her. Could they?

To her astonishment, the first thing the marines did was clap handcuffs on her.

"Is this really necessary?" she asked with Virginia aristocracy hauteur.

"Yes, ma'am," they assured her, very politely. The handcuffs stayed in place as she was led from the building. Two cars waited below. Both were white Mercury station wagons, completely nondescript except for the flashing red lights mounted in the center of the windshield.

"What about my cat?"

"We don't know anything about a cat, ma'am." She was escorted inexorably down the stairs.

"Where are you—"

The rear door of the first car opened as she stepped onto the lowest step. A hand was placed on top of her head and she was hustled inside before she could even finish her question. Then the door was slammed and the car was pulling away.

"Hello, Clara."

She looked sideways. There, sitting next to her on the blue vinyl seat, was McClain. No one had ever looked as wonderful to her in her life as he did at that moment. He was clean shaven, his aggressive chin smooth and powerful. His hair was shiny clean, neatly brushed in a military style. Like hers his clothes had been washed and pressed. The bruises on his face had faded into faint yellowish traces, barely visible beneath the swarthiness of his skin. He looked toughly masculine, a man's man in a man's world. She felt safer with him than anybody she had ever known in her life.

"They took Puff to the pound!" The words burst from her, almost accusingly. He looked at her, his green eyes unsmiling.

"Did they? Well, he'll be all right. You can get him back later."

"That's easy for you to say. What if they put him to sleep?"

McClain snorted. "I couldn't get so lucky."

"That's an awful thing to say!"

"I apologize. They won't hurt him. I can guarantee it, okay?" Clara was surprised at how certain he sounded. How could he know? In pounds across the country, stray animals were destroyed after about seven days, she knew. But Puff was not a stray; he was a blue-blooded Persian worth hundreds of dollars, any fool could tell that. Besides, he had a tag with his name, address and registration number on his collar. Surely no one would destroy a cat like that.

"You're not in a position to guarantee anything, McClain."

"Go soak your head, Thompson." McClain scowled at the man in the front passenger seat, whom he apparently knew. The other man turned around to scowl back at him.

"You're in deep trouble, McClain. You'd better remember that."

"Lay off, Thompson. McClain, that goes for you too. We're just following orders. No need to take it personally." Clearly the driver knew McClain too. Clara looked over at

McClain questioningly. Only then did she realize that his hands were cuffed behind his back. She was more fortunate; at least her hands were cuffed in front.

"Clara, let me introduce you to two erstwhile colleagues of mine. Pat Thompson riding shotgun and Arthur Knebel driving. Gentlemen, meet Claire Winston, author."

"Sure," said Thompson, turning sideways to look back at them. His left arm in its tweed sportscoat sleeve lay along the top of the seat. "You never read a book in your life, McClain. How would you know an author?"

"Rostov mistook her for Gloria. You remember Gloria, don't you, Thompson? You met her at the last Christmas party. You'd had one too many, and you were so googly-eyed over her you spilled a drink down her dress."

"Lay off, McClain." Knebel's voice held a warning. McClain ignored him.

"Clara, I want you to tell them everything that's happened to you. Start at the beginning."

Clara looked over at him with a questioning frown.

"They won't believe me. I'm hoping you can convince them. If you can't, we're going all the way back to Langley. And Rostov and company."

Thus adjured, Clara started to talk. She told the two politely disbelieving men in the front seat about the night Rostov broke into her house demanding a mysterious magic dragon. She told about how she was kidnapped and found McClain being tortured in the basement of a house in northern Virginia. She told how they escaped, and how they'd been running for their lives ever since.

"Does that convince you?" McClain demanded testily when she was done.

Thompson snorted. "All it convinces me of is that you've embroiled an innocent woman in another one of your stinking messes. Did he tell you about himself, Miss Winston? He was in charge of a sting operation in Hungary that ended up with everyone but him getting killed. He screwed up. Then he cracked up. Couldn't take the guilt of getting all those people killed, I guess. They brought him back to the U.S., finally, and he spent almost a year in a loony bin. My guess is he'd been out drinking the night he shot up that hospital. He can't hold his liquor; goes crazy when he drinks.''

''Why, you . . .'' McClain lunged forward, eyes blazing, then seemed to get a grip on himself and sank back against the seat. Clara looked over at him, her eyes wide. She didn't know whether she felt alarm or sympathy.

''Cool it, McClain. Thompson's got a point, and you know it. Last we heard you were farmed out at a desk job, labeled unfit for active duty. Then the word's out that you'd gone berserk again, shot up a lot of civilians, and were out wreaking general mayhem on the countryside. We were sent to bring you in, nothing more.''

McClain leaned forward again, his face grim as he kept himself under tight control. ''Damn it, Knebel, that's just what they want you to believe. *He* wants you to believe. Bigfoot. Whoever he is, he's high level enough to sic the agency itself on me. Christ, man, think of the operations a mole at that level could jeopardize!''

''Oh, give it a rest, McClain.'' Thompson turned back to look out the windshield in disgust. ''Keep spouting off like that and they'll be putting you in a rubber room before we get halfway to Langley.''

''Shut up, Thompson.'' Knebel was frowning. ''Miss Winston, did he tell you to say these things or are you telling the truth as you yourself saw it? Think hard before you answer, because if you lie any more you could get yourself into more trouble than you'll ever get out of.''

"Of course I'm not lying." Clara was getting angry at their attitude toward her, and it showed. She didn't go out in society much, but when she did she was accustomed to being treated with respect, if not downright deference. After all, she was a Winston and a Jolly—not to mention a published author! What she was not was a total fool. She told them so, and McClain grinned at her.

"You tell 'em, baby."

"Another of your bimboes, McClain? Somebody should warn you, Miss Winston: he's famous for them."

"Thompson, I swear to God that when I get these handcuffs off I'm going to knock your teeth down your throat!"

"Shut up, both of you!" Knebel hit the steering wheel with the flat of his hand. The resultant loud slap made Clara jump. She looked over at McClain uneasily. Of course, she knew that every word she'd said was the truth, but what about the things he had said? Maybe, just maybe, he *had* shot up that emergency room. She hadn't been with him Friday night, after all. Maybe Rostov was after him for an entirely different reason than what he said. Maybe Rostov wasn't KGB at all, but a Mafia enforcer, for instance. Who knew what McClain might have gotten himself involved in? Drugs, maybe, if a hospital was involved? After all, during the time she had known him he had not impressed her with his stability.

Her eyes were upon him, and he must have correctly read the doubt in them.

"*Et tu*, Clara?" he said softly, then settled back in his seat, his mouth grim.

"Jack . . ." Her voice was troubled. Those green eyes

were very hard as they met hers. She bit her lower lip. She wanted to tell him that if he was . . . troubled in his mind she would understand. He had been through a very difficult experience in Vietnam and apparently afterwards too, if Thompson's words were true. It was no shame that he had broken under what must have been an intolerable burden.

"I am damned well in possession of every one of my faculties," McClain ground out, glaring at her. Clara gave him a gentle smile.

"See there, Miss Winston? You're beginning to have second thoughts, aren't you? Now I don't doubt that McClain here is in some trouble, but the question is, what kind of trouble? Could any kind of a different interpretation be put on what you've experienced? After all, what did Rostov actually say to you? Admittedly, Rostov is KGB, but the point is, except for McClain's telling you so, how do you know that the man who came after you was Rostov? He could have been anyone with a personal grudge against our pal here, don't you see?"

"Bullshit!" McClain gritted. Clara looked over at him helplessly. She wanted to believe him, she did, but the whole thing was so utterly fantastic. Here were these calm, reasonable men working for the very agency that her spy claimed to represent, telling her that McClain was crazy. Who was she to believe? All her instincts urged her to side with McClain, but were her senses unfairly disordered by her attraction to him? Face it, she had never had very good judgment when it came to men, and apparently, if Thompson were to be believed, he was a past master with "bimboes." Had he made a fool of her in more ways than one?

"The point is," Thompson continued inexorably, "that

he hasn't any proof. Just what he says a supposed defector told him. And I never heard a word about that defection, by the way. Again, we have no proof except his say-so that it ever happened.''

"You damn idiots," McClain said bitterly, and turned his head away from them.

No one spoke for a while. McClain stared out the window, watching the passing scenery in tense silence. The countryside was beautiful, Clara noted in passing, but she had no appetite at the moment for the beauty of North Carolina in the autumn. She watched McClain and her heart ached for him. Poor, tormented man. His face was turned away from her, but she knew each feature as well as she knew her own. If her hands were free she would reach out and touch that harshly carved face. But as it was, all she could do was look.

"Damn it, Clara, I am not crazy!" He turned his head to catch her sorrowing eyes on him. Her pitying look must have galled him because his words were filled with suppressed violence.

"Oh, Jack, I know you're not *crazy*." The very emphasis she put on the word left room for a large but. He glared at her, then leaned forward again.

"Listen, Knebel, you can see she's not involved in this. At least let her go before you take me in. Like Thompson said, she's just another of my women. No point in dragging her into this any further.''

Knebel shook his head regretfully. "No can do. My orders are to bring you both in. Sorry.''

"Damn it, man, you realize that they'll kill her!''

Knebel sighed. "McClain, nobody is going to hurt anybody, least of all Miss Winston. Miss Winston, I hope you believe that.''

"Do you believe that, Clara?" McClain turned to look at her with a fierce bitterness. Clara stared back at him helplessly. The truth was, she didn't know what to believe. She wet her lips, trying to think of an answer. Before she could come up with one, Thompson looked in the rearview mirror and frowned.

"Hey, we've lost our backup." Just then the radio crackled. Thompson picked up the microphone.

"Where are you guys?" he barked. The answer from the radio was unintelligible to Clara, but Thompson relaxed again as he replaced the mike and spoke to Knebel. "Seems some damn fool truck tried to turn in front of them just as we went around that bend. They'll catch up." Clara realized that the two cars had a two-way communication set up.

"Shit! This is it! Man, I told you, they're not going to let you bring me in! The whole setup is KGB, you damn fools!"

"Now, McClain, calm down." But Knebel looked in the rearview mirror as he spoke, sounding the slightest bit uneasy. McClain was sitting tensely alert, scanning the surroundings with narrow eyes. Clara turned around in her seat to look back down the road. It was deserted. Nervously she wished the backup car would hurry and catch up.

"They'll be back with us in a minute." Knebel still sounded uneasy.

"Unlock these cuffs and give me a gun!" McClain's voice was urgent. He leaned forward, practically shouting in Knebel's ear. Clara shrank back against the seat. She was scared, really scared, and she didn't know if it was of McClain or Rostov or who.

"I said calm down, McClain!" Knebel roared, looking

nervously from the rearview mirror to the road in front of him. "Nobody's going to hurt—"

A moving van pulled out of a side road in front of them, its long orange length blocking the road as it executed a leisurely turn. Horizon Movers was emblazoned in black letters on its side. Another moving van was behind the first.

"Turn around, Knebel! For God's sake!" McClain was shouting, but Knebel ignored him. He approached the van, but slowed slightly, looking worried when it failed to move out of his way. Clara waited to see what would happen with a kind of horrified fatalism. Either McClain was right and it was a KGB trap or it was nothing more than a moving van, and in a moment they would be past it and on their way. Knebel sounded the horn. The driver, features indistinguishable in the shadows of the cab, seemed to notice them at last. He stuck his gloved hand out the window and gave them a wave as if to say that he would be out of the way shortly.

The truck's back door rumbled up, and four men wearing identical gray coveralls jumped out. It was only as they began walking toward the now barely moving car that Clara noticed that their faces were smudged, the features squashed in a most peculiar way. They were wearing stocking masks. And they carried rifles in their hands. Knebel and Thompson must have noticed all that at the same time, because they swore and fumbled for the pistols they wore in holsters beneath their impeccably tailored coats.

"Oh, Christ!" McClain threw himself on top of Clara, knocking her out of her seat and crushing her down on the floor behind the back seat just as the shooting started. Clara screamed as the sound of gunfire roared around her like point-blank thunder. Bullets tore through the body of the car, skewing it sideways in the road. For the first moment the agents in the front seat were returning fire, but then either Knebel or Thompson, she wasn't sure which, shrieked. The shriek died in a liquid gurgle. The other one grunted, and muttered something that sounded like damn. Then there was an awful silence.

The rear door opened. Clara heard it distinctly despite McClain's body all around and over her. Then she felt McClain's weight shift as he was dragged off her. Finally she felt an ungentle hand on her own arm. She opened her eyes as she was pulled from the car. McClain was standing by the car in the grip of two of the masked men, looking remarkably calm for a man with two rifles pointed at his heart. Another thug was holding her, while the fourth used his rifle to poke at Thompson, who was lying half on the front floorboard of the idling car and half on the ground. The thug put the rifle behind Thompson's head, then pulled the trigger. The shot at point-blank range exploded the agent's head like a grapefruit. Bright crimson blood mixed with gray brain matter spattered over the roadside. The smell of blood was strong in the air. Then the thug turned Thompson over. Clara felt her stomach heave when she saw the oozing crimson pulp that was all that remained of his face. Knebel was slumped over the steering wheel, she saw as she deliberately averted her eyes from what was left of Thompson. She assumed he too was dead. The thug who'd finished off Thompson walked around to the other side of the car, reached in and turned off the ignition. Then he plowed a bullet into Knebel. This time Clara closed her eyes before she could witness the butchery. Bile rose sickly in her throat. She thought she was going to vomit.

McClain swore. Clara opened her eyes. A figure she

remembered all too well stepped from the back of the van. Unlike his compatriots, he was not masked. The sun glinted on his sandy hair as he walked toward them, a rifle tucked negligently under his arm.

"Well, well, it seems we are destined to meet in out-of-the-way places, doesn't it, Dragon? And Miss Winston too, of course," said Rostov, and smiled. Then, as he reached them, he lifted his rifle in a quick, savage movement and clubbed McClain viciously on the side of his head.

XVII

"Now, I am going to give you a final chance to be sensible. Miss Winston, I will ask you first: Where is the microfilm?" Then he smiled at McClain. "Oh, yes, Yuropov told us all about it. Did you doubt that he would? Toward the end he was very eager to tell us everything he could." His eyes shifted back to Clara. "Well, Miss Winston?"

The moving van was rumbling down the road. Huddled half clad beside McClain on the cold metal floor, back pressed against the narrow wall at the forward end of the mobile prison, Clara felt her skin quiver with horror as Rostov looked at her. She prayed that he would not touch her again.

They were going to die, sooner or later, she knew. No one would know what had become of them. Knebel and Thompson's bodies had been loaded back into the car in which they had been killed, and that car had been driven up a ramp and inside the second moving truck, which had headed in the opposite direction from the first. The backup car, Clara's last hope, had not shown up. It had been deliberately delayed by another moving van that had pulled across the road in its path, ostensibly to turn around. By the time the occupants of the backup car figured out that the other car was not in front of them, all three vans would be long gone. And the authorities, being what they were, would undoubtedly assume that the hijacking of the agents and their car had been carried out by McClain. One more act of bloody mayhem by a crazed agent.

When McClain and Clara's bodies were found, if they ever were, they would be in the purloined CIA car at the bottom of a river somewhere. Thompson and Knebel would be discovered in the trunk.

Rostov had related this plan almost casually as they were herded aboard the first of the trailers. Then she and McClain had been forcibly strip searched in the most humiliating way possible. The two thugs with Rostov had first stripped McClain, roughly examining every part of his body and then going over his clothes with minute thoroughness before shaking their heads and tossing the garments back at him. McClain had borne the indignity with stony lack of responsiveness.

Clara had tried not to watch. But when they had turned to her, it had been a different story. She had screamed and struggled, to no avail. They removed every stitch of her clothes, ran their hands over her body, looked in her hair and mouth and ears and made her bend over so that they could check the most intimate of body cavities. When it was over, Clara was reduced to a trembling wreck of humiliation. They had allowed her to pull on her teddy, flannel shirt and sweater (simply because the items had been dangling from the handcuffs that still chained her wrists and were therefore in the way) before pushing her stumbling toward McClain, who sat impassively against the front wall, clad once again in jeans and sweatshirt. Clara huddled against him for warmth as well as what scant protection he could offer, her long bare legs drawn up in front of her to hide as much of herself as she could from these monsters who had no human feelings whatsoever. At least their actions had been impersonal—so far. Rape was a horrible spectre she refused to even think about.

Until now Rostov had been almost affable—except for that single instant when he had clubbed McClain with his rifle butt. He had said little throughout the searches, just watched keenly. He was smiling, swaying slightly with the movement of the truck as he stood before them, balanced on the balls of his feet, hands clasped behind his back. His teeth gleamed whitely in the light of the generator powered lightbulb that hung from a wire rigged across the ceiling. One of the two thugs who had stayed with Rostov had cranked the old-fashioned generator to get it going as soon as the prisoners had been taken aboard. The other two had gone into the cab as driver and lookout. With his blond hair, ruddy cheeked, classically featured face and upright military bearing, Rostov looked like the all-American boy. Even his navy wool pants and white crewneck sweater over a pin-striped button-down shirt were in impeccable taste. Never in her wildest dreams had she thought that death, when it came for her, would be dressed like a preppy!

"I don't know anything about a microfilm." Clara's voice was as steady as she could make it. She really didn't know anything about a microfilm, but Rostov wouldn't believe her in a million years. She knew that already. She cast a sidelong look at McClain. Did *he* know anything about a microfilm? He hadn't said anything about it to her.

"Admirable courage, Miss Winston." Rostov was still smiling. "Aided, of course, by your ignorance of how truly easy it will be to make you talk. What about you, Dragon? Are you going to save yourself and your lady some pain?''

''I don't know what you are talking about.''

Rostov's smile stayed in place. ''Ah, Dragon, I know what you are thinking: if I tell Rostov where that microfilm is, I am dead—what do you say, beef?—as soon as he gets his hands on it. Right? You are not a fool, my friend, so I will not attempt to deny it. You and the lady will die, just as everyone you have talked to is either dead or soon to die. The operative you and the traitor Yuropov have imperiled is too big to permit us to take chances. But what you can choose is the manner of your dying. I can make it very easy for you. Or I can make it very hard and painful. You would not like the lady to suffer pain, would you, Dragon?''

''She knows nothing about any of this, Rostov. You made a mistake when you went after her. I never saw her before in my life before that night. If she wanted to, she couldn't tell you anything.''

''Then that is her misfortune.'' Rostov turned to the goon behind him. ''Get her up.''

''No!'' Clara whimpered, huddling closer to McClain, who was motionless. Her eyes were huge as she watched them come for her. She had never felt so terrified in her life.

The stockier of Rostov's henchmen reached down to grab Clara by the arm and haul her to her feet. As she tried to resist, earning a vicious pinch for her pains, McClain made an abortive movement beside her. Almost instantly he subsided, his face impassive. Clara struggled as she was pulled toward Rostov, but to no avail. The man holding her was an ape. Shorter than either McClain or Rostov, thickset, heavy featured with a bald head so smooth Clara wondered hysterically if he shaved it, he had long since discarded the stocking mask he had worn during the ambush. Shuddering as she looked into his avidly gleaming small eyes, Clara wished he had kept it on. Then she would not be able to see the anticipation in his eyes.

"You know, Dragon, I am inclined to believe you when you say the lady was a mistake. She is too soft, too easily hurt. Not your type, eh? This one does not have the toughness of the other, Gloria?" McClain's expression changed, almost indiscernibly. But Rostov saw it and smiled. "Ah, yes, I have made the acquaintance of Gloria. It seems she wished to make up your quarrel. At any rate, she returned to your apartment a couple of days ago. But she, too, knew nothing. A pity. But one must do what one must do. For one's country, you understand."

Clara felt her throat go dry as she absorbed the implications of his words. Had Rostov killed Gloria? He would do so without compunction, she knew. Clara had a moment of thanksgiving that her mother was safely out of the country. Then she was jerked back to reality by Rostov's almost casual command.

"Break one of her fingers."

Before Clara could recover her wits enough even to scream, the other thug had his arm around her throat in a choke hold. The first one grabbed her by the handcuffs that still linked her wrists, caught her left hand in his, and wrapped his huge hand around her pinky. With a twisting motion, he wrenched it to the side. Clara screamed in agony as pain shot through her body. When he released her hand, the littlest finger stuck out at an odd angle. Already it was swelling, turning black. Sobbing, Clara cradled the injured hand with the other. Her knees gave out; the thug behind her let her slump to the floor. Clara sprawled on the cold metal, clutching her hand, unable to believe the agony. They had deliberately broken her finger! She vomited, retching until her stomach was empty.

"Such a little pain, and you see how she reacts? This one is a lady. Hurting her will be easy." Rostov was talking to McClain, ignoring Clara who was still sobbing at his feet. As he spoke she scooted a little away from the puddle of vomit, but remained huddled on the floor. Hoping against hope that they would forget she was there.

"What shall we do to her next, Dragon? We could, of course, break all her fingers and toes. But that is mere child's play. Or we could strip her naked again and let Orlov have some fun with her. He is a sick man, our Orlov. But then, I am not feeling in charity with Orlov today. I specifically asked him to save the coup de grace to your agents for me, and instead he got carried away and killed them himself. So he needs a lesson in discipline. But there are still many other choices. You know them as well as I. So I will ask you again, Dragon: Where is the microfilm?"

"Go to hell, Rostov."

Rostov shook his head. "I am sorry, Miss Winston, but as you see your friend does not value you as he should. Malik, help Miss Winston up."

The second thug walked over to pull Clara to her feet. She cowered, whimpering, still cradling her injured hand. Pain and shock throbbed along her nerve endings. She felt cold—so cold—a cold that had nothing to do with her bare feet and legs beneath the scanty edgings of silk and lace. Her throat was dry. Even the soft little cries she was making hurt. But she couldn't seem to stop whimpering. Terror filled her as she was jerked to her feet, imprisoned again in the choke hold.

"Scream all you like, Miss Winston. The trailer is sound-proof." The words were benevolent. Their effect on Clara was horrible.

"Oh, please, please..." They positioned her so that McClain could see her and she could see him. He was looking at her, his face like stone. His eyes were as hard and impersonal as Rostov's. He was not going to give them what they wanted. A dry sob racked her, then another and another. They were going to hurt her, torture her, kill her...

"What shall we do to her, hmm? Orlov, have you a cigarette?"

"*Da.*" He fished in the pockets of his gray coveralls and came up with a pack of cigarettes and a lighter, which he passed to Rostov.

"Ah, thank you, comrade." Rostov leisurely extracted a cigarette from the pack, which he then slid into his shirt pocket beneath the sweater. Putting the cigarette in his mouth, he flicked the lighter to life and held the flame to the tip, inhaling deeply. Snapping the lighter shut and sliding it into his pants pocket, he took a couple of long drags on the cigarette. Then he looked at Clara, frowning in a mock-considering way.

"Now, let us see...."

"Please, don't hurt me!" Clara's voice was a hoarse croak. She was dizzy with pain and terror. This animal was going to burn her tender skin with the cigarette, she had absolutely no doubt. It would hurt—like her hand still hurt. She couldn't bear any more pain. But there was nothing she could do; she was helpless, at their mercy. And they were merciless men.

"Where shall we start? Not the face, at first. No, the face is too pretty to mar unless we must. What about the neck? Just beneath the ear. . . ."

He pulled hard on the cigarette. The tip glowed bright red when he took it from his mouth. Clara cringed as he reached for her with his free hand, smoothing her hair away from her neck with a caressing gesture.

"Such soft skin," Rostov murmured.

Clara realized with a sick heave of her stomach that he was actually enjoying what he was doing. She strained away from him, whimpering, pressing her head back against Orlov's barrel chest in a vain effort to evade the approaching cigarette. Rostov's hand held her hair clear; the cigarette touched her neck just below her ear. Clara screamed, jerking helplessly as the cigarette burned into her white skin. The scent of charred flesh reached her nostrils as Rostov stepped back. For a moment she thought she might faint. Everything swam before her eyes . . . She wanted to faint, to hurry up and die and get it over with. But she didn't. She could only stand trembling, cringing, sobbing, to wait for another onslaught of pain.

Rostov returned the cigarette to his mouth and took another leisurely drag. When the tip was glowing bright red again he took it out and turned it over in his hands, studying it.

"Hold her up, Malik." Rostov's order was sharp.

"No, please. No." Clara barely even heard her own mindless pleading. The thugs paid no attention. Orlov tightened his grip on her swaying, trembling body.

"That's better." Rostov nodded, looking Clara up and down. Then he reached toward her, grasped the hem of her sweater and pulled it over her head so that it hung from her chained hands. Clara shook from head to toe as he began to flick open the buttons that fastened her shirt. She felt nausea churn again in her stomach as he exposed the soft flesh of her neck and shoulders, the burgeoning swell of her breasts against the silky white teddy. He pushed the shirt off her shoulders. Clara could feel the men's eyes on her breasts. She had a horrible premonition that before this was over they would all rape her, not because they wanted her woman's body but because they enjoyed inflicting pain and humiliation on the helpless. They were sick, evil men. . . .

Rostov's hand reached out, caressed her shoulder, slid a spaghetti strap down one arm. He continued to tug at the strap until her left breast was exposed. Clara cringed against Orlov as Rostov ran a questing finger over her breast, flicking the shrinking nipple.

"Very nice, very sexy. I compliment you on your taste in women, Dragon." Rostov was drawing on the cigarette again. Tears fell from Clara's eyes. She was helpless to stop him from hurting her.

She looked over at McClain to find him watching her. Those green eyes were stony in his set face.

Rostov withdrew the cigarette from his mouth and held it over her breast without quite touching it. Clara squirmed, panting and whimpering in anticipation of the pain as he moved the cigarette around in the air, seemingly trying to position it just right. Finally he stopped when it was directly over her nipple. She could feel the heat of the glowing red tip although it was still about an inch from her skin.

"Please, no! I don't know anything, I swear I don't!" Clara was babbling through falling tears. "Please. . . ." Her eyes encountered McClain's. His were such a dark green that they looked almost black. "Jack!"

"All right, Rostov. You win. Back off." McClain's voice was hoarse. Clara didn't understand for a moment as she watched the slow smile that stretched Rostov's mouth. His pale blue eyes gleamed. Then the cigarette was put back in his mouth and he turned to look at McClain. At a gesture from Rostov, Clara was abruptly released. She sank to her knees, dazed with relief. It was a moment before she could even cover herself. Then she scrambled back into the protection of shirt and sweater like a rabbit running for its burrow. Not that the garments would protect her, but she couldn't stand to be naked to their view.

"Well?" Rostov drew out the syllable, not troubling to conceal his triumph.

"It's on the damned cat."

"What?" Rostov's voice was sharp. The cigarette came out of his mouth again to be held tensely in his hand as he stared at McClain.

"You heard me. The cat. The one we've been lugging around. The microfilm is on the cat."

Rostov swore in Russian. Clara blinked, her attention caught despite the pain. McClain had hidden the microfilm on *Puff*? No wonder he had been so careful of him! Fuzzily she remembered him saying, Just because I didn't let the damned cat drown doesn't make me some kind of hero, you know. Some kind of hero, indeed! He'd been saving his precious microfilm, and not Puff at all! She looked across at him, blinking, knowing she should be angry but too dazed with pain and fear, only to find that his attention was all on Rostov.

"And where is the animal now?"

McClain smiled, a slow and mocking smile that made Rostov's lips tighten.

"Where is Puff now, Clara?" McClain was looking over at her with a kind of triumph in his eyes. Rostov's eyes followed his. Clara felt her heart lurch as those merciless pale blue eyes pinned her. He would hurt her again. . . .

"The pound. They took him to the pound," she gasped.

"Where?"

"At Camp Lejeune."

Rostov uttered another short Russian curse and turned to Malik. "Tell them to stop."

Malik pulled a walkie-talkie out of his pocket and said something into it in Russian. A moment later the truck was pulling off the road and coming to a stop. Rostov turned back to McClain.

"For your sake I hope you are telling the truth. If I go to the quite considerable trouble of extracting an animal from an impoundment office and there is no microfilm I will be most unhappy. And if I am unhappy, I fear I will vent my feelings on Miss Winston here first. Perhaps I will present her with a necklace. Like all women, you like necklaces, eh, Miss Winston? But not, I think, the kind I have in mind. You see, we take a small rubber tire and soak it in gasoline, then put it over your head so that it imprisons your arms. Then we give you a cigarette to smoke. Sooner or later an ash falls, the tire ignites, and you are burned alive." Rostov smiled as Clara paled. She had no doubt at all that he would do just as he threatened. "Think well about that, Miss Winston, while I am gone. If I return without that which I seek, that is how your life will end."

He turned, saying something in Russian to Malik. Malik in turn said something into the walkie-talkie. A few seconds later the van's door rolled up. Rostov turned to look at McClain.

"I will be back, Dragon," he said, and then jumped down onto the road. Malik and Orlov followed him. The door rumbled shut. Clara heard a clang as it was locked from the outside. For a moment she stayed where she was as the van once again got under way, unable to believe that they had gone. She was reprieved, no matter how temporarily. Then she saw McClain's bare feet beside her and realized that he was standing over her.

"Clara . . ." He hunkered down beside her. With his hands still cuffed behind his back, he couldn't touch her, but his voice was rough with concern. She lifted her head. Her teary eyes traveled over the broad chest and wide shoulders clad in soft black cotton; they touched on the thick neck, jutting chin, narrow mouth, crooked nose, and kept going until they met his eyes . . . His eyes were a dark pine green. She stared into them, saw the hurt that was in them for her, and sobbed. Immediately he was leaning over her, nuzzling her cheek with his lips, rubbing his face against her neck.

"Sh, baby."

"Oh, Jack!" She rose off the floor to press against him, her face burrowing into the hollow between his neck and shoulder, desperate for his warmth, for the solid comfort of touching him. She had been so frightened. Was still so frightened. And she hurt. Sobbing, she huddled against him, trying to get closer yet. He couldn't take her in his arms, but his warmth was all around her. She squirmed against him, her cuffed hands going under the hem of his sweatshirt to entwine in the thick mat of hair on his chest, her mouth open against the skin of his neck. Her eyes closed as she tasted the salt of his skin against her tongue, breathed in the musky scent of man, felt the satin over steel muscularity of him, the hard warmth of his chest. She needed him so much that she wanted to absorb him through her skin. Shivering, she leaned against him and cried, her tears trickling down his neck, glistening against his bronzed skin.

SWEET SAVAGE

XVIII

"Clara."

She sobbed, hiccupped, and pressed her face harder into the warmth of his neck. His voice threatened to pull her back to reality. Closing her eyes tightly, she resisted. He moved slightly, his mouth nuzzling the hair out of her face to rest against her forehead.

"Clara. Baby, stop crying. Come on."

"No." It was a resentful mutter. His mouth nuzzled her forehead again.

"Please, sweetheart. We've got things to do before Rostov gets back. We've got to make sure he can't hurt you again."

"You can't stop him." Her voice was muffled against his skin. Another hiccup punctuated the words.

"I can try. Come on, Clara, dry up, will you please? We don't have time for this. Besides, I'm uncomfortable as hell. My legs have fallen asleep."

This bit of trivia had the effect he desired. Clara lifted her head, looked up to find his face so close that she could make out every black whisker, every pore in his bronzed skin. Shakily, her hands against his chest, she pushed herself a little away from him, aware suddenly of the shooting pain in her hand where Orlov had broken her finger, the stinging of the burn beneath her ear.

"My hand hurts." Brought back to reality, she was also brought back to pain. She stared down at her hand. The little finger was shades of purple and swollen to three times its normal size; it stuck out from her palm at a forty-five degree angle.

"I know it does. I can make it better. Just hold on for a couple more minutes. Don't faint on me, baby."

Clara felt herself swaying, felt the blood drain from her face. The inside of the van seemed to swirl around her. She thought hazily that she needed to lie down. Then, like a flower left too long without water, she wilted, and lay panting on her side on the floor.

"Clara!" He was beside her, bending over her. She blinked up at him, saw his mouth tighten. Her eyelids flickered down.

"You've got to stay with me, baby. Just a little longer. Do you hear?"

He was speaking very slowly and distinctly, as if he was afraid she might not be able to understand him. Clara looked up at him, her brow wrinkling. She supposed she must be going into shock. Her eyes closed, shutting him out. Her every instinct clamored for sleep. Sleep was escape. . . .

"Clara." There was an urgency to his voice, a leashed frustration to his movements that were hampered by his chained hands. Against her will, she felt herself being pulled back from the edge of blessed unconsciousness. She was in pain, frightened, and exhausted. All she wanted was to go to sleep. But he was not going to let her escape.

"Clara. Don't go to sleep. There's something that I need

for you to do." He leaned closer, his breath warm against her cheek as he spoke almost directly into her ear. "When Rostov hit me with that rifle and I fell down, I managed to pull the keys to the handcuffs from Thompson's pocket. Do you hear me, Clara? I have the keys to the handcuffs."

"You don't." Clara's words were slurred. It was all she could do to think at all. "They searched you. They would have found them."

"I dropped them on that pile of moving pads just inside the door. They didn't see me. I knew they would search us. Come on, Clara. I need your help to get these handcuffs off. Rostov probably won't be back for a while, but we can't take that chance. We have to do it *now*."

It took the words a few minutes to penetrate the fog surrounding her. Then Clara felt a sudden tiny prickling of hope. She struggled to suppress it. To hope was too painful. It would just make her suffering worse when Rostov got back.

"Get up, Clara."

He wasn't going to let her go to sleep. She turned her head, blinking at him resentfully, trying to marshal the words to tell him how hopeless it all was. But before she could put them together in her dazed mind, he leaned over and kissed her, hard and quick, on the mouth.

"You are a pain in the ass, Clara Winston." The words were rueful, affectionate, exasperated. He clambered to his feet and stood over her, nudging her thigh with his bare toes. She liked his toes, she decided, looking at them with detachment. Long, narrow toes with a tiny tuft of black hair on the largest attached to long, narrow feet. Nice.

"Clara, stand up!" There was no affection in his voice now. It was hard, the words a command. Clara flinched, looking up into his eyes almost fearfully. He sounded too much like the men who had done this to her. Hard, uncaring men who liked inflicting pain.

"Did you hear me?" The edge to his voice made her whimper. His eyes narrowed, hardened. Clara felt nausea rise in her stomach. The brutal voice penetrated. Moving slowly, awkwardly, she stood up. For a moment everything swam around her; she was afraid she might fall down again. He swore, moving behind her, helpless to hold her up if she should fall. His cuffed hands twitched impotently.

"Don't you dare faint on me now!" The words were a fierce order. "Damn it, I don't know about you, but I refuse to just lie here and die, and you're going to help me! Do you understand?"

His harsh voice cleared some of the cobwebs that swirled through her mind. Clara nodded, and her head cleared a little more.

"All right, Jack. What do you want me to do?" Her very docility was unnatural, she sensed, but he wasn't arguing.

"The keys are somewhere in that pile of pads." He indicated a jumbled heap of quiltlike furniture pads in the rear corner. "You'll have to dig through them and then unlock my handcuffs. That's all you have to do. I'll take it from there."

Clara nodded. Anything to keep him happy, she told herself, so that he wouldn't yell at her. She could not take any more violence. It was hard to walk with her head swimming and the truck jouncing over potholes and around turns, but she made it to the pile of pads. Then, gritting her teeth against the pain that even the slightest movement brought, she began to pull the pads off the pile one by one. Finally, with a jingle, the key ring clattered into view. Another tiny prickle of hope awoke within her. This time she let it flicker.

Bending carefully so as not to jar her hand, she picked up the keys and turned to McClain. He nodded his approval.

"Good girl. Now unlock these." He turned his back to her. It took Clara a few moments and a few false tries to find the right key, and a few more false tries before she got it to click open the lock, but at last she did. The cuffs came off. He turned, rubbing his wrists, and reached for her. She went into his arms without thought, as though it was the most natural thing in the world. As though she belonged there. She felt a pressure against the top of her head and wondered if it was his lips. Looking up, she saw that his jaw was set and his eyes were that familiar brilliant green.

"Now at least we can give Rostov a run for his money," he said, his eyes glowing. Danger excited him, exhilarated him, she remembered. He got high off it, just like some people did off drugs.

"You're crazy," she muttered with conviction. He leaned down and kissed her mouth hard.

"I'm sorry I got you into this. Sorry you got hurt. Sorry I didn't stop the bastard sooner." Her head was tucked into the hollow of his neck now; the words were muttered into her hair. Clara nestled closer, forgetting everything but the security he offered. A stab of pure agony shot from her broken finger. She moaned, stepping back from him, cradling her injured hand. Her finger was aching terribly, so badly that it made her stomach heave. She felt dizzy again, and leaned her head forward to rest it against McClain's chest. His hands came up to grasp her shoulders in quick concern.

"You need to lie down, don't you? Let's get these things off first." He was unlocking her handcuffs as he spoke, gently easing them off her wrists so as not to hurt her more than he had to. Hurriedly he piled a few of the pads into a

makeshift bed next to the wall, then swept her up in his
arms and carried her over to it, staggering a little with the
motion of the truck. She mewled a tiny protest as he laid her
down, and he apologized with a quick kiss on her lips.
Folding a pad under her head like a pillow and covering her
with another, careful not to touch her injured hand which
rested on top of the quilt, he made her as comfortable as he
could. Then he smoothed the hair out of her face, straightened, and moved away.

Clara watched him as he prowled around the trailer,
checking the door to be sure it was locked, testing the
strength of the walls and corners, looking at the miscellaneous items lying around the floor. Besides the rusty looking
generator, which must have once graced somebody's farmhouse, and the pads, there were other typical movers' items:
a pair of dollies, ropes, a couple of empty boxes, and a
small fire extinguisher. There was also half a case of warm
beer. McClain lugged it over to where Clara lay on the
pallet of quilted pads, fished a beer out of the case, popped
its top, and held it out to her.

"Drink up."

Clara shook her head, unmoving. "I don't like beer."

"Now why did I guess that, I wonder?" He shook his
head at her. "A lady to the bitter end, aren't you, baby?
Will you please, as a favor to me, drink this beer? You'll
feel better, I promise you."

Before she could answer he was settling himself behind
her and propping her against his shoulder, then holding the
can to her lips. Clara could either drink or drown. She
drank, gasping and choking as the liquid came too fast. But
when he let her come up for air she had to admit she did
feel a little better. Warmer, more aware, if a little woozy.

"I told you," he said when she admitted as much. She

didn't even feel like glaring at him. Having him take care of her was too comforting. As long as he cosseted her she could pretend everything was nearly normal. That they weren't going to die when Rostov returned.

"Let me fix your finger for you, baby. I know it must hurt like hell. I can make it better if you'll trust me."

Those two little words set off warning bells in her brain, but she ignored them. When he settled her back down in her bed of pads and told her not to look, she obediently put her good arm across her face. When she felt him gently take her injured hand in his, she let him. Even when she felt his fingers probing her injured pinky while his other hand encircled her wrist she made no protest. Then he repaid her trust by grabbing the end of her poor broken finger and jerking with all his might. The pain was so excruciating that she screamed. And then at last she fainted.

"I'm so sorry, so sorry I had to hurt you," he was whispering to her, cradling her in his arms when she started the slow swim back to consciousness. "Poor sweetheart, poor baby, poor little girl. . . ."

"I am not," Clara said, revolted, "a poor little girl."

He lifted his head a little to look down at her. The smallest glimmer of a smile quivered at the corners of his mouth.

"No, you're not, are you? I beg your pardon," he said gravely, then bent to press a quick kiss on her soft lips. He disentangled himself, got to his feet and reached for another beer. Hunkering down beside her, he popped the top, then took a long swallow himself before offering it to her. Clara didn't even argue this time. She drank thirstily. Her mother might swear that ladies never, but never, drank beer, but she didn't suppose that any ladies of her mother's acquaintance had ever found themselves in a situation quite like this one.

"My finger doesn't hurt quite so much," she said, discovering that she could move her hand without a shaft of agony jolting her clear down to her toes.

"I had paramedic training in the marines. It's almost as good as new. See?"

Her eyes followed his to her hand. He had fashioned a makeshift splint out of the stiff cardboard of the beer case and a soft maroon strip wound with an inch-wide section of white elastic, both of which reminded her forcibly of his underwear. She touched the funny looking bandage with a tentative finger.

"Yours?" she asked, looking up at him. He grinned a little.

"Sacrificed to a good cause. How does that burn feel? I don't have anything to put on it, but it doesn't look too bad."

"It stings a little, but I'll live." As soon as she said it, she wished she hadn't. The truck was still lumbering through the North Carolina countryside, but it had to stop sooner or later. And when it did, Rostov would rejoin them, and despite McClain's increased mobility they would die. Even McClain was no match for five gorillas armed with rifles.

"We're going to die, aren't we?" She started shivering violently.

"No, we damned well are not. We're going to get out of this with our skins intact and live to laugh about the whole damn thing." But his very vehemence told her that he was as uncertain as she. Her shivers intensified. The thought of what Rostov would do to her—to them—when he returned was too terrifying to contemplate.

"Hold me, Jack," she whispered, scrambling onto her knees as she reached for him. His arms went around her and he cradled her against him, his hands stroking her back, his bristly cheek pressed against the softness of her own.

"Listen to me," he said. "We're going to get out of this."

But she was beyond listening. She was beyond anything but an urgent need to affirm that she was alive. That she could smell and taste and touch and see and hear and feel . . . Her shivers intensified until she was quaking in his arms, her body pressed to his from knees to chest. Her hands burrowed beneath his sweatshirt to find the heat of his skin, pushing the shirt up and over his head in her greediness to absorb his warmth so that his movements were hampered by the cloth that stretched from elbow to elbow. She was mindless now, acting solely on instinct; primitive instinct intent on affirming her body's life-force.

Her open mouth ran along his neck, down through the curling black thatch on his chest, over his hard stomach to the waistband of his jeans. She nuzzled her face lower, pressing her mouth against his crotch, biting at the swelling bulge she could feel straining against the stiff blue denim. He jerked, sucking in his breath. She didn't stop, couldn't stop. Her hands were urgent, tugging at his snap, working down his zipper so that his manhood fell free, unconfined by the underwear he had sacrificed to bind her finger, huge and hot and pulsing and alive. She took it in her mouth, cupping the soft sacs beneath with hands that shook, rubbing and stroking and caressing the twin roundnesses while her lips and teeth and tongue staked their claim to his shaft.

"For God's sake, Clara . . ." He was kneeling; her head was in his lap as she crouched in front of him. Unable to fend her off with the shirt tethering his arms, he tried to rise. Her teeth sank into him viciously, making him yelp and sink back. Then she pushed him hard, turned into a feral creature with her need to affirm life, to keep the darkness of fear away. He sprawled backward, unable to save himself without the use of his hands. Immediately she was over him, tugging at his open jeans, pulling them down around his hips as her mouth once again found and claimed him. This time he didn't try to stop her. Through the haze that she was lost in she heard the harsh gasps of his breathing, but still she didn't stop. She bit and sucked and kissed and caressed until he was groaning and jerking and needing her as she needed him.

"Ride me, baby. Please. Ride me." The hoarse plea was accompanied by urgent movements of his pelvis. Clara ran her tongue up the length of him one last time, then sat back on her heels to survey her victim. With his shirt binding his arms and his jeans down around his thighs, he was naked and vulnerable to her. His manhood jutted enormously upright from its nest of black hair, thick and pulsing and wet from her ministrations. She bent her head to kiss it again.

He jerked sideways. Her lips met the furred skin of his belly.

"Ride me, Clara." His voice was hoarse.

She stared at that pulsing shaft, felt an urgency start in her own loins, and straddled him. Her breasts were covered by silk and flannel and wool, but only the flimsiest of silk and lace kept the part of her that needed him most from him. Moving aside the wide lace-edged leg of her teddy, she held him tightly while she settled herself on him. Delicately, so delicately, the hot thick quivering shaft probed, slid inside. He gasped. She gasped. Then she closed her eyes, her muscles clenching, closing around him. He was so big, so hot.

She moaned, her fingers clenching in the hair on his chest, her head thrown back, her muscles contracting. He surged upward, violently, unable or unwilling to let her set the pace any longer. She cried out, riding him, her movements matching his, her urgency matching his. She needed him, needed him, needed him. . . .

When the release came it was an explosion. Her nails dug into his chest, her neck arched, and she cried out as exquisite convulsions claimed her. He cried out too, pushed over the edge by her ecstasy, his hips coming up off the floor as he ground himself inside her. When it was over, she collapsed limply on his chest. Beneath her ear she could hear the pounding of his heart.

"God in heaven," he said after a moment, his eyes still closed. "If that didn't kill me nothing will."

The fervent mutter brought her back to awareness. She became abruptly conscious of her position, sprawled across his lap, naked flesh still pressed to naked flesh. The haze of fear was crowding in on her again. It was hard to remember exactly what she had done. She had a feeling that, under normal circumstances, she would be mortified beyond bearing by the wantonness of her actions. But confronted with her own helplessness in the face of pain and death, she could not worry about such things as pride. She just wanted to stay alive.

"I'm scared," she whispered forlornly, starting to shiver again. His eyes opened, dark as pine forests as they rested on her face.

"Don't be scared," he said swiftly, sitting up with her still atop him and pulling his shirt back over his head. Then he rolled with her onto the pallet, careful of her injuries, and lay with her wrapped in his arms, her head pillowed on his chest. "It doesn't do any good at all. The best you can do is just concentrate on how you feel this moment, and let what happens later take care of itself."

Clara thought about that, thought about how she felt at that moment with his long hard body next to hers and his arms around her and his breath in her hair, with the memory of their passion in her heart. If she refused to think of what horrors later might bring, she felt warm, cared for, content. Happy.

"Talk to me," she murmured against his chest, enjoying the way the soft hairs tickled her nose. "Tell me everything about Jack McClain. I want to know it all. Please."

"You know most of it," he said after a moment, with an air of humoring her. His hand was stroking almost absently over her back. Her head was resting on his shoulder, her injured hand cradled carefully on his chest. "About how I grew up on a farm with five bossy sisters, and—"

"Did you go to college?" Clara interrupted.

"Yup. Texas Christian University. I was their star quarterback. What about you?"

"I hate football."

"I meant did you go to college."

"Oh. Wesleyan."

"La-de-dah."

"My mother's like that."

"Is she? Stuck up?"

Clara shook her head. "Not stuck up. Just . . . just a lady, I guess. We still have them, you know, in the South. She always knows the right thing to do, does it and looks marvelous all the while. Wesleyan was the right college to go to; her mother went there, she went there, and she wanted me to go there. So I did."

"She sounds formidable as hell. Tell me about her. From the sound of her we don't have anything like her in my neck of the woods."

So Clara told him all about her mother. About the fur

coats and pearls and men she collected like some women collected porcelain. About her four husbands and the current candidate for number five. About the ballet lessons and piano lessons and equestrienne lessons that her mother considered essential to a young lady's education and how hopeless she had been at all of them. About white gloves and white gowns and cotillions. About the battle they'd had over her debut. For the first time in her life Clara had stood up to her mother and flatly refused to be presented at the annual debutantes ball in Richmond. Her mother threw it up to her to this day, insisting that her daughter's stubbornness over the matter was the sole reason she wasn't married at age thirty. About her retreat to the world of books to escape a real world she had never felt quite adequate to cope with, and how her writing had grown from that. About her mother's feelings on her daughter's career: a nice, genteel way to pass the time until she got married. To her mother, marriage was the be-all and end-all of a woman's existence.

"Good God, how do you stand her?" McClain asked wryly when she paused for breath.

Clara shook her head. "It's not a matter of me standing her. It's more like how does she stand me? I certainly wasn't the daughter she was expecting. I'm hopeless at all the things she considers important, and I don't even have an urgent desire to get married. A total washout. But she loves me anyway. And I love her too. We're just . . . different from one another, that's all."

"My mother's not like that at all," he said after a moment. "She never wears any makeup and screws her hair up anyhow and more often than not has a rip in her dress. All the animals on the farm follow her everywhere she goes. So do the grandkids. When I was in Nam and found myself in real trouble, I even caught myself wishing my mother was there. She's a terror in defense of children or animals. I kept thinking that if she were only there she'd take care of those Cong in a second. She'd go to hell barefoot in defense of her baby boy."

"She sounds wonderful." Clara giggled; she supposed the beer had gone straight through her empty stomach to her head. "I can't imagine you as anyone's baby boy."

He chuckled, the sound rich in the darkness. "Hard, isn't it? I only revert when I'm home. Which is probably why I don't go home more often. It's tough being fussed over by six women."

"It sounds tough." Clara was smiling. She felt happy, at peace. If one just thought of the present, it was easy, she found. There was a brief pause, and then Clara bethought herself of something that needed to be said. In case she didn't get another chance.

"Jack."

"Hmm?" He sounded sleepy.

"I want to apologize."

"For what?"

"For not believing in you earlier. For doubting you. I should have known better."

"You should have."

Clara paused again. There was something else she had to know or she had a feeling she would never understand him at all.

"Jack." Her voice was hesitant. "Did you really have some sort of a breakdown? Or was Thompson making that up to get me on his side?"

There was a brief silence. Beneath her head she felt a tenseness in his shoulder. When he spoke his voice was expressionless, carefully even.

"No, he was telling the truth. I spent six months in a hospital about four years ago. I had a breakdown."

He seemed the least likely person in the world to have that kind of problem. Something horrendous must have happened to bring it on—something that he hated to remember even now. She could hear it in the starkness of his voice.

"Can you . . . tell me about it, Jack?"

There was a long silence. She thought he wasn't going to say anything, that he would refuse to talk about it. Then he sighed.

"Why not? I was working undercover in Hungary. There was a cell, a network of agents, spies if you will. My cover was a writing assignment for a national news magazine; I was really supposed to find out who in our organization there was leaking information to the other side. I found and identified the traitor; a supposed student, just as I was a supposed journalist. I reported to my superiors and was told to eliminate him. The rest of the story's a classic. While I was over there I'd met a girl, a beautiful Hungarian named Natalia. She was young and sweet, and I was so in love with her I was planning to take her back to the U.S. with me when I left. I was a deep cover operative, trained to tell no one—no one—what my job in Hungary or wherever really was. But I told Natalia. She had a family, parents whom she loved, brothers and sisters. I wanted to give her a chance to say good-bye. Whenever I left a country it was usually in a hurry, and as I said I planned to take her with me.

"My only excuse—and it's not an excuse, but an explanation for such a lapse in judgment—was that I was drinking a lot then. I'd been going on occasional benders ever since Nam, and the drinking got worse in Hungary; there was damned well nothing else to do, and I thought I could handle it, not let it make a difference to my work.

"I told Natalia the truth the night before I was to carry out the operation. So she'd have just a little time. I was tight. Not drunk, mind you, but tight. Feeling no pain. I loved her, I thought. But pillow talk can kill, and mine was deadly. Of course she had connections with the KGB. She was a goddamn *plant*, because they suspected me. I should have been on to her in five minutes. But I missed all the signs. And there were signs all over the place, I realized later. But I didn't suspect a thing. I went on with the assignment to eliminate Casanova—that was our codename for him. He was a good looking kid with a string of women. I was going to take him out from a window across the street from his flat, nail him with a silencer equipped, high-powered rifle. I got into position and waited. After two hours—the kid was normally as regular as clockwork—it became clear that something had gone wrong. I went to see my contact. He was dead, shot in the head in his flat. The backup man was dead, too. I went to the apartment that served as a meeting place for our cell and found one survivor, a sixteen-year-old kid who'd managed to hide. He told me that the entire cell had either been killed outright or picked up. The ones that were already dead were the lucky ones. The others would be tortured to death. I knew I had to get out of there fast if we'd been betrayed. There'd be time to deal with the traitor later. I went back to my own flat. Natalia was there. She confessed everything, laughing at my gullibility, and then the knock sounded at the door. The bitch had set me up all the way around. I went out a window while she ran to let the goons in. I managed to save my ass, but a lot of the good guys had gone down because of me. Then Hammersmith—he was my superior officer—found out that Natalia had betrayed us. He was going to have her taken out. I lied, told him I'd already done it. I couldn't stand the idea of any more killing because I'd screwed up. Hammersmith believed me. But the guilt ate at me, and I went on the mother and father of all benders as soon as they had me safely back in Berlin. While I was drinking, I vowed to get my own revenge on Natalia sooner or later. Then it occurred to me: I was the real traitor. I'd gone against my training and compromised my contacts. Then I went a little crazy. I think I believed I could wipe out the whole KGB singlehandedly. I sure as hell tried. The agency rounded me up, hustled me into a sanitorium, dried me out, shrank my head a little, and when I got out gave me a job. A desk job. That's all they were willing to trust me with, and I don't blame them. Once a traitor, always a traitor, they say.

"That was four years ago. Then Yuropov, whom I had known some years before, defected. He asked for me, Hammersmith, who had also been reassigned to a desk job on the strength of my screwup, vouched for me, and they gave him to me. And now this." He broke off, shook his head. "Christ, when you're hot, you're hot."

That feeble attempt at humor told Clara more than any amount of soul baring could have how much he still despised himself for what had happened. She took his hand and held it to her breast in wordless comfort. There was nothing she could say to ease his pain, she knew.

"I'm glad you told me," she said finally.

"Yeah."

"I think you're pretty wonderful." The words came out of nowhere. Clara wasn't even sure that she meant them. But the urge was strong in her to offer him what solace she could.

"Go to sleep." From the sound of his response, he didn't think she meant them either. Clara hesitated, wondering if she should say something else, try to ease the tension she felt in him. But what could she say? There was no solace she could offer for his particular brand of bruised and battered soul.

"Only God never makes a mistake, Jack," she whispered. He didn't even bother to reply.

XIX

He sat through the night, wide awake, thinking. The truck had stopped, but no one had attempted to enter the trailer. They probably had orders to wait for Rostov to return. McClain half smiled. It would take a while for Rostov to discover that Puff was not in the pound. And when he did, he was going to get very, very angry. But it wouldn't matter even if he did find the cat. Because there was no microfilm to be found on the furball.

Oh, it had been there, all right. He had hidden it in Puff's blue vinyl collar during that miserable night spent in the log in the woods. It had occurred to him while he was lying there sleepless, sneezing his head off, that if he were caught and searched, and the microfilm found, that would be the end of the story right there. There were lots of places he could have hidden it—forests are full of hiding places—but he preferred to keep it close at hand in case he should need it in a hurry. For a moment he had thought about hiding it on Clara without telling her, but he'd decided against that almost instantly. Of course, if they were taken, they would search her too. Then his eyes had lit on the furball, and the perfect solution had occurred to him. The cat's collar was rolled and stitched blue vinyl, presumably fairly waterproof, a perfect size and the last place anyone would look. It had taken some doing and a badly scratched hand to separate the cat from his collar, but McClain, with what he modestly considered real heroism, had done it, sneezing all the while. Then he had slit the end of the collar open, tucked the microfilm inside the narrow tube, pushed it as far down as he could with the aid of the screwdriver, and replaced the collar around the spitting fury's neck. Voila! And if Rostov or anyone had ever found it there he would have kissed their fannies for them.

The microfilm was in Ramsey's hands now. The general was strictly a by-the-book military man, which McClain never had been, but he was known to have an almost fatherly feeling for those who had ever served under him. McClain had realized almost at once that Ramsey was his best, and possibly his last, shot at getting someone to listen to him before he got his head blown off, as seemed all too likely. So as Clara had been led away he had requested private speech with the general in the interests of national security. And Ramsey, bless his paternalistic heart, had heeded the call of the old outfit and granted his request, posting an armed guard outside his office door but otherwise seemingly content to meet alone with the crazy McClain knew he'd been made out to be.

Not that Ramsey had believed his story, of course. That would have been too much to ask. But he'd listened without interruptions, then asked about proof. Which was when McClain had made the gamble of his life and told him about the microfilm. The general had barked an order over the telephone, and after a wait of about fifteen minutes the cat had been brought in. Puff was wrapped in a blanket so that only his head showed, but he was hissing and spitting like a demon straight from Hell. The young marine who carried him in looked like he thought he had a man-eating tiger by the tail. Which, McClain thought as the bundle was dumped on his lap with an air of relief by the young man, who saluted and hurriedly retreated, was exactly what he had. Puff was no ordinary pussy. Having learned to move fast and ruthlessly with the furball, McClain just managed to get the collar over Puff's head before he erupted from the blanket with as much fire and fury as Mount Saint Helen's. As Puff tore around the general's office like a dervish with claws before winding up crouched on top of one of a set of built-in walnut bookcases, hissing at the world, McClain succumbed to a violent fit of sneezing.

"Here, kitty." The general went to stand under the bookcase while McClain worked to extricate the microfilm, which he finally managed to do by slitting open the entire collar with the aid of Ramsey's letter opener. When at last he had the capsule containing the tiny roll of film in his hand, the general had coaxed Puff down from the bookcase and was holding him on his lap, stroking his head. As McClain gaped, Puff, who had been purring under Ramsey's ministrations, looked across the desk at him and hissed.

"I don't think he likes you," General Ramsey said with some humor.

"He hates me," McClain said, eyeing Puff with revulsion. "And I'm not too crazy about him, either."

"Ah, animals can always sense the way you feel about them. I'm a cat man, myself. Always did like them."

"He obviously likes you," McClain said. Puff's acceptance of the general's touch did more to elevate Ramsey in his mind than any of the heroics he had heard the man had performed on the field of battle. Any man who could coax a purr out of that benighted feline was a miracle worker, no less. McClain's respect for his former C.O. soared to new heights.

"So, did you find it?" Despite the enormous gray cat rumbling on his lap, the general was suddenly all business. By way of an answer, McClain held out his hand. The yellow and red capsule rested in his palm. Ramsey reached over and picked it up between his thumb and forefinger, then separated the two sides of the capsule. The miniscule roll of film fell out.

"By damn!" Ramsey sounded mildly surprised. He picked up his phone again and spoke through it, presumably to his secretary.

"Marge, get Captain Spencer in here, would you please? On the double." He put the phone down and looked over at McClain. "Spencer's a good man. I'd trust him with my life. I'll have him check this out."

McClain said nothing, just sat in the chair across the general's desk and waited. Ramsey had not been asking his permission to give the microfilm to Captain Spencer; he had merely been telling him that he intended to do so. He had handed the ball off to Ramsey now; it was up to Ramsey to run with it.

When Captain Spencer entered after a brief knock, McClain had known instantly why this was the general's assistant. Captain Spencer was spit-and-polish from the jaunty hat he carried under one arm to the shine on his shoes. Fortyish, with a balding head and a stocky but compact build, Captain Spencer was the quintessential marine.

"Davey, I want this microfilm looked at so we can see what's what with it. Also, check it for prints and anything else that might help us identify where it's come from. And do it yourself, Davey. It's top-secret, and I don't want anyone else outside the three of us in this room to have the slightest notion that the thing even exists. Got it?''

''Yes, sir.'' Captain Spencer saluted, took the microfilm from the general and tucked it carefully into his breast pocket.

''Be as quick as you can, Davey.''

''Yes, sir.'' The captain saluted and turned to leave. When he was nearly at the door, the general stopped him.

''Oh, and send someone over to the PX to get some Tender Vittles, would you? This kitty looks like he's hungry.''

Captain Spencer didn't blink an eye, just saluted and was on his way.

When he was gone, Ramsey set Puff on the desk and stood up. Puff swished his tail and fixed baleful eyes on McClain. McClain did his best to ignore the smug looking cat, succeeding admirably except for the sneezing he couldn't control as he rose to his feet along with the general.

''I imagine it will take Captain Spencer an hour or so. I will have someone show you to a room where you can shower and rest. A meal will be provided as well.''

''Yes, sir.'' The military training fell over his shoulders like a cloak. Like riding a bicycle, McClain thought with wry amusement. He even found himself saluting as the general left the room, Puff tucked securely under one arm.

The microfilm provided all that Yuropov had promised it would: names, dates, places of operations compromised by Bigfoot; agency operatives revealed; codes mysteriously breached.

''Pretty damning,'' Ramsey said two hours later as he stared through the scratchy, glaring field of the microfilm lens. ''Not a doubt that the agency's got a leak somewhere. The question is where? Who?''

''Yuropov said that Bigfoot was at the highest level,

general. It's clear from the scope of information here that that's true."

"Begging your pardon, sir, but if what Mr. McClain has told us about Bigfoot checks out, then it stands to reason that his information about a plot against the secretary of state is also legitimate. Shouldn't we get on the horn and warn Washington?" Captain Spencer's words were urgent.

"I've already done so," General Ramsey replied, his eyes still on the microfilm. "Went right through the head of the Joint Chiefs. Nick Segram and I were at Annapolis together. He'll get the word to the secretary of state. Privately. No one else is to know."

"That doesn't mean that the hit won't still go down." All the extra security precautions in the world were little protection against a man with a high-powered rifle, as McClain well knew. Providing, of course, that that man was prepared to sacrifice his own life for the good of the Cause. And they couldn't assume that whoever was charged with hitting the secretary of state wasn't prepared to do just that.

"No, I realize that. But warning the secretary himself was the obligatory first step. From what you tell us, McClain, we can't even trust our own Central Intelligence Agency with this. Which means that the little group of people who have proven they can be trusted—you, me, Captain Spencer here, and Nick Segram—are going to have to come up with a solution outside the usual intelligence channels. I have a call in to the White House. I expect to bring the president in on this. I am assuming we can trust *him*."

From the sudden jocularity in Ramsey's tone, McClain recognized that this was an attempt at a joke. He smiled halfheartedly. The little band of freedom fighters Ramsey had named sounded pitifully small when he considered that they were pitted against the vast resources of the KGB. But looking at old Wild Bill and Davey Spencer, McClain decided that they'd do. *Semper Fidelis.* To their backbones. Always faithful. As was he, whether he wanted to be or not. McClain grimaced to himself. Old marines never died. They just grunted away in different mudholes.

"In addition to the safety of the secretary of state, we must also give the highest priority to identifying Bigfoot. I would like to run this information through Big Floyd, sir. If I can access it," Captain Spencer said to General Ramsey.

"My plan exactly," McClain said, surprised into admiration. There was more to this spit-and-polish captain than appeared on the surface, apparently. Big Floyd was a widely known secret, but it was still a secret and not one that the average marine officer should be aware of. He regarded Spencer with some respect. "And I think I can get in, with the help of your modems."

"And how do you intend to do that, I wonder?" General Ramsey asked with a fleeting grin. "No, don't tell me. I don't want to know what lawless act you're planning. You are in a peck of trouble already, McClain. Everyone from the police departments of fifty states to the FBI to the National Guard to the CIA to the KGB wants a piece of your ass for everything from car theft to mass murder. Are you going to add breaking and entering a computer to the list?"

"You only live once, sir."

Ramsey laughed and agreed. McClain worked with Davey Spencer all through the night trying out different combinations of access codes. Finally they broke in. An hour later they had what they wanted. The list of individuals who had had access to every piece of information that Bigfoot had passed on was narrowed down to five: Tim Hammersmith, who was dead and thus effectively eliminated; Eugene Matlock, head of Counterintelligence; Oliver Simonis, deputy director of the agency itself; Brandt Rowe, head of the Consular Operations within the agency; and Michael Ball, retired director of the CIA, who nevertheless still received weekly briefings on everything in which the agency was involved. And of course, as McClain sourly observed, he could add to that the entire Senate Intelligence Committee and the president and his key aides. Not more than two dozen or so, although as Spencer pointed out the five names selected specifically by Big Floyd were the most likely candidates.

"I was going to take this to Michael Ball," McClain said, frowning over the list.

"Good thing we brought you down, then," Spencer said cheerily, punching one last command into the enormous computer which ran the length of the room. At that early hour of the morning Camp Lejeune's computer center was almost deserted. General Ramsey had ordered everyone out and posted a guard outside the door as McClain and Spencer worked. When summoned at last, after the two finally hit paydirt, General Ramsey was impressed with the speed and efficiency with which the computer spewed out information. He was a secretary and typewriter man himself, he said. McClain barely managed a grimace at the joke. He was dead on his feet.

Finally it had been agreed that things must go forward just as they would have if McClain had not convinced General Ramsey of the truth of what was happening. If the KGB got wind that their plot was coming unglued they would bury Bigfoot so deep that it would take years to find him. The plan was to keep up the pretense that everyone accepted wholeheartedly the story that McClain had gone off his rocker. So he was to leave Camp Lejeune in the morning; General Ramsey had already been notified that an escort of agents was arriving to conduct the prisoner back to Langley. McClain would be assisted to escape before he got there— Ramsey was working out the details of that with Nick Segram—and then he would be brought back to Camp Lejeune in the greatest secrecy where he would assist in the identification of Bigfoot. Rostov, meanwhile, would be scouring the country for McClain, but Bigfoot would have no idea that McClain was anything more than a hunted fugitive and thus would consider himself safe. And therefore would be far easier to expose.

But it hadn't worked out that way. McClain shook his head wryly at his own naiveté at imagining it would. Wishful thinking, he supposed. He'd done a hell of an acting job with Knebel and Thompson if he did say so himself, playing the reluctant prisoner desperate to convince a skeptical audience of the truth of what he said. They would report everything to their superiors, he knew. Hell, there had probably been a tape recorder in the car. All so Bigfoot wouldn't get suspicious. And he'd been counting on that escape.

But Bigfoot apparently had an ear in Camp Lejeune as well. McClain told himself that he should have suspected it, should have known that the KGB wouldn't be shaken off so easily. That Rostov might take him from his escort before Ramsey's men could liberate him had occurred to nobody. The only comfort was that the Soviets apparently didn't know that he had passed the microfilm on to Ramsey. If they had, he and Clara would already be dead. Even Rostov, sadist that he was, would not go through this charade if he already knew that McClain could not give him what he wanted.

A rattle sounded outside the trailer's garage-type door. Speak of the devil, McClain thought, tensing as he was brought back to the present with a start. But apparently one of the thugs who had stayed with the truck just wanted to make sure that the door was still securely locked. If Rostov were back he would have burst in, murderously angry at having failed to find Puff. But the door stayed closed.

When Rostov returned, they would have just one chance to take the bastard off guard, and a slim one at that. And it was all they would have. McClain knew suddenly that he wanted it to work. Wanted it with a desperation he hadn't felt about anything in years. And the reason he wanted it to work so badly was for Clara far more than himself. He had been playing Russian roulette with death for years. Dying wasn't anything he courted, but it came with the territory. But Clara—he couldn't stand watching Clara suffer. He thought of how Rostov had had her finger broken, of how he'd burned her, of how he'd humiliated and terrorized her, and he felt a fierce anger burn in his gut. Rostov would pay for that.

Talking to Clara earlier had been a mistake. It had opened him up to emotions he'd kept buried for four years, buried deep beneath carefully built layers of indifference. Natalia's face swam in his mind's eye. He didn't want to remember Natalia, whose dark hair and pretty smiles had blinded him to a murderous bitch. Deliberately he banished her image. Gloria's face immediately rose to replace it. He hadn't loved Gloria, just lusted after her body, but he had never meant to get her killed. But he had thought she was safe enough. When he had started seeing her he had been a desk jockey, for God's sake. He'd had no idea that he would get mixed up in something that would cost her her life. Always assuming Rostov was telling the truth about that, of course. The KGB was a past master at playing head games.

Now there was Clara, sleeping warmly at his side. She

trusted him, more fool she. He had an idea she still thought
he could get her out of this in one piece. She had more
confidence in him than he did in himself. But he would do
his damnedest to succeed—for her sake.

Damn the woman, she appealed to him! He liked everything about her, from her sassy mouth to her gentle blue
eyes to her Southern belle manner to her sexy body. He
liked the way she smiled, her fierce loyalty to her cat, the
way she said Oh my God like it was the worst epithet ever
invented when she thought she was in trouble. He liked her
femininity and her courage under fire. In a pinch, she had
never once let him down. He'd discovered that there was an
awful lot of steel in this particular magnolia.

And he liked making love to her. In fact, he loved making
love to her. And that worried him, now that he thought
about it. His taste usually ran to what his mother would call
fast women. And Clara was far from that. Clara was a lady.
At least until he got her in the sack. Then she was as hot as
any female he'd had. And she got him hot, too. Randy as a
ram. Horny as a goat. In bed, that lady was no lady. His
mind boggled at the saying that brought to mind. And there
was another one, too. One about the ideal wife being a lady
in the parlor and a whore in the bedroom. In that respect,
Clara would certainly make a hell of a wife.

The very notion of himself with a wife appalled him. All
right, he liked Clara. More than liked her if he was honest.
And she turned him on. But that was a far cry from
marriage. Marriage wasn't in his game plan. Since Natalia's
betrayal, he'd never met a woman he could imagine himself
living with for the rest of his life. He'd decided that he just
wasn't cut out for marriage, for a normal family life. He had
to live free.

But she felt good nestling against him, her body soft and

trusting. He felt good holding her. And she'd been very sweet when he'd confessed to her the darkest secret of his life, which was something he'd never talked about to anyone but the shrinks at the hospital. Only God never makes a mistake, she'd said. He hadn't answered her then. Now the words came back to lodge in his mind. Was it possible, that after all these years, he could let the dead go? Write it all off as exactly what it had been, a misjudgment on his part, a tragic mistake?

Maybe, just maybe, if he got out of this alive, he'd think about that some more. Right now there didn't seem much point in forgiving himself. It was far more important to figure out a plan that would give them at least a chance of getting out of this mess alive. He was no Superman; hell, he wasn't even close. He'd have to outmaneuver five KGB agents armed with Kalashnikov rifles, Skorpion machine pistols, and God only knew what else, all in the confines of a ten-by-thirty-foot trailer. Completely impossible. The odds were maybe five billion to one against success. If he were smart he'd probably give up the fight right now, strangle Clara in her sleep to save her from what Rostov and his apes would do to her when they returned, and then hang himself from that hook in the ceiling. Death wasn't so horrible, he knew. It was the dying that was the bad part.

Clara stirred beside him. He looked down at her, at her lovely face flushed with sleep, her tousled blonde hair, her voluptuous body that turned him on even now, just looking at it. His eyes touched on the small circular burn beneath her ear and then traveled to the ridiculous bandage on her hand. He remembered how sick and helpless and at the same time blindingly furious he'd felt when they'd hurt her and she'd cried . . .

A rush of protectiveness so strong that it amazed him

flooded his veins. She did not deserve this. He had gotten her into this mess and it was up to him to rescue her—if he could. Easing his shoulder out from under her head, McClain shook his head at himself. Lost cause or not, he would put everything he had into saving her life.

Who had ever said he was smart?

XX

"Clara. Wake up!"

The urgency of the whisper penetrated her warm, cozy fog of sleep. Clara surfaced reluctantly. For some reason she wasn't yet aware of, her mind did not want to rouse itself.

"Clara!"

The voice that was whispering in her ear was male, and familiar. Its deep rasp sent an anticipatory tingle down her nerve endings. She associated pleasure with that voice . . . Her eyes blinked open to find brilliant green eyes not more than six inches away. Jack. Of course, Jack. She smiled with sleepy invitation into those eyes, noticing with purely female satisfaction how they darkened to emerald. Of its own accord, her hand rose to touch his stubbled cheek. Not much more than twelve hours after he had shaved, he already had a thick growth of black bristles covering his cheeks and jaw. Stroking lightly over the sandpaper roughness, Clara decided that the Miami Vice look became him. It enhanced the rugged, vibrant maleness that was as much a part of him as the green eyes.

"What are you trying to do, turn me on?" He caught her

hand as it dreamily stroked his face and carried it to his mouth. His lips were warm on her palm; Clara felt the sweep of his tongue against her skin and shivered. Never had she dreamed that a man's slightest touch could do that to her. Never had she dreamed that her whole body could be set to trembling by one long, sexy look out of a pair of male eyes.

"Kiss me, Jack." Her eyes closed as her lips yearned upwards. She felt heat shoot down to her toes as he obliged, his mouth hot and hard on hers. Then his mouth was withdrawn, and at the same time she felt the sting of a hard slap on her silk covered bottom. Yelping, she started into a sitting position, rubbing the injured portion of her anatomy as she glared at him.

"Get up, sleepyhead. We've got things to do." He was standing over her now, fully dressed even to his sneakers, his fists balled on his hips. Clara looked around, suddenly remembering where they were and what had happened. Had Rostov returned? Of course not. Jack would not be standing there like that if he had.

"Is Rostov back?" The words were wrenched out of her. Maybe he was outside, even now on his way in. Maybe that was why Jack had awakened her.

"Not yet. But we have to get ready for when he does get here. We shouldn't have long to wait."

"Oh my God." Clara moaned. She had been so comfortably asleep, lulled by Jack's solid warmth and reassuring presence, made pleasantly tipsy by the beer. Now she had been dragged awake to face an aching hand, a throbbing burn, a growing sense of embarrassment as she remembered just how she had come to be cuddling so intimately with Jack—good Lord, had she practically raped the man?—and overriding all, the realization that nothing had changed: their lives were still in the deadliest peril.

"Come on, baby, get dressed. I have a plan." Jack reached down and grabbed her good hand. Clara allowed herself to be hauled upright.

"What time is it?"

Jack shook his head. The goons had smashed his watch when they searched him, hoping, she supposed, that the microfilm might be hidden inside it.

"I don't know. But Rostov's been gone about six hours. Which means that it should be about two A.M."

Unspoken between them was the thought that he shouldn't be gone much longer. Clara felt her chest tighten as she picked up her jeans. With her injured finger dressing was awkward, but she managed to struggle into the jeans and boat shoes that Jack had placed beside their makeshift bed. Sliding into one shoe and hopping sideways to put the other on her foot, she discovered Jack's eyes on her. From the expression on his face, he had been watching her dress.

"Nice ass," he said with an exaggerated leer. Clara got her foot in her shoe at last and straightened, eyeing him. He was grinning a little, waiting for her reaction. So he thought he'd put her out of countenance with chauvinistic remarks, did he? She walked over to him, patted the tight little masculine rear she really did admire tremendously, and said gravely, "You too."

He looked so surprised that she had to grin. He grinned back at her, leaned over to kiss her, quick and hard, then straightened.

"Remind me to do something about that smart mouth of yours when we get out of this mess," he said, and then he was all business. As Clara listened to his plan her eyes widened. She couldn't do what he asked—could she?

"Just don't forget how to operate the damned thing. And for God's sake, don't shoot me."

Clara eyed her weapon with strong misgivings. She was supposed to shoot Rostov with *that*? Her heart sank at the very idea. But she had to admit, when pressed by Jack, that she couldn't come up with a better plan. So, heart pounding, she sat back down on the floor of the trailer, furniture pad over her lap to conceal the weapon, a roll of furniture pads next to her in the hope that, for a moment anyway, Rostov might mistake them for Jack. The only thing in their favor was that Rostov would suppose them still to be handcuffed, and the assault Jack had in mind would take him totally by surprise. The details of it even surprised her, and she was rapidly learning the way his mind worked.

Once in position all there was to do was wait. Clara felt herself get more and more frightened, too frightened even to talk. If Jack's plan didn't succeed, the consequences were too terrifying to contemplate. Rostov would be livid, ripe for vengeance. At the thought of what he could do to her Clara felt the familiar nausea start to churn in her stomach. Then she thought of what he had done to her previously. And she realized that whatever happened, unless this plan worked, she would die. And what death could Rostov dream up in vengeance for their attack on him that would be more horrifying than being burned to death by a rubber tire?

Finally, icy calm descended. Her shattered nerves flatly refused to feel. She would do what she had to do, just as Jack would do what he had to do. Both their roles were vital to the operation's success. Operation. The word stuck in the track of her mind and was repeated. She was even starting to think like Jack.

"Clara, get ready." The soft warning was hissed from

where Jack was perched high up on the steel door guides. He gave her a quick thumbs up sign.

Clara knew that the showdown was about to begin. The flickering light from the bulb cast eerie shadows on the metal walls. A tremendous tension charged the air.

The click of the door being unlocked shot along her nerve endings like electricity. She was more alert than she had ever been in her life, but still the icy calm held. She would do her part. Her life as well as Jack's was on the line.

The door rumbled open. Rostov heaved himself up, rifle in hand, silhouetted against the deep gray of the moonlit night outside as he straightened, looking around for his prisoners.

"You play a game with me, Dragon." His icy blue eyes found Clara huddled beneath the furniture pad as he spoke. They narrowed. Orlov came up behind him, still on the ground outside, head and upper trunk shadowy but visible as he laid his hand on the floor of the van to heave himself inside.

Overhead there was a crash as McClain's feet slammed into the top of the door. The heavy metal door shot for home with a furious rumble. Orlov jumped back, cursing in Russian as the door clanged shut. Rostov whirled, looking up and shouldering his rifle at the same time. Clara came up off the floor with the fire extinguisher in her hand. She ran toward Rostov, squeezing the lever. Rostov heard her footsteps rushing across the floor and started to swing back around, rifle zeroing in on Clara. Overhead, McClain shouted. Rostov automatically flinched and looked up. White foam spewed over his face. McClain dropped from above, landing square on the Soviet's back. The two went down in a flurry of blows and curses. The rifle went skittering across the metal floor, throwing up a shower of sparks as it went.

Clara scrambled after it. The sounds of a furious fight spurred her on. It was impossible to know who was doing what to whom with her back turned, but Clara knew that it would be a fight to the death. She had to help Jack—and herself. All her life she had thought of herself as a coward; well, here was the true test.

The sounds of blows accompanied by grunts and groans punctuated her desperate search for the rifle. Where had the damned thing gone? A furious banging on the door from the goons outside told her that Jack's plan to lock the door by snapping a handcuff through one of the holes on the guide after kicking the door closed had worked. Orlov and Malik and the others could not get in—for the moment.

She found the rifle at last, its barrel protruding from beneath the generator. Fishing it out, she lifted it, surprised at its weight and the cold solidity of it in her hand, and turned. The men were flopping around on the floor like landed fish. Rostov had Jack in a headlock; Jack was punching Rostov's kidneys. Blood spattered both distorted faces. Their expressions were murderous. Each was out to kill. She had to do something; there was no one else. Jack might win or he might not. It would be foolish to take that chance. Lifting the rifle to her shoulder, pointing its ugly black mouth at the twisting, grunting, gouging pair on the floor, she walked forward until she was only a few feet away. Then she stopped. It occurred to her that Rostov might seize the chance to try to grab the rifle away from her, and that would be disastrous. For a moment she stood irresolute. What should she do? They paid her not the least attention, fighting in deadly earnest and a frightening silence punctuated only by the sound of blows and pained grunts. Rostov once again got Jack in a headlock.

For a split second Clara considered firing the rifle. It

would give her tremendous pleasure to shoot Rostov point-blank in the head. But she wasn't sure exactly how to fire it, and even she knew better than to shoot off a gun in a metal enclosure. The ricochet could very easily kill any one or all of them. Besides, she had never fired a gun in her life. As entwined as Jack and Rostov were, there was every possibility she might shoot the wrong man.

There was, it seemed, only one thing to do. Taking a deep breath, Clara lowered the rifle, grasped it firmly with both hands around the barrel, lifted it high overhead and brought the heavy metal butt crashing down onto Rostov's blond head.

XXI

"Moy tvoyou mat!" Rostov was rasping out a stream of Russian interspersed with English curses. "Bastard! Son of a bitch! Bitch!"

"Sticks and stones, comrade," Jack taunted with a grim smile. Clara, sitting on the pile of mattresses, could hardly believe that the plan had worked. So far.

Rostov was hanging from the ceiling, his feet not quite touching the floor, the muscles in his arms bulging as they bore his weight. Handcuffs passed over the middle of the steel door tracks overhead were locked onto each wrist. He was naked. Clara stared at his gently twisting body with detached interest. It was pale, lean, well-defined if not as muscular as Jack's, and sprinkled with reddish hair. Not unattractive as male bodies went, she supposed, then wondered at herself. Five days before she would have been embarrassed at seeing a naked man. But there she sat, prepared to witness the very intimate kind of torture that Jack had devised with grim satisfaction.

Jack was delicately wrapping a piece of thin wire around Rostov's testes. The wire was connected to the generator.

Jack would ask Rostov questions, and if the answers weren't satisfactory would crank the generator. Sooner or later the resulting jolts of electricity traveling through Rostov's genitals would be enough to make him tell them anything they wanted to know, Jack assured her. Clara didn't ask how he had come by the knowledge. She was only glad that Rostov had not thought to use such a method on her.

They were safe inside the trailer for the moment. The banging at the door and sides had stopped; it was apparent that the goons couldn't get in. Rostov was completely at their mercy, and as Jack had said, they weren't likely to get a better chance to find out what Rostov knew. Once they made a break for it anything could happen. The goons, knowing that they were trapped in the trailer, were likely to try to wait them out. For a while, anyway.

Rostov kicked at Jack's head as he finished wrapping the wire. Jack ducked, catching the blow on the top of his head, then straightened, unhurt.

"You don't have much in the way of brains, do you, comrade?" he asked. Then, without warning, he slugged Rostov hard in the stomach. The Russian screamed, writhing like a worm on a hook.

"That was for Hammersmith," Jack said. Rostov heaved and gasped, trying to catch his breath. Jack waited until he almost succeeded, then without warning slugged him hard in the stomach again. Rostov gagged, flopping about like a hooked fish.

"That was for Gloria."

Rostov's breath wheezed and rasped in his throat. His face was blue. He sounded and looked like he was dying. Jack smiled. Then he slugged Rostov as hard as he could in the groin.

"And that," Jack said, "was for Clara."

Then he turned his back and walked over to the generator while Rostov was violently sick all over the floor. Jack waited patiently for the spasm to pass.

"Now, comrade, you will tell us what you know about plans to assassinate the secretary of state."

"*V'nebrachnee!* Capitalist idiot of a pig! Have you forgotten that four of my men are right outside this trailer at this moment? Undoubtedly they have sent for backups. You can never get away. They will storm this truck at any minute. You will be killed, or better yet, not killed. I will make you pay with a thousand screams for this."

"That reminds me," Jack said, and picked up the walkie-talkie that Rostov had been carrying when he entered. "You will tell your goons that they are to do nothing—nothing—without orders from you. Do you understand? Tell them we are negotiating. Clara, hold this thing up to his mouth. Keep the button depressed so they can hear him. When I tell you."

"If you think I will . . ." Rostov said with contempt, his pale blue eyes icy with rage as Clara scrambled up to do Jack's bidding. She had to stretch to bring the transmitter level with Rostov's mouth, suspended as he was, and took care to stay clear of his feet. She was surprised at the eagerness she felt to make him pay for what he had done to her.

"Oh, I think you will," Jack said. He picked up the pistol that Rostov had been wearing in a shoulder holster under his clothes and pointed it at Rostov's knee. "If you don't, I'll blow your kneecap off."

Rostov spewed another stream of mixed Russian and English invectives, which stopped abruptly when Jack cocked the pistol. Glaring malevolently at Jack, he began to speak rapidly into the transmitter.

"In English, so we don't have any mix-ups," Jack directed smoothly. "Clara, now press the button."

Clara pressed the button so that Rostov could transmit. Furiously, Rostov did as he was told. When Clara lowered the transmitter, his ice cold eyes met hers.

"I will very much enjoy making you pay for this, Miss Winston," Rostov promised softly. Clara felt a frisson of fear shoot down her spine, but tried not to let it show. After all, she and Jack had the upper hand—for now, at least.

"Last chance, Rostov." Jack moved back beside the generator. Clara sat on the moving pads. Both watched the sweating, naked man suspended from the ceiling, but with very different expressions.

"Go to hell!"

Jack turned the crank. Current zinged along the circuit of wires. Rostov screamed. Clara flinched, wincing. She knew that Rostov deserved everything Jack did to him and more, but she still hated to hear the sounds of a human being in pain. Even Rostov. Who was not, in her opinion, qualified for the designation of human.

The procedure went on for some time, but at last Rostov broke. First he started to sob, then as Jack turned the crank again he screamed and began to babble. The secretary of state would be hit on Seabrook Island as soon as he arrived for the secret summit on the evening of the sixteenth. The assassin would be a sleeper—an agent planted years before to give him time to worm himself into a position of trust—just recently activated. As to Bigfoot, Rostov's knowledge was sketchy. He knew that the mole was very high in U.S. intelligence circles and that he himself had orders to protect him at all costs.

The only new information he professed to know was that Bigfoot was the head of a vast network of sleepers planted in the country years earlier. He was activating them, one by one, on orders from Moscow. Some years before, the first had loosed the virus that caused what was subsequently named Legionnaire's Disease at a convention in Philadelphia to test the efficacy of the virus as a biological weapon; the second had poisoned Tylenol capsules in Chicago to weigh the vulnerability of the United States to attack through their consumer market; the assassination of the secretary of state was to be carried out by the third. Rostov didn't know how many more there were. He only knew that the sleepers were to be activated by Bigfoot as the need arose.

"Why, you monsters!" Clara sputtered, dumbfounded and horrified at the revelations.

Jack silenced her with a wave of his hand, then turned his attention back to Rostov. His hand rested threateningly on the crank.

"Who is Bigfoot?"

"I do not know his identity. I swear to you, I do not!"

Jack turned the crank. Rostov screamed.

"All I know is that one of the *Nachalstvo* once referred to him in my hearing as the black hawk with the yellow eyes!" Rostov stumbled over the words in his haste to get them out. Sweat rolled down his brow; his eyes were fearful as they watched Jack's hand.

"The black hawk with the yellow eyes," McClain said slowly, his eyes narrowing. Then he shook his head, reaching for the crank again. "It tells me nothing."

"It is all I know! I swear to you! I know no more!"

Jack's hand hovered. Then he looked at Clara and shook his head. "I think he's telling the truth. In any case, we're out of time. We have to get out of here before dawn. Darkness gives us our best chance to make it. We have about an hour left."

"You will...never make it, Dragon." Rostov's voice was weak, but he had recovered some of his defiance.

"If I don't you can make sure you won't." Jack was stripping. In response to Clara's questioning look, he indicated the clothes they had removed from Rostov.

"If they can't tell which one of us is which, we'll gain a little time. A minute or two while they figure it out."

Clara watched him pull on the navy slacks and button-down shirt, its collar spotted with blood from the fight. The pants were a little long, the shirt a little tight. He left the shirt half unbuttoned to allow his shoulders moving room. Then he strapped on Rostov's shoulder holster. The white sweater, also daubed with crimson splotches, went on last. Jack kept his own sneakers. When he was dressed, Clara was impressed. In nice clothes, even with red-rimmed eyes, a black stubble of beard, and miscellaneous bruises, he was a strikingly attractive man.

"Try anything funny, comrade, and I'll blow you straight back to the Kremlin." Jack's voice was as wintry as Rostov's eyes. Picking up his jeans from the floor, he slid them efficiently up Rostov's legs, fastening them around the other's middle. Then he tied an arm of his sweatshirt around each of Rostov's ankles to form a primitive hobble. Finally he took the wire which he had stripped from Rostov's genitals and refashioned it into a loop which he passed around Rostov's neck. The other end he wrapped around the rifle, which he then pressed tight against Rostov's neck.

"Now unlock the handcuffs from one of his hands, Clara."

"You will pay for this, Dragon," Rostov promised through clenched teeth. He was drenched with sweat and pale from his ordeal. A pool of vomit had formed beneath his feet, and more had spattered his chest. He stunk of vomit and body odor. Clara crinkled her nose as she obeyed Jack's order.

Rostov dropped to the ground, his knees sagged, and he fell forward so that his forehead rested against the floor. With a sound of disgust, Jack shoved the muzzle of the rifle hard into his neck.

"I always knew you were a pansy, Rostov. Get your hands behind your back."

Rostov did. At a sign from Jack, Clara snapped the open handcuff shut so that Rostov's hands were chained behind his back.

"We're going now, and you're coming with us. You're our hostage to fortune, comrade. If anyone tries to stop us, takes a shot at us, whatever, you'll be the first one to die. At this range a Kalashnikov AK-47 would blow your head clean off, as I'm sure I don't need to remind you."

He let Rostov feel the muzzle of the rifle for emphasis. Rostov said nothing, but Clara could feel the hatred emanating from him in waves.

"Now get on your feet, asshole. Clara, bring the walkie-talkie over here. Rostov is going to tell his comrades that the negotiations were successfully concluded. We are coming out, and they are not to try to stop us. Tell them that you will be leaving with us. And to make sure the keys are in the cab. In English."

Rostov rose slowly and awkwardly to his feet. He swayed, then with sheer force of will seemed to make himself stand upright. The wire around his neck dug into his flesh, causing the skin to redden and bulge out on either side. Grim-faced, hands in firing position on the rifle that dug into the back of the Russian's neck, Jack stood less than a foot behind Rostov. The tableau looked eerily like a picture Clara had seen in the *Washington Post* not long before with a story on a hostage taking. It seemed such a dreadful, barbaric act when someone else did it. But now Rostov was their hostage, all that stood between them and a barrage of bullets. It was a terrifying thought.

Clara brought the walkie-talkie and held it to Rostov's mouth. His eyes were feral as he glared at her. But he said what Jack told him to say.

"Ask them if they understand."

Rostov repeated the question.

"*Da*, Comrade Colonel." The voice crackling back over the walkie-talkie could have belonged to Orlov or Malik or any of the others. It was impossible to tell. If the goons had disobeyed Rostov's previous instructions—which she thought they would have done if they were smart—a whole army of KGB thugs could be waiting for them outside. Jack might open the door to a hail of gunfire.

"Tell them to get behind the trailer where I can see them from the door. Tell them to lay down their weapons. If they don't, if I see anything that looks halfway lethal in their hands, I will kill you."

"You will then be killed within instants yourself, Dragon." Rostov's voice was recovering its strength. Jack jammed the muzzle hard against his neck. Rostov grunted in pain.

"You won't live long enough to enjoy it, I promise. Now tell them."

Rostov told them. Jack reached up and unfastened the set of handcuffs that had been locking the door. Then he turned to Clara.

"Turn off the light. We don't want to make it too easy for them. Then get over here between us. In the middle. You'll be harder to hit."

Clara did as she was told, half turning the crank on the generator so that the trailer suddenly became as pitch black as the darkest cave. She made her way to Jack's side on blind instinct, then wedged herself between his sweatered chest and Rostov's naked, sweaty back. Her skin crawled at the idea of being so close to the man who had hurt her, but she did it anyway.

"And take this. If anything goes wrong, use it. It's an automatic, all you have to do is pull the trigger and hold it down. It will keep firing."

"Jack . . ." She felt the gun pressed into her hand. It was cold and heavy. She was suddenly, terribly, afraid.

"Don't worry, baby. I've been in tighter spots than this and lived to tell about it." He whispered the words into her ear, his breath warm on her skin. Then she felt the brush of his mouth as it widened in what she sensed was, incredibly, a smile. "Besides, think how good this will sound in one of your books." Her fear didn't lessen, but her heart warmed. Please, God, she prayed feverishly, please don't let anything happen to either one of us, Jack or me.

Jack straightened. Clara caught her breath, knowing that it was time to go.

"Tell Orlov to open the door. Then tell him to step back where I can see him."

Rostov obeyed. Clara tensed. Behind her she could feel Jack's body take on an added alertness, like a prowling tiger in the dark.

The door rolled open. In front of them, in the grayish cold darkness of the predawn, four men stood in the clearing in which the moving van was parked. Orlov's stocky body was easy to identify, as was Malik's thinner form. The other two were with reasonable certainty the same goons who had been with Rostov from the beginning. Clara breathed a little easier. At least they weren't faced with an army of KGB agents. The moonlight glinted off the gray metal of weapons piled neatly in front of the trailer.

"Tell them to stay where they are." McClain hissed the order at Rostov. He hesitated, and McClain prodded him hard with the rifle.

"*Stoy!*"

The goons continued to stare up at them, unblinking.

"All right, we're all going to sit, and put our feet over the side. Together. Now!" The hissed command was meant for Rostov and Clara.

It was awkward, but they managed to get on the ground without altering their basic conformation. Clara's mouth was sour with fear; behind her she could feel the slow, steady pounding of Jack's heart. In front of her, tight as bread on a sandwich, was Rostov's bare back. She could feel his heart pounding, too. The next few seconds would tell the tale. Would the goons allow them to proceed to the front of the truck and get in the cab? Would the rifle wired to Rostov's neck persuade them? Did they have any inkling of what was going on? There was an air of confusion about them as they peered at the closely pressed trio that maneuvered around the corner of the trailer and backed toward the cab, closely hugging the trailer's side, protected by its deep shadow. The night itself was shadowy and cold. A thin sickle moon floated overhead, obscured for the most part by rushing clouds. Clara had to concentrate to keep from stumbling over the frozen tufts of grass. Her hands rested on Rostov's damp bare back; despite her revulsion she had to keep them there for balance.

"Almost home," Jack muttered. Clara felt him reach up and behind him for the door handle as they reached the cab. There was a click as the handle turned. The goons hadn't moved. Their heads turned as they followed every little movement. Clara prayed that they would stay confused just a few seconds longer.

"Stop them!" Rostov shouted as he threw himself violently forward. Jack's attention had been distracted by opening the door; the Kalishnikov was pulled from his hands before he could squeeze the trigger. Rostov hit the ground, scrambled away on his hands and knees, reaching behind him for the rifle as he went. The other KGB men, after a split second's astonishment, began to run toward their rifles. It was all over. . . .

"Jesus H. Christ!" Jack yelled, grabbing her around the waist and throwing her up on the van's vinyl seat. Shocked, terrified, she nevertheless retained the presence of mind to scramble out of the way. He leaped in the truck beside her, banging the door closed, feeling for the keys. Thank God they were in the ignition! He turned the engine over just as the Russians rushed up, their rifles blasting. The bullets whacked into the metal cab. Clara screamed, ducking. The windshield shattered.

"Oh shit!" McClain muttered as his body jerked. His hand clapped to his chest and dark liquid that Clara knew was blood spurted through his fingers. Clara stared at him with horror; the driver's side door was jerked open. A black shape loomed in the space.

Clara lifted the pistol and pulled the trigger. A spurt of fire shot across the cab just above Jack's lap. The shape screamed and fell back.

"That's my girl," Jack managed with a half smile even as he nearly fell out of the cab reaching for the swinging door. Clara grabbed for him, but he recovered, slamming the door as he trod hard on the accelerator. The huge truck shot forward; a goon jumped out of the way. Another was mowed over, screaming. The truck bucked and slid out of the muddy clearing onto the dirt road. Bullets whacked into the trailer behind them; Clara could hear the whistling as they ricocheted off the metal.

"Jack! My God, Jack!" She moved closer to him, terror in her eyes as she touched his shoulder. His face was dead white. Blood still oozed between the fingers he had pressed to his chest. To her horror, she discovered that she could hear blood bubbling. The smell of gunpowder was strong in the air. He was swaying; his left hand was locked to the wheel, but he blinked once or twice as if he was having trouble keeping his eyes open. "Jack, you're hit!"

"You better drive," he muttered, his voice thick. Then his eyes rolled back in his head and he collapsed on the steering wheel. The horn blared with his weight. The huge truck skewed wildly across the muddy track. Terror stopped her breath. They were going to crash!

Hand closing over his shirt collar, Clara yanked Jack sideways, off the wheel. He slumped onto her lap. There was no time to move him out of the way. She grabbed for the wheel, hung on to it, fought the urge to close her eyes as the cab hurtled toward the densely packed trunks of sturdy pines. With all her strength she yanked the wheel to the right. The truck obeyed, skidding madly in a new direction. They could jackknife, turn over... Clara swung the wheel back to the left, her heart in her throat. Somehow the truck ended up back on the road, hurtling furiously forward. Clara heaved a sigh of relief. By the grace of God and nothing else she had managed to keep them from crashing. Jack's foot was a dead weight on the accelerator. Of course, that was why they were still traveling at such a speed. Kicking Jack's leg aside, she was relieved to find that the truck slowed on its own. Then she remembered Rostov and jammed her own foot down on the gas. The truck shot forward again. Still there was no time to move Jack out of the way. Hampered by his deadweight across her lap, she leaned sideways, stretching her arms to the utmost to get a firm grasp on the wheel, exerting every ounce of her strength to keep the lurching, swaying truck on the narrow dirt road. As the dark shadows of the woods shot past on either side, Rostov and his goons fired furious, impotent shots after the speeding truck. Clara realized that she had been too frightened even to pray.

XXII

"Please don't die. Please don't die. Please don't die. God, please don't let Jack die."

The litany ran over and over again in her brain. Clara had managed to wedge herself between Jack and the door and shove him off the steering wheel. Now he slumped, inert, on the bench seat beside her. Her right hand was pressed tightly over the hole in the bloody sweater. Blood oozed through her fingers, oily and frightening, its volume increasing and declining with each pump of his heart. She was so afraid he was going to die. And there was nothing she could do to save him but try to stem the flow of blood with her palm. She felt like the little Dutch boy with his finger in the dike.

A little while back the dirt road had opened onto a paved one. The forest was still thick all around them, just barely starting to lighten as the sun came up. The smell of dewy evergreens was everywhere. Clara wondered where on earth they were. Where could she take him? Where would he be safe from Rostov? She had to stop before long, before he bled to death.

A small green sign ahead proclaimed they were approaching

Highway 58. It was a four-lane road. As she turned on to it, the rising sun was straight ahead. Which meant that they were traveling east. It seemed as good a direction as any. The thing was to put as many miles as possible between themselves and Rostov. They had left him without transportation, but she had no illusions that that state would last long. He was probably in touch with confederates. Maybe he could even call them on that walkie-talkie they'd had. She had no idea of its range.

She was going to have to stop soon. Casting a worried glance at McClain, she saw that beneath his stubble of black beard his face was as white as a corpse's. He was still, so still that she had a momentary horror that he might not be breathing. Then she felt the rhythmic pump of blood beneath her hand and dismissed that worry. His heart was still beating; he was not dead.

Minutes later 58 connected with 24, and the Atlantic Ocean loomed before her. She turned south on instinct, rumbling down the ocean road. The scarlet sunrise turning the foamy breakers to pink was a gorgeous sight, but she was too frightened even to notice. She had to find a place to stop, a place where they could hide.

A large sign informed her that she was leaving the Croatan National Forest. She drove over a bridge and found herself in the town of Swansboro. A large truck stop with a gleaming neon sign and a shabby looking motel caught her eye. A dozen huge semis were parked in front; more were in the back. If she parked around to the rear, where the truck couldn't be seen from the highway, this might be as good a place as any to hide. Rostov wouldn't be expecting them to stop so soon. Anyway, wasn't there a saying about the best place to hide being in plain sight?

She swung off the road, maneuvered the truck behind the

buildings without doing anymore than scaring a stray cat that happened to be crossing the parking lot, and parked between two semis. Turning off the ignition, she bent over McClain. He was breathing strongly despite his pallor. Lifting his sweater and yanking his shirt from his pants, she got her first look at his wound. His chest hairs were matted with blood. Blood covered him from his collarbone clear to the navel. He was losing a lot. . . .

"Jack! Jack, can you hear me?" There was no response. Should she take him to a hospital? But there was a good chance that they would recognize him there. After all, his picture had been on the front page of the *Washington Post*, and there was no telling how many other papers. And for all she knew they'd even run it on TV. No, she couldn't risk it. But what risk was it, she argued with herself, if he was going to die in any case?

Jack would not want her to take him to the hospital. She knew that. He would prefer to take his chances with her. She would just have to do the best she could for him herself. Gritting her teeth, she pulled her sweater over her head and stripped off her shirt, thanking God that the parking lot was deserted of people so early in the morning. Then she pulled her sweater back over her head and folded the shirt into a pad. This she crammed under his sweater and shirt, holding it tightly against the wound. That might slow the blood a little.

She needed to get him inside. Clara felt a frission of fear as she realized that she would have to talk to a real live person face to face to get a room, but of course it would be safe for her. Her picture had not been in the newspapers and on TV. Jack was the one the police were looking for. She hoped.

Money. To rent a room she needed money. She had not a

penny on her. Did Jack? She had a notion that he'd spent his last cash when he'd bought the paper and their crackers at that roadside store three days before. Maybe there was money in Rostov's pockets.

She needed something to hold the makeshift bandage in place. Clara thought for a moment, then remembered the expensive looking snakeskin belt around Jack's waist. It was Rostov's, and she pulled it free of its loops with satisfaction. Rostov had tried to kill Jack. It was only fitting that something of his should be used to save him.

The belt would not fit around Jack's chest. Clara stared at the five inches or so of muscled flesh keeping the two ends from meeting and felt herself grow savage. She had to find something. . . .

The seat belt. The seatbelts were wedged between the seat and the back, but she managed to extract them. Pulling the passenger belt out as far as it would go, she wrapped it around Jack's chest. Then she clicked the end into the lock.

It worked like a charm. The belt contracted until it was pressing tightly against Jack's chest. Already Clara thought the blood flow was beginning to stem. At least her shirt was not turning red as fast.

She watched him for a minute, then thrust her hand into his pants pocket. She needed money for a room. The first pocket was empty, but the second yielded paydirt. A wallet with nearly two hundred dollars in it and a fistful of credit cards. All in the name of Andrei Rostov. Clara began to smile grimly. Rostov was being more of a help than he knew.

She didn't dare use the credit cards, but the cash was perfectly acceptable to the disinterested, sleepy looking woman who was manning the front desk. Clara handed over twenty-eight dollars for a double, and was given a blue-handled key in return. Room number 38, around back as she had requested, ground floor. Now all she had to do was get Jack out of the truck and into the room.

In the end she managed it by maneuvering the truck until the passenger side door was no more than five feet from the room door. She pushed, dragged, and shoved, and somehow managed to get Jack inside. The pressure of the seatbelt had staunched the flow of blood, she had been relieved to see when she'd returned to the truck. But all her jostling started the wound to bleeding again. Her shirt was stuck fast to the drying blood on his chest, and Clara feared what would happen if she tried to free it. Instead she stripped the top sheet from the bed, chewing the edge until she could rip it across. Tearing strips from the sheet, she wrapped them around his chest, tying a hard, tight knot directly over where she judged the wound to be. The bandage might not be sanitary, but her first priority was to stop the bleeding again. She pressed her hand down hard over the knot until her wrist began to ache. Then, cautiously lifting her palm and peeping under the edges of the bandage, she judged that the bleeding had once again stopped.

Getting him into the bed by herself proved impossible. He weighed a ton. Regretfully, Clara left him on the floor with a pillow tucked under his head. Then she wrapped a blanket around him, tenderly tucking the ends in around his bare feet, from which she had removed the raunchy sneakers, and went into the small bathroom. Looking down, she was shocked to find that her hands were covered with blood to the wristbones. She had always hated the sight of blood. Her stomach heaved, but Clara refused to allow herself to be sick. Jack had only her to care for him; she had to be strong for him. Taking a deep breath, she methodically washed the blood from her hands. She would have to be careful. It would raise too many questions if people should see her coming and going covered with blood.

She had done the best she could for Jack for the moment, but there were other problems to be considered. To begin with, the truck had to be moved away from their door. Pulled diagonally across six parking spaces as it was, it was sure to invite a lot of comment.

When Clara returned from moving the truck back to its hiding place and buying a take-out meal as well as a few necessities at the small drug and gift store next to the truck stop's restaurant, Jack still lay on the floor exactly as she had left him. For a moment she again feared the worst. Then she knelt beside him and saw the uneven rise and fall of his chest. He was still alive.

"Jack! Jack, can you hear me? Jack, it's Clara."

He didn't move, didn't make any sign that he heard her. Clara sank back on her heels and looked at him. She didn't know what to do. If he didn't have medical attention he might die, but she couldn't call a doctor. She couldn't call anyone. She would have to care for him as best she could herself. If his condition worsened, then maybe she would take a chance on taking him to a hospital. But they would know at once that it was a bullet wound, and then they would almost certainly call the police who were sure to recognize him.

Clara had another worry, too. Rostov could find them at any time. He probably had agents scouring all roads leading out of the Croatan National Forest by now. It was just a matter of time until someone spotted the truck, with its distinctive orange color and the words Horizon Movers emblazoned across the side. There couldn't be many on the road like that, certainly not in this neck of the woods.

She ran out to the truck and fished the pistol from under

the seat. Then she locked and chained the motel room door, and jammed a chair under the knob. If someone looked like breaking in, she decided that, no matter what, she was calling the police. At least that would give them some time.

There was no help for it, Clara knew. She had been putting the moment off, but it had to be done. She, and she alone, Miss Weak Stomach herself, was going to have to do what she could for Jack's wound. She had never been much good at nursing, never had to be. Her mother never got sick, and she was blessed with the same iron constitution. But Jack had only her to take care of him, inexperienced and inadequate as she was. She was going to have to do her best, and to hell with the queasiness that threatened to overwhelm her whenever she was faced with a little blood.

Gripping her lower lip between her teeth, Clara extracted the scissors from the bag of supplies she had bought and proceeded to cut the thick Irish wool sweater across the shoulders and down the center. She didn't want to risk lifting his arms to pull it over his head. The bleeding might start again. When the sweater was off, and the shirt was carefully unbuttoned and laid open to expose the bandage of sheets and her flannel shirt, Clara hesitated. It was imperative that she clean out the wound. Even she knew that from the books she had read. She had bought some antiseptic for that very purpose. But the strips of sheet, not to mention her shirt, were already stained scarlet and black with fresh and dried blood. When she cut through the binding of sheets and tried to pull it away, she found that it as well as the shirt was stuck fast to the wound. Frowning with concentration, she cut away as much of the material as she could. Then she filled the flimsy ice bucket with warm water from the sink, soaked a washcloth in it, and proceeded to lay it over the stuck cloth. After several tries it worked.

She was able to gently lift the blood soaked shirt away from the wound.

A small amount of blood still oozed from the blackened hole that was no bigger than a dime just beneath his ribcage. It occurred to Clara that a bullet was lodged in his chest. It should be removed, but she could not do it. She might kill him. It would have to stay where it was, and she would hope for the best. The edges of the hole were puffy and white, grotesque. Already the flesh around it was swollen and discolored. Dried blood matted the hairs on his chest. More blood had smeared his belly and crusted in his navel. His right hand was covered with it where he had grabbed and held the wound just after being shot. Blood spattered Rostov's once immaculate trousers. In all, there was more blood than Clara had ever seen—or wanted to see—in her life.

In a book somewhere she had read that when one didn't know what to do he should just do the next thing. The next thing seemed to be to clean away as much of the blood as she could, so that's what she did. By the time she had finished, she had gone completely through the meager store of towels allotted to the room, and had changed the water in the ice bucket six times. But finally there was left on him only the small amount of blood still oozing from the wound, and the spatters on his pants.

Still going by the principle of doing the next thing, she swabbed the wound with the antiseptic, then opened a tube of antibiotic ointment she had bought at the same time and smeared it liberally over the wound. Then she ripped open the package of large sterile gauze squares and put one over the oozing hole, securing it in place with a roll of gauze, which she wound around him. After she tied the knot so that it would apply pressure directly over the wound, she sat for a moment looking down at him. Was there anything else she should do?

He was deathly pale. His skin felt cold to her touch when she laid her hand against his cheek, and for some reason that frightened her more than it would have if he felt hot. Quickly she got up and stripped the bed, piling blankets and the bedspread over him. After that, there didn't seem much more she could do. She knelt for a moment beside him, then leaned forward to press a quick kiss to his chalky white, sandpapery cheek. Then she sat down at the small rickety table in front of the tightly curtained window and forced herself to eat the meal she had bought for herself at the restaurant. The coffee was stone cold, and the cheeseburger which the woman had zapped in the microwave was nearly as bad, but she ate them anyway. Funny, just the day before she had been starving and now she had to force herself to eat. She looked down at the man sprawled at her feet. Because of Jack. . . .

She gathered up her styrofoam cup and cellophane wrappers and threw them away. Then she stood over him, indecisive, looking worriedly down at his waxy face. There was a bullet in his chest. Could he get lead poisoning? Would the wound get infected? He would never get well as long as it lay in there festering. Now was the time to call a doctor if ever she was going to do it. She moved toward the telephone and picked up the receiver. A woman's voice answered.

"Front desk."

Clara took a deep breath. "Wrong number," she said, and replaced the receiver in the cradle. Maybe she could try, just a little, to get the bullet out of the wound herself. She had played "Operation!" a lot as a girl. The object of the game was to extract a plastic organ from a gameboard patient with inch deep openings in his body where the organs lay in wait. The openings had metal sides, and the tool of extraction was a pair of electronic tweezers. If the tweezers touched the metal sides during the operation, a buzzer sounded and your patient died. She'd been pretty good at it as a girl, but Jack was no gameboard patient. He was a living, breathing man, and utterly important to her. She couldn't go poking about that hideous little wound with a pair of tweezers! But if she didn't, who would? The next thing to do seemed to be remove the bullet, and there was only herself to do it.

The gift store had tweezers. An omen? Clara bought them, bought some rubbing alcohol, cotton, and some more gauze. Maybe she would just probe around a little bit. If she was lucky the bullet might be right beneath the surface and she could remove it with no trouble at all.

She would just probe a little. Clara kept repeating the words over and over as she unbandaged the wound, swabbed the area with alcohol and soaked the tweezers in the smelly liquid. Then, steeling herself, she took the tweezers in hand. Should she do this? Or would she harm him more by trying? She didn't know. But her instincts told her that the bullet had to come out. If she could not do it, then she should summon a doctor. But she couldn't do that, either. Clara knew as well as if he were conscious and could speak what Jack would say to her: Go for it! And he would grin that lopsided grin.

She would just probe a little, Clara repeated as she tentatively brought the edges of the tweezer together and inserted them in the hole. Fresh blood oozed forth. Clara winced, feeling her stomach churn with revulsion, expecting at any moment to hear Jack scream with pain. But he lay unmoving, mercifully oblivious to her amateur ministrations. So, taking a deep breath, she sank the tweezers a little deeper into his flesh.

By the time she had worked the tweezers inside him until they were buried nearly to the tip in his flesh, she was sweating like a rain forest and covered with blood. Blood had a distinct smell to it, she discovered, a sweetish odor that didn't help the state of her churning stomach. She fought to hold back wave after wave of nausea, concentrating instead on feeling her way inside, following the path the bullet had taken. She was about as deep as she was prepared to go. Besides, the tweezers were in so far that she could barely manipulate them as it was.

Just then the pointed end of the tweezers struck something hard. Something metal. Clara felt a rush of excitement. Unbelievably, it seemed she had found the bullet!

The tweezers were inside too far to permit her to open them and grasp the bullet with the pointed ends. Instead she had to work the ends beside the bullet and nudge it upwards a little at a time until at last she could manipulate the tweezers. After that, it was only a matter of a minute or two. She opened the tweezers, probed carefully, felt metal on metal and closed them. Then, gently, she withdrew the tweezers holding their prize. Blood poured forth in the bullet's wake. Clara had just a moment to look at the blackened, twisted lump of bloody metal on her palm. Then, with a shudder, she threw it across the room and applied herself to stopping the bleeding again.

By the time that was accomplished, antibiotic ointment was worked into the wound and a fresh bandage was applied, Clara felt as if she had been run over by a truck. Every muscle in her body ached. But she had done it! She had really done it! Pride in the accomplishment warmed her. She was smiling faintly as she pulled herself to her feet and stumbled into the bathroom to wash off as much of the blood as she could. By the time she came out she was no longer smiling. It had occurred to her that just because the bullet was out did not mean that Jack would recover. He could die from infection or internal injuries the bullet had caused. She had no idea how severe they might be.

But just then she couldn't worry about it. She had done what she could. Her body and mind were far beyond the point of exhaustion. Dragging the other pillow from the bed, she dropped to her knees at Jack's side. If he worsened, she wanted to be near enough to know it. Then she drew the covers a little away from him and crawled in beside him. He still felt as cold as a corpse . . . She shivered at the comparison. Curling as close to him as she dared, hoping to share her warmth with him as she wrapped her arms around him, she closed her eyes. Moments later she was asleep.

XXIII

He was burning hot, and she was terrified. It was the middle of the night and he had started muttering and thrashing an hour before. Clara couldn't make out anything he said. The jumbled phrases made no sense. But once he called her name.

"I'm here, Jack. Lie still, darling. Please lie still. You'll reopen the wound."

But he hadn't given any indication that he had heard her. He continued to thrash, kicking off the covers she piled on top of him, flailing his arms about until she caught his hands and lay across his stomach to hold them still.

"Jack. Jack, please be still. Please." She was crying as she begged. She had never felt so helpless or so alone in her life. He was dying, right there in her arms. She knew he was. No one could burn so and live. And there was nothing she could do. No one she could call. No help she could give him.

"Please don't let him die!" She turned to God, that solace of her youth. As a child she had spent every Sunday morning in church, and said her prayers every night of her life. As an adult she was not nearly so conscientious, but now, when there was no one else, she turned to He from whom all blessings flowed. And she prayed as she had never prayed in her life.

Her arms were resting across the hard flesh of his stomach. His skin was so hot that it burned to the touch. He was groaning in pain, and she had nothing to help ease it. Then the groans turned to whimpers, pitiful helpless whimpers like a hurt child. There had to be something she could do for him, there had to be. She could not just let him die! Clara gritted her teeth. She would not.

His fever had to be brought down, and he had to be kept still. Those were her immediate priorities. Straddling him to keep him as still as she could, she reached for the torn top sheet, ripping long strips from it. Those she tied together to form a rope. That done, she scooted down so that she was sitting on his thighs, and quickly wrapped one end of the rope around his twitching wrists. His head thrashed from side to side as she wrapped the rope around him until he was bound like a mummy from his navel to his ankles. His hands were caught inside the binding. Knotting the rope at his ankles, she only hoped that her makeshift straitjacket would hold. Then she got up, grabbed the ice bucket, and ran outside to the ice machine in the little cubicle three doors down. In the quiet hours before dawn the area was deserted. Clara looked uneasily around at the shadowy darkness beyond the yellow motel lighting, but saw nothing out of place. Still, she thought of Rostov and her heart pounded.

When she let herself back into the room she forgot all about Rostov. Jack's entire body was jerking, rising off the green carpet in spasmodic heaves. Oh, dear God, don't let him die!

Dumping the ice in the sink, she filled it with cold water and soaked the fitted bottom sheet in it. When the sheet was dripping wet, she carried it back over to Jack, kneeling as she wrapped the icy wet cloth around him, leaving only a small opening for him to breathe and another around his wound. She wanted to keep the wound as dry as she could, but the priority had to be bringing down his fever.

She soaked and wrapped and soaked and wrapped, and at last he was still. His skin was still overly warm, but not as fiery hot as it had been. His breathing seemed easier. Clara was exhausted, but she could not leave him lying there soaking wet. He needed to be dry.

Every muscle in her body ached. She was so tired that she could barely lift her arms. Her left hand with its broken finger was killing her. Looking down, she saw that the splint Jack had made for her out of his underwear was soaking wet. But she was too tired to unwrap her finger and deal with what was underneath. Swallowing two aspirin, she set herself to untying and unwrapping the makeshift strait- jacket she had put on him. Finally she had the last of it off. Still he lay without moving. She prayed that he had passed from unconsciousness to sleep.

His pants were soaked, as was the open shirt. Unbuttoned and unzipped, they still clung to him, the wet material loathe to leave his body. She yanked and pulled and tugged until she had them off. Then she cut off the shirt. He was naked except for the bandage, legs sprawled, left arm outflung, right arm, the one nearest the wound, close to his side. Carefully she dried him with a blanket. His nakedness seemed as natural to her as her own. When she was done, she pulled off her own sweater and jeans. Wearing just her teddy, she lay down beside him, pulling the rest of the covers over them both. Nuzzling her face against his side and wrapping her arms around his middle, she whispered another prayer for his life. In the middle of it she fell asleep.

Forty-five minutes later his restless mutterings woke her. For a moment she was groggy, not knowing quite where she was or what had happened. Then she felt the burning heat of his skin. The fever had returned. Groaning, she got up and repeated the process she had been through before, fetching ice and soaking sheets and wrapping him in them. And as before his fever went down, she dried him and went back to sleep.

Before morning she repeated the procedure twice more. By the time the sun rose she was sitting on the floor near his head, her own head flopped back on the mattress, back propped against the end of the bed. She was boneless with exhaustion. Bright spots of white floated in and out of her vision. She had never worked so hard or so desperately in her life, never prayed so fiercely nor willed anything so much. He was going to live. She would not admit any other possibility.

It occurred to her, in her half somnolent state, to wonder why it mattered so much. After all, she had only known him five days. How could a stranger—a violent, tormented stranger who played this horrifying game of kill or be killed like one born and bred to it—have come to mean so much to her so quickly? He was not her type at all. She wasn't sure what her type was, but she was sure it was not him. He wasn't even handsome, or at least she remembered she hadn't thought so at the beginning. Now she found him wildly attractive, but she suspected that it was the result of some kind of chemical effect he had on her hormones. With him she was as uninhibitedly passionate as any of the heroines in her books. It was not something she had ever expected of herself, and she did not like it. Craving a man's body like an addictive drug just was not nice. Certainly it was nothing to make her fall in love. . . .

Her mind winced away from the thought. She could not, would not, fall in love with him. It was ridiculous, impossible. He was crazy, for God's sake, and she wasn't referring to his past breakdown. He liked violence, liked danger; she knew he did, could see it in his eyes whenever they were in a tight spot. He had torn her from her home, endangered her life every half hour, been rude to her, insulted her, manhandled her—and he hated cats! She could not be in love with him.

She had always had the feeling that somewhere in the world was a man meant by fate just for her, her soulmate. A gentleman, a knight in shining armor, someone with whom she could fall madly, irretrievably in love. Someone with whom she would blissfully spend the rest of her life. Clara's head lifted from the bed and she stared down at Jack in a kind of horror. Pale, unshaven, breathing stertorously through an open mouth, black hair standing up around his head in spikes, he looked dearer than all the world to her. Her heart warmed, but her mind shuddered with horror. Please, dear God, she added an addendum to her original prayer, don't let my soulmate be him!

He was muttering. Clara sighed, pushing the unwelcome thoughts away. Whether he was one of life's little dirty tricks or not, he had only her to care for him. And his fever was up again.

It was late afternoon. Clara was sprawled wearily on the floor beside Jack, too tired even to sleep. She had battled the fever all day, and at last she thought she might be winning. He was sleeping now, really sleeping. She wished she could. But she had passed beyond that point. She was tired to death, but sleep refused to come.

"Clara." The mutter was indistinct, and for a moment she thought she had imagined it.

"Clara." He was calling her! The knowledge banished her tiredness. Scrambling over beside him, she touched his cheek.

"Jack, I'm here. Right here, darling."

He opened his eyes. His green eyes were feverish and bright, but aware.

"What . . . happened?"

"Don't you remember? You were shot. When we were escaping from Rostov and his men."

"Ahh." He was silent for a moment, eyes closed. Then they flickered open again. "I see we . . . made it."

"Yes. We're safe. Don't worry." She wanted to soothe him. Impulsively she bent down to kiss his cheek. His eyes adjusted to look at her as she straightened. His lips moved in what might have been meant for a smile.

"You're a good egg, baby."

Clara didn't know what encomiums she had been expecting, but that brief compliment made her want to laugh and cry and bash him over the head and hug him at the same time. When she thought back over the battle with death she had waged for the last twenty-four hours, to be greeted with You're a good, egg, baby seemed like something of an anticlimax. But what had she expected, anyway? Protestations of undying gratitude and devotion? Not from Jack.

"You're a good egg, too, Jack," she told him with a rueful smile, and gave him a thumbs up sign. This time his smile looked more like the real thing.

"You got the bullet out, didn't you?"

Clara blinked at him. "How did you know?"

"I know you. Nothing you can't do if you put your mind

to it. Remarkable—remarkable woman.'' His speech was slurring. His eyes blinked once, then closed.

"Jack!" She was panic stricken, leaning over him. She hadn't known how much she needed his conscious presence until that instant.

His eyes flickered open again.

"Call Ramsey," he said. And then they closed. Clara called to him, even shook him a little in her fear, but to no avail. He was either unconscious or deeply asleep. She sat back on her heels, chewing her lower lip with worry. Call Ramsey, he'd said. He must mean General "Wild Bill" Ramsey from Camp Lejeune. But was General Ramsey on their side? True, he had not shot them down when they had been in the stolen helicopter, but he had not helped them other than that, as far as she could see. But Jack had told her to call him. Had he been out of his head? She didn't think so. Clara pondered a while longer. Then she made up her mind and picked up the phone.

"I want to place a call to Camp Lejeune," she said into the receiver.

XXIV

General Ramsey arrived within the hour. Waiting for him, Clara had been so nervous that she had paced the room, alternating between staring down at Jack and peeping out the window. When she had placed the call to Camp Lejeune, Ramsey's secretary had answered the phone. Clara had almost hung up, but instead she had nervously given her name. The secretary had seemed to have no idea who she was. Clara had begun to doubt that the general would even speak to her. But in seconds he had been on the line.

"Where the hell are you?" he had barked.

Far from being taken aback at such a greeting, Clara had felt relieved. He sounded almost as if he were scolding an errant soldier, not as if he were talking to one of a pair of wanted criminals.

"At a truck stop in Swansboro. I—I think it's called the Stop and Eat. At least that's what the sign says."

"Good God!"

Not sure whether this bellicose interjection had to do with

290

the place they were staying or with some other matter, Clara had gone on.

"General, Jack told me to call you. He's quite badly hurt."

"What happened?" Then he had snorted. "Never mind. Save it. I'll be with you in an hour." He had paused. "Miss Winston, don't open the door to anyone else."

"No, I won't," Clara had agreed with fervor. And she had kept the pistol close at hand as she waited for General Ramsey to arrive. But she had spent the entire hour praying she wouldn't have to use it. She'd shot it once, in extreme terror, but she couldn't remember quite how she'd done it. And she wasn't sure if she could count on renewed terror to remind her.

When the two nondescript station wagons pulled up out front, Clara felt her heart pound so wildly that it was all she could hear. But her fear was assuaged in an instant. There was no mistaking General Ramsey. Uniform and all, he was the epitome of a high ranking marine officer. He exited from the passenger door of the first station wagon while a balding, fortyish officer who was obviously his subordinate exited from the driver's side, and another, younger officer stepped out of the rear. As the senior officer moved around the car, Clara recognized more than his uniform and breathed a sigh of relief. She'd only had a brief glimpse of "Wild Bill" Ramsey, but there was no mistaking that leathery face or grizzled crew cut.

While General Ramsey and the other officers strode toward her, four other marines, ordinary grunts as Jack would doubtless call them, got out of the other car and closed ranks behind the general. It looked like the general had brought his own private army. Thank God! Clara moved quickly to pull the chair from beneath the doorknob.

She had it open before General Ramsey and his men reached it.

"Miss Winston." He nodded his head. "Where's . . . Ah."

This last came as she stood back to let him enter and he saw Jack huddled beneath his pile of covers on the floor.

"What happened?" he asked grimly, surveying Jack and then the bloodstained towels and pieces of sheet and clothing littering the room. As Clara told him, jerkily, the second officer entered to be introduced as Captain Spencer. He was followed by the third officer, who was introduced as Captain Kryzanski, physician. Clara was so glad to see a real live doctor that she could have hugged him. General Ramsey called her sternly back to account as the ordinary grunts deployed themselves outside the door, which he then shut and locked. Feeling almost dizzy with relief at such reinforcements, Clara told him all that had occurred from the time they left Camp Lejeune.

"Jack's told the truth about everything, General, I swear it. The KGB is really after him, and there is a mole and microfilm and—" Her desperate attempt to convince General Ramsey of Jack's innocence before Jack could be carted off to some kind of prison was cut short with a brusque wave of his hand.

"I know that," he said curtly. Then, "McClain and I reached an understanding while he was at Camp Lejeune. No one was to know. But I think you're in it as much as anyone now. You may as well know what the hell's going on."

"Why, thank you, General," Clara said, taken aback. Jack hadn't told her about any accord with the general. She cast a dark look down at him. He hadn't told her about the microfilm either, until he'd had to. She wondered what else he was keeping from her.

"Somebody did a good job of patching him up." The doctor straightened from where he knelt over Jack. "The bullet's out, and as far as I can tell it hit a dead spot. No vital organs. Missed the heart, lungs, liver, the works. He's a lucky SOB. Oh, sorry. He's a lucky guy."

"That's all right, doctor."

"You get the bullet out?" General Ramsey was regarding her with keen eyes. Clara nodded. "Well, he said you were a damn fine woman."

Her eyes widened at that. But before she could reply Jack stirred, calling her name.

"I'm here, Jack," she said, moving toward him just as his eyes opened. They touched on her face briefly, then widened as they took in the doctor and Captain Spencer. She saw his muscles tense. Then General Ramsey moved forward. Jack saw him and seemed to relax.

"Good to see you, General." He frowned, concentrating. "The hit's going to take place on Seabrook Island itself. First day of the summit, just as the eagle lands. The hit man's a sleeper in a position of trust."

The colonel was visibly excited. "How the hell did you find that out?"

Jack tried another of those weak smiles. "I had a little conversation with Rostov. Ask Clara. She'll tell you all about it."

General Ramsey nodded, then jerked his head in the doctor's direction. Captain Spencer led the protesting man out of earshot. General Ramsey bent over Jack and spoke in a low tone: "I personally spoke to the president yesterday to brief him on what was going on. On my say-so he took it seriously. He's passed the word on only to his most trusted aides. No one else knows. The security for all the president's senior advisors has been tightened so as not to let on that we're expecting something to happen to the secretary of state in particular. Now that we know precisely where the hit will be, and when, we'll take care of it. Security on that damned island will be tighter than a matador's pants. And we'll see that you're taken to a hospital, and later get your name cleared. Don't worry about a thing. Your part's done for now. And a damn good job.''

Jack shook his head. "You're not counting me out because of a little hole in my side." Concentrating for the length of his conversation with Ramsey had clearly taken a toll on him. His words were slurring. But he made an obvious effort. "You need me. The agency's no help while Bigfoot is on the loose. Even the secretary of state's own secret service guard is suspect. Everybody is suspect; the sleeper could be anywhere. I want to be there. At the hit. On the Island. It's my baby, General.''

General Ramsey frowned. "There's no need. You're not up to it. And what about Miss Winston?''

"I go with Jack," Clara interjected. Jack looked up at her for a moment, hugging herself as she stood near his head, then his eyes shifted back to General Ramsey and he nodded.

"You heard the lady. She stays with me.''

"It's damn foolishness. You're wounded, you need to be in a hospital.''

Jack shook his head. "I won't be safe in a hospital. Not at Lejeune, not anywhere. Not until Bigfoot's uncovered. And you know it, General. Besides, I have some more information for you. Might be vital. I'll give it to you when you get me to Seabrook Island.''

General Ramsey looked angry. "That's blackmail!''

Jack's eyes narrowed. His shoulders moved in what might have been a shrug. "Whatever works."

General Ramsey stared down at him for a moment, his bushy salt-and-pepper eyebrows working furiously. Clara held her breath. . . .

"You've got balls, McClain, I'll give you that. You always did." He shook his head and suddenly grinned. "All right, boy, you've got it. We're going to Seabrook Island."

XXV

Seabrook Island was gorgeous. It was a twenty-two-hundred acre private resort of lush flowers, moss draped trees and rain forest vegetation located off the South Carolina coast twenty-three miles from Charleston. Breakers crashed against the resort's white sand beaches. Three-story balconied villas of silvered timbers faced the ocean on one side and a central, porticoed lodge on the other. Other groups of villas were situated on the edge of the golf course fairway and in the maritime forest. Small inland waterways rife with birds and wildlife meandered across the island to spill into the sea. Manmade lakes glittered in the verdant setting like sapphires. A great salt marsh of tall rushes growing thickly on acres of mud and water separated the island from the mainland. The island paradise was the perfect spot for a dream vacation—or a very hush-hush summit meeting.

Three days after they had arrived with General Ramsey in rented cars (the military variety having been deemed too conspicuous), Jack was already sitting up in bed in the three-bedroom villa that had been provided for the two of them. He was an aggravating patient, but Clara was so relieved that he really wasn't going to die that she didn't mind. She fetched and carried for him uncomplainingly, feeding him his meals when he was too weak to eat himself, giving him sponge baths in bed when he very loudly preferred her ministrations to those of the doctor. When General Ramsey appeared for his twice daily huddle with Jack, she either sat in on the meetings or vanished for a walk along the beach, according to the gentlemen's preference. She could always tell by General Ramsey's eyebrows if he wanted to be private with Jack, and she had no objection to leaving the two of them alone. She loved walking along the lonely stretches of seawashed white sand, which were almost deserted now during the resort's off-season. She didn't like to leave Jack alone, and he didn't like being left to Captain Kryzanski's tender mercies, so the general's confidential visits were about the only free time she had. If Clara asked, she was sure that Jack would tell her what went on during those meetings, but Clara didn't ask. She didn't particularly want to know all the details of the plots the two of them were hatching. She had an uneasy feeling that whatever it was they were getting so excited about would end up involving a lot of bloodshed. Jack seemed to thrive on violence, and Wild Bill Ramsey wasn't much better. But Clara had had her belly full of death and guns and bloodshed. She just wanted Jack and herself safe and together, far away from the whole mess.

The notion that she, might be falling in love with him unsettled her. He was too much of a loner, an outcast from all she'd been raised to hold dear. She wanted a nice, ordinary man with a nice, ordinary job so she could have a nice, ordinary life with nice, ordinary children. All of which seemed impossible with her crazy spy.

When they had first arrived on the island, they had no sooner gotten settled into the villa than General Ramsey came across the ten feet or so of scrub grass and sand that separated their villa from his, which was next door. Clara quite liked General Ramsey, helped no doubt by his pronouncement that Puff, who was staying with his wife at Camp Lejeune until Clara could reclaim him, was a cat with *personality*. Jack had told her that General Ramsey was a cat lover, and described how Puff had reacted to him. In Clara's opinion, anyone whom Puff liked couldn't be all bad. So when he banged on their front door, Clara let him in with a smile. But the general obviously had something on his mind. With scarcely more than a grunt he took himself up to the bedroom where Jack was being examined by Captain Kryzanski, who along with Captain Spencer and a small platoon of marines had accompanied them.

"These kids I can trust," General Ramsey said when Clara had questioned their presence. And she could see the sense of that. In civilian clothes, as were the general and the other officers, the grunts were deployed around the villas to keep supposedly inconspicuous guard. Clara didn't think they were very inconspicuous, but then she knew they were there. She supposed if one didn't, they might pass for gardeners, or sunbathers, or whatever. As protection against Rostov and his men, if they should by some horrible mischance discover their prey's hiding place, Clara feared that the grunts would be outclassed. But Jack did not seem particularly concerned. He had laughed when he saw General Ramsey's own private security detail, and said old Wild Bill was a careful man.

"So where's the information you promised me?" General Ramsey bellowed as soon as Captain Kryzanski, in response to a scowl, had left the room. Clara had remained behind that first day, and stood, arms crossed over her chest, at the foot of the luxuriously appointed king-sized bed in the villa's master suite. She thought that Jack, who could not even sit up at that point, might need her. And so she stayed despite Ramsey's beetle-browed look.

That meeting took place less than thirty-six hours after General Ramsey had spirited them from the motel. It was Friday the ninth of October. The planned assassination of the secretary of state was exactly one week away. Jack was still very weak, but as General Ramsey gruffly told Clara there was no time to let him recover in peace. Matters were getting urgent. Time was growing short.

He was lying propped up on pillows, his aggressive chin clean-shaven and his hair neat. He was bare from the waist up, a professionally applied white bandage around his chest. His right arm was in a sling. His skin beneath its surface tan was nearly as white as the bed linen. But his eyes were bright, that familiar emerald green, and he even managed a weak grin.

"Good morning, General."

"Don't bother me with that malarkey. You promised me information. What is it?"

By way of a reply, Jack manipulated his tongue inside his mouth. He raised his hand to his lips, and seemed to spit something into his hand. While Clara watched wide-eyed, he held up a tooth with an air of triumph.

"What the hell is that?" General Ramsey spoke for them both. Looking from Jack to the tooth in his hand, Clara saw a definite gap in his pearly smile where his right cuspid had been. Jack had a false tooth!

"You didn't think the furball was the only trick I had up my sleeve, did you, General?" Jack's eyes twinkled at Ramsey as he unscrewed the root from the crown section of the tooth. Nestled inside, a perfect fit, was a red and yellow capsule.

"Well, I'll be goddamned!" The general sounded both amazed and affronted. Jack twisted the capsule to reveal a tiny microfilm, which he shook out into the palm of his hand. "Another microfilm? You've been holding out on me, McClain!"

"Sorry, sir, but I didn't know at that point if I could trust you or not. I didn't want to put all my eggs in one basket. I've lived as long as I have because I'm a cautious man."

"Humph!" The general said, and took the microfilm from Jack's palm. "Where'd you get this one?"

Jack screwed the root back on his tooth and popped it into his mouth like a man taking a pill. He wiggled his tongue, and Clara was amazed to see the cuspid fit right into the dental arch as if it was as natural as the ones on either side of it. And maybe, she thought, frowning at Jack suspiciously, maybe it was. Her spy was chock full of surprises!

"It's half of the original microfilm Yuropov had. He cut it in two in case one half should be discovered, and I thought he had the right idea. No one was looking for *two* microfilms."

"By damn!" Ramsey sounded excited, staring down at the tiny piece of brown film as if it were a holy relic. "I'll get Davey on this right away!"

"I'd like to get a look at it, too, sir."

Ramsey looked at him. "You don't have any more surprises, do you?"

McClain grinned. Clara could see that, as weak as he

was, it cost him an effort. General Ramsey was tiring him. She frowned.

"That was my last one."

"It better be! Hold out on me, will you?" Ramsey was grumbling as he turned to look at Clara. "Miss Winston, you take care of this two-timer, hear? If you need anything, you send one of my boys for it. No need for you to go running errands yourself."

"Thank you, General."

General Ramsey stomped toward the door. "As soon as we get one of those microscope things you look at these with over here I'll let you know what's on it. Take care of yourself, McClain."

When he was gone, Clara walked over and stood frowning down at Jack. "Is there anything else you haven't told me?"

"I don't think I've told you how lovely you look today," he answered with a seraphic smile, reaching for her hand. Clara allowed him to take it and press it to his lips, but her frown increased in severity.

"You never told me about the microfilm at all, not one word from the beginning. You let me think you were saving Puff's life for altruistic reasons when all the time you were really saving your damn microfilm! You never told me that General Ramsey was on our side after Camp Lejeune; I nearly died of nervousness trying to make up my mind whether or not to call him. I couldn't decide if you'd been out of your head or not! And now this! More microfilm hidden in a false tooth! Next you'll tell me that your name isn't really Jack McClain!"

"Well, to tell the truth . . ." Jack said with a roguish grin.

"Arrgh!" Clara jerked her hand away from him and turned on her heel, marching from the room.

"I was just teasing!" he called after her hastily. "Of course my name's Jack McClain! Clara, baby, come back. Please!" And he went into a splendid fit of coughing. Clara weakened, turning back at the head of the stairs. Then he spoiled it by calling after her, "Don't you trust me?"

He was laughing, but she wasn't. The truth was, she didn't trust him. Not one inch.

◆

XXVI

◆

It was nine o'clock that night when General Ramsey came banging on the door. Jack, who at this stage of his recuperation was easily exhausted although he didn't like to admit it, had just fallen asleep. Clara, clad in robe and nightgown charged to the villa at one of the resort's exclusive boutiques, was in the living room-kitchen combination downstairs brewing a fresh pot of coffee. She was nervous despite the general's marine guard, and when the knock sounded at the door she jumped.

"Not going to bed so early, were you?" General Ramsey greeted her as he barged on past. "McClain awake? That microfilm contained material that will blow his socks off!"

"He's sleeping," Clara said, but with a wave of the manila folder he carried in his hand General Ramsey was up the stairs. Clara, shaking her head, closed and locked the door behind him, then followed him up.

"Thought you'd want to see this right away." Ramsey had already switched on the bedside lamp and roused Jack when Clara stepped inside the door to the bedroom. Jack looked bewildered for a moment, blinking and shaking his head to come awake. His black hair was tousled and his chin was covered with black bristles. Looking at him, Clara felt a little ache grow in her heart. How could she ever have thought him less than handsome?

"What is it?" Levering himself up against the pillows, sounding groggy, McClain nevertheless accepted the folder from Ramsey. He couldn't seem to get himself situated comfortably in the bed. The mobility in his right arm was severely restricted. Clara hurried over to arrange his pillows for him. He leaned forward, permitting her to do so as he opened the file.

Taking her attentions for granted already, was he? she mused with one eye on his bent black head. But then he let out a whistle, and her attention shifted to the folder in his hands.

It contained two xeroxed pages. One was a grainy black-and-white head and shoulders shot of a young man in the high-collared gymnasterka uniform of the Soviet army. He was lean, with strong features and a long, hooked nose. In the picture his hair was slicked close to his head, but it appeared to be jet black. His eyes were surprisingly pale for such dark hair, but their exact color could not be determined. A caption under the picture identified the man as Nikolai Andreivich Bukovsky. The other page was Bukovsky's biography. Clara skimmed it rapidly.

Nikolai Bukovsky was born on August 17, 1922 in the village of Gorlovka in the eastern Ukraine. His father was a coal miner and a soldier in the Red Army. His mother was of mixed Latvian and Polish descent. He was the oldest of four children, had excellent grades in school and a passion for aviation. In June 1941, when Hitler attacked the Soviet Union by bombarding the port of Sevastopol, Bukovsky joined the Red Army. He was put into training in the fledgling Air Force. He flew throughout the war, first in antiquated wooden planes and later in modern fighters. In October 1944 he was shot down near Warsaw by German antiaircraft guns. He was first listed as missing in action. His family was later officially notified that he was dead. He was twenty-two years old.

"Who is Nikolai Bukovsky?" Clara asked, frowning. She knew the folder must have major significance from the way General Ramsey was behaving, but she could not quite figure out what it was.

"I think," Jack said slowly, his eyes dropping to the picture once more, "I rather think we've found Bigfoot."

"My conclusion precisely," General Ramsey agreed, beaming.

"But how can Nikolai Bukovsky be Bigfoot?" Clara still didn't understand. "It says in the file that he was killed in 1944."

"That's what it says," General Ramsey confirmed with cheerful good humor.

Jack took pity on her. "Just because someone's official file says that they died doesn't really mean that they did. The KGB often changes files on its agents to read the way they want them to. My guess is that Bukovsky didn't die at all. He was recruited as an agent. He was sent to the United States as a sleeper after the war, and he's here now. As Bigfoot."

"But how could he be? How could a man like that have reached the kind of level in our intelligence network that Bigfoot supposedly has? Don't they do background checks, for goodness sakes?"

"Obviously he's taken on another identity. But now that we know what we're looking for, it shouldn't be too hard to find him. We need to run background checks on our list of suspects, look for information that doesn't hold water before 1944. Forged high school and college transcripts, for example. Phony birth certificate. No friends or family who knew him prior to 1944, that sort of thing.''

"Wouldn't it just be easier to compare this picture with the suspects? Surely he couldn't have changed that much."

Both men looked at her pityingly.

"If he's a sleeper, he'll almost certainly have had plastic surgery, Clara," Jack said. He was frowning, seemingly thinking of something else.

"Davey's running those background checks now. Then we'll start checking official facts against real life. Shouldn't take more than a couple of days, would you think, McClain?"

Jack was still frowning. He looked distracted.

"I don't know, General. Bigfoot is certain to have covered his tracks well. It may take more than a background check to smoke him out. But I agree that that's the first step."

"Yes, well, we'll get him, one way or another. Now that we know he's there, and where he came from, it's just a matter of time."

"Time's what we don't have too much of, General. The hit on the secretary of state will take place in less than a week. And he's compromising security every day."

"The secretary of state thing is all taken care of," General Ramsey said, reclaiming the file and tucking it beneath his arm. "Simplest damned thing in the world, when you think about it. The hit will go through all right, only they won't get the secretary. We've got a substitute all lined up. Same general height and build, arriving in the secretary's limousine with the secretary's security detail. Nobody will know the difference. If the hit goes down, they'll be shooting the wrong man."

"The poor man!" Clara gasped.

General Ramsey grinned at her. "He'll be wearing bullet-proof armor under his clothes. He'll be fine. And we'll catch the gunman in the act. If the background check doesn't turn up anything, maybe he can lead us to Bigfoot."

"Yeah." McClain still sounded distracted. Ramsey frowned at him, and said heartily that he must be off. Clara accompanied him down to the door.

"Still feeling pretty rocky, isn't he?" the general asked. Clara nodded.

"Well, he's done his share. You keep him in bed now, you hear? No need for him to worry about anything. Between us, Nick and Davey and I have things under control."

When Clara shut the door behind him and went back upstairs, Jack was still sitting up in bed, frowning.

"What's the matter?" she asked, crossing to him and pulling a pillow from beneath his head so that he was lying on just one.

"Hey!" he protested her action, then settled back, brow furrowing. "I've got a funny feeling about this one. Like there's something there that I know that I don't know I know. Know what I mean?"

"Yeah, I know." Clara was gently mocking him. He gave her a lopsided smile.

"The whole thing's too damn easy," he muttered.

"Quit worrying and go to sleep." Clara leaned over to turn out the bedside lamp.

He reached over and caught her hand, drawing her down so that she was sitting on the edge of the bed beside him. His fingers traced the scalloped edge of her cream colored quilted robe.

"I like that. Where'd you get it?"

"At the Columbella. It's a very exclusive boutique, and this robe cost a small fortune. General Ramsey told me to buy what I needed there and charge it to the villa, so I did."

"Nice." His hand slid beneath the neckline of the robe to stroke the silky skin just below her collarbone. Even that slight touch jolted through Clara like electricity. She caught his hand, pulled it from her skin, and held it firmly.

"Why'd you do that?" He sounded injured. Clara tried to release his hand, but his fingers twined with hers.

"You need to go to sleep."

"Sleep with me."

Clara's eyes widened. "You've got to be kidding. With that hole in your chest?"

She could see the gleam of his teeth through the darkness as he grinned.

"My, you do have a dirty mind. I meant just sleep. You know, zzzzz?"

"Sure you did."

"I did. To tell you the truth, I don't like to sleep alone anymore."

Clara looked at him suspiciously. His voice was wistful, plaintive. Not like Jack at all.

"Why not?"

"I have horrible nightmares." It was a tremulous whisper. She wasn't falling for *that*. If he was really having nightmares, he'd let himself be tortured on a rack before he would admit it to a soul.

"Every one of which I'm sure is well deserved!" She responded tartly and tried to stand up. He shouted with laughter and kept her beside him. As weak as he was, his grip was surprisingly strong. Clara didn't want to struggle for fear she might hurt him, so she allowed him to hold her in place.

"I like you, Clara Winston," he told her when his laughter had quieted to a broad grin. Then he brought her hand to his mouth and pressed his lips against her palm.

"Sleep with me. Please? Nothing else, I promise. It's foolish to mess up two beds when we can make do with one perfectly well."

That wasn't much of a reason, but Clara allowed herself to be persuaded. To tell the truth, she knew she would miss him if she went to bed in the other room. She'd grown accustomed to his presence, solid and warm beside her, when she slept.

"If you'll give me back my hand, I'll take off my robe," she said, capitulating. She didn't want him to know how much she wanted to join him in that enormous bed.

"I can't wait." He watched her slide out of her robe, expressing lecherous approval of the pretty pink nightgown beneath. Falling to mid-calf, edged with creamy lace around the neckline and hem, it was a lovely, feminine confection that, if she were honest, she would admit she'd bought with him in mind. Curling up beside him, careful not to touch his injured side, she thought about telling him so. But she was leery of giving him an idea of the extent of the hold he was getting on her heart.

"Kiss me good night, baby," he murmured, his good arm pulling her close. Obediently she reached up to kiss his lips. She intended it to be a soft, butterfly kiss, but he caught her mouth with his, parting her lips and kissing her with an intensity that shook her soul. When he let her go she was trembling.

"I want like hell to make love to you." His hand was sliding over her bare arm, rubbing up and down, creating a delicious friction.

"We can't," she whispered weakly. Lying shivering

beside him in the dark, the imprint of his kiss on her lips, she caught herself wondering just how much his wound would hamper his activities. Maybe if she made love to him. . . .

A soft snore put an end to those musings. Staring at him through the darkness, Clara realized that her sexy spy was fast asleep. For a moment she felt affronted. Then she had to grin.

"I like you too, Jack McClain," she whispered into the darkness as she curled closer to his side.

XXVII

By Wednesday of the following week the background check had turned up nothing. General Ramsey ordered Captain Spencer to probe deeper; Captain Spencer vowed to do his best. Jack seemed preoccupied, when he wasn't closeted with General Ramsey, which was most of the time. The gears were already turning to foil the assassination of the secretary of state; they worked instead on identifying Bigfoot. But so far they'd had no luck.

"We'll have to plant some disinformation, see where it comes out," Jack said finally.

"It could take quite a while," Captain Spencer objected. "We'd have to feed totally separate bits of false information to every single suspect on our list. Counting the members of the Senate Intelligence Committee and the President's aides, we're talking about a lot of time and a lot of trouble. And there's no guarantee that Bigfoot would even pass on the information we gave him."

"It would have to be something urgent, something that he would have to pass on immediately."

"They don't know that we know that they broke our VKR

code. We could pass that information along in a top secret memo and include a new code. A different one for each suspect. Then all we'd have to do is wait and see which one was used."

General Ramsey and Captain Spencer stared at him with something approaching awe.

"Brilliant!" Captain Spencer said with an air of congratulation. "That will work perfectly."

"Do you know the codes?" General Ramsey inquired. "The new ones would have to be legitimate, something we could trace."

"Oh, yeah," McClain said grimly. "I know the codes."

General Ramsey and Captain Spencer were closeted with Jack far into the night. They even ordered in a room service meal, so intent on what they were doing that they barely took a break to eat.

Clara ate a solitary dinner in front of the TV. She was lonely, damn it. Her spy was not being much in the way of a companion. She'd be glad when this whole mess was over and she could go home. Suddenly she longed for Jollymead with an intensity that brought tears to her eyes. It was hard to believe that twelve days before she had spent a peaceful day finishing up her book and had never dreamed that any of this was about to happen. in the wildest reaches of her imagination she would never come up with anyone like Jack.

The late news went off. Clara clicked off the TV and went upstairs. The door to the master bedroom was still firmly closed. She eyed it with disfavor and decided to take a bath. A long, relaxing soak in a hot tub was just what she needed.

She turned on the taps, added some lilac scented bath salts thoughtfully provided by the hotel, and went into the second bedroom where she kept her new clothes. At the

Columbella she'd bought only what she needed, but for someone who had possessed only a grubby pair of jeans, a torn shirt, a borrowed sweater, and a well worn silk teddy, all but the teddy liberally stained with blood, it came to a considerable number of garments. Besides the quilted robe, she had bought two nightgowns, one pink and one cream, a gorgeous raspberry lace bra and several pairs of panties in the same luscious shade, a vanilla satin teddy with a plunging vee neck and high cut thighs filled in with cascades of café au lait lace that she'd fallen in love with, three pair of pantyhose, a pair of flat sandals and a pair of heeled sandals, a gorgeous yellow halter sundress splashed with white flowers, a broad-brimmed sunhat, and two pairs of shorts and matching tee shirts. Most of the clothes she never would have bought two weeks earlier; they were too flashy, too bright, and too revealing. But she had slimmed down and firmed up wonderfully what with everything that had happened, and even she had to admit that her body looked nice. And something had happened to her inside as well. Before she had been content to hide in the shadows; now she had the confidence to walk boldly in the sunlight. To what she owed the change she wasn't sure, but she expected it boiled down to one person: Jack.

She pulled the cream nightgown and her robe from the closet, armed herself with the creams and cosmetics she had charged at the drugstore, and went into the bathroom. The water was almost ready. Piling her blonde hair on top of her head and securing it with bobby pins, she creamed her face, rinsed it, then applied a thick layer of moisturizer. With all the abuse her skin had taken lately, it could use a deep moisturizing treatment. She would let the steam from the tub help it penetrate her skin.

Turning off the taps, she peeled off the lime green shorts

and top and the lacey raspberry underwear and stepped into the tub. Washing herself languidly, she thought what a luxury a hot bath was. She had never really appreciated it before she'd gone adventuring with her spy.

The hot water was making her sleepy. Finished washing, she lay back against the rolled porcelain lip and closed her eyes. The lilac scented steam wafted around her nostrils; she breathed it in with pleasure.

"You look like Caspar the Friendly Ghost."

The familiar but unanticipated voice made her sit bolt upright, her eyes flying open. The door had opened without her hearing it. Jack stood leaning against the doorjamb, barechested except for the white bandage, lean hips clad in a pair of pale blue cotton pajama pants. His feet were bare. Her eyes flew back up to his face. Those green eyes gleamed at her. Clara remembered the inch of thick white cream she had slathered on her face and her hands immediately flew to her cheeks. Then she saw where his eyes rested. Her bare breasts, gleaming with bath oil and water, were well above the water line. Not that the rest of her was much better covered. The water made a very inefficient shield for her modesty.

She dropped her hands from her cheeks to cross them over her breasts and glared at him.

"What are you doing in here? You're not supposed to be out of bed."

He grinned, his eyes shifting back up to meet hers. He knew how embarrassed she was, the devil; she could tell he did from the mocking smile that curved his lips.

"Wild Bill and Davey finally went home. I got lonesome. Then I got worried. Suppose Wild Bill's baby green marines had slipped up on security? Suppose Rostov had crept into the villa and spirited you away? Suppose you'd guzzled too much of the orange liquor the hotel provided and were passed out cold on the kitchen floor? I had to see.'' His grin widened. "And I do see.''

"Would you get out of here?'' His obvious amusement was annoying her. Embarrassment was quickly being replaced by good, healthy anger. She scowled at him.

He sniffed the air, ignoring her. "Mmm, nice! Flowers?''

"Lilacs. Jack, I'm taking a bath. Please leave!''

He cocked an eyebrow at her, his green eyes sparkling devilishly.

"I haven't had a real bath in weeks.''

His hands were on the snap fastening of his pajama pants. Clara began to get an inkling of his meaning. Her puritan soul was horrified.

"Jack, don't you dare! You can't get in here! What about your bandage?'' The last was an almost wailed last ditch effort to stop him. But he paid no attention, stepping out of the pajama pants and into the tub with her. Clara squeaked, drawing up her legs as he sat down.

"Quit splashing. You'll get my bandage wet. Clara, baby, what is that mess on your face?''

Clara had been so preoccupied with the ramifications of his presence in the bathroom while she was taking a bath that she had completely forgotten the white cream on her face. Mortified, she scooped up water in her hands and splashed it off. When she had finished, blinking her eyes against the stinging combination of perfumed water and face cream, he thoughtfully passed her the small towel that had been sitting on the tiled floor beside the tub for just such a purpose. She dried her face with it, then eyed him over the top of it. The ends of the towel trailed down into the water, effectively shielding her body.

"You're not shy, are you?" he asked in a teasing tone, tugging on the edge of the towel. Clara clutched it tighter.

"Certainly not!"

He grinned. And tugged on the towel again.

"I bet this is the first time you've ever had a man in the bathtub with you."

Clara glared at him. "If it were, I certainly wouldn't tell you!"

Jack gave a jerk and the towel flew from Clara's hands to land in a sodden heap on the floor.

"Oh!" Her eyes were wide as they met his. She stood up abruptly. Water streamed down her body as she stepped from the tub, reaching for the towel. Jack had an excellent view of full white breasts crested with velvety pink nipples, a narrow waist, curvaceous hips and a flat belly with an adorable round navel just above a triangular nest of ash brown hair. Her legs were long and lovely and well-shaped too. And when she turned her back on him, her round little ass nearly gave him palpitations.

"Baby, you turn me on," he said, meaning it. She had wrapped a towel around herself by that time and turned back to frown at him severely.

"You should be in bed."

He manuevered himself so that he was sitting back against the tapless end of the tub. Resting both arms along the side, he smiled at her. The charm of that lopsided smile took her breath.

"I told you. I got lonely. Besides, I need a bath."

"So take one." She turned and started to gather up her nightclothes prior to leaving the room. He watched her, his eyes gleaming over the long bare expanse of her legs.

"I could use some help," he said plaintively. "After all, I

don't want to get my bandage wet. Think of the complications that could lead to. I could *die*."

She turned to look at him.

"You are so full of buffalo chips, McClain, that I'm surprised you haven't experienced spontaneous combustion by now."

That surprised a laugh out of him. She eyed him with disfavor, then turned on her heel and marched out of the bathroom, towel still wrapped around her body and nightclothes in hand.

"Clara, wait!"

There was a tremendous splashing as he clambered out of the tub. Then Clara was horrified to hear a yell, an enormous thud—and silence.

"Jack!" She rushed back into the bathroom to find him sprawled flat on his back on the floor. His eyes were closed, his head resting near the toilet. Had he hit his head as he fell?

"Jack!" She dropped to her knees beside him, touching his shoulder, his face, her fingers slipping gently through the hair on the top and back of his head as she sought for visible signs of an injury. "Jack, say something!"

"Something," he said, his eyes popping open even as his hands closed over her arms.

"You cheater!" Those green eyes were sparkling with laughter. "You no-good, dirty polecat! You—"

"Keep talking, sweet thing," he murmured, still grinning as he pulled her closer. "Your words are music to my ears."

"Filthy pig!" Clara wailed, even as he tugged her close enough so that he could catch her lips with his. He had to lift his head from the floor to do it; his fingers were tight around her upper arms. She knew she could pull away; a sideways turn of her head would at least free her lips of his mouth.

But his warm, soft lips on hers were so tantalizing, gently seductive, promising better things to come. Clara felt her eyes closing and didn't even fight it. She could imagine nothing she wanted more than to have him kiss her.

"You smell nice," he whispered as his mouth left hers to trail a string of fiery kisses along her neck. Clara pressed her lips to his shoulder and had to repress a giggle.

"So do you," she said unsteadily. The scent of lilac was intoxicating mixed with his musky aroma.

"Mmm, I could eat you up." His mouth was trailing along her collarbone, moving lower. His hands released her arms at last to slide around her back. With a quick tug the towel parted in front, baring her breasts to him.

Clara looked down at herself, saw the soft white globes with their strawberry nipples suspended over his face, saw too the darkening of his eyes to emerald as he took in her bounty.

"God, you're beautiful." His voice was a husky growl. Clara felt the force of it like a tremor along her spine. Then his lips were trailing along the upper slopes of her breasts, his bristly chin moving back and forth over the swelling softness until she was gasping, on fire for him to take her nipples in his mouth. At last he did. He licked and bit and suckled her like a babe, while Clara watched him through a smoky daze. He was so dark and she so fair. . . .

She was kneeling beside his prone body, leaning over him. His hands slid down to knead her bottom. His hands were so large and warm and strong against her silky curves; his mouth was hot and wet and powerful on her breasts. A clamoring started deep in the pit of her belly, a quickening that grew and grew and demanded more.

Her hands were on his chest, careful not to go near the bandage as they tested his muscles, ran over each hard sinew, tugged on the forest of curly dark hair. His chest was so wide; his belly with its arrow of black hair was so hard and flat. She loved his belly, she thought, stroking it while his hands explored her bottom and his mouth caressed her breasts.

Then his hand slid lower, slipping between her thighs from the rear, creeping and stroking along the hot womanly flesh of her until they found the opening and his fingers slid inside.

"Oh, Jack!" She was leaning over him, completely open to his mouth and his touch, her eyes closed as her body caught fire for him. Trembling, she lay against his chest, not even thinking about his wound now, or hurting him or anything else except the marvelous way he was making her feel. His fingers moved inside her. She made a little mewling sound and sank her teeth in his shoulder. Blindly her fingers reached for the swollen proof of his desire.

"Hold it!"

Clara blinked as Jack sat up, bringing her up with him.

"Jack!" Her hands clung to him; her body craved him. He couldn't stop now!

"I'll be damned if I'm going to make love to you on a hard bathroom floor when there's a perfectly good bed in the next room," he gritted, standing up. Clara knelt naked at his feet, looking up at him with dazed eyes. She wanted him. . . . Naked, towering over her, he was beautiful, all bronzed skin and muscles and black curling hair. Her eyes riveted on the part of him that stood out from the rest of his body. It was huge and hot looking and pulsing for her.

"Come on." He reached down, pulling her to her feet, then slid his arms around her and lifted her against his chest. Clara came out of the daze she was lost in as he started to stride from the bathroom.

"Jack, put me down! Jack, your wound!"

"To hell with the damn thing," he muttered. Then it was too late to argue because he had reached the bed and was tumbling her down on it. She landed against cool sheets, lying sideways, legs dangling over the side of the bed. He came down on top of her, hard and fast, and she spread her thighs to accommodate him. Then he was inside her, plunging deep, surprising sharp cries of ecstasy from her as he took her with furious need. Her arms were around his neck and her legs were around his waist and she was trembling, shaking, dying with the bliss of what he was doing to her.

His mouth found her nipples, pulling one into his mouth and closing his teeth around it, suckling and biting until she thought she would go crazy, and all the while he was slamming into her like a jackhammer gone wild.

"Clara! My God, Clara!" He called her name as he drove into her one final time, shuddering. The force of his climax drove her over the edge, and she cried out too, holding him tight as she was whirled away.

XXVIII

By the time morning rolled around Clara was so exhausted that all she wanted to do was lie in bed with her head under the pillow and sleep the day away. She had lost count of the number of times she and Jack had made love during the night. He'd been tireless, and despite her occasional feeble remonstrations about his wound she'd been more than willing. They hadn't closed their eyes until dawn was sneaking bright pink fingers across the sky.

Beside her, Jack was snoring. She listened groggily to the sound, wondering if that was what had awakened her. Then she heard it again: the imperious pounding on the villa's door.

"Oh, no!" she groaned. She buried her head beneath the pillow again, attempting to ignore General Ramsey's morning summons in hopes that he would go away. But the pounding sounded again, forceful enough to shake the walls of the villa, accompanied by the general's bass voice calling, "Miss Winston, is everything all right?"

Clara sat up in bed, giving Jack a baleful glare. He was still blissfully asleep. Clara didn't see how any normal human being could sleep through the racket the general was making, but Jack was doing a good job of it. She shook his shoulder. He didn't move, so she shook it again, harder.

The snoring stopped. One green eye peered out from under his arm to blink at her.

"Baby, you're the sexiest thing on two legs, but I'm going to have to take a raincheck for now. I'm dead beat," he muttered. Then his eye closed again. Clara stared down at him, amused in spite of herself.

"You are a conceited soul, Jack McClain," she told the back of his black head. Getting out of bed, she pulled on her robe and went downstairs to let General Ramsey in before he had one of his grunts break down the door.

After she let the irate general in, she went into the kitchen to make a pot of coffee as he stomped up the stairs. If Jack felt as wiped out as she did, he would need the caffeine jolt to make sense of a word General Ramsey said. When the coffee was ready, she put the pot, sugar, cream, cups and saucers on a tray and carried it up the stairs. Jack was just dragging himself to a sitting position while General Ramsey glared at him.

"None of the codes have been used," she heard the general say as she entered with the coffee. Jack, bleary-eyed, grinned at her as she set the tray down on the bedside table. Clara gave him a narrow look. Raincheck, indeed!

"Coffee, General?" she asked civilly as she passed Jack a cup. Jack took his black with one spoonful of sugar, she already knew.

"Thank you. Just a little cream." Clara poured the coffee and passed it to him, then poured herself a cup. She would take it into the bathroom with her as she dressed.

"We'll have to—" the general began, only to break off

abruptly and sniff the air. Clara, already heading toward the door, saw his eyes widen as they focused on Jack.

"That's the damned wimpiest smelling aftershave I've ever come across in my life, boy," General Ramsey said, glaring at Jack. "It smells like *flowers!*"

Jack, in the act of swallowing some coffee, choked. Clara grinned when she saw the tip of his ears go red as his horrified gaze met the general's. She was still grinning as she left the room. After that, Jack would think twice before climbing into a scented bathtub!

By the time night fell Clara was dead on her feet. Jack had gone next door to the villa General Ramsey shared with Captain Spencer to work with some of the sophisticated computer equipment the general had had brought to the island. She made herself a light supper, thinking that she would wait up for him. But by the time he came in, she was fast asleep on the couch.

"Wake up, sleepyhead," she heard him say. Groggily, she tried a smile. But her eyes would not open. She was so tired she couldn't swim through the dense layers of sleep. She felt his arms go around her, and then he was picking her up and carrying her up the stairs. Clara roused herself enough to slide her arms around his neck and rest her head against his shoulder. He dropped a quick kiss on her lips as he laid her on the bed.

"I'm beat, too. Go on back to sleep, baby," he murmured. Clara tried another smile at him, felt him ease her out of her robe, vaguely heard him shed his clothes and felt the solid warmth of his body as he climbed in beside her. Snuggling close to him, she gave herself up to sleep.

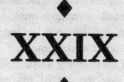

XXIX

"Clara!"

"Hmmm?"

"Clara!"

She felt the nuzzle of a mouth against her neck and instinctively stretched her chin out of the way. The mouth dropped lower, traveling over the smooth upper slope of her right breast before coming to rest on the nipple. The hot moistness of that mouth burned through to her skin. Clara opened her eyes.

Jack lifted his mouth from her breast to grin at her.

"Let's go swimming."

"What?" The suggestion so surprised Clara that at first she wasn't sure she heard it correctly. Jack obligingly repeated himself.

"In the middle of the night?"

"Haven't you ever fantasized about swimming in the ocean by moonlight?"

"No."

He laughed. "Think of it as another experience for your books."

Clara groaned, but when Jack got out of bed she watched him with sleepy eyes. He was not kidding, she saw to her surprise as he shucked off his pajama pants and stepped into a pair of bermudas and a white sweatshirt that had been charged for him at the gift shop.

"You can't go swimming with a hole in your chest."

"Captain Kryzanski says I'm ninety percent recovered. Not even lilac scented bathwater will hurt me."

"When did he say that?"

"After he noticed my peculiar smell today."

Clara smiled into her pillow. Jack saw it and pulled her up into a sitting position on the side of the bed.

"I don't have anything to wear. I didn't buy a swimsuit."

Jack sighed. "Why is it women think they must be perfectly dressed for every single thing they do? Baby, nobody cares if you don't have a swimsuit. It's dark outside. That thing you have on will be perfect. It even looks like a swimsuit. A sexy one."

That thing was the new teddy, which she had put on to wait for Jack in before she had fallen asleep on the couch. Clara looked down at it. So Jack thought it was sexy, did he? It faithfully revealed every curve and hollow of her body. Her nipples pressed against the shimmery silk and frothy lace spilled out of the high cut sides that made her legs look impossibly long and slender. She *felt* sexy in it.

"Come on. It's almost dawn. I want to watch the sun come up from the beach. The sun rising over the ocean is one of the most beautiful sights in the world."

Clara groaned. But she got out of bed, pulled on her robe, and allowed Jack to pull her down the stairs.

The beach at night was a beautiful, mysterious place. The moon rode low on the horizon, a hazy white sphere; stars were sprinkled thickly over the midnight blue velvet sky, lighting their way. The white beach stretched before them like a ghostly ribbon, while the white-capped waves rolled in toward shore, one after the other, with a rhythmic roar that was hypnotic. The smell of the sea was everywhere; a briny smell that made Clara think of oysters.

There was a brisk wind blowing. Clara wrapped her arms around herself, glad she had worn the long quilted robe. Looking over at Jack in his bermuda shorts and sweatshirt, she wondered if he was cold. But he didn't seem to be, strolling along beside her with his eyes on the ocean and his hand gripping hers. A young man in the uniform of a motel employee materialized behind them as they passed the end of the line of villas. Jack motioned him back with a curt wave of the hand.

"Who's that?"

"One of Wild Bill's baby green marines. I don't think we need him, do you?"

Clara shook her head. Leaning against Jack's side, her hand entwined in his, she didn't need anyone else in the world. This was another of those times that was just for the moment, she thought. Danger and treachery and death were pushed out of her mind; she would enjoy the night.

The sand was cool and gritty beneath her feet. They were walking close to the ocean's edge, just beyond the place where the tide ebbed and flowed. The sand was wet with spray. Looking behind them, Clara saw the set of twin footprints that marked their path: Two sets of long, narrow feet walking close together and in harmony down the long stretch of moonlit sand. That line of footprints blazed itself into her memory. She knew that she would remember how it looked when she was old.

They walked until the villas were distant gray castles on the horizon, until the beach curved outward along a grassy promontory, forming a small, sheltered cove. Jack stopped, peeling the sweatshirt over his head.

"You're not really going to swim, are you? The water must be freezing!"

"Don't be a pussy," Jack said chidingly, and tugged at her robe. "Come on!"

"Uh-uh," Clara shook her head, crossing her arms over her chest. "You can lead a woman to water, but you can't make her swim. You go ahead. I'll wait right here."

"Pussy." He grinned at her, then ran down to the ocean's edge and waded out. He looked magnificent against the breaking waves. Clara felt a heartstopping frisson of pride that this was her man. Then he was swimming, his strokes strong and vigorous. Clara watched him for a while, worried that he might get beyond his depth, but he stayed parallel with the beach and eventually headed back. When he waded out of the shallows, water streaming from his body, black hair as sleek and shiny as a seal's, he was grinning and shaking the water from his body like a dog. He had lost his bandage during his swim, Clara saw as she hurried down to the water's edge with his sweatshirt. His wound was a puckered black circle surrounded by a yellow and gray bruise.

"It's not cold once you get in, Clara. Come on." He wiped his face on his sweatshirt as he spoke. Clara looked at him suspiciously.

"You wouldn't lie to me, would you, Jack McClain?"

"On my honor, the water's great. Don't you trust me?"

"No!" Clara retorted, and he grinned. Their private joke, she thought, and had to grin in return.

"All right, you bully, I'll try it, but if it's cold I'm coming out."

She shed her robe, letting him take her hand as she waded

gingerly into the sea. The first incoming wave poured gallons of water so cold it must have come straight down from the Arctic Circle around her bare legs.

"Brrrr! It's freezing! Now I remember why I don't trust you, Jack McClain!"

"It's not cold once you get used to it," he protested as she started to scamper back to the beach. Catching her by the wrist, he whirled her back into his arms. Laughing, struggling, she felt his arms slide behind her knees and around her shoulders and shrieked.

"Jack! What are you doing? Put me down! Don't you dare drop me in this freezing water! Do you hear me? Jack!"

He was wading out to sea with her in his arms. She clung to his neck, certain that he meant to drop her at any minute, half laughing as she scolded. He held her carefully out of the water as it churned around his hips.

"What will you give me if I take you back without dropping you?" he asked with a wicked grin.

"That's blackmail!" she gasped.

"Whatever works," he said, shrugging, and she had to laugh.

"A dollar," she suggested, grinning.

He shook his head. "A kiss."

That certainly wasn't any hardship. With the moon glinting off his black hair, black stubble sandpapering his cheeks and chin, and those green eyes gleaming wickedly in the ghostly light, he looked as devilishly handsome as the pirates she wrote about. Twining her arms tightly about his neck, she lifted her lips to his. He let her kiss him for a minute, his lips still under hers while she nibbled with her teeth and teased with her tongue. Then, without warning, the kiss changed. He drew in his breath, slanting his mouth across hers, kissing her with bruising intensity so that her head fell back against his shoulder and the world whirled away around her. There was nothing left but him, his mouth, his arms holding her safe.

Then he dropped her.

Clara screamed, the sound drowned in a gurgle of icy water as it closed over her head. Furious, freezing, she found her footing and shot spluttering to the surface. Jack was laughing. She went for him with a roundhouse punch that would have taken his head off if it had connected. Unfortunately, he ducked.

"You creep! You low life! You . . . !" she raged, plunging after him through the waist-high water, throwing punches right and left. He retreated, laughing, holding his arms up in front of his body to ward her off. She could barely see where she was going. Her soaking wet hair blinded her. Sweeping it back with one hand, she aimed one more punch at the no-good dog before turning her back and tromping off toward land. The ebb and flow of the waves made walking difficult, dragging her back one step for every two she took, but she made it to the shallows and kept going, feet splashing through the icy froth. She wrapped her arms around herself, shivering with cold, gritting her teeth with rage. Not even the white-hot blast of her anger could warm her. Jack, who apparently didn't care if he got back to the villa with a whole skin, trailed along behind her, still laughing.

"Don't be mad, Clara."

"Don't be mad? Don't be *mad*? I'm not mad, I'm furious!"

"I'm sorry, Clara. Really. I just couldn't resist."

"Go to hell!"

"Damn it, Clara, it was just a joke! I said I was sorry!"

"Sorry? *Sorry?* I'll make you sorry, you . . ." With that she swung around, both hands clenched into fists, to find him right behind her, grinning from ear to ear. Realizing that his wide grin was probably largely on account of the ludicrous picture she must make, clad in the sexy silk teddy that was nearly transparent when wet, her hair in dripping rattails, teeth chattering, flesh ridged with goosebumps, she saw red. This time the roundhouse punch connected solidly with his cheek.

"Yow!"

"Serves you right!" She turned around, stalking toward the beach. No sooner did she set foot on solid sand than she heard him coming after her. Glancing over her shoulder, she was surprised at the fierce gleam in those green eyes. Instinctively she started to run. Before she had taken more than three steps he downed her with a flying tackle that sent her tumbling to the sand.

"Let go of me! Don't you dare manhandle me! Did you hear me? Let me go, you bully!" Her struggles were useless. Despite her attempts to prevent him, he pulled her backward until she was eye level with green eyes that promised vengeance. She turned onto her back, trying to kick him to free herself. He prevented her by the simple expedient of throwing one hard wet thigh over her thrashing legs. Then she tried to punch him again. He grabbed her hands and had her trapped. Looming over her, he supported himself on one elbow while the other hand held both her wrists prisoner against her waist. Helpless, panting, she glared at him. Suddenly he grinned.

"If I'd known you had a right like Mohammed Ali's I would have ducked. From the feel of it, I'm going to have a black eye."

Clara felt some of her anger fade as she stared up at him

anxiously. As far as she could see there wasn't a mark on him. She didn't even think her fist had gotten anywhere near his eye.

"Now you're going to have to kiss it better," continued her tormentor, leaning closer. "Right there." He turned his head until her lips were approximately two inches from his right eye. Clara looked up at him a minute, contemplating the possibilities. Then she sweetly lifted her head the required two inches and nipped his cheek with sharp little teeth.

"Ouch!" He jerked back, letting go of her hands to touch his abused cheek. His green eyes gleamed down at her. "That's going to cost you, baby. Now you're going to have to kiss me properly."

"Would you please let me up? I'm getting sand down my back!" She wriggled, pushing at his shoulders, trying to free herself. He shook his head, recapturing her hands and pinning them to the sand over her head.

"Not until you kiss me."

"Would you stop being so childish?" He merely looked at her, a grin lurking at the corners of his mouth and his green eyes gleaming. "Oh, all right!" She reached up and pecked his lips with hers. He shook his head, the gleam in his eyes brightening.

"You call that a kiss? *This* is a kiss." With that he lowered his head and took her mouth with his. And he was right: *that* was a kiss. Clara wrapped her arms around his neck and closed her eyes, kissing him as if she'd die if she didn't. The surf pounded in the distance and the stars twinkled overhead as he slipped her out of the teddy and shed his own shorts. They were naked in the sand, the brisk air around them turned to steam heat by the blaze of their passion. He made love to her with a growling intensity that reduced Clara to quivering jelly. And when she had melted in his arms he made love to her again.

Afterwards, he lay sprawled on top of her, his big body warming her as well as any blanket. It took Clara quite some time to return to an awareness of exactly where they were. Never in her wildest imaginings had she thought she would some day find herself lying naked on a public beach with her love while dawn broke around them.

"Look!" He lifted his head to stare at the sky. Then he rolled off her onto his back, shielding his eyes and pointing to the east. His arm around Clara pulled her close to his side. She cuddled against him, warmed by his heat, glad to be curled up in the depression they had found in the sand. Her white robe was nearby. Stretching, she managed to catch hold of it and pull it over them.

"See? Here she comes!"

Clara looked in the direction he pointed and found herself in awe. On the east horizon, the midnight blue velvet of the sky was coming alive with glorious pinwheels of deep pink, crimson, yellow, and orange. Purple ribbons curled through the colorful display while fleecy lavender clouds floated across the surface.

"It's beautiful," she said with awe.

"I knew you'd like it." He sounded smug. Clara looked over at him, lying with one arm bent beneath his head while he marveled at one of nature's wonders. His black hair was already dry; beneath it, his crooked nose and jutting chin were bathed in an orange glow. Clara watched him instead of the sunrise, mentally tracing each blatantly masculine feature, each stubby eyelash, each stubborn whisker. In less than two weeks this man had become her whole world. The thought scared and warmed her at the same time. Looking at him, she felt a tremendous swelling of emotion. Then he turned his head and smiled at her with those incredible emerald green eyes.

"I think I love you, Jack McClain." The words came out of nowhere. Clara blinked at him, as taken by surprise as he.

There was a brief silence as his green eyes bored into hers. His hand came up to trace the outline of her lips. They quivered beneath that butterfly touch.

"Then marry me," he said. Clara caught her breath, her eyes widening. Her crazy, sexy spy wanted to marry her.

"Oh, no!" she breathed in a panic, terrified at the sudden urge she had to throw her arms around his neck and laugh and cry and kiss him and promise him anything. "I can't *marry* you!"

His face went as cold and hard as the rocks behind them. He sat up abruptly, then stood up as Clara gaped at him. She hadn't meant to say the words aloud. What she'd meant to say was that she needed time to think. But he'd caught her by surprise. Never had she given serious thought to becoming his wife. James Bond didn't have a wife.

"Jack, I didn't mean it like it sounded," she said, desperate at the look on his face as he pulled on his soaking shorts and sweatshirt.

"I don't think there's much room for misinterpretation," he said savagely, glaring at her. Clara scrambled to her feet, pulling on the robe and securing it with nervous hands.

Jack was already stalking back in the direction of the villas. Clara ran to catch up with him, grabbing his arm. He shook her off furiously, continuing his angry march.

She caught up with him and grabbed his arm again.

"Jack, I really do love you," she babbled, desperate to make him listen to the jumble of emotions rioting inside her.

"Yeah, you love me so much that the very idea of

marrying me sends you into a spasm,'' he growled, shaking her off again.

"I *do* love you,'' she insisted desperately. He whirled suddenly and caught her by her arms in a grip that hurt. Clara hung suspended from steely fingers, mesmerized by the savagery in those green eyes.

"Baby, what you feel for me isn't called love. It's called *lust*. You got an itch that you need me to scratch, and that's the end of it,'' he bit out. Then he let her go and stalked away.

Clara stood where she was, staring after him, angry, hurt tears slowly filling her eyes. Behind her, some distance away, the crumpled teddy lay forgotten in the sand.

XXX

Friday, October 16, 4:55 P.M.

The secretary of state's limousine was due to arrive in five minutes. The Secret Service was already present in force, having gone over the villa on the golf course where he would be staying and the surrounding area with a fine-tooth comb, and secured it. The Chinese premier was due at approximately the same time, so that neither side would seem to be taking precedence over the other. Of course, the man who stepped out of the secretary of state's car when it arrived would be a decoy, but only a select group knew that. The real secretary of state had arrived earlier, with the bare minimum of escort, in great secrecy.

Clara waited with Captain Spencer and Jack inside the glass-walled meeting room that overlooked the circular drive where the dignitaries would alight. General Ramsey and Admiral Segram were at present closeted with the secretary of state. Security was tightly in place, things were going just as they should, but Clara could not help but be nervous. Would the ruse work? Would an attempted assassination

really take place, or was the whole thing an elaborate
nightmare? If shots were fired, would the decoy survive?
Would the gunman be captured and, if so, could he lead
them to Bigfoot?

Davey Spencer and Jack were as silent as she. All three
of them stood at the floor-to-ceiling window, looking out
over the drive as they watched for the arrival of the cars.
Clara had not seen Jack since he had stalked away from her
on the beach that morning. Now, after a single wintry glance
from his green eyes, he did not so much as look in her
direction. Clara was quietly miserable. She had to talk to
Jack in private. But now was not the time.

"Here they come." Davey Spencer's eyes were alight
with excitement as he announced the appearance of a long
black limousine around the curve in the driveway. Two
white sedans followed the limousine. Clara pressed her nose
to the window as she watched the procession of cars. They
were pulling up to the curb where the secretary of state
would step out.

The time was at hand. The limousine stopped. The two
cars behind it stopped. A man in a uniform sprang from
nowhere to open the rear door of the limousine. A double
line of Secret Service agents formed from the limo door to
the hotel door and looked warily about. A man in a trench
coat with a hat pulled down well over his eyes stepped out,
the supposed secretary of state. He paused for a moment,
looked around, then was joined by another man who had
ridden with him. The two of them walked slowly inside
the building together, surrounded by the small army of
agents.

"Nothing happened!" Clara turned to look at Jack. He
was frowning, his eyebrows knit together in concentration.

Davey Spencer turned away from the window as well. He too looked perplexed.

"They must have found out that we were on to them."

"But how?" Clara chanced to look out the window again. "Look, the Chinese premier is arriving. Oh, well, at least they can have the summit in peace."

"Mmmm." Jack, too, turned to look out the window. The second limousine pulled up in the same spot as the first. Again a uniformed man opened the door. The double line of agents formed. A slight figure in a Western business suit stepped out. A heavyset man in traditional Maoist dress stepped out of the following car and walked toward the first man.

"Deng En-lai," Jack identified the first man as the premier. Losing interest, Clara started to turn away from the window.

Pop! Pop! Pop! Pop!

Gunfire! She would know that sound anywhere! She whirled back around to find pandemonium on the ground below. Deng En-lai was sprawled on the pavement, agents bent frantically over him. A few feet away, more agents overpowered one of their own, who still brandished a pistol.

Pop! Pop! Pop!

More gunshots. The knot of agents who had been wrestling with the gunman fell back. He fell to the pavement, his feet beating an involuntary tattoo on the concrete as he lay, apparently mortally wounded. The heavyset man in the Maoist suit was running from the site of the shooting, heading toward the trees at the side of the grounds.

"No! Don't kill him!" Jack yelled through the glass, though it was doubtful if anyone outside the room heard him. But the agents were chasing the man, dodging his fire, before one brave soul downed him with a football tackle.

There was a moment of appalled silence as the three of them stared at the bloodbath below.

"My God," Davey said slowly. "They weren't after the secretary of state at all. They meant to assassinate Deng En-lai all along. And they've done it!"

XXXI

Friday, October 16, 6:00 P.M.

"We now have an international crisis on our hands." The speaker was the secretary of state, Franklin Conran. "When the word gets out about the assassination of Premier Deng—and the information must be released within twelve or so hours or we face a worse crisis—our relations with China will deteriorate to an all-time low. Premier Deng was in this country secretly, on a highly sensitive peace mission. Most members of his own government were not aware of his intentions. Now he has been murdered on American soil, by an American Secret Service agent. The repercussions will be enormous."

"Is the president aware of the situation?" Admiral Segram leaned forward in his chair, his fingers drumming on the polished wood top of the round table around which they all sat.

"I just finished speaking with him over the telephone."

"And so Bigfoot wins." Jack spoke under his breath. They were in the newly dubbed "situation room" in the

339

basement of the golf villas' main lodge. General Ramsey and Captain Spencer were also present. The secretary of state overheard Jack's comment and nodded.

"Bigfoot wins. Unless we can identify him and expose the assassination to the world as a KGB plot. Is there any chance of that before the information is released?"

"The assassin was a sleeper activated by Bigfoot, a sleeper with such a good cover that he survived even the stringent background checks required by the Secret Service. The second gunman is one of Premier's Deng's aides. He is claiming that he shot the assassin in an excess of emotion upon witnessing the murder of the premier. Of course he is a KGB asset too. His involvement indicates that Premier Deng was the target of the plot all along. However, both Rostov and Yuropov sincerely believed that you, Mr. Secretary, were the target of the plot. Whoever is masterminding this in the Kremlin obviously believes in playing his cards close to his chest. Bigfoot must have waited until the last possible minute to activate the sleeper, or word of the change of target would have trickled back to somebody. Sources have been keeping their ears open. The sleeper was probably not informed of his real target until shortly before the hit." Jack summed up the situation in a thoughtful tone, thinking as he spoke. He threw a narrow-eyed look at Ramsey. "In other words, what we have here is an elaborate game of bluff and double-bluff."

"Has Premier Deng's aide said anything?"

Davey Spencer shook his head. "Not yet. He's being interrogated now. We'll get whatever he knows out of him, don't worry."

General Ramsey looked at Jack. "Any luck with the false information?"

Jack shook his head. "So far none of it has turned up. That could change at any time."

A knock sounded at the door. Davey Spencer got up to answer it. When he came back, he whispered something to General Ramsey, who became visibly excited.

"Mr. Secretary, I've just been informed that the prisoner has broken: he has confessed his involvement with the KGB and states that he has been in contact with Bigfoot since arriving in this country with Premier Deng. His instructions were to call a certain number upon arrival in Charleston. A man answered who knew the code. This man was, we believe, Bigfoot. The prisoner feels he can identify the voice of the man he spoke to."

Franklin Conran's hands tightened on the arms of his chair. "Excellent. Have you checked out the number?"

"A pay phone in Washington."

"Of course the son of a bitch would be careful." Conran sighed. "Well, all we can do is let Premier Deng's aide listen to our suspects' voices and hope he can make a positive ID. How many suspects do we have at this point?"

Jack answered. "Three, Mr. Secretary. The rest we were able to eliminate through various means."

"Who are they?"

"Oliver Simonis, deputy director of the CIA; Michael Ball, retired director of the CIA, and Senator Adam Chandler, chairman of the Senate Intelligence Committee."

"Whewwww!" Admiral Segram whistled through his teeth. "Those are some pretty big fish. Are you sure?"

"That one of them is Bigfoot? Reasonably. Which one? It could be any of the three."

"We need to get those men down here. First so our pigeon can listen to their voices. If he can identify the man he spoke to, we'll be halfway home. Bigfoot can be taken into custody without the media getting hold of it until we've taken steps to minimize the damage. All hell is going to break lose when the public finds out that a Soviet spy has managed to worm his way into a position of such responsibility in our government. Won't look good for the administration.'' Admiral Segram was drumming his fingers on the tabletop. ''We'll have to find a solution. After we've caught Bigfoot, of course. But our first step is to contain the three of them until this thing can be sorted out. Thank God, with the help of Wild Bill and his boys we can do that here. If we can get them here.''

The secretary of state's taut face relaxed into a grim smile. ''I'll ask the president to place a personal call to each of them telling them that we have an international crisis and they have been appointed to the Crisis Containment Committee. The emergency meeting will be held here within the next six hours.''

General Ramsey snorted. ''Do you think Bigfoot will buy that?''

Franklin Conran shook his head. ''He already knows we're on his trail. If he runs, then he reveals himself to us. He can't be sure that he is not being summoned for precisely the reason the president gives. Although there has been no announcement, and the other two members of the Crisis Containment Committee will not be aware of the assassination of Premier Deng, Bigfoot will. Therefore he knows the crisis is genuine. My bet is that he'll come and try to bluff his way through. To have succeeded as well as he has already, he must be a master actor.'' He looked around the table. ''Is there any further discussion?''

The men shook their heads.

''Then let's do it,'' he said, and pushed back his chair.

XXXII

Saturday, October 17, 12:01 A.M.

The group in the situation room had reconvened. In addition to the original members, four new faces had been added: Oliver Simonis, deputy director of the CIA; Michael Ball, recently retired director of the CIA; Senator Adam Chandler, chairman of the Senate Intelligence Committee, and Clara, who had been drafted by General Ramsey to take notes. Her shorthand was not the best, but she used it sometimes in her work and it was serviceable. General Ramsey said that would be fine; they didn't want to bring anyone else into this who was not already directly involved. The consequences of a leak would be severe.

"Gentlemen, please bear with me on this. Two of you are about to be gravely insulted. I apologize for that in advance. But the situation we face requires grave measures and quick action if we are to salvage anything from the debacle." Franklin Conran quickly described the assassination of Premier Deng. Simonis, Ball, and Chandler all looked suitably horrified.

Conran continued. "But the reason that the president asked you to come here is this: we believe that the assassination was carried out with the aid of a high-level mole in the intelligence network. Our suspects have been narrowed down to three: Mr. Simonis, Mr. Ball, and Senator Chandler."

"This has got to be some kind of a joke!" Oliver Simonis protested furiously, rising from his chair.

The other two remained seated, but looked like they agreed with Simonis. Clara looked first at Jack and General Ramsey and then at the flushed or set faces of the suspects in astonished disbelief. She had not realized that the purpose of the meeting was to identify Bigfoot. It was impossible to believe that one of these distinguished public servants had been betraying his country for years. Why, she even knew Senator Chandler! He had been a friend of her mother's for years. When he had entered the small, brightly lit room and greeted her with the same surprise she had felt at seeing him, she had had no idea that *this* was the purpose for which he was present.

"Unfortunately, it is not, Mr. Simonis. Please sit down." Oliver Simonis' face purpled, but with a furious look at the serious faces around the table he sat down. Like the rest of them he could not fail to be aware of the contingent of marines standing guard outside in the hall. No one would leave the room without General Ramsey's clearance.

"It's a damned insult," Simonis muttered. Clara watched him, wondering if he was protesting too much. Was that the sign of a guilty man? Oliver Simonis was a tall, thin man with a tanned, lined face, a hawklike nose and a slightly receding chin. He was in his mid-sixties, as were the other suspects. His once dark hair had turned iron gray. Clara stared at him, wondering if this was the man that Nikolai Bukovsky had matured into. He bore little resemblance to the photo Clara had seen, but then of course he wouldn't. Jack had mentioned plastic surgery. But surely there should be some resemblance to the man Bukovsky had been? Clara looked suddenly at Simonis' eyes. They were hazel. Of course, it was hard to tell in a grainy, blurry Xerox of a black-and-white photo, but she had the impression that Bukovsky's eyes had been lighter than that. If nothing else, surely the eyes would be the same.

"Secretary Conran already apologized for the insult, which I'm sure he recognizes is extreme," Adam Chandler said to the fuming Simonis. Although Senator Chandler didn't look any too pleased himself, he conducted himself with restraint. His drawling voice had only a slight edge to it. Like herself, Adam Chandler was from an old Virginia family. He looked every inch the aristocrat: not overly tall—Clara guessed he wasn't much more than an inch or two above her own five-feet-five inches—but well-muscled and solid, his thinning gray hair impeccably groomed, his dark blue suit clearly from an expensive tailor. *He* could not be Bigfoot, she found herself thinking as she took in his highly polished cordovan wingtips. Why, her grandmother had been acquainted with his parents! All three were long dead, but her mother knew the genealogy of everyone who had ever been born into a prominent family. There was no way Nikolai Bukovsky had forged a background like that! But he must be under suspicion for some reason. Clara looked at his eyes. They were a deep, piercing blue. Like Simonis', the eyes were not right.

"Let's get on with it, shall we?" Admiral Segram was brusque. Franklin Conran nodded.

"What exactly is it that you want us to do, Frank?" Michael Ball, a round little man with a balding head fringed by graying black hair, clearly knew the secretary of state well. If they were friends, or even longstanding associates, Franklin Conran was in an awkward position. But no hint of it showed on the secretary of state's jowly face. Looking carefully, Clara decided that Michael Ball's gray eyes weren't the right color, either. Although they were closer than the other two.

"Probably take a lie detector test." Simonis' face was red with indignation.

"No," Franklin Conran shook his head. "I want each of you to repeat this sentence, please: Comrade, the horsemen are mounted."

"What kind of damned nonsense is that?" Simonis looked like he was on the verge of a stroke.

"It is the code which was used to activate the assassin's murder. Do you refuse to say it?"

"Damn right I—" Simonis looked at the hardening of the faces around the table. "All right, I'll say it. But you better be prepared to make a hell of an apology when this is over, Conran."

"What about you, Mr. Ball?"

"I'll say whatever it takes to get this settled."

Franklin Conran looked at Adam Chandler, who nodded brusquely.

"Very well. Mr. Simonis, if you would go first, please."

"I feel like a horse's ass," Simonis snorted, but he repeated the phrase.

"Mr. Ball."

Michael Ball repeated the phrase.

"Senator Chandler."

Adam Chandler repeated the phrase.

The telephone by Franklin Conran's elbow rang. He picked it up, listened a moment, then nodded to General Ramsey. General Ramsey stood up at once, crossed to the door, opened it and beckoned to the armed guard outside. Six uniformed marines entered and stood at attention in a line barring access to the hall.

"Our man has made a positive identification. Michael Ball, you are under arrest for treason."

"The hell I am!" Michael Ball jumped to his feet, eyes wild, fists clenched. Adam Chandler, who was seated beside him, jumped up too and placed a restraining hand on his arm. The contingent of marines rushed forward. Everyone at the table leaped up as the marines surrounded the struggling, cursing suspect. Ball got off one roundhouse punch, which caught Senator Chandler on the temple. The senator staggered back, hand to his head. The marines forced Ball down on the floor, cuffed his hands behind his back, and it was over. Bigfoot was caught at last.

XXXIII

The room was emptying. Clara stood up, feeling numb. She had given the notes she had made to Franklin Conran, who would have them typed up Monday in his office after the news of the assassination was made public. With the arrest of Michael Ball the nightmare she had been trapped in had finally ended. It was over.

"Clara Winston? That is you, isn't it? What on earth are you doing here?" Senator Chandler walked around the table toward her, frowning and blinking as though he had something in his eye. A reddened circle on his left temple marked the spot where Michael Ball had struck him. Perhaps the blow was causing his eyes to water. "I thought I recognized you as soon as you sat down, but I wasn't sure."

"It's a long story, Senator," she answered with a sigh, shaking his proffered hand. He blinked again, rubbed his left eye, then looked alarmed.

"Is something the matter, Senator?"

"I—I seem to have lost my contact lens. I . . ." He was peering at her through one eye, presumably the one with the lens still in it, and looking slightly panicked.

"Oh, dear," she said, looking down. Lena wore contacts, and Clara knew from experience what an annoyance it was when one got loose. A glint on the linoleum floor caught her eye. She knelt. Sure enough it was the contact. With a careful finger she picked up the tiny hard circle of plastic, straightened, and held it out to the Senator.

"Thank you," he said, taking it from her and turning slightly aside as he popped it back in. Lena had always cleaned hers first. . . .

Over the Senator's shoulder, Clara saw Jack head out the door with Davey Spencer.

"Excuse me, Senator, I have to talk to somebody," she said quickly, almost running as she went after Jack. She was afraid, now that everything was over, he might vanish into the night like a ghost.

"Jack, wait!" Her heels clicked on the linoleum as she hurried after him. Dressed in the white-flowered yellow halter dress and heeled leather sandals she had charged at the Columbella, she knew she looked good. And she desperately wanted to look good for what she had to say to Jack. "Jack!"

"What is it?" He turned, his face stiff as she caught up to him, tugging on his sleeve so that he had to give her his attention. His green eyes were twin shards of ice. Clara hesitated, acutely conscious of the listening ears of Davey Spencer, who had stopped with Jack, and Senator Chandler, who had come out of the situation room and was walking toward them.

"I need to talk to you," she said urgently.

"I don't believe we have anything to say." He started to pull away. She clung to the sleeve of his tweed sportscoat, her eyes pleading.

"Won't you at least give me a chance to explain? I—I didn't mean what you thought."

"It doesn't matter what you meant. The offer is withdrawn." He let out an impatient hiss. When he spoke again his voice was low and rough. "Look, Clara, don't you know enough to know when it's over? It was good, baby, as long as we had the excitement of the chase to fuel it. But the chase is over, and we have to go back to real life. We're not right for each other. Be proud that you had the good sense to recognize it first."

"McClain!" General Ramsey's voice called him from down the hall. "We've got something interesting coming from the wire. Come take a look at it."

"Excuse me," Jack said formally. Freeing himself from her grip on his sleeve, he turned on his heel and walked off. Clara, looking helplessly after him, felt her cheeks start to burn with angry embarrassment as Davey Spencer gave her a pitying look before hurrying after Jack.

"I'm sorry, my dear," Senator Chandler said quietly, coming up behind her. "I couldn't help but overhear."

Clara shook her head. Tears were burning in her throat, but she would be drawn and quartered before she would make an even worse fool of herself by crying. If Jack didn't want her . . . The thought made her eyes blur with tears despite her best efforts.

"Isn't that the man who's been in all the newspapers? The one they said was responsible for that hospital massacre? How did you ever get involved with him?" Clara had the impression that Senator Chandler was just talking to cover up the fact that she couldn't. She sniffed and swallowed, and with a valiant effort managed to find her voice.

"It's another long story, Senator."

"I see." He hesitated a moment, then said, "I have to be

back in Washington tomorrow in time for a luncheon in my honor. I'll be leaving right away. You're welcome to a lift home, if you like."

Home. The word conjured up a picture of Jollymead, of her mother who would be returning from her cruise and her manuscript which was unmailed and Iris and Amy and Puff, whom she would have to ask the general to send to her. . . Suddenly she longed to be at home more than anything in the world. It was, she acknowledged with a sad sniff, the place she always ran to when she had wounds that needed licking.

"Thank you very much, Senator, that's very kind of you. I would like a lift," she said. With a fatherly pat, he tucked her hand in the crook of his arm and they started down the hallway.

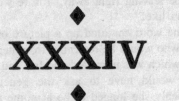

XXXIV

Saturday, September 17, 2:15 A.M.

Clara sat in the back of the limousine beside the senator trying not to think of Jack. She had blown it all around. If she had it to do over again she would have snapped up his offer of marriage so fast that he would have felt like a fly with a turtle after him. But she didn't have it to do over again. Like the rest of the whole fantastic adventure her romance with Jack was over. They weren't right for each other he had said. And she knew he was right. But oh, how wonderful being wrong for each other could be!

"There's a chartered jet waiting for us at the Charleston airport. Once we get on it you can sleep. You look worn out." Senator Chandler's voice roused her from her thoughts. She smiled at him, though the smile took an effort. The inside of the limousine was dark. They were still on the island, heading for the bridge over the swamp that connected it to the mainland. Outside lighting was limited to right around the resort area.

"It's very kind of you to offer me a lift, Senator," Clara said again. "I really wanted to get home."

"I guessed as much." Senator Chandler leaned forward to pick up the receiver from the telephone built into the door as he spoke. Besides the telephone, the limousine was equipped with every conceivable luxury from a fully stocked bar to a TV. "But please don't thank me. I'm glad of the company."

Clara smiled at him. He smiled back. "I hope you'll forgive me," he said, holding up the receiver, "but I want to tell my housekeeper I'm on my way home."

"Please go ahead," Clara murmured, her eyes shifting to the darkness outside the window, an instinctive courtesy to afford him as much privacy as she could while he made his call. The phone made little beeping noises as the senator punched in a number. Without the distraction of conversation, her thoughts drifted back to Jack.

"Damn, I guess I'm getting old. Or maybe it's my contacts that are getting old. I'd like to think so, anyway. I can't make out the numbers on this thing." Senator Chandler grimaced ruefully as he squinted at the receiver he held in his hand. "Would you be so kind, my dear?" He held the receiver out to her.

Recalled from her unhappy thoughts, Clara smiled at him. "I'd be glad to."

With an answering smile he passed the receiver to her. "Thank you. Good eyesight is one of the first of the many advantages of youth to go."

"What is the number?"

"Area code 301-244-3668."

It was hard to see the numbers in the darkness. The tiny buttons were lighted, but Clara still had to hold the phone close to her face and squint as she punched in the number. There was a busy signal. She told the senator so.

He frowned. "Try again, please. That's the line to my private retreat, and it shouldn't be busy, certainly not at this time in the morning."

"Perhaps I got a wrong number."

"Yes, that's possible. 301-244-3668."

Clara tried again, holding the phone close as she squinted at it. Above the little buttons the letters corresponding to the numbers danced, actually more visible than the numbers themselves because of the intensity of the light in the darkness of the limousine's interior. She'd always played a little game with herself when she'd dialed a phone, checking to see if the letters corresponding to the number spelled anything in particular. Businesses especially seemed fond of numbers that spelled out a word. For example, the last four digits of a weight loss center she'd gone to once spelled out diet.

"2-4-4-3-6-6-8," Clara muttered to herself, punching the numbers in with painstaking care. Suddenly her eyes widened with horror, and ran back over the sequence twice. There was no mistake. The letters that corresponded with Senator Chandler's personal phone number spelled out Bigfoot. For a crazy moment she thought it might be a coincidence. But the hope died as she lifted her eyes to see the look on Adam Chandler's face. As Jack had once said, in this business there was no such thing as coincidence.

"So you picked up on my little conceit. I always thought you were an exceptionally intelligent young lady. I'm pleased to have my opinion validated," he said conversationally, taking the receiver from her limp hand and replacing it on its rest.

"But—they arrested Michael Ball," she protested stupidly, staring at him with dawning horror.

He smiled. "They did, didn't they? I've always been a lucky soul. My luck continues to hold."

"Your eyes are too dark." She was whispering.

"My, my, you have been thorough, haven't you?" he asked with a sneer. Lifting his hand, he cupped it under first one eye and then the other as he blinked. When he looked up at her again, she sucked in her breath. His bright blue eyes were blue no longer; they were an unusual light hazel, almost yellow.

"The contacts! They're tinted green!" She had noticed that tinge of color when she had handed the tiny object back to him, she realized. It just hadn't registered on her consciousness until now. At the time she had thought that the terrifying game was over. And she'd been thinking of Jack. . . .

"Pity I had to lose one back there, and you had to pick it up. That was unlucky. For you."

The black hawk with the yellow eyes. That was how Rostov had described him. Clara stared at him with the fascination a rabbit must feel for a cobra.

"You're Nikolai Bukovsky," she breathed. "But how can you be? My mother knows your family. Adam Chandler isn't an alias. He's *real*."

"He was real," the senator corrected. "He's been dead these forty-two years, God rest his soul. He died in a Russian field hospital in 1944. He was on a secret mission behind enemy lines when he was captured and tried to escape. He was badly wounded in the attempt. But I, who escaped with him, was not, and I carried him on my back to the Russian front. We were your allies at the time, you know. The officer in charge of the field unit was veteran

KGB. As I recovered from my wounds and Chandler expired of his, he took note of the similarities in our height, build, and coloring, and our friendship, which meant that I knew a great deal of Chandler's life before he went off to war. Our features were different, as was the color of our eyes, his being dark blue and mine, as you see, being hazel, but the basic similarities were there. This officer had tremendous foresight: he guessed that the friendship between the United States and Russia would not long survive the war. He checked into Chandler's background, found that he was indeed as wealthy and well connected as he had boasted to me, and decided that it might be useful to have such an operative in the United States when our relationship should once again grow distant. He put the proposal to me, I consented, and underwent the plastic surgery and training necessary to become Adam Howard Chandler IV. There was nothing they could do to change my eye color without damaging my eyes, however, and that I would not consent to. So I have been wearing colored contact lenses since 1944. They were made by Soviet scientists just for me, and have been replaced regularly over the years. Now, of course, colored contact lenses are available in every corner store. I've been quite a trendsetter.'' This was accompanied by a small chuckle.

"Oh my God!" Clara breathed. The extreme danger she was in had just started to occur to her. This was Bigfoot. She knew it and he knew she knew it. He could not let her live.

"That I should be elected to the senate was a dividend not expected by my superiors. The chairmanship of the Senate Intelligence Committee was the icing on the cake. But as Adam Chandler, wealthy war hero, every door was open to me. I have been invaluable to my country; I will continue to be so now that the search for Bigfoot has been successfully concluded." He chuckled again. "To think I seriously considered fleeing the country when I received the president's summons. I almost went back to Russia. One day I will. When I do, I will be greeted as one of the greatest heroes our country has ever known."

He took a deep breath and released it with a sigh. His yellow eyes blinked regretfully at Clara.

"I'm very sorry that you got involved in this, my dear. I still don't understand quite how it came about. I had hoped to be able to spare you. Indeed, if you hadn't seen the contact . . . Ah, well."

"What are you going to do?" Her lungs felt stifled, as though someone were pressing a pillow down on her face.

"Why, have you killed, of course. Don't worry, I'll give them instructions to make it painless."

"I told General Ramsey I was leaving with you. I had to give him instructions about where to send my cat. They'll know you did it." She was clutching desperately at straws, instinctively shrinking into the corner of the luxurious leather seat as her body tried to put as much distance between the two of them as she could.

"Did you?" He frowned, sounding annoyed. "Well, no matter. I will of course see that you get home safely despite your despondency over the defection of your lover. Once there, I cannot be blamed if you take your life in an act of despair."

Clara stared at him with horror while he appeared to work out the details of her demise. Her own brain revived from its state of frozen terror to work with lightning speed. The driver. Could he be involved in this, too? It was likely, or the senator—Bukovsky, she still had trouble equating the two in her mind—would not speak so freely. She could not

count on him to help her. It was a better than even chance
that Bukovsky was not armed. He would have been searched
before being admitted to the secretary of state's little confer-
ence, and he'd had no reason to arm himself afterwards. Of
course, he might have a gun in the limousine.

Bukovsky reached down to retrieve his briefcase from the
seat beside him.

"It's extremely fortunate that I am an insomniac, though
I never thought so before now," he remarked, extracting a
pill bottle from the briefcase and closing it again. He
removed a glass from the rack beside him, opened the
refrigerator, and extracted a bottle of vodka, which he
proceeded to open and pour into the glass. When the glass
was full he recapped the bottle and put it back in the
refrigerator.

"You don't take Seconal, do you, my dear?"

Clara shook her head, her eyes on the two red capsules he
extracted from the pill bottle.

"Excellent. Two of these and a shot of vodka and you'll
sleep like a baby. Such deep sleep that you must be carried
onto the plane will be taken as another mark of depression.
And it's to your advantage, too, my dear. When the time
comes for you to hang yourself, you won't feel a thing."

"I won't take them." Clara shrank even further against
the seat as he extended the pills toward her in his outstretched
palm. She looked around desperately in search of the door
handle. Finally she found it, nestled deep within a shadowy
recess. The car was moving along the dark curving road at
about forty miles an hour. They were on the bridge now;
beneath them, Clara remembered from her own trip over,
was the swamp. It was said to be impassable. . . .

"You will," Bukovsky answered positively, setting the
glass down on the small table in the middle and reaching

down to pull off his shoe. Beneath Clara's startled eyes, he twisted the heel until it turned at a ninety degree angle from the sole. Nestled inside was a small derringer.

"I really would rather not shoot you now, but I will if you force me," Bukovsky said, picking up the derringer and pointing it at Clara. "Now take the pills."

He held out his hand. Swallowing hard, Clara looked at the derringer. Meekly she allowed him to pour the pills into her palm.

"Take them."

"Could I—have a drink of the vodka first? My—my throat's so dry I don't think I can swallow."

"Very well. Get it." The derringer followed her as she leaned forward to pick up the glass from the table. With a quick look at him, she lifted the glass to her lips and took a sip.

"Now the pills."

Clara lifted the hand the pills were in to her mouth. Then, knowing it was now or never, she threw the contents of her glass in his face.

Bukovsky screamed, clawing at his face. The derringer went off, the bullet whistling over her head to crash with a tinkle of shattering glass through the passenger window. The driver, made aware of the altercation by the gunshot, stood on his brakes. Clara and Bukovsky were thrown forward. Even as she was scrambling from the floor, her hand was on the door handle. She jerked. It was locked.

The limousine was skidding sideways along the road, tires squealing in protest at the suddenness of the stop. She had to save herself . . . A hand was on her leg. Clara looked around, saw Bukovsky coming up off the floor of the limousine at her, murder in his yellow eyes.

Of its own volition, her hand thrust through the shattered

glass, not even feeling the pain as it was sliced in a dozen places. She felt for the doorhandle, found it, pushed the button, leaning her weight against the door at the same time, and then she was flying free, rolling down a steep grassy embankment as the car slewed past and Bukovsky's head appeared in the swinging door.

She landed in three feet of icy water at the bottom of the embankment. Tall swaying reeds towered above her head. Gasping as she surfaced, half blinded by mud and slime that covered her, she lifted a hand to dash it from her face and dared a terrified look up toward the road. The limousine had stopped. Bukovsky was standing on the gravel shoulder, staring down at the marshy field where she lay. His driver was getting something from the trunk. Clara began to scramble away, half swimming, half crawling, the bottom of the swamp slippery ooze beneath her hands and feet. The water was black with an oily sheen on its surface. She was shivering already, teeth chattering. The horrible stink of swamp gas threatened to steal her breath away.

"There she is!" she heard Bukovsky cry. Instinctively she glanced back. The driver was lifting a rifle to his shoulder. Taking a deep, shaking breath she went under. As she went she heard a zinging sound overhead. Then another one. The rifle was equipped with a silencer. There was no chance that someone at the resort would hear the shots and come to her aid.

She pulled herself frantically along the bottom, holding her breath as long as she could. When at last she had to surface, she was terrified to hear splashing behind her even as she gulped in the rotten smelling air. Looking back over her shoulder, she saw a darting light. For a moment she was puzzled. Then it came to her: Bukovsky was in the marsh, behind her and to her left, searching for her with a powerful flashlight. She could just make out the dark gray bulk of him behind the light. He was carrying a rifle tucked beneath his left arm. She thanked God for the shadowy darkness and the tall reeds. He did not see her as the light flashed over her head. She cowered amongst the reeds, her heart beating so hard that it was all she could hear. Where was the driver? She turned her head in the direction of the resort, realizing that she could, just faintly, see its lights. Then she saw the driver behind Bukovsky. He too carried a flashlight. And a rifle. She could make out the peaked chauffeur's cap quite clearly. He was between her and the resort. He and Bukovsky seemed to be weaving back and forth, sloshing in intersecting paths along the way she had come. Heart sinking, Clara realized that they were beating the swamp for her as hunters beat the heath for birds. There would be no cowering amidst the reeds, praying that they would pass her in the dark. She would have to flee before them like any hunted creature.

Carefully, quietly, she began to pull herself along, using handfuls of swamp grass for purchase. They were crossing and crisscrossing behind her, lights slicing through the darkness as they moved back and forth, their very silence more menacing than any threats could have been. Clara realized with a sickening sense of fear that Bukovsky would hunt her to the death. Only one of them could emerge alive from that swamp.

To her left she heard a swish and a splash. Head slewing around, she watched in horror as an alligator slithered from a tussock of swamp grass and passed close beside her. Clamping down hard on her tongue, she had to fight back a panicked scream; the memory of the deadlier beasts behind her killed the sound aborning. She would stand a better chance with the alligator than Bukovsky. The alligator paid her no mind. Heart pounding, Clara hoped his kinsfolk would be as forbearing.

"There she is!" The bright beam of a flashlight blinded her. Bullets whizzed over her head, slamming into the water around her and ricocheting off with a whiny screech. Stomach churning with terror, she dove beneath the surface of the oily black water, scrambling forward on her belly like the gator that had just passed as bullets spat into the water around her, praying that by some miracle she would be spared.

Surfacing, she realized that they were close behind her. The beams from their flashlights crossed and crisscrossed in the darkness. Over the harsh pounding of her heart she could hear their frenzied splashings. Scrambling forward, sobbing with terror, she looked over the acres of black water and blacker mud for a place to hide. The darkness was her ally; shifting shadows and rustling reeds disguised her passing.

The flashlight passed over her again, then froze.

Zzinng! Zzing! Oh, God, they had her pinned in the light! Flinging herself face down in the icy water, she pulled herself toward where the reeds grew thicker in the middle of the channel, at a right angle to their path. She would need a miracle to escape.

Daring a look back, she saw that they were not far behind her. She had managed to elude them for the moment, but she did not delude herself that she could do it for as long as it would take. It was just a matter of time until one of them got a bead on her back and put a bullet through her even as she scrambled frantically to escape. Wouldn't it be easier just to stand up and let them see her, to end this frantic terror, this misery? At least then maybe she would buy herself a few hours. Instead of being shot to death in this slimy swamp, maybe Bukovsky would follow his original plan of taking her home to Jollymead to die.

Oh, God, she was so afraid to die! Please save me, she prayed, pulling herself along with desperate strength as the two men behind her closed in. Please save me! Please! Please!

"There she is!"

Clara dived without even bothering to take a breath. With frantic desperation, she changed her direction one hundred and eighty degrees, moving back toward them under the protection of the water and the reeds. They wouldn't be expecting that. Moving as quietly and quickly as she could, feeling as though she would die if she didn't breathe soon, she pulled herself along. At any second she expected to feel a bullet ripping into her flesh.

When at last she had to breathe or drown, she poked her head up through the surface. To her amazement, she saw that God had heard her pleas one more time: while she had been submerged, a fog had rolled in.

XXXV

"Clara!"

The hoarse whisper made her shiver with horror. She did not know how long she had laid hidden in the icy swamp; it could have been minutes or hours. All she knew was that they still stalked her, their flashlights turned off now as they sought her in the shifting fog. Some time ago Bukovsky had started calling her name. The mere sound of it on his lips made her shiver with horror.

"Clara!"

Despite the muffling fog, she could hear them sloshing through the marsh. The thick soupy mist distorted sounds as well as blinded her. They could have been ten feet away or a hundred.

"Clara!"

Her name on his lips unnerved her. She knew the voice was Bukovsky's, but it sounded so horribly familiar that she was having trouble not responding to it. The voice still seemed to belong to Adam Chandler, longtime family friend. She had to fight back panic, senseless, sobbing panic. Her fear was that the fog which she had thought was her savior had instead merely been the agent to prolong her torment. Her entrapment in the dreadful world of icy mud and terror could only end in her death.

"Clara, you're being very foolish. Come out and let me take you home."

It sounded tempting, horribly tempting, whispered in that voice with its slow cadence of Virginia drawl. Clara quivered, holding onto reason with an effort. She must not respond, must not respond.

"Emily is waiting for you at Jollymead, Clara. Let me take you home to your mother."

Clara had to bite back a scream. He was moving closer to her. The whisper was growing more audible. She could hear the splashing as he moved toward her through the water.

Slowly, carefully, she began easing herself backward, away from the tempting voice that promised only death. She slithered backwards through the ooze like an eel, fleeing from the familiar horror that stalked her. Around her the swamp bubbled and sighed, releasing its gas with tiny pops that made her heart pound through her chest.

"Clara!"

She slithered faster, staring mesmerized in the direction of the sound. Her foot bumped something solid.

"I've got her! I've got her!"

Clara screamed with mindless terror as the chauffeur whose leg she had bumped into while escaping from the other hunter grabbed for her. His arms slid around her, dragging her up out of the icy mud that had been her protection for so long, hauling her high like a landed fish as she struggled and fought and screamed.

"Hold her, I'm coming!" Bukovsky's voice was like a torch to the already flaring blaze of her terror. She fought against the arms that struggled to hold her like a wild thing,

kicking and biting and scratching until without warning she
was free, falling into the water with an enormous splash
while the sound of furious curses filled the air over her
head.

"Don't let her get away!"

She was slithering frantically through the water, but she
knew that they were close behind her; she could feel them
gaining on her. Reason fled. Stumbling to her feet, sobbing
in high-pitched gasps that sounded to her ears like banshee
wails in the darkness, she fled like a doe before the hunters.
Splashing through the hip-deep water, stumbling, falling,
picking herself up to run some more, she felt with an icy,
numbing certainty that her death was close at hand. Then
she heard the rasping slide of metal against metal as, near at
hand, a rifle was readied to fire.

She threw herself into the swamp just as the jet of fire
sang over her head. Scrambling forward, bent almost double
now, she still fought to elude what she knew was inevitable
even as more bullets whined past her.

Her feet touched solid ground. Before she thought, she
had scrambled up on a mud bar. It took her above the
sheltering reeds.

"There she is!"

Clara heard the cry, the splashings that told her that they
were only feet behind her, and scrambled for the other side
of the mud bar. But her feet, frozen after hours in the icy
water, betrayed her. They slipped and she went sprawling
flat on her face.

"You were foolish to run, Clara."

"No!"

With a little cry of dread, she turned over to find him
looming a mere three feet behind her. The fog was lifting
now; she could see him clearly. Chandler—Bukovsky, with

his terrifyingly familiar face and those feral yellow eyes gleaming at her through the shifting mist.

"Don't shoot me! Please! I'll go with you! I won't cause you any more trouble, I promise!" She was babbling, scrambling backward across the grassy mud, her terrified eyes fixed on the rifle that he was slowly lifting to his shoulder.

"You've been a great deal of trouble already, Clara. I'll be late for my luncheon now." The rifle was on his shoulder. He was aiming it at her heart.

"No!" Clara cried, cowering. His hand moved on the trigger. With a terrified sob she shut her eyes.

The world exploded around her. Clara screamed, a high-pitched shriek of terror. Panic of the most primitive sort claimed her, and she screamed again and again. . . . There was another scream, but it was not hers. It was a man's.

The explosion sounded again. Clara's eyes flew open. In front of her, almost touching her feet in their mud-and-slime caked sandals, sprawled Bukovsky, his rifle lying useless by his side. His eyes were open. He was looking beyond her with those dreadful yellow eyes, one hand stretched toward her, opening and closing like a bird's claw. An expression of pure hate crossed his face, then he shuddered and was still.

Gasping, shuddering, Clara looked around to see what it was that had prompted that last blast of evil from Bukovsky's eyes. To her surprise, she saw the sun was rising at last. Pinwheels of vivid pink and yellow and orange swirled across the sky. Silhouetted against their vividness was the dark figure of a man. He was lowering a rifle.

"It's all right, Clara," Jack said grimly. "I'm here."

Epilogue

◆

Clara spent two weeks in Saint Mary's Hospital in Richmond, Virginia, suffering from pneumonia as a result of her night in the swamp. Her right hand, which had gone through the window of the limousine, required seventy-five stitches. It was swathed in white bandages and looked like it should more properly belong to a mummy.

She had visitors galore in the hospital. Her mother and Lena were fixtures. Mitch came by nearly every day. Even his mother stopped by twice, bringing an offering of an apple tart each time. The primary topic of conversation was the hunting accident death of Senator Adam Chandler in Georgia. Out stalking deer early in the morning on an impromptu vacation, he had been accidentally shot by his own chauffeur, who had then killed himself in an excess of remorse. A terrible tragedy, and a terrible loss to the nation, everyone agreed.

Clara made no attempt to alter those perceptions. As General Ramsey had told her on his one visit (made when he returned Puff to Jollymead), things were not always what they seemed.

To begin with, Premier Deng was not dead. With fore-knowledge that an assassination attempt on the secretary of state would take place—as was then supposed—it had been deemed wiser to postpone the secret summit. The man who was mistaken for Deng and shot (though not killed, or even wounded; as a precaution, he had been wearing a bulletproof vest) was a stand-in for the premier, just as there had been a stand-in for Franklin Conran. The supposed crisis had been seen as an excellent opportunity to trap Bigfoot, as none of the principals in the assassination attempt were aware that it had not succeeded.

Jack had been the first to suspect Adam Chandler. A routine background check had turned up the interesting information that, from the time he was reported Missing in Action to the time he came home from the war, his entire family had died in a series of accidents: His parents killed together in a car accident; his sister and her husband killed in a house fire; his brother falling over a cliff while hiking. Five deaths within eighteen months was peculiar, to say the least. A girl with whom Chandler had been close had also died. By the time Adam Chandler had returned from the war, everyone who had known him intimately was dead.

He had had access to the information that was passed.

Then, just as the meeting in which Michael Ball was arrested had concluded, a piece of false information that had been planted for each of the suspects to pass along had been acted upon. The information was that given to Adam Chandler.

Under increasing duress, the premier's aide confessed that he had misidentified Michael Ball as Bigfoot. He had greatly feared for his life if he told the truth. The KGB had long arms and long memories. But the true possessor of the voice he had heard had been the third speaker. There was no mistaking that Virginia drawl.

Adam Chandler had already left the resort. Orders were

given to pick him up at the airport in Charleston or Washington. Failing that, agents would be waiting at his Georgetown townhouse and his weekend place in Maryland.

Jack had gone back to the villa and missed Clara. It had been nearly three hours before it had occurred to him that she might have left with Chandler. A quick phone call to the Charleston airport had revealed that the plane Chandler had chartered had not yet left.

Jack and General Ramsey and some of his baby green marines had immediately set off to search the road between the resort and the airport. They had found the limousine parked at the side of the road, trunk still open, rear window broken, and had immediately spread out and begun to search the swamp.

Jack had found Clara, who had promptly fainted. He had carried her out of the swamp, and she had been treated at the resort for shock and blood loss. Then she had been airlifted to the hospital in Virginia.

Mary Hammersmith had hanged herself in jail immediately after being arrested for the murder of her husband. It was suspected that she was one of Bigfoot's "sleepers," assigned to get close to Hammersmith soon after his recruitment into the CIA with no certainty that she would ever be activated. When the activation came, she was ready. When she was no longer useful, she was terminated.

Rostov had been deported. He was protected from prosecution by diplomatic immunity.

And thus the nightmare truly ended.

There was just one fly in the ointment of her giddy relief: the one visitor Clara wanted more than anything in the world to see never came. Jack was conspicuous by his absence.

"Going back to Tennessee, he told me," General Ramsey

told her when Clara, embarrassed to ask but desperately needing to know, asked about Jack's whereabouts. "I think he said something about raising chickens."

The general did not know where in Tennessee. But Clara, her research techniques honed by years of writing novels, took only three hours to find McClain's Chicken Ranch in the phone book of a little town called Fork Mountain about forty miles west of Knoxville.

"I knew there was a man involved!" Emily squealed when Clara told her, as soon as she was released from the hospital, that she was flying to Tennessee to mend some fences. "Is he *the one*? At last?"

"If he'll have me, Mother," Clara said, grimacing at her mother's excitement.

"He'll have you if I have to drag him back here by the ear," Emily said grimly, and Clara had to laugh. The image of her elegant little mother dragging Jack anywhere by the ear was ludicrous—but endearing at the same time.

With her mother's blessing she made the evening flight to Knoxville. Then she rented a car, bought a map, and headed for Fork Mountain. By the time she finally saw the sign that proclaimed McClain's Chicken Ranch, it was nearly midnight. She had gotten lost six times.

There was a light in a window around the back. Gathering up the peace offering she had brought and taking a firm hold on her courage, she walked toward it.

The house was huge, an oversized white clapboard farmhouse with gingerbread trim. The light was coming from a window over the back door. Climbing the pair of wooden steps, she knocked before she could lose her nerve. Then she looked through the gap in the curtained window. As she had suspected, the light was in the kitchen. Like the house, it was huge. And it was also full of people.

"Oh no!" Clara murmured, wishing she'd looked before she knocked. Hastily she stepped down from the steps, knowing she had to retreat. She could not possibly talk to Jack in front of all those people.

The door opened. A cheery, dark-haired, middle-aged woman looked out. For a moment she frowned, seeing no one, and then she caught sight of Clara on the verge of flight, looking guiltily up at her. Her eyebrows went up.

"Why, hello," the woman said.

"Hello." There was nothing for it but to walk into the light. She couldn't even hide her ridiculous peace offering behind her back. It was much too big. Why, oh why had she imagined that Jack would be alone? "I—I've come to see Jack. He—he is here, isn't he?"

"He sure is. Come on in, I'm his sister, Janey. My goodness, what's that you have in your hand? You didn't bring those for *Jack*?"

Clara was already walking into the kitchen. Immediately she was the cynosure of all eyes. At first glance there seemed to be dozens of people in the room. Then the crowd resolved itself into five women and assorted children.

"Look what she brought for Jack!" Janey tittered, and the women at the table, all apparently his sisters from the look of them, hid smiles behind their hands or giggled openly depending on their various natures.

"Roses! For Uncle Jack?" One of the children, a girl of about eleven, piped up. Then she went running out of the kitchen. "Uncle Jack! Uncle Jack! A lady's here and she's brought you *roses*!"

Clara wanted to sink through the floor.

"Come on in and sit down," one of the women suggested kindly, standing up and offering her chair.

"Don't mind us," another one chimed in. "It's just so funny that you'd bring Jack *roses*."

"It was just a—joke," Clara explained feebly, moving toward the proffered chair.

"Let me get you a cup of coffee," Janey said, bustling over to the stove.

"What the hell's this nonsense Katie's been—" Jack strode into the kitchen, the little girl who had run for him clinging to his hand, only to stop dead at the sight of Clara.

"See? I told you, Uncle Jack," Katie said importantly.

"She's brought you *roses*, Jack," one of his sisters pointed out with suppressed hilarity.

Wordlessly Clara held them out. Going red to his ears, Jack took them. His eyes locked with hers. His face worked. Then he let loose with a tremendous sneeze.

"You're allergic to roses, too?" Clara asked, light dawning in a tremendous flash. No wonder his sisters had reacted with such hilarity.

"I hate roses," Jack said, scowling and thrusting the gorgeous mass of two dozen, bloodred long stemmed roses at his sister.

"And cats and cheese and—"

"Sally, would you shut up, please?" Jack's tone was more vicious than polite. Sally laughed, but obligingly shut up.

"Jack, there's a card with these roses." Clara's eyes widened with horror as Janey dug it out. She hadn't bothered to put it in an envelope. On the flower-edged front, it said simply—

"To Mr. Irresistible," Janey read aloud. The room erupted in a chorus of giggles. Jack stared at Clara, his eyes turning suddenly emerald. Clara stared miserably at the floor. Never in her life had she suffered such an agony of embarrassment.

"Ladies, could we have some privacy, please?" Jack fixed his sisters with monitory eyes.

"Aren't you even going to introduce us before you sweep her off her feet, Jack?"

"This is Clara Winston. Clara, as you have no doubt guessed, this gaggle of giggle boxes is my sisters. And they are going to bed."

The room emptied in a hurry. Giggles floated back to them from the hall. Jack turned and carefully closed the kitchen door. Then he looked at Clara, his arms crossed over his chest, his head cocked to one side. Those eyes still blazed a vivid green.

"Did you mean it?"

"What?"

"That Mr. Irresistible stuff."

"Yes."

"Do I take it you're proposing?"

Clara felt her heart speed up. "Do I take it you're accepting?"

"If you're proposing, then I'm accepting." He grinned suddenly, holding out his arms. "Come here, baby."

Clara went to him. His arms closed around her. His mouth came down on hers. Clara kissed him back with giddy abandonment. She felt like she'd finally come home.

"You really are my Mr. Irresistible, you know," she murmured when at last he lifted his mouth from hers. Opening her eyes, she smiled languidly into eyes of emerald green.

"Baby, what I am," he said, punctuating his words with kisses, "is irresistibly yours."

And then he kissed her again. As Clara wrapped her arms around his neck, she thought she heard a chorus of giggles from just beyond the kitchen door.